Sweet Afton

a novel by

CLENT MOORE

Indigo River Publishing

Indigo River Publishing
3 West Garden Street Ste. 352 M
Pensacola, FL 32502
www.indigoriverpublishing.com

Cover Design: My Custom Book Cover, LLC

Ordering Information:

Quantity sales: Special discounts are available on quantity purchases by corporations,
associations, and others. For details, contact the publisher at the address above.

Orders by U.S. trade bookstores and wholesalers: Please contact the publisher at the
address above.

Printed in the United States of America

Library of Congress Control Number:

ISBN: 978-1-948080-05-7

First Edition

With Indigo River Publishing, you can always expect great books, strong voices, and
meaningful messages. Most importantly, you'll always find ... words worth reading.

This story is dedicated to the memory of Molly Grace Mordic.

ACKNOWLEDGEMENTS

I wish to thank my wife, Danielle, for her tireless efforts and endless support during this project. Without her, Sweet Afton would never have been finished.

I also want to thank my lifelong friend Sonya Humphries Thompson for being the one to say "You should write a book." Without her constant encouragement, Sweet Afton may never have been started.

Many thanks to my editor, Liesel Schmidt, who patiently and carefully maintained my vision for this novel.

I would also like to thank Dan Vega and all of the staff at Indigo River Publishing for taking a chance on me and affording me the opportunity to share this story.

To all my friends and family, thank you for your undying support on this project. I hope to make you all proud.

Last, but certainly not least, I want to thank my mother, Sue Taylor Moore, for telling me that I would never finish. Mother, it's done.

"The sea cannot be tamed, nor contained. At best, it can only be reckoned with . . . it owes no explanation for what it gives or for what it takes. It just is."

1920 - SAVANNAH, GA

WILLIAM EDWARDS STOOD IN THE DOORWAY TO THE BEDROOM, HIS MUSCULAR FRAME SEEMING TO DO LITTLE TO BLOCK THE PAIN FROM RAMMING INTO HIS HEART. He paused for a moment, breathing deeply and wiping his face and eyes before walking into the room. He hated to see his wife in pain. Sometimes the pain was more physical, but today it seemed to join forces with emotion, as well, doubling the weight on her heart. If only there were a bartering system in the universe, a way to take all of this from her. He would be there, the first in line, ready to make a deal.

The windows were open, letting through a light breeze that moved the sheer curtains, and he could hear the school children passing by outside. Massie School must have dismissed for the day.

Such bad timing, he thought, the sound of their childish laughter bringing a grimace to his face.

She'll hear their innocent squeals and hurt even more.

The worst part was knowing she'd feel guilty for it. Her sweetness was matched by her determination, and inside—all mixed together— was longing and love, intertwined like best friends. They each took turns having the upper hand. Today, it seemed the longing was winning.

His wife lay there, so quiet and small, her face turned toward the wall as if no one seeing her tears meant that they weren't there—as if that meant there were no pain in this.

If only her strength in spirit could make up for her lack of strength in body, he thought.

He touched her arm and spoke softly. "Hey, honey, I'm here. Do you need anything?"

She turned toward him and shook her head, her throat too tight for words to come.

He felt compelled to say it one more time. "Everything will be okay, sweet girl. You'll see. You'll have another baby—I just know it."

Her shoulders shook slightly, and her lips trembled as she covered her face with her hands. She wanted so badly to believe him. She grabbed a handkerchief from the nightstand, wiped her face, and sat up just enough to no longer be "lying around." She knew that she didn't have time to stay in bed hoping that her heart would heal. There was a war being fought inside of her as she desperately tried to look stronger in front of him, willing herself to believe that his words were true. She attempted to push herself out of the bed.

"*No.* No, you don't," he said with quiet force. "You stay right there—doctor's orders."

Knowing there was no use arguing, she sank back into the pillows, sighing deeply. Watching him pick up *the book* from the bedside table, her lips relaxed into a small smile. He leaned in close and gently kissed her forehead.

"Always remember—a calm sea never made a good sailor."

It was something that he often said whenever a situation created adversity, and the confidence and strength in these few simple words always eased her. She loved him for that.

"I love you," she whispered with tears slipping down her cheeks.

"I know," he said gently, wiping the tears from her face. "Just listen, my love . . ." and he began to read slowly—with his calming, gentle spirit—something she'd always cherished about him.

Though his voice was deep and raspy, to her it sounded soft and easy, a comfort only he knew how to give her.

"'Afton Water,'" he read, "written by Robert Burns."

"Flow gently, sweet Afton, among thy green braes,
Flow gently, I'll sing thee a song in thy praise;
My Mary's asleep by thy murmuring stream,
Flow gently, sweet Afton, disturb not her dream.

Thou stock-dove, whose echo resounds thro' the glen,
Ye wild whistling blackbirds in yon thorny den,
Thou green-crested lapwing, thy screaming forbear,
I charge you disturb not my slumbering fair.

How lofty, sweet Afton, thy neighboring hills,
For mark'd with the courses of clear winding rills;
There daily I wander as noon rises high,
My flocks and my Mary's sweet cot in my eye.

How pleasant thy banks and green valleys below,
Where wild in the woodlands the primroses blow;
There oft as mild Ev'ning weeps over the lea,
The sweet-scented birk shades my Mary and me.

Thy crystal stream, Afton, how lovely it glides,
And winds by the cot where my Mary resides,
How wanton thy waters her snowy feet lave,
As gathering sweet flow'rets she stems thy clear wave.

Flow gently, sweet Afton, among thy green braes,
Flow gently, sweet river, the theme of my lays;
My Mary's asleep by thy murmuring stream,
Flow gently, sweet Afton, disturb not her dream."

He looked at her, and his eyes welled with the love that he felt. A
little of it spilled down his cheek and onto the book he still held open.
As it often had before, the rhythmic cadence of the poem had gently

rocked her to sleep, as if she were on a boat with the slow, undulating water's movement beneath her. He felt a sense of relief as his Mary lie sleeping soundly, just as he'd hoped. She was a picture of beauty and peace in this still, quiet moment. He stood slowly, closed the book for the night, and carefully placed it on the bedside table. He quietly closed the window and curtains, wishing to keep the room darkened so that his sweet Mary could rest.

She'll feel better tomorrow, he thought hopefully, *and then I'll read to her, again.*

May 2012

John Callaway sat behind his ornate mahogany desk on the plush forty-second floor of a midtown high-rise office building. The desk was a finely crafted masterpiece that had dutifully served his father, the founder of the company, as well as a former President of the United States. And now, it was his.

Quite the pedigree for an inanimate object, he thought as he leaned back in his chair, its leather skin feeling to him like a soft, worn glove.

He was fully embracing the realization that he had truly *arrived.* Twenty years had passed since the untimely death of his father, John Callaway Sr., thrusting him headlong into the world of commercial development and construction at the mere age of twenty-five. He now stood firmly at the helm of one of the fastest growing and most successful companies of its kind in North America—certainly the largest in the Southeast.

Since taking control of Callaway Development in the spring of 1992, John and his business partner, Michael Bloom, had grown the business more than tenfold, generating revenues in excess of $200 million each year—said revenues boosted, in part, by Michael's encouragement and guidance to take greater risks and capitalize on construction speculation projects during the housing and building boom of the prior decade.

Granted, it had been a risk that John's conservative father would have never allowed the company to take, but it had been one that had paid off handsomely. Callaway Development had been one of the more fortunate companies and was able to "get out" at the peak of the market, and so the company had suffered little—if any—in the way of losses. In fact, the overall P&L sheet for the past twelve years or so reflected record gains in every department of his thriving corporation.

Michael had been John's roommate in college, someone whom most considered to be a mathematical prodigy of sorts, and there was absolutely no doubt of Michael's extraordinary ability when it came to numbers. Though his methods were unconventional at times or even a little circumspect, the outcomes were always the same—highly advantageous.

Fortunately, Michael possessed other skills, as well. For one, he had always been very adept when it came to estimating and calculating risk factors. Some might even go so far as to say that he was the luckiest guy in the world, but Michael would always adamantly defend himself—believing that every problem, no matter how big or small or in which category it belonged, could be resolved through a simple—to him, yet otherwise complex—web of arithmetic only *he* knew how to calculate.

It was his way with women, too. If Michael wanted her, it didn't matter who she was or what current circumstances may have surrounded her, he always seemed to "get the girl." Whatever gifts Michael did or didn't possess had made them both very rich, and John felt grateful to have him by his side. It was indeed a new world at Callaway, and John felt like he was holding it all in the palm of his hand.

He was alone, staring out the large plate-glass windows of his corner office, surveying the ever-growing skyline of the "new" South's capitol—Atlanta, Georgia. Lost in thought over the next big deal, John snapped back to the present when Joan Taylor, the COO and oftentimes John's personal assistant, placed a beautifully wrapped gift on the edge of the desk in front of him.

In her mid-fifties, Joan was an average-looking woman, but one who was always well put together, even if her conservative style did seem a bit gloomy at times. She had been his father's protégé, having begun working for John Sr. straight out of college. There was no doubt that Joan knew this business, and John had always considered her to be one of his greatest assets.

In fact, there had been a special provision in his father's will regarding Joan's employment at the firm. Upon his death, she was appointed COO with full access to the inner workings of the company— executive-level knowledge and privileges. Joan was to remain actively employed by the company for as long as she so desired and would be paid in perpetuity, until the time of her own death. Obvious to John was his father's trust and faith in Joan; thus he never questioned the arrangement.

In her own way, she had always seemed more like a big sister to him, standing up for him and supporting him early on when he first took over his father's company. He was lucky to have her, and he knew it. The only problem was that *Joan* knew it, too.

"What's with the gift, Joan?" John asked. "Is it my birthday? Because if it is, I didn't get the memo."

Joan half-smiled as she replied, "No, John, it is *not* your birthday. Don't worry, though; I'll be sure to let you know when that glorious day arrives. It *is*, however, your anniversary."

"Really?" John said, "Like . . . *today?*"

"I'm afraid so, my dear boy." She had a way of pursing her lips when she made comments like that, making him feel as if he were being scolded by his mother for failing to remember something important. "Of course, John, you don't have a thing in the world to worry about. You went over the top on Molly's gift, just as you *always* have." The sly half-smile had returned to her lips. "Trust me, she's going to love it. I know, because you bought *me* the *exact* same thing. Unknowingly, perhaps—but I certainly do love mine. That's how we do things around here, isn't it, you and I?"

She emphasized her last words just enough to make sure he knew they were a serious statement and to remove any inference that they might actually be a genuine question. She then held up her wrist to reveal a stunning diamond tennis bracelet. It appeared quite expensive and somehow very out of place when paired with her plain light-gray business suit.

"Believe me when I tell you, John, I deserve mine *just* as much as Molly deserves hers—maybe more so." She sighed and made her lips appear pouty. "We have both taken *very* good care of you for the past twenty years, wouldn't you agree?"

Joan began making her way around the desk to stand behind him, placing one hand on the back of his chair while using the other to gently pat his shoulder—much like a mother would do to soothe a fussy child. She leaned down close to his ear and spoke softly. "My dear boy, just where do you think you'd be today without me?"

This, of course, was another rhetorical question, and she squeezed his shoulder for emphasis as she let her words linger heavily in the air. John stared far into the distance without blinking; then he finally spoke. "Yes, I suppose you're right, Joan. Where *would* I be today without you?"

Although his tone was without expression, Joan could sense that it carried with it the weight of sarcasm, even if ever so slight. Though she did not let it show, she was almost amused by his words, as well as by the situation itself. She rather enjoyed reveling in her assumption of always having the upper hand and was especially pleased with herself when she knew that John could feel it, too. With the exchange hovering thickly in the atmosphere, she began making her exit, then abruptly turned back toward John.

"By the way, you have an anniversary dinner reservation at The Optimist for eight o'clock tonight. Nice choice. How very thoughtful of you to remember to do such a wonderful thing . . . considering it's your wife's favorite, and all." The sarcasm spread heavily atop what remained of her contrived superiority. "Oh, and, John, you should consider wearing your navy-blue pinstripe with the new silk tie you picked up specifically for this most auspicious occasion. I'm sure your dear Molly will more than appreciate your thoughtfulness."

Joan's accent was pure Southern sophistication, and she could dial it up or down, depending on the circumstance. Today, she allowed her words to carry with them an equal amount of derision that she, of course, made zero effort to conceal. John had learned over their years together that Joan never did anything casually nor on a whim. Everything that she ever said or did was deliberate and meant to be noticed.

Whether it was an instinctive skill or an acquired one, he admired it in her most of the time, and Joan's cunning had served him well on more than one occasion. He actually appreciated her professional inappropriateness as she slinked her way out of the room, her face remaining stoic as her eyes cut slowly to a small table near the door. At some point upon entering the office, she had placed a small box there without his notice, but now he could see that the bold black letters embossed into the lid read "Armani."

The new tie, he guessed. *She's good at doing things like that.*

She was, in fact, very good with details, even the smallest ones— the ones that he usually overlooked. She seemed to think of everything. Even if it *had* just cost him an extra ten thousand dollars or so, he knew that he was lucky to have her. And because of that fact, he allowed many of her eccentricities to go unchecked.

He also knew that he was lucky to still have Molly.

Sometimes he wondered, if he had to choose, which one of the two did he feel the most fortunate to have?

He looked at the card attached to the gift. Joan had even written it out for him.

Happy Anniversary,

John

The words, although elegantly written, were short and to the point—much like their marriage had been for the past few years. It had been so long since he had written anything personal to his wife, he wondered if she would even notice that he had not filled out the card himself. Joan had signed his name for him so many times over the past twenty years that it was often difficult for even him to discern the real thing from the imposter.

How pathetic.

He turned his chair back around to face the window, staring at nothing and remembering too much.

CHAPTER ONE

JUNE 1988

JOHN LOWERED THE TOP ON HIS FIRE-ENGINE-RED '74 TRIUMPH SPIT-
FIRE AND TOSSED A TIGHTLY PACKED DUFFLE INTO THE PASSENGER SEAT
BESIDE HIM. Warm and cloudless, the day was perfect for a drive to
the coastal empire of Georgia and the crown jewel that presided over
it—Savannah.

It was the summer before he was to begin his senior year at the University of Georgia in Athens, and although John was majoring in fi-
nance and was poised to follow directly in his father's footsteps at his
family's company, he had opted to take a summer elective course in
marine biology.

The ocean and the mysterious world beneath the waves had always
been of interest to him, and this course being offered at Skidaway
Institute of Oceanography in Savannah had been a tempting idea—if
for no other reason than to avoid going home to stay with his parents
in Atlanta. His mind went back to the previous summer, when his
father had put him to work in the mailroom at Callaway, a ploy to
teach him that hard manual work still existed for those who, in his
eyes, failed to succeed. The way John saw it, eight weeks at the beach
seemed more like a vacation than school, anyway.

Although the Triumph had been purchased new in the fall of '73
by his father after he'd closed his first deal at the newly formed company, its reliability often left something to be desired. John had driven
the car to its limit and beyond since his sixteenth birthday, and col-

lege life had taken its toll on the aging British convertible, as well. Today seemed to be a rare exception, though, and as he sped along Interstate 16 to the sound of Don Henley's "The Boys of Summer" blaring from the stereo speakers, John reveled in the feel of the wind in his hair.

Life was good and his plan was simple—keep driving until the map beside him turned blue.

...

It was late Sunday afternoon when John arrived in town. With plenty of daylight left, he decided to drive around what appeared to be the older part of the city and soak in some of the historic flavor that had been synonymous with this settlement by the sea for more than two centuries. As he turned off the highway, it was as if he had somehow been instantly transported to another place in time. Had it not been for the bustle of cars and the occasional convenience store and flashing traffic signals, it could have easily been a hundred years or more before.

Although he was sure that he had never visited this particular part of the city before that moment, John could not deny a strange but calming sense of familiarity. The stoic houses and moss-draped oaks lining the streets and squares were not like that of most other cities in Georgia. Sure, there were mansions spread all over the South, and Atlanta had its fair share of big houses. But these were somehow very different, with a soul and character all their own—something that only time could invent. A lot of the structures seemed to have been built around the same time period, but no two were just alike. Each row of houses and each street had a unique personality—qualities that were nonexistent in the large track-built developments around the other larger cities in Georgia like Atlanta, Macon, and Columbus.

Continuing south on Bull Street, John recognized a progression as the homes grew in grandeur and scale.

This must be where the old money lives, he thought as he twisted his way through the streets and around the oak-packed squares that created small, individual parks.

Noticing a small tour bus, he remembered having taken one of those with his parents years before, when he had been here on summer vacation. Back then, these historic homes, streets, and churches were passed by unnoticed. His realization now was that with age comes a greater appreciation for certain things he had hardly paid attention to before. He decided right then that he would take another tour before he left Savannah, this time not taking for granted the historical significance and magnificent architecture unfolding before him.

He neared the end of Bull Street where it intersected with Highway 80, also known as Victory Drive—so named after America's victory in the first world war. It was a division between old and new, of sorts. If not exactly new, it was certainly less dramatic than the area through which he had just driven. He turned left and headed east, driving along a palm-lined street that seemed almost like a dotted line on an old map guiding him closer to some hidden treasure on the coast. He saw a sign that read, "Tybee Island—13 miles."

Remembering that Tybee had been where he had spent time on the beach with his family, he decided to drive there and take a quick look around the island before checking in at the institute. He was growing hungry, his mind envisioning a dozen oysters and some fresh shrimp that would be sure to fit the bill. No doubt Tybee would provide ample opportunities for each, but it would also be a good place to reminisce over his childhood memories of the beach and watch the sun paint the sky as it made its retreat from the early summer day.

Driving along Victory Drive, John passed through a section of town littered with used-car lots and strip malls. This seemed far removed from the opulence that he had been immersed in only a few blocks before, and he wondered for a moment if maybe he had taken a wrong turn somewhere. His apprehension was relieved when he crossed over a high bridge on the eastern edge of the city, near the small fishing village of Thunderbolt. The bridge descended into a large expanse of marshland and live oak trees, and he soon began noticing signs that advertised beachside and island vacation rentals, dolphin tours, and even airboat rides. He also saw a sign mentioning a nearby Civil War fort and lighthouse, two more things to be added to his growing list of things to explore while he was here in Savannah.

John knew he must be getting close to the edge of the map when he first caught sight of the ocean, and a flood of memories immediately came rushing back to him as he thought of that summer week he'd spent here with his parents many years before. His father had wanted to rent a small boat to take John and his mother out for an afternoon cruise around Tybee and the other small islands that were near to it, but his mother had been more interested in the local boutiques and art galleries. John, being a typical teenager, had preferred listening to his Walkman and watching girls on the beach.

He crossed the final causeway that led onto the island and continued following the road as it made a sharp right turn and began to parallel the ocean. Even though the quaint island was strewn with the typical assortment of hotels, restaurants, and t-shirt shops, it didn't seem as overly developed as some sections had been in the panhandle of Florida, where he'd recently spent a week-long spring break with his friend and roommate, Michael Bloom.

Tybee still has charm, he thought, taking note of the presence of that special something that had been lost in most seaside communities now given over to tourism and heavy commercialism. John found a local restaurant near the end of Tybrisa Street with a large deck for dining, and he chose a seat that offered him a partial view of the Atlantic. He ordered the oysters that he'd been craving since leaving Athens earlier in the day, along with a shrimp sandwich that was boasted to be one of the house specialties.

He began to relax and soak in the sights, sounds, and local island flavor surrounding him, while above him the sky was washed in streaks of orange with blues and greens, stretching as far out into the horizon as he could see. The salty air hovered around him, heavy and warm against his skin.

An older man with a graying beard and long, braided hair was playing Buffett tunes on an acoustic guitar at the edge of the deck, his feet bare and a skull-and-crossbones earring dangling loosely from one ear, that gleamed when it caught the light. Even if the man wasn't exactly Jimmy, the atmosphere lent the music a certain authenticity, just the same. John joined in with the crowd on the chorus of "Come Monday" and clapped right along with all the other impromptu back-up singers as someone shouted out their next request.

After dinner, he walked back to where he'd parked his car near the pier and grabbed his camera for a quick shot before the last of the day's light faded away. Photography was only a hobby to him, but he had gained somewhat of an interest in it after taking a course during his freshman year at UGA, and this gorgeous sky was tantalizing his photo-eye. He focused along the pilings of the pier as the waves crashed against it, hoping for some sort of "artistic" shot—the kind he had so often seen in magazines and on billboards advertising some version of paradise.

John was working the lens to adjust focus when he saw her for the first time.

She wore a yellow sundress, with her hair pulled back into a tight ponytail, each step she took bringing her closer toward him as he stood frozen in place under her spell. She walked down the steps and right past him, giving the merest hint of a smile when she briefly looked back and saw him still standing there motionless. He was clutching his camera, as if he were an action photographer at some sporting event, and he hoped that she had looked back at him out of interest and not because he looked utterly ridiculous.

He would probably never know.

Assuming she was one of the many tourists that flocked to the island this time of year, John was sure she probably thought the same of him, as he tightly gripped the camera in an effort to suppress his giddiness.

When the girl in the yellow dress neared the end of the footpath, he instinctively snapped the shutter closed on his Nikon.

John got back into his car and began driving toward Skidaway. He needed to check in at the institute and get settled at the cottage dorm that would be his home for the next two months. He enjoyed the picturesque drive in silence; and his thoughts, though now scattered, left him with a smile.

I've spent my first afternoon in Savannah, and it's been nothing less than perfect. A scenic drive with the top down, fresh oysters, live music sung by a modern-day pirate . . . and a glimpse of perhaps the most beautiful girl I've ever seen. I think I'm going to like it here.

CHAPTER TWO

JOHN'S NEW ACCOMMODATIONS WERE SPARSE BUT ADEQUATE, AND THEY
REMINDED HIM OF BEING AT SUMMER CAMP WHEN HE WAS A KID. The
cottage was located next to a tidal creek and was raised up about
four feet off the ground with pilings. It consisted of a common room,
a bathroom, and a small kitchen in addition to two bedrooms, each
of which contained two beds, a dresser, and a small writing desk. Off
the back was a small screened-in porch with an old table and four
mismatched chairs.

No roommates were currently assigned to the cottage with him,
so for now it was like having his own private house all to himself—a
much-needed break after sharing a dorm and then an apartment with
Michael. Admittedly, while Michael was considered by most to be a
pretty decent guy and the proverbial "life of the party," the old saying "too much of a good thing" seemed highly applicable, in his case.

One thing was for certain, though: despite Michael's carefree attitude, late-night behavior, and lack of proper social etiquette, he was
an excellent student. He never seemed to study much yet consistently
carried a 4.0 GPA or better. When it came to mathematics, Michael
was, for lack of a better term, a virtual human computer, often challenging his professors' methods and teaching abilities to the point of
becoming a regular distraction to the entire class. For the sake of the
other students, Michael was usually only required to show up to take
exams, which he passed with what appeared to be little effort, earn-

ing him the envy of his peers for his possession of this *particular* set of skills—John included.

After a long, hot shower, John put his personal effects away in the dresser drawers and closet, then set his alarm clock for 7:00 a.m. He turned off a reading lamp on the desk and flopped on the bed, feeling only slightly tired, which was odd, considering that his non-stop day had begun nearly fifteen hours earlier.

Maybe the soft smell of the sea had worked its magic and somehow managed to rejuvenate him.

Maybe the sight of the girl in the yellow dress at the pier had released a surge of adrenaline, causing his heart to race.

Whatever the reason, it kept him wide awake as he lay sprawled out under a rusty, old ceiling fan, listening to its low hum as it tirelessly made circles above his bed.

Giant bullfrogs in the creek were fully immersed in deep conversation, as were the crickets right alongside them, adding background vocals to the natural melodic orchestra now in full swing. The low moan of a ship's horn far in the distance could be heard warning of its impending approach. As John's mind replayed thoughts of his day, a light rain began to fall, its steady cadence making a soothing sound as the drops landed on the metal roof above him. The rain also brought with it a feeling of cool and calm, and he was soon asleep.

...

Somewhere in the early morning hours, John was startled awake, his body involuntarily sitting up as he processed the loud crash that had broken his sleep with a jolt. His blurry eyes caught the glow of the bedside clock showing 6:00 a.m.

Slowly crawling out of the bed to investigate, he cautiously made his way toward the door, then took a quick step back as his rational mind caught up with him.

What if it's a burglar or some kind of wild animal? Are there wild animals in this part of Georgia that I don't know about?

He slowly reached for the knob on the bedroom door, trying to be as quiet as possible. This, of course, was a futile attempt, as the old wooden floorboards creaked loudly under the strain of each cautious step—so much so that he might as well have used a bullhorn to announce his presence. He quickly jerked the door open and was greeted by a guy who looked to be about his same age, unexpectedly sporting a jovial smile.

"G'day, mate. How do you take your tea?" His accent was undeniably Australian, and he seemed to be in way too good of a mood for this early in the morning.

John stumbled over his own words. "What? Who are you? And where did you come from?"

The energetic Aussie quickly replied, "I'm Ben from Sydney, mate. Where do you hail from?"

"What?" John asked, the shock of it all still thick in his voice. "I'm from here. I mean—not *here*, exactly. But I'm from Georgia. Atlanta, actually." He paused, scratching his head as he tried to get his bearings. "Who did you say you are, again?"

The newly arrived stranger—ostensibly his new roommate—began explaining to John that he was a fourth-year student at the University of Sydney in Australia and that he was at SkIO for the same summer course as part of a studies abroad program. Ben was majoring in marine biology, and John found himself thinking that if he had to share the house at all, it couldn't hurt to share it with someone who actually knew what they were doing. John began to introduce himself.

"I'm John. It's nice to meet you." He extended his hand toward Ben, but before he could get it there, Ben responded with a booming laugh, "Ah, bring it in for a hug, mate. After all, we're gonna be bunk mates . . . right?"

He grabbed John in a strong, one-armed embrace and patted him sharply on the back with his free hand. Craning his neck and peering into the bedroom, he said, "Looks like you're already settled nicely into this one. Guess I'll take the one over there."

With that, Ben spun on his heel to attend to his whistling teakettle, leaving John to try shaking his head clear of cobwebs. Realizing there was no sleep left to be had, he went back into his room and began dressing for his first day of class.

John walked out of the cottage only to discover he had left the top down on the Triumph. This wasn't the first time this had happened; and while he felt a slight annoyance at himself for the oversight, the soaking rain last night had done little to further harm the well-worn interior of his aging convertible. Fortunately for him, the day was bright and clear, with a crisp freshness in the air that afforded him the option of walking to the nearby institute rather than having to subject himself to a soggy car that would, no doubt, be less than kind to his clothes.

As John neared the end of the driveway, Ben sped past him on a road bike, one not unlike the kind he had seen being used by serious riders and racers in the Tour de France. The happy Australian certainly had a lot of energy.

Must be the tea.

He meandered down the narrow road leading from the cottage to the SkIO campus, noticing that off to his right was an expanse of marshland and seagrass as far as the eye could see.

A true savannah, he thought, with a smile.

It was, in fact, a perfectly fitting name for the city that was to be his temporary home. Directly ahead in his path was a concrete bridge slightly rising over a body of water that was about 200 feet or so across, and he walked to its crest and leaned against the side railing, peering down into the brackish water—a murky mixture of freshwater and saltwater constantly blended by the incoming and outgoing tide.

Two men stood on part of a very old dock below the base of the bridge that appeared to defy gravity as it hung precariously out over the water's edge. The men were casting nets out into the open water in a fashion that looked more like a choreographed dance than the actual act of catching fish, their round nets about eight feet in diameter and held aloft by both their hands and their mouths. A swaying one-two-three rhythm ensued before the net was released. Then it flattened out into a perfect circle before landing on the surface of the water, sinking rapidly under the heavy pull of lead weights attached along the perimeter of the net. A nylon rope attached to each man's wrist was quickly pulled tight to enclose and capture all that had the misfortune not to escape the net's boundary. Today's catch seemed to be plentiful and the nets were laden with mullet, the flopping silver fish dragged in by the dozen. It was much more than just a task to catch fish—it was a methodical, yet somehow graceful, performance to watch, almost hypnotic.

Yet another item added to his list of things to try while he was in Savannah.

A glimmer of light caught his attention and caused him to look upstream, and John watched intently as a medium-sized sailboat slowly made its way toward the bridge where he stood. There was a man and a woman onboard pulling lines and turning crank handles, and he found himself lost in admiration of the way that the couple worked in sync until the sails were in exactly the right position. The pair looked up and waved as they passed beneath him. He waved back and quickly made his way to the opposite side railing in time to see the boat emerging into the morning light, the sun's rays shimmered onto the rippling water before the bow, bouncing hard off of the perfectly polished stainless rigging.

Although John knew virtually nothing of boats, it was obvious to him that this one was well cared for. Once she had gracefully navigated clear of the bridge supports and pilings, he could read the name of the vessel neatly painted in gold leaf on the stern.

Absolut Heaven, Key West, FL.

The boat was a long way from its homeport, and he pondered the possibilities of where their excursion might be taking them. The prospects were limitless, really, once they'd made it through the pass and out into the open sea. With a sturdy vessel and the wind at your back, the world was yours to explore. His gaze remained fixed until she faded out of sight around the long, far bend.

The near-mile walk to the campus was an easy one, with so much to see and experience along the way that John decided at that moment to make it a regular part of his daily routine—weather permitting, of course.

CHAPTER THREE

THE FIRST DAY OF CLASS WAS MOSTLY SPENT GETTING TO KNOW THE
TWENTY OTHER STUDENTS AND DISCUSSING THE COURSE GOALS THAT
WERE TO BE ACCOMPLISHED OVER THE NEXT TWO MONTHS. A lot of it
sounded very interesting, and some of it even sounded like fun. But
none of it sounded easy. It was completely foreign to John, who had
spent much of the past three years studying economics and building
mock business models, not learning about the migration habits of ti-
ger shrimp and moon jellyfish. He looked over at Ben with an overwhelmed expression on his face, expecting to see some sign of mutual
confusion; but Ben just smiled, seeming unfazed by it all.

"No worries, mate—nothing to it," he said with a shrug.

His casual demeanor gave John a sense of relief, and he relaxed
some after that.

The next couple of days passed by at a leisurely pace, something
that he was unaccustomed to at UGA. He had always taken an ex-
tra-heavy class load—a "suggestion" from his father that had felt less
like a request and more like a command from a drill sergeant—so he
could, as his father had put it, "Excel and push beyond his peers."

His father would say things like, "I'm not going to just *give* you
my company one day, John. You're going to have to *earn* it, just as I
have!" Another one of his father's favorites was, "In this business, we
take no prisoners. It's war—kill or be killed!"

John thought about how he and his mother had rarely ever seen his father at home before 9:00 p.m. on weeknights, and his Sunday afternoons were usually spent on the golf course, schmoozing potential clients and closing business deals. It was true that John Callaway Sr. had made a name for himself in big business, but was it *really* worth all that he had sacrificed to do it?

Mid-afternoon that first Wednesday, John was at the cottage, lying shirtless on the old couch in the common room as he dug his way into a copy of Hemingway's *The Old Man and the Sea*. The worn book had been hiding under some old papers left in the writing desk, and he was trying his best to escape the heat of the day by use of an ancient window-unit air conditioner perched directly above his head. The tired, rusty machine squealed and strained to push out air that was only slightly cooler than the overheated air already in the room, and he laughed to himself as a cool drop of condensation fell onto his forehead and ran down the side of his face.

He looked up at the sad unit and spoke. "You know, I'm not sure if you're sweating or crying, but I really couldn't blame you if you just gave up!"

Another drop fell, this time directly into his open eye. He sat up sharply, staring at the vibrating vents and knobs, laughing out loud as he rubbed the moisture from his eyelid.

Ben entered the room from the porch. "I've got an idea, mate. Whaddaya say we take a ride to the market? I need to pick up a few things, and I was thinking that maybe we could get something for the barbie. My treat."

John looked back over his shoulder, addressing the air conditioner. "We'll finish this later!"

"What's going on? Has the heat driven you mad?" Ben asked, shooting him a puzzled look.

Fifteen minutes later, they were in the cool supermarket, taking their time near the frozen-foods section.

"Now *this* is what I'm talking about, Ben. I wonder what it would take to get a new AC at our place?"

"I don't know, but maybe we should look into it. I'm starting to worry about you!" Ben said with a laugh.

They continued shopping, both grabbing odd things to fill their baskets. On a shelf near the end of the hardware aisle, a small selection of fishing tackle was on display.

Perhaps I should get a rod and try my luck in the creek behind our cottage, John thought as he passed by. *Better yet, I'll get one of those throwing nets like the guys near the bridge were using.*

An hour later, two ribeye steaks were sizzling over a fire they'd built back at the cottage. Ben insisted on grilling them his way, and John gave no argument otherwise. He had neither the energy nor the inclination to put up a fuss. After all, weren't Australians supposedly adept at grilling things?

"I'm going to walk down to the water and show you how the men that I was telling you about were using this thing." John held up his newly acquired eight-foot-diameter cast net, showing it to Ben. The nets he had seen at the store came in several sizes, and he had chosen the largest one, assuming that its size would afford him the best chance of catching the most fish.

"Who knows, maybe I'll be back in a couple of minutes with a fresh catch for the grill!"

How hard could it be? The men at the bridge filled an entire bucket with fish in a matter of minutes!

"Give it a go, mate! See how ya do," Ben replied, knowing full well it would be a lot more difficult than John was anticipating. He had learned this back in Australia after making a similar attempt and had figured out quickly that net fishing was a masterful skill, acquired through patience and repetition. But he would hate to discourage his new friend from trying, so he kept quiet and watched in silence as calamity ensued.

John stood at the water's edge, grabbing a handful of net with each hand and holding up the middle section with his mouth, just as he had seen the men do. He swayed back and forth in a one-two-three motion and then allowed the net to slip from his grasp as he watched the tangled mess fly through the air and land in one large heap about twenty feet away from where he stood.

That's not at all what it was supposed to look like, he thought with a frown, watching in frustration as the net sank from sight. Realization struck him as he recalled a missed step in the careful process that he had observed the two men do, while he watched them from the bridge. *How in the world did I forget to slip the end of the retrieving line over my wrist?*

John stood there for a full minute in disbelief as to what had just happened. He turned and walked back up the porch stairs of the house in silence, then slowly pulled a chair from a rickety old table and sat down, still without uttering a sound. Finally shooting a defeated look at Ben—who, by contrast, stood capably manning a smoking grill—John listened as his roommate offered words that did little to soothe his bruised ego.

"I reckon there's no fresh catch on the menu, then?" Ben said with a good-natured laugh.

Realizing that Ben was not taking delight in his failure but rather commiserating with him, John shrugged it off and joined in the laughter.

"Nope. No fresh catch," he replied, eyeing the hefty portions of meat that Ben was pulling off the coals. "Thank God for cows!"

The next morning, the class was surprised to be given a field project. The assignment was to collect water samples from various parts of the inland marsh, bring them back to the lab on Friday, and analyze them for their content. The class was divided into four groups and given different areas from which to collect their samples.

Anytime there was an opportunity to do things outside of the class-room, the level of excitement grew for the students. The professor had chosen the members of the small groups at random; and, unfortunately for John, Ben was not included in his group. John had hoped to be able to benefit from Ben's previous experience, but there was no such luck on this day.

When John's group arrived at their designated stop, it was low tide. The marsh bottom was black and soft looking, made up of sand, clay, and other decaying organic material that had the consistency of tar and oil more so than of mud. The smell was strong and sour, akin to a bucket of dirty mop water sometimes found in a roadside rest-stop bathroom or in a school cafeteria after lunch. The instructor for the group asked for a volunteer to put on a pair of rubber waders and cross to the other side of the now-empty tidal creek where some water had been trapped in a small pool. No one seemed overly eager to accept the challenge, and John found himself to be the lucky individual given the task.

As John eased himself into the marsh, his boots sank into the mud halfway to his knees. It was a laborious journey just to cross the ten feet or so of marsh to reach the area from which he would extract the samples; and with each step, he was fighting the suction that was trying to hold him captive within the muck. After reaching the tidal pool, John gathered five individual water samples into small plastic bottles, one for each person in the group. Part of the exercise would be for each student to analyze their own sample and then compare their findings with the rest of the class to see what, if any, differences existed.

John made his way back to the edge of the creek and was mulling over his best option for climbing the four feet back up the bank to reach solid ground. As he neared the top, he reached for the offered hand of one of his fellow classmates, losing his balance as both his feet slipped from underneath him. Unable to catch himself, he fell back into the mud, momentarily disappearing from everyone's sight.

He came back up with a gasp, struggling against the pull of the mud as he finally made his way back up onto the bank. The rest of the group seemed overly amused at his blundering escapade, and after a few seconds John's initial shock and anger gave way to laughter of his own.

He was standing at the rear of the school van, removing his useless waders and attempting to clear away some of the sticky black mud from his face and hair when an old pickup truck rolled slowly by on the gravel road next to him. It was driven by an older man, with a lone passenger catching John's eye.

Their eyes met, and a bolt of recognition shot through him.

From what he could tell by the look on the girl's face, John knew that she had recognized him, as well. Once again, he stood frozen under the spell of her gaze, only his eyes able to move and track the path of the truck as it passed by him. The girl's curious expression changed to laughter; and she covered her mouth with her hand, leaning her head out of the open window to look back for one last glance.

Faded white letters were painted on the tailgate of the truck. *Thunderbolt Marina.*

...

When John arrived back at the cottage, Ben was out front making adjustments to his new racing bike. Taking stock of John's mud-covered appearance, he stared at him with a bewildered expression as John made his way from the Triumph to the front steps.

"Rough go, mate?"

"Don't ask," John replied, holding up his hand to ward off any further questions and stopping to strip his mud-dried clothes off, leaving them on the porch.

After a half-hour-long, scalding shower, the water finally ran clear at his feet. With his eyes closed tight and water spraying directly into his face, John's mind began forming the image of *her*, as clear as if the two of them were standing face to face.

Who is she?

What is she like?

Where is she from?

How can I find her?

The questions filled his thoughts, staying with him even as the very last of the water swirled down the drain.

CHAPTER FOUR

CLASS WAS RELEASED AT NOON ON THE FOLLOWING DAY, AND IT WAS AN
ADDED BONUS TO BE ABLE TO HAVE MOST OF A FRIDAY OFF. *This* was
the part of the summer that he had signed up for, and he had been
looking forward to his first full weekend in Savannah. He had thought
of little else that week other than the girl from the pier who had temporarily stolen his ability to move or breathe on his first day in town.

The very same girl who had seen him, just yesterday, looking more
like the creature from the Black Lagoon than a human being.

John drove east, back toward the high bridge that he had crossed
on his way to Tybee Island the previous Sunday. He again found the
sign that read, "Thunderbolt Village," noting that the small "village"
was actually little more than a collection of docks serving a few shrimp
boats that had long since passed their prime, along with a sailboat in
dry dock storage and in obvious need of a complete restoration. There
was a restaurant or two and a few shops, along with a post office and
a town hall, and at the end of a narrow road that separated the village
from the intercoastal waterway was the Thunderbolt Marina.

The marina wasn't very large and consisted of a set of slips that
was home to about a dozen boats. There was a two-story wooden
building at the water's edge; and although it was desperately in need
of paint, it seemed to be sturdy and well constructed, as did most
other structures in Savannah. There was a large sign attached to the
front of the building, advertising fuel and bait, as well as sundries

and supplies. A smaller sign hung below it that read, "Bill Edwards, Owner. Closed on Sunday."

The old truck was parked out front and was currently being used as shelter by an aging golden retriever who wisely seemed to be seeking relief from the midday Georgia sun.

John thought the chances of *her* actually being there weren't likely. Even so, if there was a chance—*any* chance—he certainly wanted to make use of it. And why not? He hadn't ever had a problem meeting girls or talking to them before, and he was considered one of the more popular guys at his high school and college. But for some reason, this felt totally different, and he found that slightly unsettling.

As he walked toward the door, he noticed that his hands were sweating, his mouth was dry, and he felt himself tighten inside. He took a deep breath and exhaled as he reached to open the door. Once inside, he did a quick scan of the room, but he didn't see her. He made his way to a drink cooler that caught his eye and took out a Coke, trying to gather his thoughts and his composure.

And then it happened.

The sound of a voice—*her* voice—reached his ears for the first time. She was at the front counter speaking to an elderly gentleman, but he only caught the tail of their conversation. The man looked a bit concerned.

"We'll be glad to add this to your account, Mr. Davis. You can settle up with Dad at the end of the month, if that's okay?"

The man's voice sounded grateful. "That'll be fine, Molly. I'll square this with Bill no later than next week. You be sure and tell your father that for me."

John could hear the smile in her voice as she replied. "I sure will, Mr. Davis. You have a good afternoon, and please tell Mrs. Davis that we hope she feels better soon."

John was still facing the cooler, appearing deeply in thought over the particular drink that he'd chosen. He stared at the Coke and thought how the bubbling carbonated wonder mirrored the state of the nerves in his stomach. He attempted to clear his throat and began a mumbled practice of his introduction.

"Hello, Molly. I'm John . . . Nice to meet you." He shook his head and tried another. "I'm John . . . Haven't I seen you somewhere before?"

You sound like an idiot.

He shook off the thought and squared his shoulders, trying to regain his usual confidence—the confidence that had never before failed him when it came to meeting a girl. Finally feeling that he was ready to make his move, he turned around and found himself facing a broad-shouldered man at least three inches taller than himself, eyes squinted as he peered suspiciously out of a face that was well weathered and baked brown by the sun.

"Is there something I can help you find, son? You seem to be having an awful hard time deciding on just what it is that you're here after."

"Um . . . no, sir," John stuttered, stumbling over his words. "Uh, thank you, though. I think I have what I need."

He stepped around the imposing figure and made his way to the front of the little store, feeling the man's eyes boring a hole into his back the entire time. After placing his Coke on the counter, John finally looked up at Molly. Their eyes locked again, and this time he was close enough to see that her eyes, like his, were blue.

Third time's a charm?

She was only a few feet away from him. He could smell her perfume, and he felt dizzy and awkward. He hoped that she couldn't hear the pounding in his chest or the ringing in his ears, like he could.

She was the first to break the awkward silence. "Well, I can see that you've showered since the last time I saw you."

He smiled and let out what was little more than a nervous chuckle. "Yes, I have. More than once, actually."

Molly smiled and said, "You know, when I saw you by the marsh yesterday, I figured out that you were one of the students at the marine institute. But what I *haven't* quite figured out is . . . why on earth are you here in Thunderbolt?"

John was scrambling for a plausible answer when he noticed a photograph pinned to a bulletin board on the wall behind the counter, with what appeared to be a much younger Molly standing on the bow of a sailboat. There were words printed beneath the picture, and he hardly had a moment to rethink the prudence of his words before he blurted out a reply.

"Sailing lessons! Yes, I was thinking about learning how to sail!"

Molly's frown made his heart catch.

"Oh, well, we haven't done *that* in quite a while. I'll have to ask my dad if he would be interested in teaching you." Molly had delivered the line sounding certain that it would make him rethink his question.

John could feel his plan falling apart in front of him, a sinking feeling in his gut.

Not her father!

"Well, that's alright. If he can't, though, I understand," he said, trying to sound nonchalant. He paused, trying to build the pretense of a thought just having occurred to him. "Hey, if you're not busy this weekend, would you like to hang out and maybe see a movie or something?"

Molly smirked. "Well, I don't usually *hang out* with strangers."

He realized then that, in his bumbling attempt to meet her, he had failed to even introduce himself.

"Oh, gosh, I'm sorry. I'm John Callaway," he said, putting out his hand to shake hers and trying his best not to over-smile. "Pleasure to finally meet you." She laughed a little as he continued a lengthy, awkward handshake.

"Hi, I'm Molly."

"Yeah, I know."

She tilted her head slightly, looking perplexed.

"I mean, I don't really *know*," John said, feeling an urgent need to backtrack. "I just overheard you talking to that man a while ago." He loosened his grip and she was finally able to retrieve her hand. "Well, now that we're not strangers anymore . . . what do you think about this weekend?"

Molly looked toward the back of the store and watched her father as he pretended to organize items on a shelf, knowing full well that he wasn't missing any of this. She leaned forward onto the counter and spoke quietly.

"Well, John Callaway, I usually paint at the pier on Sundays until sunset. Why don't you meet me there, and then we'll see." She smiled at John, and he could feel his face turning red.

"Until Sunday, then." John walked out of the store biting his lip, attempting to hold in his burst of excitement. He felt as though he had just taken his last step at the summit of Mt. Everest. He drove back toward Skidaway, smiling and singing along with the radio, completely oblivious to his surroundings.

"Who was that?" Molly's father asked as he walked by the counter. "Do you know him?"

She tried her best to contain her smile when she turned and answered. "Don't worry, Daddy," she said with a shrug. "He's just a boy."

CHAPTER FIVE

JOHN SPENT SUNDAY AFTERNOON WASHING HIS CAR AND TALKING TO BEN ABOUT WHAT LIFE WAS LIKE "DOWN UNDER." It didn't take much convincing on Ben's part to get him to agree to a visit sometime after graduation from college. Really, John liked to travel and had always been interested in going somewhere far away like Australia. Now he had the perfect excuse *and* a personal tour guide.

Around six o'clock, John shaved and showered in preparation for his date with Molly. He could tell his nerves were getting the better of him when none of his clothes seemed quite right and he found himself trying on one shirt after another, finally settling on one that seemed to win only by default of having the fewest wrinkles. He took one last look in the mirror, ran his fingers through his hair, decided that it was about as good as it was going to get, and left the cottage. He started his car and began driving toward Tybee.

John arrived on the island just over half an hour later and parked his car near the pier before setting off in search of Molly. He walked along the beach and up the steps that led to where he had first seen her, and it only took a minute to spot her about halfway down the boardwalk. He took a deep breath and began making his way in her direction, his heart racing again at the sight of her and his stomach clenching.

Relax, John–she's just a girl.

"Well, hello, John Callaway," Molly said with a sly smile. "I wasn't sure if you were going to make it."

Are you kidding me? he thought. *I wouldn't have missed this for the world!*

He hoped his words—and his tone—would be more casual than the thoughts running through his mind, so he took a moment to compose himself before he spoke. "Of course, I made it. I really didn't have anything better to do, anyway." He gave her a look that said he was obviously joking, but still offhand enough that she wouldn't be able to gauge his true level of interest—if he was lucky.

She playfully reached out with her paintbrush, as if she were going to add a dash of bright orange to the dark-blue polo shirt he had given in to wearing.

"I'll get you for that one, mister."

They both laughed. The ice had been broken.

He looked at the seascape she was painting, impressed at how good it was, and he was effusive in his compliments. Molly was clearly flattered.

"Thank you. For now, it's really nothing more than a hobby—but I've enjoyed painting since I was a child." She shrugged. "I guess I've always used art as an outlet."

She proudly told him about her mother, an artist of some renown back in the seventies whose works now hung in several museums around the South. Molly also told John that, back when he'd been governor of Georgia, former President Jimmy Carter had purchased one of her mother's early paintings of the Tybee Lighthouse.

"Someone told her that he even took it to Washington with him when he became the president a year later," she said with her eyebrows raised, as though the thought still amazed her. "I like thinking of my mother's artwork hanging somewhere famous like the White House, and I often wonder if it's still there," Molly said with a faraway look in her blue eyes. "I'd like to think so."

John listened as she spoke and found himself not only impressed but genuinely interested.

"Amazing. I look forward to meeting her someday."

"That's kind of presumptuous, don't you think?" Molly asked wryly.

"Maybe a little," John said with a half-grin. "But I have a good feeling about you."

Molly smiled. *I have the very same feeling.*

After she finished putting her final details on the canvas, Molly put her things away and asked John if he would like to take a walk on the beach. They strolled along the water's edge for nearly a mile as dusk settled around them, neither of them ever at a loss for words. She felt at ease with him and talked about her life growing up in the secluded seaport of Savannah, explaining that, even though it was one of Georgia's major cities, it seemed to her like it was its own separate little world. She felt that somehow it had been cut off and protected from any outside influence; and because of that, it had remained much as it had been since its first foundations were laid.

"I like to think of Savannah as having an old soul," she said.

John thought about her words and how eloquently she had described life in her hometown. It was the same feeling that he had experienced when he'd arrived in town a week earlier.

He told her about the summer vacation he'd spent there with his parents when he was thirteen and how much different things looked to him now, just seven years later. As he was recounting some of the highlights of the trip, he suddenly realized that had been the last time he and his parents had been together on vacation. Maybe that was why the memories of that time together were still so vivid—there had been no new ones made to dilute or to replace them.

He went on to tell her about his new friend Ben and how he had nearly scared him to death the morning he had arrived at the cottage and about the teakettle and even the cast net debacle. Fortunately for his ego, she laughed with amused pleasure as John described the incident just as it had unfolded.

He enjoyed seeing Molly smile and especially liked hearing her laugh. From what he had seen so far, she did it easily and often—even if it was sometimes at his expense. Not that she didn't return the favor. She gave him reason enough to laugh at her, as well, when she made a futile attempt at mimicking Ben's accent, butchering it completely and making them both burst out into uninhibited giggling. An onlooker would have thought they were seeing two people who had known each other for years. Like this one seemed to be, some connections were effortlessly made and never lost.

Molly somehow made it easy, slipping into ready tales about her life. "My parents are a lot older than most of my friends' moms and dads, since they were both in their early forties when I was born. They were told by doctors early on in their marriage that it would be nearly impossible to have a baby, but"—she spread her arms wide and tilted her head ever so slightly to one side, a broad smile on her face that seemed to light up the world around her, as if to say *ta da!*—"here I am! They called me their miracle baby." She shot John a sheepish smile. "Sometimes Dad still does. I think that's why he's a bit overprotective of me. He's a great dad, though, and he's worked very hard all of his life for everything he has and to give us the best life."

John watched her, thinking about the man who had so intimidated him in the marina store a couple of days before. After hearing Molly talk about him in *her* way, Mr. Edwards' behavior made more sense, and he made a mental note to be more mindful of that in the future.

"How long has your family owned the marina?" he asked.

"My grandfather built it himself when my dad was a little boy." She paused for a moment and then continued. "It's a sad story. He was lost at sea when my dad was in his early twenties, and Dad has been running the marina himself ever since."

Her words had an unexpectedly sobering effect on him.

"I usually try to help out on the weekends, but things aren't as busy as they used to be. Most times it seems like more money is going out than coming in, but Dad has always been happy doing it. I guess that's what matters most, after all. Right?"

She looked his way, and John nodded his silent agreement, his thoughts wandering to the glaring difference between Molly's dad and his own father. While it was true that both men were passionate and driven when it came to their work, their definitions of success were as opposing as night and day.

"Sorry to hear that about your grandfather, Molly," he said at last. "I'm sure that must have been tough for your family."

Her face became pensive as she looked toward the wide-open Atlantic. "Yes, it was. I'm told that my dad took it especially hard. The two of them were very close, and Dad was an only child," she said, her voice full of reflection. "My grandmother had a very hard time during her pregnancy with him, and it was pretty much a miracle that he was even born. Kind of like me." She shrugged and went on. "When he got older, my dad and my grandfather built a schooner together and planned to sail it throughout the Caribbean someday. Granddaddy took the boat out alone for a sea trial in late December that year, but he never came back. I think Dad still feels some sense of guilt for not being with him that day. The boat was found partially submerged down near Cumberland Island about a week later, and no one knows what really happened."

John was immersed in her story *and* the way that she told it.

"That's terrible, Molly. I'm truly sorry for your loss—for your whole family's loss."

"Thanks, John. Of course, that was long before I was ever even thought of, so I never got the chance to actually know him. But I've heard my dad tell many stories about him, and he was obviously quite the character. He was what some might call "a man's man"—salty and hardened by the sea. But my grandmother used to tell me of the man *she* knew, the one that read poetry to her and gave her a bouquet of fresh flowers every week for more than thirty years. He even named the boat that he and Dad built *Sweet Afton*, after his favorite poem written way back in the 1700s by a man named Robert Burns. Grandma used to recite it to me when I was a little girl, and I remember thinking how beautifully written the words were. The way that she spoke them is something I'll never forget. She loved Granddaddy dearly, and she always said that they were *kindred spirits.*"

John watched her smile soften, and he could sense her heart warm as she talked about her family and the love they obviously shared for one another.

Her next words were almost a whisper. "I wonder if real, true love like that still exists? If two people can somehow be so connected in spirit? I'd like to believe so."

John smiled and was imagining that Molly had probably inherited some of her own sweet spirit from the grandfather she had never known. She told him that her dad still owned the boat and, although it hadn't been in the water for more than forty years, he had always planned to restore it back to the original beauty it once was. John recalled the old wooden schooner in dry dock back in Thunderbolt and wondered if it was the same one.

An hour together had passed in a blur, and the two made their way back up the beach to the pier as he walked Molly to her car. Drawing closer to the car, they both stopped and turned to face in the direction of the wind.

Hair blowing behind her, Molly looked at him. "Thank you for meeting me here tonight, John. I enjoyed your company very much, and I'm so glad you had nothing better to do," she teased, playfully punching his arm.

John searched for an excuse to delay her departure and extend their date, but he realized it had already surpassed his every expectation.

"Can I see you again?" he asked, somehow sure that he would not be disappointed at her reply.

Molly's face gleamed under the brilliance of her smile. "I imagine so . . . if *I* have nothing better to do." Her easy smile broadened and John felt something he had never felt before.

Not quite like this, anyway. He felt himself falling . . .

CHAPTER SIX

2012 - Atlanta, Georgia

John finished drafting a business proposal he had been working on, then went into his office dressing room and changed into a navy pinstriped suit. He made a perfect knot with the light-blue tie that Joan had so generously purchased with his credit card earlier in the day and then picked up the gift from the edge of his credenza. On his way to the elevator, he placed the rough draft of the proposal in the center of Joan's desk. He knew that she would see it first thing in the morning and recognize any possible changes that needed to be made before retyping it and submitting the final draft.

We're a good team, he thought.

And they were. Joan more than pulled her weight at the firm, and she had made John's life a great deal easier for the past two decades. Needless to say, she was very well compensated.

John found his Mercedes SL63 in the parking garage. It was hard to miss—bright red and conspicuous. It had the AMG package, and he loved the feel of it. It reminded him of his old Spitfire from twenty-five years ago. Both cars were red two-seater convertibles, but, fortunately in this case, that's where the similarities ended. He turned left on Peachtree Street and began driving toward home on the northern end of the city.

The house was located off West Paces Ferry Road in the affluent community of Buckhead. A few years after they were married, John and Molly had purchased an older home with an adjoining lot.

A year later, the existing home was torn down, and they had built a Georgian style mansion based on ideas drawn from some of their favorite homes in Savannah. Now, *this* house was definitely a show place and certainly one of the finer homes ever built in Atlanta. It had even been featured in a couple of books *and* several magazines over the years, including *Architectural Digest* and *Southern Living*. Although no expense had been spared building the mansion itself, the house never quite *fully* captured the essence and personality inherent to the grand homes John and Molly had fallen in love with on Bull Street in Savannah.

John arrived home a little after 7:30 p.m. Knowing their reservation at The Optimist was at eight o'clock sharp, he quickly scaled the interior staircase in search of Molly, wholly anticipating the need to encourage her to hurry. He was met at the top of the stairs by their seven-year-old daughter, Afton, who ran right past him and into her room. The sitter, Abby, was close behind and appeared out of breath. Obviously, a game of cat-and-mouse had ensued. As usual, Afton appeared to be winning.

John entered the bedroom where Molly was putting on the last of her jewelry. He thought that she looked as amazing as she ever had, but, for some reason, those were not the words that formed.

"Are you almost ready?" he asked impatiently. "We need to leave in the next five minutes or we'll be late."

Molly sighed as she struggled with the clasp on her necklace. "Almost, John. I just need another minute."

"Okay, but hurry up. I'll see you downstairs."

As John turned to walk out of the room, he removed his iPhone from his pocket and began pressing the screen, composing an email. Seeing his distraction, Molly stomped her foot in frustration, her fingers still struggling with the clasp. All of it escaped her husband's notice as he continued down to the car.

The drive to the restaurant was spent mostly in silence, the only interruptions being two "critical" phone calls—one from Michael and one from Joan. Because a significant business deal was set to close on the following day, it was easy for John to justify his distracted state as Molly sat beside him, staring pensively out her window. She bit her lower lip, then forced a smile as they arrived at the restaurant and were led to their reserved table.

So far, the entire evening seemed to be playing out as many had as of late—awkward silences occasionally interrupted by trivial comments, yet no real substance of conversation. It seemed that John was spending more and more of his time at the office these days and less and less time with her and Afton. And even now that he was with her, his mind was not. Finally feeling the need to speak, Molly broke the uncomfortable silence that had almost become their status quo.

"I talked to Dad today. He still refuses the idea of the assisted living facility that we looked into last year. He's just *so* stubborn. It's hard to believe that he's going to be eighty-eight soon—did you know that he still goes to the marina almost every day?"

It was clear that John was only half listening to Molly as she rambled on about her father and his ailing health, his mind focused on his phone and the response to the email he had sent earlier.

"What? Oh, yeah. He's a tough man, Molly. You know that he's not going to give up *that* easily."

Molly sighed. "I know, but it's not safe for him to be alone anymore, John. You know we're going to end up having to go down there to do something."

John momentarily looked up from his phone to Molly. "I know, sweetheart. It's a hard thing. Listen, I need to run and call Joan for a minute and give her a heads-up about this deal tomorrow."

Molly stared at John, the hurt and contempt etched plainly on her face. "Can't it wait until after dinner? I mean, it *is* our anniversary."

John rose from the table. "I'm sorry, hon. I won't be long but Michael keeps making changes, and I need to be on top of it." He kissed Molly lightly on the cheek and made his exit through the front door.

Molly sat and finished her meal alone, her husband's absence cutting deep. She closed her eyes and leaned back in her seat, the weight of truth hitting her hard.

She missed her dad.

And her husband.

When John and Molly arrived back home, she went in and checked on Afton, who was sleeping soundly. As she thanked Abby and paid her for the evening, she asked the girl if she might be available again for the weekend.

"Sure, Mrs. Callaway. I'm happy to watch Afton anytime. You know how much fun we have together, and she's no trouble at all."

Molly thanked her again and locked the door behind her. John walked through the foyer as Molly made her way to the stairs that led up to their bedroom. Halfway up, she stopped.

"Alone at last," she said, attempting a smile and an inviting tone. "Are you coming up?"

John didn't even give her the courtesy of a backward glance. "I'll be up soon. I have to check on something first."

Molly went into their bedroom, changed out of her new dress, and lit some candles. She placed John's anniversary gift underneath his pillow. Early on in their marriage, they used to hide little notes and things for the other to find, and she prayed this would be a sweet reminder of better days.

It was a gift she hoped he would appreciate for the sentimentality and the significance, a rare antique book entitled, *The Poetical Works of Robert Burns.* It was a first edition that had belonged to her grandfather and contained his favorite poem, "Afton Water." The name was indeed one that echoed through her family—first, as the namesake of the sailboat he had built with her father; and then, as the reason they had chosen the name for their precious little girl.

She slipped her hand under the pillow, feeling the wrapped book, willing it to work its magic. She had come across the book nearly a year before while clearing out some of her dad's old things.

Has it really been so long?

She felt emotional already, thinking about her mother's passing seven years earlier *and* her dad being alone. It was all weighing heavily on her now. She knew it was time to encourage her aging father again to consider moving into a retirement home, one that would be better suited to help take care of him, but the last conversation about it had infuriated him. He was adamantly opposed to the proposition— so much so that he'd asked her to leave him alone and never to mention it to him again.

She had left Savannah in tears and hadn't seen him since. Only recently, she had begun speaking to him again on the phone. It was ridiculous, really, and a situation she was determined to change. These were her last thoughts as she drifted off to sleep, still waiting for John.

...

John walked into his study, logged onto his computer, and spent the next three hours going over accounting documents and making adjustments. He emailed the changes to Joan, then went upstairs and looked in on Afton before walking into his bedroom. He sat in the wing-backed chair that faced Molly's side of the bed and watched her as she slept.

She really was the most beautiful woman he'd ever seen. Sometimes it was hard for him to believe that it had been almost twenty-five years since he had seen her that first day, at the pier in Savannah. He thought that she looked even prettier now, if that was possible.

He knew that their marriage had been strained for the past few years, and she often complained about his preoccupation with work. It dawned on him then that he hadn't heard her complain much lately and wondered if she was *really* okay with the way things were now or if maybe it just didn't matter so much anymore. He felt guilty for not paying as much attention to her as he used to, and he knew that it hadn't been easy for her to deal with their daughter and her father all on her own. He hoped that someday he could find time to make it all up to her, but—for now, at least—the firm was dominating his life. And consuming *him*.

. . .

Molly awoke around 7:00 a.m. the next morning.

Alone.

Not that she was surprised to find that John wasn't in bed with her, since he usually left the house by six every morning. He had always prided himself on being the first one at the office each day. He was an overachiever, just like his father had raised him to be. She looked at his undisturbed pillow and the gift still lying underneath it—untouched.

Beside her on the bedside table, she noticed the trademark blue box from Tiffany & Co. Reading the small card attached, she thought how far removed it seemed from the wonderful, heartfelt letters that he had written to her many years before. She opened the gift and admired the craftsmanship and beauty of the neat row of diamonds embedded in gleaming platinum links.

It was an ironic gift, she realized, as there was a symbolism to the strength and clarity of diamonds that somehow felt tarnished under the current circumstances hanging over her marriage like a dark cloud. She placed the box back onto the side table and slowly pulled herself out of bed. Dropping her satin gown to the floor, she stepped into the shower, her tears intermingling with the hot spray of water upon her face.

No, last night was *not* how she imagined it should have been—not at all.

CHAPTER SEVEN

JOHN ARRIVED AT THE OFFICE JUST AFTER 6:00 A.M.
He had slept little the previous night, and he felt it. In fact, he had dozed off in the bedside chair, never actually making it into bed at all.

He would be meeting with his new clients in the conference room at 9:00 a.m. to go over the proposal that he'd finished drafting the day before—hoping Joan would be in early, as well, to finalize the changes he had made. Callaway Development had been slow to move on many projects in the past couple of years due to the slump in the economy and a lack of demand for new business space. Even so, the firm was still viable and had begun exploring partnerships in other areas outside of the continental United States where the economy was strong and still growing.

Today's deal, once closed, would be the single largest contractual partnership that they had ever entered into, especially since this partnership consisted of Callaway Development being the financial backer. In fact, the $90-million investment was primarily for the construction of an exclusive, high-end resort on what was now a private island in the Bahamas. Michael had made initial contact with the chief developers of the project nearly three years before, and the deal had taken all the firm's resources to procure. It was a big risk for them, and John had done everything in his power to guarantee its success.

When John exited the elevator, he could see Joan already at her desk, with Michael sitting across from her, typing on his laptop. He was surprised to see them *both* there so early, but he was glad that they seemed to be taking this deal just as seriously as he was.

"What's up—did I miss the meeting?" he asked, his jocular words belying the knot of anxiety forming in his gut.

Michael and Joan both looked at him and spoke at the same time.

"No, we just wanted to get here early and make sure that all of the details were ironed out and that we haven't overlooked anything important," Michael said, his voice overriding Joan's.

"*And?*" John asked.

"*And* everything looks as it should." Michael forced a smile as he closed his laptop and excused himself from Joan's office.

John sat down in the chair that Michael had vacated.

"You don't look so good, John," Joan said, leveling her gaze at him. "Something you ate?"

She always knew exactly how to push John's buttons, but one of John's strengths was a good poker face, and he never let on that it bothered him.

"To tell you the truth, Joan, I barely ate anything at all last night. I was on the phone with you and Michael for a good portion of the evening *and* I hardly slept. Something about this deal bothers me, but I can't exactly say what—or why."

"John, you know as well as I do that this is a good deal for everyone involved. Sure, there's some level of risk, but you know that you have to take big risks in order to reap big rewards."

John knew that she was right and that she had never given him bad advice. Still, he found himself wishing that his father could have been here to sign off on this one. He rose from his seat and turned to leave Joan's office.

"By the way, John—what did Molly think of her gift?" Joan asked.

"Honestly, Joan . . . I have no idea," he replied with a shrug that was far too casual, walking out the door and into his own office to begin preparing for the day.

Promptly at 9:00 a.m., John entered the conference room and greeted his new client, Greg Kline, President of Kline Construction, who was already seated and speaking with Joan and his attorney, Mark Walker. He thought for a moment that the man looked vaguely familiar, but he couldn't recall where they might have previously met—although certain they had not collaborated on any former deals. Realistically, he had met so many company heads over the years that he could hardly keep track, so he dismissed the feeling.

"We look forward to working with you on this project, Mr. Kline," he said, bypassing introductions and any other formalities. "You and your company came highly recommended to me by both my COO and my CFO. Thank you for choosing to partner with us on this exciting endeavor."

Kline remained silent as he smiled, nodded, and shook John's hand.

Obviously a man of few words. Just as well, I suppose. This is business, and I have enough friends in my life already, John thought.

Michael came into the room only a few moments later, accompanied by a tall and very attractive brunette, whom he introduced to everyone as Erica Payne—his new assistant.

John was caught completely by surprise, unaware of the new hire. Not to mention her uncommon, striking appearance. John thought it shocking that Michael would have chosen someone without considering her *actual* possession of business skills, and he guessed that her abilities were likely yet to be determined. Michael's previous hires had always been based on appearance first, competency second. This had been an area of contention between them on more than one occasion, but John hoped this time it would be different.

After all the necessary introductions had been made, everyone took their places around the finely polished conference table. Erica seated herself directly across from John and, after adjusting herself in her chair, gave him what could only be described as a "winking smile."

This obviously intentional seating arrangement and semi-flirtatious introduction from Erica did not go unnoticed by John—nor by Joan.

After two hours of reading through the details of the contract, all the pertinent documents were signed and authorization was secured to transfer a portion of the funds—a sum of $21 million—into three working accounts so that the process of development and construction could begin. With a sense of relief from both parties, everyone shook hands, and the meeting was adjourned.

When Kline walked past John, he gave him a soft pat on the shoulder and said only one word.

"Thanks."

John looked at Michael with his eyebrows raised in mock amazement. "It speaks!"

Michael laughed. "Of course he does—when he feels the need to, I suppose. Don't worry about it, though. Just let Joan deal with him. She says he's fine, go figure!"

Michael began walking away, shaking his head in mild confusion.

John spoke up again. "Hey, can I see you in my office for a minute before you leave for lunch? *Alone.*"

"Sure thing, boss. See you in a couple of minutes."

John hated it when Michael used the term *boss* to refer to him—he did it in such a way that it always came across as patronizing. He had made every attempt over the years to make *both* Michael *and* Joan feel more like partners than employees; but, when it came right down to it, it was still John's signature on the paychecks.

At least, he *thought* it was . . .

When John returned to his office, he had several messages waiting for him, including one from Molly.

"Hey, honey, it's me. I know you're probably still in your meeting, but I just wanted to give you a call and thank you for my beautiful bracelet. It's perfect. I love it."

John smiled to himself as he listened to the cheerfulness in her voice, and her voice continued. "I'm sorry that last night was less than perfect. I know you have a lot on your plate right now, but if you have some time for lunch today, I'd love to meet you somewhere and thank you in person. Just call me back when you get this and let me know. I love you. Bye."

John stared at a picture that sat on the corner of the credenza behind his desk as the message concluded. The photo showed the three of them at Disney World, celebrating Afton's fourth birthday. He was remembering how much fun that trip had been, finding it hard to believe that three years had passed since the picture had been taken.

Just as he began dialing the number to call Molly, Michael walked into his office and sat down.

John placed the handset back on the receiver and leveled a sober gaze at his partner. "What are you doing, Mike?"

Michael feigned a look of innocence. "What are you talking about?"

"You know *exactly* what I'm talking about. What's with the new girl?"

"She's *hot*, isn't she?" Michael was grinning as he spoke.

John stared intently at him and didn't blink.

"That's not what's up for debate, Mike. But what *is* is your judgment."

"I'm not sure I follow you. What are you implying?"

"The girl, Mike. *The girl.* Who is she, and how did she come to be working here? More importantly, how did she land herself right in the middle of my deal?"

Michael laughed out loud, sarcasm thick in the sound.

"*Your* deal? John, if it weren't for me, you wouldn't have even *known* about this deal! Look—just *calm down.* I know what I'm doing." He dropped his gaze to his hands, folded loosely in his lap, as he continued. "Yes, I admit that Erica's looks *may* have helped move her résumé to the top of the stack. But she's more than qualified to do the job. She has a master's in economics from Auburn, with five years of experience at Merrill Lynch, on top of that."

"That's great, Michael. So, what does that make her—about thirty?"

"Twenty-nine, actually, I think. But you have to admit—she *is* gorgeous." Michael was still grinning without the slightest hint of shame. He had changed little since college.

"She *is*," John admitted. "Just be careful, Michael. We've been down this road before."

"Nothing to worry about, John; it's all good. Hey, we're going to go grab some lunch at The Cheesecake Factory. Why don't you join us, and you can see for yourself that there's more to her than just great legs."

John reluctantly agreed to meet them for a quick lunch and decided that he would go home afterwards to crash. He was exhausted.

...

By early afternoon, Molly still hadn't received a call back from John about her lunch invitation.

While she was slightly wounded, she wasn't overly surprised, as she rarely heard from him during the day. She assumed, of course, that he was probably still in his meeting or possibly tied up on a conference call, which was usually the case. She called her friend Katie and asked her if she would like to get some lunch and run a few errands before they picked their girls up from school. Katie had twin daughters who attended Pace Academy with Afton, and she readily agreed and told Molly that she would pick her up in an hour.

...

John was seated at a table on the outside patio at The Cheesecake Factory on Peachtree Street and sipped a sweet tea with lemon while he perused the restaurant's extensive menu, already knowing that he would be having Key lime cheesecake for dessert, his absolute favorite. After settling on the Caribbean jerk chicken with black beans and mango salsa, he put the menu aside and awaited Michael and Erica's arrival, his mind caught up in reflection on the day's events thus far. As for the deal closing, he felt better now that the contracts had been signed and everything was moving forward.

As for Michael's new assistant, he thought, *the jury's still out on that one.*

John looked over at the door that adjoined the interior dining room to the patio. He watched as a server walked through, quickly followed by Erica.

"Well, hello there, Mr. Callaway. Do you mind if I join you?"

It was a rhetorical question, and Erica did not wait for a response as she took a seat at the table.

"Where's Michael?" John asked, not appreciating her presumptuousness.

"Well, it seems that Mr. Bloom won't be joining us right away. He was on the phone with Joan on the way here, talking about some problem with a wire transfer or something from the Bahamas deal this morning. He dropped me off at the door and said he would try to make it back after he got it fixed."

"*What?* What kind of problem?" John picked up his phone and pressed the screen to call Michael.

"I'm not sure. It *is* my first day—remember?"

John stared blankly at Erica as Michael's cell went straight to voicemail. He pressed redial, getting the same result.

"I told him that I would wait here with you and that it would give us some time to get acquainted," Erica said.

John barely acknowledged the woman's attempt to distract him as he made a call to Joan. Thankfully, she answered right away.

"I was expecting your call. You're so predictable, and you always worry about things too much!"

"What's going on with the account, Joan?" John's tone was stern and the question was direct.

"Nothing that can't be fixed. Don't panic. One of the routing numbers was entered incorrectly, that's all. I've almost got it taken care of, I promise. Enjoy the rest of your afternoon with Molly." Joan hung up.

Molly? What did she mean by that?

...

When Katie arrived to pick Molly up for their lunch date, she was already outside enjoying the warmth of the day.

"It's *so* good to see you, Katie! I've missed you, and I've been going out of my mind alone in the house lately."

"What's been going on with you and John? Haven't things gotten any better?"

Molly had pulled the visor mirror down and was putting on lipstick before she answered. "I don't know, Katie," she finally said with a sigh as she put the lipstick away. "Some days I think things are better, and some days I'm just not so sure." She turned to face her friend, her concerns spilling out in an anxious stream of words. "Last night was a *total* disaster, and this morning, I woke up to find *this*." Molly held up her arm and showed Katie the shining diamond bracelet on her wrist.

"Oh, Molly! That's incredible—I love it!"

"Thanks," Molly replied, her friend's enthusiasm not quite assuaging the unease she felt. "It *is* quite beautiful, isn't it?"

"It's *gorgeous*," Katie exclaimed giddily.

Molly looked contemplative and shook her head slowly, a heaviness settling in the pit of her stomach. "It's just that last night we really didn't connect. I had a vision of what the night was going to be, and I was hoping—Oh, Katie, pull in here," she broke off. "I want to pick up a dessert for tonight to celebrate John's deal closing. He absolutely loves their Key lime cheesecake."

John flagged down his server and handed him a ten-dollar bill, thanking him for the bread and sweet tea and stood up to leave. He told Erica to get her purse and that they were going back to the office to make sure the accounting problem had truly been resolved. He was afraid Joan might have downplayed the severity of the situation to ease his anxiety over the deal—the deal that she had been so eager for him to pursue.

...

Molly was getting out of Katie's SUV when she saw a red SL63 being delivered to the rear door of the restaurant by a valet. Noticing the personalized tag, she knew without a doubt that it was John's. Her brow furrowed in confusion as she watched John exit the building with a tall brunette, get into his car, and drive away.

Molly's heart sank.

She got back into Katie's car and paused for a moment before speaking.

"Will you please take me home, Katie? I think I'm going to be sick."

...

When John pulled back into the parking garage at the firm's office building, he could see Joan at the exit as she was leaving. He stopped next to her BMW and lowered his window. Erica was still in the car with him, and he didn't want to go into great detail—but he *did* want to ask Joan what had happened.

He could read Joan well enough to know that she was surprised to see Erica in the passenger seat, but she didn't show it.

"John, I told you not to worry about this. I've already handled it. Anyway, I thought you were going home for the rest of the day?"

"I *was,* Joan. But when things like this happen, I somehow find it hard to relax."

"It was just a *typo,* for goodness sake—not the end of the world, by any means. Disaster averted, now *go home.* I'll see you on Monday."

"Okay, but if anything like this happens again, I want to be made aware of it. *Immediately.*"

"*You're* the boss," Joan said with a mock two-fingered salute. "I will, but you need to stop worrying about things so much. That's what you pay *me* for." Joan raised her window and began to drive away, giving Erica a hard stare before speeding off.

John dropped Erica off in front of the bank of elevators, telling her that she could spend the rest of the day organizing her desk and familiarizing herself with the office and whatever else that Michael had asked her to do. He apologized for cutting lunch short and told her that, if she wished, she could order something from the building's cafe and charge it to the firm's account. She placed her hands on the top edge of the driver's side door and leaned down to John's eye level.

"How about I just let you make it up to me some other time?" She gave the same brazen wink and smile she had given him earlier that morning in the conference room.

"We'll see, Erica. I'm going home. When you see Michael"—he corrected himself—"when you see *Mr. Bloom,* tell him to call me on my cell, please."

"Sure thing, *John,*" she said, walking toward the elevator and pressing the call button. She looked back at him and held her stare as he drove away in the direction of home.

CHAPTER EIGHT

JOHN TURNED INTO THE CIRCULAR DRIVEWAY AND PULLED UP IN FRONT OF THE HOUSE. He couldn't remember the last time that he'd been home before sundown during the week. He noticed Katie Sutherland's SUV parked in front of the garage, which was not unusual. He knew that Molly and Katie sometimes rode together to pick up the kids from school. He entered the house through the front door and called out.

"Hello—anybody home?"

Hearing no reply, John went upstairs and checked the bedroom, still finding no one. He stopped his search long enough to change his clothes and went back downstairs, finally finding Molly and Katie sitting on a small sofa in the keeping room, just off the dining area of their kitchen. Both women stopped talking and looked up at him. Molly was obviously upset, and he could tell that she had been crying.

John felt a sudden sense of panic.

"What's wrong, Molly? Did something happen?"

She sat there in silence, staring at him.

"Is Afton okay? Tell me what's going on!"

It was Katie who finally spoke, though it was not in response to his question. Instead, she looked at Molly as she rose from her seat.

"Molly, I'll pick up the girls from school, and Afton can stay with me as long as you need her to. Just call me later, okay?"

Molly nodded her head. "Thank you, Katie. I'll call you in a little while."

Katie hugged Molly and left the house—never acknowledging John's presence.

Assuming the worst, John spoke again, this time with more urgency. "Did something happen to your dad?"

Molly glared at him, her eyes red and swollen from crying. "How would *I* know, John? I haven't seen him in six months!" she spat, pulling another handful of tissues from the box on the table in front of her.

As John sat down on the sofa and attempted to put his arm around her to console her, he noticed that she was shaking. Molly pulled away from him and turned her head.

"*Don't* touch me!" she exploded.

Still utterly confused, John felt himself becoming even more distraught by her behavior.

"What's *wrong*, Molly? Have I done something to you? Because if I have, I'm sorry."

"You *should* be, John! You should be. . . ." Her words, final though they were, trailed off—their meaning left hanging in the air, filled with accusation.

Molly stood up, snatched the tissue box from the coffee table, and went upstairs. John heard the click of their bedroom door as Molly closed and locked it behind her. Still, he followed her up the stairs, knocking on the door and calling out to her.

"Molly, open the door, please! I want to talk to you," he pleaded. "Please tell me what's going on!"

"Go *away*, John! Just go away! I don't want to talk to you right now. I need some time. Leave me alone!" her disembodied voice called through the door.

"I'm not leaving until you talk to me, Molly," he insisted. "I'm worried about you."

There was no response. John slumped onto the floor with his back to the bedroom door, shaking his head and racking his brain as he tried to figure out just what was happening.

He could still faintly hear the sound of her muffled weeping. She must have been crying into her pillow.

After an hour had passed, John heard only silence, so he gently tapped on the door once more and spoke.

"Molly, I don't know what's wrong with you because you won't talk to me." His words elicited no response. "I'm going downstairs to give you some time, but when you're ready to talk please come down." He hesitated, then added, "I love you."

Molly lay on the bed, staring up at the ceiling fan as it slowly turned above her. Wrapped in an old family quilt, she lay there with a stack of yellowing envelopes in an old shoebox on the bed beside her—cards and letters that John had written to her in the early years of their relationship.

Like the quilt squares, each letter was a scrap of her life, piecing together who she was.

Who *they* were—*together*.

One was open, and she clutched it close to her chest, the words he had penned piercing her heart. Molly was trying to swallow the lump in her throat and slow her tears. Her mind circled in an endless loop, playing and replaying scenarios as she tried somehow to put the puzzle together in her mind—all the late nights, the business trips, the constant phone calls and messages, the lack of attention. And—most of all, now—the *woman*.

She didn't *want* the pieces to fit, but it was becoming more obvious to her that they did.

Another hour passed, and Molly, bleary-eyed and tired, came downstairs and walked into John's study. He sat sunken down in a soft leather chair, randomly clicking through television channels with the remote. When he saw her, he turned off the TV and rose to stand in front of her.

"Please tell me what's wrong, Molly," he begged, her evident pain cutting him to his core. "I feel terrible."

Instead of his words softening her, they made her bristle as their seeming selfishness hit her ears. She sounded almost robotic when she finally spoke.

"Who is she?"

John's confusion was evident. "What are you talking about?"

"The *woman,* John. Or maybe I should call her a *girl.* She certainly looked young enough. Who is she?"

"Molly, I really have no idea what you're talking about."

Molly's shaking head was a clear display of her disbelief. "I *saw* you, John," she insisted. "I *saw* you with her today." Her passion escalated with her next words. "I asked you to go to lunch, but you couldn't because you were *already* at lunch with another woman!"

John suddenly felt a sense of relief. This was all a big misunderstanding that could *easily* be explained.

"Molly, baby—I stopped to meet Michael and his new assistant for lunch on my way home today," he replied, the knot of tension in his stomach beginning to unclench.

"John, I saw her leave the restaurant with you in *your* car! And *Michael* was *not* with you!"

John was looking at the situation with more humor than anything, at this point. Really, this was laughable—and she would surely see that soon enough.

"Molly, we had an emergency at the office. Michael went back to help Joan fix the problem. I just gave Erica a ride back—that's *it.* We never even had lunch," he said, his head shaking as a smile slipped into place—he hoped, reassuringly. "I realize how it must have looked, and I'm sorry for that. But you *have* to believe me! You have to *know* that I would never do anything like that!"

Molly was trying to process the scene once again in her mind, desperately wanting to believe that he was telling the truth.

It seems plausible, I suppose, she thought.

But with everything else going on lately, she just wasn't sure anymore.

"I *don't* know, John. I don't know what to do or what to think or what to believe anymore," she said quietly, the sadness heavy in her voice. "You've changed so much. You've become a stranger to me. You're *exactly* what you promised me that you would *never* be—you're just like your father."

And *there* was the truth—barreling toward him like a heavy bowling ball and then wobbling toward the gutter.

He heard the proverbial thud before he actually felt it, unable to stop her words from stealing his breath.

The worst part was knowing that she was right.

"I need some time to think about things, John. I'm going to get Afton." She paused slightly before she spoke her next words, letting them settle on him. "I don't know yet when we'll be back."

With calm and surety, she walked out of the room and headed for the door leading into the garage.

His feeling of panic returned as he followed her. "What does that mean, Molly? You can't just leave!"

Molly turned and said with cool clarity, "I need this, John. I need to be away from you right now."

John shook his head, willing this to change, for her words to reverse themselves. "Don't do this to me, Molly! Where are you going?"

"We're going to the mountains. Maybe I'll come back sometime on Sunday, but I'm not sure yet," she said with a shrug. "I'll let you know that we're safe, but *don't* call."

The finality of her command seemed to echo in the house behind her.

Molly backed out of the garage and drove to Katie's house to pick up Afton. Her plan was to drive up to their cabin in Big Canoe, about an hour and a half north of the city. The cabin, which John and Molly had nicknamed High Cotton, sat on the highest point of Sanderlin Mountain. It was supposed to have been a family retreat, but for the past few years she had mostly gone there alone to paint. For her, it had become a place of quiet solitude.

Pulling up to Katie's house to get Afton, she prepared to pretend—for her daughter's sake—that they would be taking a great weekend adventure. Katie looked at her with sad eyes, full of empathy and admiration at the weight Molly could shoulder to shield her daughter. She hoped that her parting hug could transfer some much-needed strength to her friend.

Even so, as Molly wound her way through the familiar landscape toward the cabin, she could feel her strength and her resolve begin to weaken. Exhaustion settled in as she turned the car off and carried a sleepy Afton inside. It took every ounce of strength Molly could muster just to carry her daughter—one more reminder that John wasn't there.

After tucking Afton into bed, she collapsed onto her own bed, the tears coming, unwelcomed.

Finally—*mercifully*—sleep came.

...

John stood helplessly in the driveway and watched as his wife drove away.

What he thought was going to be a pretty decent afternoon at home with his family had now, somehow, turned into a disaster.

How had things gone sideways so quickly?

For the first time in his life, he felt defeated and utterly lost. His mind was whirling, feeling like a ship without a sail that was being tossed about in rough seas.

Finally, he walked blindly back into the house.

It was quiet. *Too* quiet.

He wondered if it felt this way to Molly when she was home alone.

He'd never really thought about anything like that before—what things were like from her perspective. He was realizing, for the first time, perhaps, all that he had taken for granted in Molly and their life together. She had given up so many things to be with him.

When he had proposed to her more than twenty-one years ago, she had answered him with an immediate and resounding *Yes!* And yet, somehow, he'd never really stopped to consider all of the decisions that she was actually making just by accepting his proposal. She was choosing to leave her home, her friends, and—most importantly—her family. And she had done these things without hesitation because she loved him with all her heart.

His promise to her was that he would always do the same.

Now, he felt like a kid trying to miss the cracks in the sidewalk. Once he landed on one, being off track, he stepped on so many more.

John wandered around the empty house for what seemed like hours, looking at all the things they had acquired together over the past two decades of their marriage. Some of it held great sentimental value, but mostly it was just *stuff* to him.

Noticing that his throat was dry, he went into the kitchen to get something to drink. As he grabbed for the handle on the refrigerator, his eyes focused on the artwork held in place by two magnets—masterpieces made by his daughter. It was obvious that she had inherited the creative gene from her mother and grandmother.

He was so proud of her work and wished that his little girl were there so he could tell her.

John's phone vibrated on the counter, interrupting his reverie.

It was a text from Molly.

"We're here safe," it said simply.

His reply was just as simple, though he could certainly have allowed a flood of words to escape beneath his fingers as they moved over the screen on his phone.

"I'm glad. Please be careful. I love you. I'm sorry."

She didn't respond.

It was almost sundown, and he was completely exhausted, so he went to lie down on his bed. Adjusting his pillow, John found the package that Molly had placed there the night before.

He felt a rush of emotion as he read her words on the card attached.

To my dear husband on our anniversary–

This book belonged to my grandfather William Edwards. It was his dearest possession. I hope that the words written in this book will inspire and comfort you as they did him.

Your loving wife,

Molly

John admired the book—both for its age and for its content—and he wondered when and where she'd gotten it. He knew how special it must be to her and how thoughtful she had been to give it to him.

He lay there alone in the deafeningly silent emptiness of the house and wept, the weight of the book sitting heavily on his chest.

CHAPTER NINE

THE FOLLOWING MORNING, JOHN DROVE TO COLUMBUS. IT WAS ABOUT
A HUNDRED MILES SOUTHWEST OF ATLANTA, AND HE KNEW THE DRIVE
WELL. The city was built on the banks of the Chattahoochee River,
bordering Alabama. He had many childhood memories here, visiting
his grandparents. It was his mother's hometown, and she had moved
back there shortly after his father's death in the early nineties. His
parents had been separated for a few months prior to his father's passing, and although they had begun taking steps to reconcile, she had
not dealt well with so many things left undone—unresolved.

After his father's heart attack, his mother had felt that she needed
to be as far removed as possible from the business and the lifestyle that
she blamed for the destruction of their marriage—and, ultimately, for
her husband's death.

John realized now that he hadn't visited his mother in more than
a year, and he knew it was time to start making more of an effort to
be a better son.

Not to mention a better husband and father.

He felt a dichotomy of emotions, a tug on his heart that wanted
desperately to please both his mother *and* his father. It was a complicated task, to gratify them both in their expectations of him. In a way,
it had been much easier when his father was alive, since his father had
been such a commanding presence and so sure of everything.

Unfortunately, his mother seemed to be the casualty in this war. As a result, John wasn't quite sure what to expect when he saw her now. Especially under *these* circumstances.

When he arrived at his mother's home just after ten that morning, she was outside pruning flowers at the edge of the driveway. She had always taken great pride in her rose bushes and hydrangeas, never letting anyone else tend to them. They were her babies, and she spent most Saturday mornings nurturing them, always making sure that they looked their best.

John pulled up alongside where she was working and switched off the ignition.

"So . . . I'm guessing Molly left you?" she deadpanned, eyebrows arched knowingly and garden-gloved hands seemingly fused to her hips, as the words precluded any greeting from her son.

He didn't speak, and his mother returned to her task as she continued mercilessly. "It was just a matter of time, I suppose. To tell you the truth, son, I'm surprised that she put up with you as long as she did. Lord knows I put up with your father longer than I should have!" This last phrase was stated with fierce honesty, the sound of her pruning shears adding ironic emphasis.

His mother's words pierced his soul and felt extremely harsh, doing nothing in the way of comforting him. His face fell with obvious disappointment, perhaps more in himself than in his mother. John felt utterly drained and unspeakably weary.

"I imagine you haven't eaten anything, either," his mother said, not looking up from her work. "Go on up to the house and Martha will fix you something. I'll be along soon enough."

She was referring to the housekeeper and cook who had worked for his family for more than forty years. Martha had moved to Columbus right along with his mother without needing the formality of a request in order to continue her services. Although she was in the employ of his mother, the two had always shared more of a mother-daughter relationship than anything else, despite the fact that Martha was only eight years his mother's elder.

It was true enough that Mrs. Callaway had always *owned* the house, but no one could dispute the fact of who actually *ran* it.

John restarted his car and continued up the winding path that led to his mother's stately home.

When he entered through the side door leading directly into the kitchen, Martha was standing in front of the sink washing a large pot. Now well into her seventies, she still looked exactly to him as she had when he was a child. She had dark chocolate skin, and even darker eyes, and a way about her that made you feel like she was looking *into* you rather than *at* you.

"Good Lawd!" she squealed, raising her arms high. "Look what da cat done drugged up in here! Just look at you, child—*skinny as a rail!* You sit right down here and let me fix you up some biscuits and gravy that'll stick to those ribs," she tutted.

It was the first time that John had smiled in days. "Thank you, Miss Martha. I would love that." He gave her an affectionate hug and told her how good it was to see her again.

"Alright now," she said, shooing him off. "You gonna get this dirty dishwater *all* ov' ya. Go sit down and let me tend to my bizness."

With that, he took a seat on a stool at the end of the counter, watching as she began adding ingredients into a large mixing bowl, then stirring them together. Without breaking the steady progression of her movements as she spoke, her mouth formed the words John had been dreading.

"Where's that pretty baby girl and Ms. Molly this fine mornin'?" Looking up from the bowl and hardly pausing before her wisdom perceived his anguish, she spared John the trouble of a reply. "*Lawd, child! She done up and left you!*"

It was more a statement than a question, and John was hit by the realization that *both* Martha *and* his mother had somehow known exactly what had happened, without him having to say a word.

"Boy, you gonna have to work *hard* and get dat girl back—you hear me? Don't you go off from here and make dem same mistakes yo daddy did with yo mama!"

He wondered now if his mother had purposely sent him ahead to the house, knowing the lecture he'd no doubt receive from Martha, who continued preparing breakfast as she hummed part of the old familiar hymn "Does Jesus Care."

John had grown up listening to Martha sing old Negro spirituals and hymns, and it had always made him feel at ease whenever she sang in the house. She continued on, in her uniquely soulful way:

"Does Jesus care when my way is dark, with a nameless dread and fear? As the daylight fades into deep night shades, does He care enough to be near?"

Her mixture of humming and singing took him back to a simpler time in his life, and he could feel the sting of forming tears. She knew exactly what she was doing, all right—she was probably the smartest lady that he had ever known. She stopped cooking and singing for a moment and shot him a slight smile and a wink. John got up from his stool and walked up behind her, pulling her into another big bear hug before she had time to swat him away with her dishcloth.

His mother walked into the kitchen, and the two ladies looked meaningfully at each other. Martha gave a knowing nod, an unspoken confirmation to his mother that she had done her job—and that she had done it well.

The three of them sat down together at the table and ate in relative silence. An occasional comment was made out of politeness, but there was no real conversation. When they were finished, Martha cleared the table and insisted that John and his mother leave the kitchen. They complied, knowing better than to argue.

John walked around the house now from room to room, enjoying a peacefulness that came somewhat unexpectedly. Although this had never been his home, it had a familiar feel to it; perhaps being surrounded by all the things that he had grown up with made him feel at rest. Everywhere he looked, there were reminders of his life, things that his mother had collected since she had married his father so very long ago.

Among the treasures and trinkets was an oil painting, hung above the fireplace in the living room. The piece depicted a sailboat and a lone sailor in the midst of a turbulent storm, and it was one that was particularly sentimental for John and Molly. His mother had purchased it from an artist in Savannah when he and his family had vacationed there when he was thirteen. He remembered his mother recounting the story that she had been told by the artist on the day she had acquired it.

Years later, while he and Molly were dating, he found her in his father's study, mesmerized by the painting. Molly had her hand over her mouth, shaking her head in disbelief. It was only then that the connection had been made.

The painting was one of her mother's.

It had been her mom's vision of Molly's grandfather, William Edwards, and his last voyage out to sea.

In that moment of realization, John and Molly knew—without a doubt—that it had been more than coincidence drawing the two of them together that first evening at the pier.

It had been *fate*.

No further confirmation was needed—they had been destined to find each other.

He stood now, once again staring at the painting, and found himself mesmerized, much like Molly had been. His mother's approaching footsteps sounded softly on the floorboards behind him.

"I want you to take that home with you," she said.

"What?"

"It belongs with you and Molly. Really, I should have given it to you years ago." Her voice sounded reflective, almost regretful. "I think that if I had, you wouldn't be standing where you are right now.

It's a good reminder of where things are supposed to be—and *how* they're supposed to be."

He knew that she was right about how things were supposed to be. And *where* he was supposed to be.

Now, more than he might have ever been before, he was grateful for the gift.

John hugged his mother and thanked her.

She hadn't said much while he had been there, but sometimes it only took a nudge to be pointed in the right direction.

He said goodbye to Martha and promised them both that he would bring Afton back to see them soon. He loaded the painting into the trunk of his car and left, relieved to find that he was feeling somewhat better than he had felt when he arrived.

...

On Sunday, the minutes seemed interminable to John, taking what felt like hours to pass. He was anxious for his girls to come home, wanting to hug them both. He wanted Molly to see the painting that had always meant so much to them, hanging now in its rightful place in his study.

He desperately wanted to feel like everything was going to be okay, and he felt sure that Molly would come to realize that the situation with Erica had all just been a silly misunderstanding. All he needed was to talk to her, to reassure her. It would all be repaired simply enough when she returned.

So confident was he in this that John was not prepared for what she told him when he saw her, at last, on Sunday evening.

CHAPTER TEN

John checked in at the Ritz Carlton Buckhead later that evening, telling the desk clerk that the length of his stay would
be . . . indefinite.

He was courteously shown to his suite and his luggage deposited inside the door—a glaring reminder that he was, at this point, unsure of
his true place.

Sitting on the edge of an immaculately made bed, John ran his fingers through his hair, feeling exasperated. He decided to text Molly.

"I don't understand how this has happened to us. When did we
stop believing in each other? I never meant for things to be this way.
I'm sorry. I love you."

He sat staring at the phone, waiting and hoping for a response, but
none came.

Later, he ordered a pizza that was delivered to his room, and he
mindlessly watched TV for an hour before falling asleep, not bothering to set an alarm.

. . .

On Monday morning, John awoke a little after eight. He was late,
but tardiness was the least of his concerns. He checked his phone to
see if there was a message from Molly.

There wasn't.

John walked into the Callaway office just over an hour later, exiting the elevator and headed directly toward his corner office, without speaking to anyone along the way.

As Joan looked up from clearing a paper jam out of the printer, her raised eyebrow and speculative sweep of his appearance left no doubt that she had quickly assessed trouble brewing.

"Hold all my calls," John mumbled as his office door closed behind him.

Joan waited for about hour before attempting to make any contact with him, lightly knocking on his office door and slowly opening it to peek inside. John sat motionless in his chair, staring out the large windows behind his desk, and she silently walked up to where he was sitting.

He neither responded to her nor acknowledged her presence in any way.

"John, what's going on with you? Are you okay?"

He remained frozen and silent.

"John, answer me. What's wrong with you? Did something happen at home?"

Without looking at her, he said flatly, "Molly's leaving me."

Joan's face grew pale as the information he just divulged rendered her speechless.

"*What*? You *have* to be joking! What happened?"

"I wish I were, Joan. She says she's had enough and that I'm not the man she fell in love with. She says I'm not the man she married."

When Joan finally ventured a reply, her tone was almost that of a coach prodding a team to win a championship, pepping them with inflated confidence. "You're a grown man now, John. *Of course* you're not the same man that she married. You are powerful and successful, and you have more than most men can ever dream of having. You should be *proud* of who you are and what you've accomplished," she insisted.

Despite her insistent tone, however, Joan's words seemed hollow and empty to John's ears. His voice was still flat as he replied, "Sure, Joan. I really do have it *all*, don't I?"

Joan replied sincerely, hoping that his agreement meant that he was coming out of this fog of disillusionment that he seemed to be mired in. "Yes, John. You *do*. And if you would take time to look around, you would realize that."

He cut his eyes toward her, his face showing no trace of emotion, as he watched her place a large, decorative envelope on the corner of his desk and leave the room. John turned away and continued to stare unblinkingly—unseeingly—out the window.

...

Molly dropped Afton off at school and then joined Katie at a nearby coffee shop to talk about what had developed between her and John the night before.

"Katie, the truth is, I feel like I'm living with a stranger." She looked uncertainly around her, clearly not wanting anyone to hear. "We don't talk or do anything together anymore. We hardly even *see* each other at all, for that matter."

Katie was worried, thinking how tired and exhausted her friend looked.

"I told him last night that I wasn't sure that we could stay married if something didn't change drastically," Molly whispered, trying to keep her emotions in check. "It wasn't an ultimatum so much as an attempt to be honest—for *one* of us to finally be *honest* about the way things are between us."

"Oh, honey," Katie murmured, feeling her heart break for Molly. "What did he say when you told him that?"

"He started ranting about how I was overreacting—'*as usual*'—and that he's worked *very hard* to take care of us." Angry tears spilled from her blue eyes as she spoke. "You know, Katie, I don't deny that he *has* worked hard and that he's done well for our family. But when is it ever going to be *enough?*"

"I know Molly, and I know this isn't easy for either of you," Katie soothed. "Brad and I have both noticed a big change in John over the past few years. Honestly, we're surprised that something hadn't happened before now."

Molly wasn't at all shocked by Katie's words.

She knew that she and John rarely did anything social with friends anymore, and a lot of them had even stopped calling to invite them to do things.

"I know. Things are just so different than they used to be." She shook her head sadly. "But in the past four or five years, it's gotten so much worse. I told him last night that I needed time to think about what was best for Afton and me. He got really upset by that, and things started to escalate, so I asked him to leave." She dabbed at her tears with a napkin she had pulled from a dispenser on their table. "He did—reluctantly."

"Where do you think he went?"

"Probably to the Ritz—that's where the firm usually accommodates all their visiting clients and team members. I'm not exactly sure when I'll see him again. I didn't tell him when to expect a call, either." Tears spilled from her eyes again, this time too quickly to stave off with a paper napkin.

Katie hugged her, at a loss for words and reluctantly saying goodbye only after noticing the time. "You may not feel like it right now, Molly, but it really was a good step to be so open and honest with John," she said, squeezing Molly's shoulder in reassurance. "I'll check in on you in the morning."

Molly sat in the same spot, motionless for a while, feeling numb and weary. Her coffee had grown cold. Even so, she held it clutched between her hands, her fingers wrapped around it tightly as though it were still hot and she was in need of its warmth.

Her mind wandered off to places in her past, playing the video reel of her life with John. She saw the John she had fallen in love with, remembering the nuances of what made them the "perfect" couple. She couldn't help but think it would be so much easier if she could just somehow forget it all.

The strange, truthful reality of love and all its costs sobered her for a moment.

She breathed in deeply, letting the thought sink into her soul.

While the truth was painful, it also empowered her.

Love doesn't ever really let you go or leave you unchanged, does it? It's changed me like the sand shifting with the tide, and I can't ever really go back. It's not possible. I just have to decide how *to move forward.*

...

John opened the large envelope that Joan had left on his desk. It was an invitation to attend an annual business gala that was being held in Atlanta the following week. He was to be honored at the event with an award for CEO of the year for the top fifty Southern-based companies.

It would be his first time receiving the prestigious award.

The honor had been bestowed twice before to his father, when he ran the company. But while it was certainly a great achievement, John found that he was less than excited at the thought of pretending to be happy in front of a thousand of his peers.

He couldn't help but wonder, too, if he would be attending the event alone.

As John left his office and began walking toward the elevator, he paused at Joan's desk to tell her that he was going to lunch and that he wasn't sure when he would be back. Joan tried to delay his departure by congratulating him on his upcoming award, but he was already pressing the call button for the elevator, and it opened immediately.

Just as he was stepping inside, Joan informed him that there were some documents that needed his signature before the end of the day.

Seconds before the doors slid closed, he looked up at Joan and said, "Handle it."

Joan sat glaring at the elevator doors, willing them to open again and feeling helpless when they did not. She had never seen John act this way before—so detached and seeming without care for the firm, for himself, or for *her*, even.

She was also becoming increasingly irritated at the fact that he was no longer confiding in her about his affairs outside of the office. Joan thrived on knowing that John depended on her for so much. But as of late, that dependence had begun to diminish, and she had begun to feel very unappreciated. She hoped that all of this would sort itself out sooner rather than later. More importantly, she didn't like the feeling that things were out of her control. John seemed to be acting very differently around the office lately, and he seemed to be becoming more paranoid and obsessed with details that, in the past, had always been left up to her discretion.

A moment later, Erica walked past Joan's desk on her way into John's office. Joan stopped her short with a snapping comment. "He's out at lunch. What do you need?"

"Okay, thanks." Erica spun around and walked directly into the elevator, pressing the button for the parking garage as she gave her signature winking smile to Joan, while the doors slid to a silent close in front of her.

...

John was opening his car door when Erica approached him in the garage.

"Hey, John. Where are you going in such a hurry?"

He turned to see her walking toward him. "Ms. Payne," he replied distractedly, not bothering to correct her overly familiar greeting, despite the fact that he still considered it inappropriate. He had more important things on his mind at the moment. "I'm going for a drive to clear my head for a while."

"Would you like some company? We could grab that lunch we missed the other day," she offered, her tone persuasive.

John looked at her standing there in front of him, noticing that she had moved in closer as she spoke. There was no denying that, on the surface, she looked flawless. Her eyes were piercing, even in the dim lights of the garage, but her attractiveness gave him no pause and held no interest for him.

"No, thank you. I need some time alone away from the office to think."

Erica made no attempt to hide her disappointment and walked away pouting like a spoiled child who had failed in getting her own way.

She probably hasn't had much experience with rejection, John thought, watching for a moment as she retreated toward the elevator.

Without consciously deciding on his destination, John drove north on I-75 toward Big Canoe and the mountain cabin. He sent a brief email to Joan that he would be out of the office for the rest of the day and that he was only to be contacted in the event of an emergency.

...

Joan was not pleased to read John's instructions and made a grunting sound out of sheer frustration. She continued what she had been working on through lunch and then decided that she was at a stopping point until he let her know how to proceed further.

A short while later, Michael approached her office and asked if she would mind calling a courier to pick up some documents for the Bahamas deal that needed to go out next-day air. She merely looked at him, trying her best to disguise the disdain she had always felt for the man. The two of them had never really been close, and it seemed that they were always in competition for John's attention.

She *wanted* to say, "*Mike*, I am *not* your personal secretary. I work for *John*. And, for that matter, I am not *his* 'secretary,' either. Where's your supermodel-wannabe Erica, or whatever her name is?"

Instead, she kept her response civil and noncommittal.

"Where's your new assistant?"

"She called me at lunch and said that she wasn't feeling well," he said with a shrug. "I told her to take the rest of the afternoon off. I don't want her bringing anything into the office." He offered a sparkling smile, one that no doubt was his go-to for charming "the ladies."

Joan stared intently at Michael for a few seconds before snatching the envelope from his hand. He gave her a sarcastic *Thanks* and walked back down the hall to his office.

Joan turned back to her computer and began typing with sharp keystrokes, mumbling obscenities under her breath.

...

John arrived at Big Canoe mid-afternoon. He looked around the outside of the house for a few minutes and picked up several limbs that had fallen near the cabin before going in. When he opened the front door, he could still detect faint signs of Molly's recent presence, the fragrance she wore lightly perfuming the air. He walked from room to room in the cabin, trying to find any other traces of her. He looked at her easel, noticing that it held an unfinished painting of the seemingly endless view from the rear deck of the house.

Sometimes on clear nights, the glowing skyline of Atlanta could be seen some seventy miles to the south. He and Molly had spent many wonderful days and nights at this cabin over the years, and he wondered why it hadn't occurred to him to escape there more often. He didn't realize just how much he'd missed the little house on Sanderlin Mountain.

He piddled around for a couple of hours, making some minor repairs to the screen door on the back porch and tightening a loose handrail that led down the back steps. Feeling that everything was in order, he closed up the house and drove back down the mountain to eat dinner at a local restaurant called Appalachia. It had always been a favorite of theirs, his and Molly's, and the freshly grilled rainbow trout was on par with any fussily created dish from one of the five-star restaurants in the city.

After dining alone, John began driving back toward Atlanta and his new temporary home at the Ritz, having chosen not to stay at the mountain house. Being there only made him miss his girls even more, a feeling that he hoped would be short-lived.

When he called home, Molly answered, and he nervously asked her how she was doing. She told him that she had certainly been better. He was momentarily at a loss for his next words, and he could feel the hurt and disappointment in her voice as she spoke.

"Molly, I want you to know that I am truly sorry for everything I've put you through." His voice quieted then, and he said softly, "I never, ever intended to make you feel this way. I know that I haven't been myself lately. I have no excuse for that—there's just been so much craziness going on at work these days, and things have gotten a little out of hand." Silence hung over the line as he continued. "You have to know in your heart, though, that I would never, *ever* betray you with another woman."

Molly could feel the sincerity in his voice, and her impulse was to tell him that she believed him and that she wanted him to come home. Even so, she remained silent. Regardless of her feelings about Erica, she was still angry with him for putting so much importance on everything *but* her and their daughter.

"Molly, please tell me that you still believe in me—in us," he implored.

"I want to, John. I really do," she said, still unable to give him any further words of consolation. "Would you like to speak to Afton before she goes to bed?"

"Of course," he replied, feeling unresolved. "Molly—" he stammered, trying to hold her on the line a little bit longer. "Molly, I'm receiving an award next week at the gala. I would really like it if you were there—*with* me."

"We'll see, John," she said uncertainly. "Here's Afton." She handed the phone to their eager little girl.

"Hi, Daddy! Where are you? When are you coming home?" her cheery little voice chirped.

"I'm close by, baby girl. Don't worry—Daddy will be home soon." He was praying with all his might that what he was telling his daughter was the truth.

"Okay, Daddy. I love you. Nite-nite."

"Goodnight, sweet girl. You be good and give Mommy a big hug from me."

After that, the connection was broken.

Sitting alone in the silence of the hotel room, John could feel the heartache closing in.

CHAPTER ELEVEN

THE FOLLOWING DAY, JOHN WALKED INTO THE OFFICE SHORTLY AFTER FIVE IN THE MORNING. It had been a restless night, and he had been unable to sleep. His natural instinct had always been to pour himself into his work and forget about everything else in the world around him. And, while it was something that had always worked for him in the past, it had seemed less effective lately. For an instant, when he sat down at his desk, he thought that he smelled Molly's perfume.

Funny how the mind works, he mused.

He clicked his computer mouse to log on and was surprised to see that he had inadvertently failed to log out of the system the day before when he left the office early. He had obviously been distracted.

Thankfully, this was a rare occurrence. However, to him, it was an unacceptable mistake, and he made a note to mention it to Joan. He wanted to ask her to make sure that the office was secure before she left each day. Sensitive information could be accessed or, at the very least, compromised by anyone willing and interested enough to look for it. Only a year before, in fact, a nighttime security guard had used one of the company computers to access an online-dating website of a questionable nature. As a result, a virus had infected the system, causing considerable damage in an amazingly short amount of time.

In light of the new developments at the firm, this was hardly the time to be less vigilant about such things.

For the next two hours, John read through the monthly financials and drafted notes for the weekly Wednesday-morning board meeting. Once satisfied with his plans for the next meeting's agenda, he began to work on a rough outline for his award acceptance speech. This sort of thing had always been easy for him to articulate, but, given the current state of his personal life, he felt that he was at a loss for words.

Writing this now was anything but easy.

...

Promptly at eight o'clock, he heard Joan arranging herself at her desk. He called out for her to step into his office for a moment but was greeted with no response. After a second attempt, he got up and made his way toward where she sat.

"Did you hear me call for you?"

She looked up at him with feigned surprise. "Oh, sorry, John. I didn't realize that you were at work today."

It was a game that he had grown accustomed to over the years, one that his father would have never tolerated. Now, it tried his patience, as well.

"I'm at work *every* day, Joan. What's with your sudden question of my work ethic?"

Joan shrugged. "I know you're having problems at home. I'm just trying to remind you that you have duties here, as well. The proverbial ship needs to stay afloat."

"I'm a good skipper, Joan. I always *have* been, so don't question my dedication now." It hardly seemed the ideal time to mention his computer security issue and admit his level of distraction. Instead, he issued a reminder to be diligent in making sure that the office was fully buttoned up and locked down when she left at the end of each day.

"Noted," she said with an eyebrow raised and her tone cool. Trying to placate her somehow, he asked her if she would like a cup of coffee. She offered a minimal refusal, turning away as John headed off for the breakroom at the end of the hall.

When John entered the room, he found Erica there alone, busily scouring the refrigerator shelves for some item that seemed to elude her.

"Is there something in particular you're looking for, Ms. Payne? Maybe I can point you in the right direction," he said, his voice breaking the silence of the room.

The young woman looked up with a start.

"Oh! You nearly scared me to death!" she exclaimed, letting her hand flutter to her chest.

"Sorry about that. It wasn't intentional—scout's honor." He smiled slightly and gave the familiar two-fingered salute.

"Thanks, John, but I think I've found *just* what I was looking for." She paused dramatically before removing a package of cream cheese from the side shelf.

She locked eyes with him for a moment and displayed an award-worthy smile, revealing two gleaming rows of bright white teeth. He thought it likely that her cosmetic dentist had some awards of his own. Her perfume wafted through the room and filled the air around them.

"Dolce & Gabbana—Light Blue, am I right?" he asked.

Erica smiled again. "We have a winner. *Very* impressive. For that correct answer, I'll let you take me out to lunch or dinner—or Paris. Your choice," she said, laughing coyly.

Joan could be heard clearing her throat in an over-the-top manner, like a schoolteacher whose class had become too rowdy.

John held his finger up to his lips. "Uh-oh—we'd better get to work," he whispered conspiratorially. "You don't want to get called into the principal's office on your first week."

"Maybe I do," Erica replied, her mouth tipped in a suggestive smile. "After all—aren't *you* the principal?"

John was caught off guard for a moment by her blatant flirtation.

"Well, yes. I guess I am . . . but, in this case, I was actually refer-ring to *her*." He nodded his head in the direction of Joan.

He quickly realized where the conversation was heading and de-cided that it would be a good time to excuse himself and return to the safety of his corner office, securely positioned behind his gatekeeper and protector, Joan Taylor.

"Have a good day, Ms. Payne. When you see Mr. Bloom, please ask him to send me his financials for this month. They're past due, and we meet about them tomorrow."

Erica stood up straight, giving John a jaunty salute and a wink. "Aye, aye, Captain. At your service."

John walked back up the hall under Joan's unblinking stare. As he passed in front her, he simply said, "What?"

Her silent glare spoke volumes, making her lack of amusement evident, as it followed John into his office, as though she had spoken her disapproval out loud.

When he sat back down at his desk, John tried to gather his thoughts. For a moment, he pondered Erica's comments in the break-room and thought about her silly reference to his role as a captain and her mock salute. Had she heard his earlier conversation with Joan when he'd referred to himself as a skipper? He quickly dismissed the thought as trivial and moved on to tackle the next item on his long list of things to do.

. . .

Joan retrieved her phone from her purse and excused herself to the ladies' room, dialing Molly's cell number once she was safely en-sconced in a stall.

"Hello, Joan. What can I do for you?" Molly's tone was cold.

"Hi, Molly. I know this might be unexpected, but I was just won-dering if you would consider meeting me for lunch this afternoon? I have a few things to discuss with you that I think will be very helpful, in light of everything you're going through at home."

Molly hesitated before answering. She and Joan had always had what might be considered a tenuous relationship, but she was hardly naive to the fact that Joan knew as much about her husband as she did—maybe even *more*.

"Sure," she replied, still feeling unsettled at the idea. "I'll meet you someplace and we can talk. But I do have to pick Afton up from school by three."

"Oh good, Molly. Thank you—I won't keep you long. How does twelve-thirty at ECCO sound?"

"That sounds fine," Molly said, feeling somehow anything *but* fine. "I'll see you then."

"Very good. I'll call ahead and get us a table—see you there."

They both hung up, and Joan dialed the number for the restaurant to reserve a table for two.

A moment later, she rapped lightly on the doorframe of the open door and entered John's office, sitting down in one of the high-backed leather visitor's chairs directly in front of his desk. She looked at him with the very serious expression that seemed permanently etched into her face.

"John, we need to talk."

...

Molly left her car with the valet at ECCO and made her way inside the restaurant. She found Joan sitting at a corner table just beyond the bar, and the older woman greeted her with a warm smile and thanked her for agreeing to the meeting. Without even glancing at the menu, both ladies ordered grilled-salmon salads and handed their menus over to the server.

As the server left them, Joan began the conversation that she had obviously been holding until they were alone.

"Molly, I'm sure that you must be wondering why I asked you to join me here today—I'm very aware of the fact that this meeting is hardly a normal occurrence for the two of us."

"Yes, Joan," Molly said with a slow nod. "I *am* wondering. I do hope that it's something positive, but prudence is making me prepare for the worst. I know that you're well aware that things aren't the best right now between John and me." Molly took a small sip of the water that sat before her, the ice tinkling softly as it clinked against the side of the glass.

"Yes, I'm very aware—and that's why I wanted to talk to you today. Molly," she paused and folded her hands on the table as she leaned forward, fixing Molly with an intent gaze, "I want you to reconsider your decision to separate from John."

Molly drew back, offended by the intrusiveness of Joan's words. "Joan, I don't see this is really *any* of your business."

"It *is* my *business,* Molly!" She practically spat the words. "And *you* of *all* people should understand and appreciate that!"

Molly snatched up her purse and began to rise from her seat. Joan reached over and touched her arm, her manner suddenly softened.

"Molly, I'm sorry," she soothed. "I didn't mean to sound so harsh. Please, sit down and just hear me out."

Molly slowly settled back into her chair, and Joan removed her staying hand from Molly's arm.

"Look, Molly . . . you and I both know that John is always putting himself under extreme pressure to succeed. He never lets up, and he's always strived to be the best at everything that he does. He can't help it—it's who is and it's what he was *born* to be."

"I'm failing to see your point, Joan."

"My *point* is that John needs your support now more than ever. I've never seen him so unfocused at work. He's a wreck, and he's miserable without you and Afton."

Despite her own best efforts to maintain her resolve, Molly felt her heart begin to soften as Joan continued to speak.

"I know that he loves you and would never do anything intentionally to hurt you or his daughter. I also understand that you need him to be his best at home—just like I need him to be his best at the firm. That's why I'm asking for you to give him a chance to make things right again. I spoke to him this morning and suggested that he take some time off and get his act together. I think a nice, long vacation might be just what the two of you need."

Molly was trying to process all that she was hearing from Joan. It seemed so out of character.

"Did John put you up to this?" she asked, suspicion heavy in her words.

"Absolutely not, Molly," Joan insisted. "I promise you that he has no idea that I'm here with you, and you know as well as I do that John is not the kind of man who would ask anyone to do his bidding for him."

Molly's eyes began to well with tears, and her voice began to shake as she spoke. "Joan, I know that you think it's your job to protect John and the firm, but I need you to be completely honest with me. Do you think that something could be going on with this new girl at the office—Erica?"

Joan felt a pulsing surge run through her body like a jolt of electricity.

"Heavens no, Molly! Why would you even think such a thing?" she said resolutely, trying to pass the whole idea off as utterly preposterous.

"I don't know, Joan. He's just seemed so distant lately and not himself, always on his phone or his computer when he's at home." She paused for a moment before she continued, saying her next words almost as though she was afraid of speaking them into reality. "And I saw him leaving a restaurant with *her* in the middle of the day."

Joan maintained her composure, accustomed to keeping herself calm and collected even under the most unsettling of circumstances.

"Molly, I can assure you that if you saw John with Erica—or anyone else, for that matter—at any time of day, it was strictly business related. I have never been a witness to any impropriety on John's part that would give me reason to believe anything to the contrary." Even as she spoke the words, Joan was wondering if this had been the day that she had seen them pulling into the parking garage—or perhaps it was the day that neither of them had returned to the office after lunch?

Molly thanked Joan for her care and concern and told her that she would consider all that they had discussed. She also asked that she keep their conversation in confidence. Joan assured her that it would go no further, offering her help anytime that it may be needed—for any reason.

"I love John—*and* you—like family, Molly," she said as she took the younger woman in a brief embrace before Molly left the restaurant. Joan paid the check as their food was delivered to their table, leaving it untouched as she gathered her belongings and summoned the valet for her car. As she waited for her BMW to be delivered to the curb, Joan pulled her phone from her handbag, quickly typing a message before she pressed *Send*.

CHAPTER TWELVE

JOHN SAT ALONE IN THE QUIET OF THE OFFICE DURING HIS LUNCH HOUR, SEARCHING THE INTERNET FOR POSSIBLE VACATION DESTINATIONS, OR PERHAPS JUST FOR AN EXTENDED WEEKEND GETAWAY.

Either way, he hoped that he would be able to convince Molly to take him up on an offer of leaving town with him. He was thinking along the lines of something tropical and serene. He had long agreed with the notion that saltwater was soothing—not only for the body but also for the mental abrasions inevitably acquired on land, in the everyday reality of the harsh world.

His first thoughts were of the Bahamas, reasoning that he could use the recent development deal there to justify his absence from the office. This, of course, was a self-imposed guilt, since he answered to no one else at the firm but himself. He eventually dismissed the idea of trying to mix business with pleasure, knowing—when he admitted it to himself—that it would only serve to defeat his true purpose in winning Molly's heart back.

Moving on in his search, John found a website that offered sailing excursions as well as sailboat rentals for qualified skippers. The company listed a number of vessels for hire in all sizes and classes, with rental periods available from as little as half a day up to a full month.

He focused in on a thirty-two-foot Morgan sailing yacht, a medium-sized craft that was well-fitted and could be easily managed by just the two of them. As he became lost in thought, the computer screen seemed to fade out in a blur before his fixed stare, a memory rising to the surface and overtaking his vision.

It played out in his mind, full of color and so vivid that it could have been unfolding right in that very moment. Molly was standing on a boat, her face aglow in such a look of utter happiness that it was breathtaking—unforgettably so. He thought then about all of the sailing excursions he and Molly had taken from her father's marina in Thunderbolt when they had first begun dating. They had even taken several overnight trips at sea during the early years of their marriage. It had been instrumental in deepening, then cementing their relationship.

The dynamics of who they were as a couple had been learned out on those waves, and they had navigated together like sea-weathered shipmates using a trusty compass. He realized now that in those times they had become each other's compass, each relying on the other's strengths to fortify their own.

John needed Molly, and he hoped with all his might that reliving the experience could help them reclaim at least *some* of what had been lost in the recent years. He couldn't help but pray that she needed him, too.

Finally turning his attention back to the present, John looked at the details of the boat he had found to lease for their trip. It was located in a private slip in Key West, Florida. He scribbled down the owner's name and phone number, then logged off his computer.

Michael passed by John's office on his way to the elevator without speaking or acknowledging John sitting at his desk. They briefly made eye contact with each other as Michael waited for the elevator car to arrive, and John motioned for him to step into his office for a moment.

"Hey, Mike—where are you headed?"

Michael's response was aloof. "To lunch, boss—if that's okay with you."

Feeling his nerves set on edge by Michael's words, John forced a smile. *"Of course,* Mike. You're entitled to lunch—just like everyone else around here. But I need your month-end financial reports by the end of the day. I need to go over them with you before we meet in the morning."

Dismissing John with his tone, Michael responded, "Don't worry. You'll have them—just been running a little behind. Erica will help me pull things together when I get back." The familiar ding of the elevator's arrival seemed almost to sound on cue. "Gotta run, John. I'm late." He stepped into the waiting elevator and disappeared, safely ushered away from further questioning.

John wondered if the change he was seeing in his partner was all just his imagination, or perhaps it was somehow a response to the fact that he had been so distracted with all that was going on at the firm and at home. Whatever it was, Michael seemed disconnected and unconcerned with work, and John hoped that this newly acquired assistant of his was not the cause of Michael's obvious lack of attention to detail. It was unlike him not to be on top of the numbers.

John began to call Molly, both to check on her and Afton and to feel out the potential of her openness to the suggestion of a getaway, an attempt to work on things between them. As he picked up his phone, it vibrated in his hand. He looked at the display.

Molly.

"Hey, Molly—I was just about to call you."

She sounded upset when she spoke. "John, it's my dad. He's not doing well—he fell again today out by the mailbox. Mr. Davis from across the street saw him and went to help, but Dad refused to let him call 911, so he called me instead. I have to get down there and try to do something!"

John sighed. He had known that it was only a matter of time before she would receive a call regarding her father's failing health. He was a strong man and had outlived all his friends, siblings, and Molly's mother, but things like the fall today were happening more often. In some ways, this made John feel helpless because he knew that, right now, he was not in a position to comfort Molly in the way that he felt he should, the way that he would have been able to *if* their marriage wasn't on shaky ground.

He searched for the right words, for the right thing to do.

"Molly, I think you should be with him. I'll make a call to Charlie—he'll meet you at the airport, and he can fly you down as soon as you're ready to go."

The firm held a corporate lease on a Cessna Citation X that was hangared at nearby Brown Field. It was a luxury that the firm had acquired five years earlier, and John had been a certified pilot for the past three years. The only other time that the plane had been used for non-business-related travel was the trip that he and Molly had taken Afton on a few years earlier, when they'd all gone to Disney World.

"I would go with you, Molly, but I have a very important meeting tomorrow, and I can't afford to miss it. Maybe I could come down afterwards—if you need me to."

There was a pause before Molly spoke. "Don't bother, John—with the plane *or* with coming to help. I didn't expect you to, and I've already made arrangements for Afton to stay with Katie and the twins through the weekend. I'm driving down after I get my things from the house. I'll let you know if I need to stay any longer."

She didn't wait for him to respond, and the line fell silent. John felt a cold blanket of disappointment fall over him. It was obvious that she had not been pleased with his response; moreover, he was less pleased with himself for how he had responded. He was starting to feel as though every time he turned around, he was banging his head into another wall.

Molly packed enough clothes to last her through the weekend and then gathered some things for Afton to put into a separate suitcase. She loaded the bags into her car and drove to Pace Academy. She wanted—*needed*—to see her daughter before she left town to let her know that, despite all that was going on in her little life, everything was going to be okay. After Molly had spoken to Katie for a few minutes in the pick-up line at school, she hugged and kissed her beautiful little girl goodbye and began the drive south toward Savannah—toward *home*.

...

John drafted an email that was addressed to multiple recipients, and after he was satisfied with it he clicked *Send*. He logged off his computer, placed a stack of papers into his briefcase, and left the office. He drove directly to the Ritz, went to his suite, and packed a light bag.

...

Joan returned to her desk after lunch with Molly and a quick stop at a local couture dress shop to be fitted for a gown that she would wear to the business gala the following week. She usually bought her clothes straight off the rack, but she felt as though she might just need a special gown for such a special evening. After all, she believed that all eyes should be on her—just as much as they would be on John—since she had been such a huge part of his success. *Surely*, he would acknowledge that fact in his acceptance speech.

When she logged onto her computer, she was alerted to an email:

Dear Staff,

Due to circumstances beyond my control and a recent illness in my family, tomorrow's board of directors meeting has been postponed until a later date. I will be absent from the office for an undetermined period as I attend to these matters. During my absence, all matters concerning Callaway Development will be handled through Michael Bloom, CFO, and/or Joan Taylor, COO.

Thank you for your continued hard work and understanding during this time.

Kind Regards,
John Callaway, CEO

John parked his Mercedes inside the hangar at Brown Field and found Charlie, his longtime friend and pilot, in the midst of a preflight inspection on the Cessna. Having given everything the once-over, Charlie went into the FBO office adjacent to the hangar and filed a final flight plan for (SIA), Savannah International Airport. Ten short minutes later, they were airborne and climbing to altitude. From his seat in the copilot's chair, John used his phone to make arrangements for a rental car to be ready for him at the airport when they landed in twenty-five minutes. His plan was to surprise Molly when she arrived at her father's house, and he could only hope that he was doing the right thing.

It had been a while since he felt like he had.

. . .

Molly pulled into a service station on I-75 just north of Macon to fill-up her SUV with gas. As she waited for the pump to finish filling the tank, she went into the small convenience store to buy a bag of chips and a Diet Coke for the road. While she stood in the checkout line, she stole a quick glance at the covers of the magazines on a rack beside the register.

Her eye was drawn to one in particular, an issue of *Coastal Living* whose cover featured a beautiful photo of the Tybee Island Lighthouse and a caption that read, "Love in the Low Country." She grabbed a copy and paid for it along with her snacks, and a minute later she was back on the road driving south.

After seeing the photo of Tybee, Molly's mind was instantly transported back to another time when all seemed right with the world around her. She thought of the afternoon when she had first seen John at the beach, remembering how cute she'd thought he looked standing there, petrified and clutching his clunky camera for dear life . . . The day he'd first come into the marina store and how nervous he had been . . . and, of course, of their days spent out on the water when she had taught him the finer points of sailing a ship.

She smiled as the memories surrounded her like a soft, familiar blanket.

"Well, John, if you really want to learn how to sail, I suppose that I could take you out this weekend and show you a few things on a small boat that we sometimes rent out. She hasn't been out in quite a while, and it would do her good to stretch her legs–so to speak."

"That would be great, Molly! I'd really like that!"

That grinning, adventurous boy had been up for anything, it seemed. He'd fallen in love with the ocean quickly, and for the next eight weekends they'd spent much of their time together on the water. It was a great time for both of them to learn so much about each other, without all of the ordinary daily distractions. Molly thought about how John had taken naturally to the boat and to the sea, right from the start—much like her father had, and his father before him.

"Maybe someday we'll have our own boat, Molly. We could sail away together and never come back."

She had seen instantly the realization on his face that he felt like he'd said the wrong thing, and he had apologized immediately.

"I'm so sorry, Molly. I didn't mean that how it sounded. I wasn't thinking about your grandfather."

She had smiled.

"That's okay, John. I know you didn't mean anything by that. I actually liked the part about us *having our own boat together someday."*

Molly smiled now at the memory. It was near sunset—just like it had been that night with John—with the sky brush-stroked red, soft pink, and orange. Inching her way nearer to the coast, she caught the scent of the salty ocean and the humid marsh hanging heavily in the air.

At her first sight of water, Molly half-expected to catch a glimpse of that young couple in another place in time. She couldn't help but remember the way John had touched her face and how he had leaned in for that first kiss. She wondered if she had ever told him that, even now, just thinking about the beauty and innocence of that kiss still made her cry.

How could he not *know that I need him now, more than ever?*

She wanted to feel it again, feel him loving her like he did back then.

Driving toward Thunderbolt, Molly relived it all, especially the night she had made a promise to herself to never forget—and she hadn't. It was the night that she had fallen in love with John.

...

John's plane landed at SIA shortly after six that evening. The rental car that he'd requested was waiting for him in a reserved space near the private aviation hangars, and he sent a quick text message to Molly asking her if she was okay and how near she was to Savannah. She responded almost immediately that she was fine and that she was still about half an hour out. He told her to be careful and to let him know when she arrived.

There was no response to the last message.

Once he had the rental all loaded and ready to roll, John began the drive toward Thunderbolt. It had been almost three years since he'd last been to Savannah, but as he entered the western edge of the city, it felt as familiar to him as the back of his own hand.

CHAPTER THIRTEEN

WHEN MOLLY ARRIVED IN THE VILLAGE OF THUNDERBOLT, SHE WENT DIRECTLY TO HER PARENTS' HOUSE, ASSUMING THAT HER DAD WOULD BE THERE.

Hopefully, he'd be resting easy in his bed.

Even so, she couldn't say that she was completely surprised when she didn't find him there. Knowing her father, the possibility of his *actually* resting was a slim one. Oddly enough, however, her next thought was not to check the hospital—it was to go to the marina. She got back into her car and drove the short distance over to the docks. When she pulled up, she saw the old truck parked out front—just like always. Beside it was a shiny, new black Cadillac Escalade.

Pretty fancy for this little town, she thought.

Molly entered through the front of the marina store and saw no one inside, but she heard voices and the boom of laughter coming from the back-porch area that connected to the main dock. She walked through the open doorway and was shocked to see her dad and Mr. Davis, sitting in rocking chairs, talking to John.

"And there she is, running down here every time her old dad gets a little bump on the head!" her father's deep voice thundered when he caught sight of her.

Even though her dad had a sizeable bandage stretched across his forehead and a swollen black eye, he hardly seemed worse for the wear. But then again, he had always been a robust man, his age something that never seemed to slow him down—and his mind as sharp as ever. John stood up and reached out for her.

Admittedly, Molly was surprised to see that her father was not in the immediate peril that she had imagined and even more surprised at John's presence. Not to mention the fact that both men were here and enjoying such easy companionship.

Her father spoke again, his resounding voice sounding like an old pirate with a belly full of rum.

"Sorry to be disappointin' ya little lady, but there'll be no burial at sea today for this salty old dog!" His words were punctuated by more eruptions of laughter.

She stood there for a moment, shaking her head with her hands on her hips and knowing that whatever she said to him would be met with another quick-witted, sarcastic response. She turned around and stomped back through the store and out the front door. She could hear John's footsteps close on her heels as he urged her to stop.

"And there she goes . . ." Her father's voice could be heard from the parking lot on the other side of the building.

Molly's fingers fumbled for her keys as she hurried to her car.

"Molly—stop! Please stop!" John's voice had an impact this time, and she whirled around to face him.

"What are you *doing* here, John? What is all of this about?" She gestured wildly toward the marina as she spoke, breaking down into hot tears of confusion and anger.

John reached out and wrapped her tightly in his arms, hushing her tears. "Molly . . . honey, I'm so sorry. I'm sorry that I didn't drop everything when you called me today. I knew the moment that you hung up that I was wrong," he soothed softly. "I guess I should be sorry for a lot of things. I know how disappointed you've been with me lately, and I know that I've let you down. The truth is, I didn't think that you would want me here with you—but I knew in my heart that I had to come."

She pushed away from him a little, but he didn't let her go completely.

"What happened to us, John?" she asked, looking up at him with tears staining her cheeks. "Where did you go? Why did you leave me? Why did you leave *us*?"

John could feel a lump beginning to grow deep in his throat as he spoke. "I don't know, Molly." He shook his head sadly. "I don't know. I feel like I've been caught up in a whirlwind, and I don't know how to get out of it."

"Just walk away, John. We don't need *any* of it. I don't care about any of this stuff. I want my life back the way it used to be. I want *our* life back! We deserve that, don't we? And so does Afton."

"I know you do. You *both* do, but I honestly just don't know how."

"What's not to know, John? You decide what's really important in your life and just *do* it!"

John looked at her and wanted so much to say the right thing, to just make it all go away, but he couldn't find the words. The silence was deafening, and after a moment Molly pulled completely away from his grip and continued walking to her car.

"I really hope you can figure it out, John. I really do, before it's too late!"

She got into her car and sped away from the graveled parking lot, out onto the road that led away from the marina in the direction of Tybee.

...

John kicked the gravel at his feet, a hot mixture of anger and frustration coursing through him. He grabbed a handful of the rocks and threw them with all his might toward the tall shed next to the marina. They made a loud clanking sound when they hit the side of the metal building, sending a small flock of seabirds out of the rafters to escape John's wrath. As his eyes were drawn to the commotion and then to the bow of a sailboat, his gaze became fixed. It was as if a sleeping giant had been awakened and had raised its head to see what had stirred him. He walked closer to the shed, and more of the boat came into view.

But not just any boat.

The boat.

John had first laid eyes on her twenty-five years earlier when he'd made his first trip to the marina to meet Molly. He thought that he had probably noticed the boat a dozen times or more since then, but this was the first time that he was actually *seeing* her. He walked alongside her, lightly dragging his fingers against her rough hull, feeling the lines that gave her shape.

She is *beautiful,* he thought.

And unique, as well.

A completely original, one-off design that had been quietly hidden away from the rest of the world, just like the city that was her home. As he made his way to the stern, John was imagining that the name *Molly* could have easily been written there. Although the letters were faded and barely visible in the dusk light, he could still make out the words: *Sweet Afton, Savannah, GA.*

...

Molly found a space near the pier and parked her car. She sat there in silence for a few minutes, then took in a large breath and exhaled slowly before getting out and walking to the steps that led up to the wooden structure jutting more than a thousand feet out into the Atlantic. It was such a familiar and dear spot to her for many reasons, and every time she came here, it felt to her like she was visiting an old friend. She walked its length as she had done many times before, each step carrying her farther out to sea—farther from home—farther from John.

When she reached the pier's end and turned back to face the shore, Molly felt a sudden rush of panic wash over her, and she wondered what was causing it. She certainly didn't feel unsafe on the pier that was so sturdily built and firmly anchored. She began walking back toward her car, her pace quickening with each step. She had a feeling of urgency, and she wanted to call Katie and check on Afton. It was the instinct of a mother whose child is in danger. Or the instinct of a woman who senses danger for the one she loves. She got back into her car and quickly dialed Katie's number.

"Hey, Mommy!" Afton squealed when she came on the line. Katie had obviously seen Molly's name flash on her phone's display and had let the little girl answer.

Molly felt a great sense of relief when she heard the sweet sound of her daughter's voice.

"Hey, sweetheart! I called to check on you! I'm at Grandpa's making sure that he's okay. How're you doing, sweetie? Are you being a good girl for Ms. Katie?"

"Yes, ma'am! I'm being *extra* good. When are you coming home?"

Molly tried to sound as positive and reassuring to her daughter as she could. "Soon, baby. Mommy and Daddy will be home very soon." She had spoken naturally without planning her response, and it felt right when she said it.

Now, she knew that it needed to be true.

"Yay!" Afton cheered. "We're having fun, Mommy. So much fun! I have to go now, okay?"

Molly laughed, and she was relieved to realize that her daughter's happiness had swept her up in its joy. The smile on her lips now could be heard in her own voice, as well. "Okay, my special girl. Go have fun. I love you!"

"Love you, too, Mommy! Bye!"

Katie came on the line, her adult voice a stark contrast to Afton's cheery little chirp. "How're you doing, sweetie?"

"Actually, Katie, I think I'm doing okay. Believe it or not, John is *here*! He was waiting for me when I got to Dad's," Molly said in a rush. "Thankfully, other than a bump on his head and a black eye, Dad is actually as good as I've seen him in a long time."

"That's great news about your father. I know you must be so relieved. But—how do you feel about John being there?"

"To be honest, I was shocked at first. But I think it's going to be good for us, Katie. At least he's trying. I'm on my way back now to talk to him."

"I think that's wonderful news! Sometimes it takes something like this to bring people back together, back to where they're supposed to be." Katie's voice sounded hopeful to Molly's ears, and she was glad to know that she had her friend's support.

"Thank you, Katie—for keeping Afton and for all of your encouragement. I'll call you back soon. Love you."

"We love you, too. And Molly? You're going to be okay."

The impact of Katie's words held tremendous weight, and for the first time in a long time, Molly felt that she just might actually be.

When Molly pulled back into the parking lot at the marina, it was after sundown. She saw John walking from the old boat shed back toward the store, so she pulled up beside him. He stopped short and looked at her intently but didn't speak. She noticed now that he looked different to her somehow.

Not different *entirely*—but certainly different than he had looked earlier.

There was something there that had changed—something in his eyes.

They seemed softer.

Kinder.

Molly had been drawn to his deep blue eyes from the moment she had first been locked in their gaze. She had always thought of them as eyes that she could get lost in, and she often had.

She spoke first. "Have you eaten dinner?"

"No, I haven't. I've been kind of . . . waiting on you."

They both smiled.

"I only ate a bag of chips on the drive down, so I'm *starving*!" Molly admitted.

John's smiled deepened. "Well. We'd better get going, then, hadn't we?"

Molly watched as John made his way around to the passenger side and slid into the seat next to hers. "Take us anywhere you want to go."

Molly nodded and once again pulled out of the marina's parking lot—this time with John belted in *beside* her rather than *behind* her in the rearview mirror. She turned onto the main road leading into the heart of downtown Savannah and its historic riverfront.

Although only a ten-minute drive from Thunderbolt, the ride felt much longer. Neither John nor Molly could find a way to break the awkward silence, and they both seemed to be taking the time just to breathe.

For John, there was both a sense of relief and of nervous anticipation with how to make this night a true turning point in his relationship with his wife.

For Molly, there was hope that John would finally be able to say and do the things needed to mend her broken heart and to save their troubled marriage.

...

At the same time that John and Molly were being seated at their favorite restaurant on River Street, Joan Taylor sat across from Michael Bloom at a small table in a restaurant bar situated in Atlanta's midtown area. She had sent him an email earlier in the day asking him to meet her there after work, telling him there were some things that needed to be discussed away from the office. Her request had sounded urgent, so he had complied without argument.

"Michael, I'm going to need you to listen to me very carefully, and I'm going to need for you to agree that this discussion will go no further than this table." Her voice was a mixture of care and concern along with frustration and anger.

"Okay, Joan," he said with a cool nod, his eyes holding her in a shrewd gaze, as though he was assessing her motives. "I'll listen to what you have to say, and then *I* will decide if it needs any further discussion."

Joan squinted her eyes a little and tightened her lips, sizing Michael up and tearing him down, all at the same time. Despite his best efforts to show her otherwise, Joan had always been good at intimidating Michael—just as she did with most all of the other employees at the firm.

The look that Michael gave her in return was one that pleased her—one of defeat and submissiveness, reluctant though his admittance of both might be.

Holding her unblinking stare until she felt sure that she had gotten her intended point across to him, she began to speak.

"I'm worried that John is losing his grip at the office, Mike. At this point, I'm even wondering if he's competent enough to be in control of the business *at all*. There have been too many careless mistakes made in the past few weeks, and we cannot afford to lose our edge at this point in the game."

Michael sat up straight in his chair, shock running through him like lightning. "I'm not sure I follow you, Joan. Just what is it that you're suggesting?"

After glancing very deliberately to her left, then to her right, Joan braced her arms beneath her on the table and leaned in closer toward Michael.

John and Molly sat on an outside terrace at Huey's on River Street, a particularly favorite spot for them both. The food was always outstanding, and their view beyond the cobblestone-paved street was of the Savannah River, the waterway that was the lifeblood of the city and for much of the South.

As a major shipping port and one of the busiest in the country, Savannah provided the perfect place for watching enormous cargo ships pass by in eerie silence. John and Molly had spent many hours talking, in this same spot, as they watched the busy port come alive. They used to play a game and try to guess where the mighty vessels were from and what cargo might be held within the many containers onboard.

It felt good to be back here again, back at Huey's, back in Savannah. Back with each other.

Molly was about to speak when John's phone rang. She froze as he pulled it from his pocket, her breath catching when she saw the name that flashed on the screen. Only when John pressed the button to send the call directly to voicemail did Molly breathe again, relief flooding over her when she realized that John was—in this moment, at least—putting *her* ahead of work.

Maybe he really *was* trying to change.

He powered the phone off completely before putting it back into his jacket pocket and looked back at Molly with a soft smile.

"Were you about to say something, hon?"

CHAPTER FOURTEEN

JOHN AND MOLLY SPENT THE NEXT TWO DAYS WITH HER FATHER MAKING SURE THAT HE WAS REALLY WELL ENOUGH TO BE ON HIS OWN. When they were satisfied that he was—or, at least, having to admit to themselves that, even if he wasn't, there was nothing either of them could do about it—they told him they would leave him alone on the condition that he would agree to move into an assisted-living facility should another incident occur.

In his own sort of way, he gave them a half-hearted—and half-convincing—agreement; and John, knowing they were at an impasse, convinced Molly to accept her father's words. She was less than pleased at the idea of leaving him alone again, but she realized she really didn't have any other option. It would be just a waiting game, now. They *did* make arrangements, however, for a housekeeper who had basic nursing skills to come in twice a week.

It wasn't much, but it did give Molly *some* peace of mind.

Before they left, John told Molly that he would like to speak to her father on his own.

"What's this about, John?" she asked, puzzled and more than just a little bit worried. She felt her brow furrow.

"Don't worry, Molly," John said, reaching out to smooth the wrinkles between her eyebrows. "It's nothing bad—and it has nothing to do with what's been going on with *us*. I'm not *that* foolish!"

Molly laughed. "I don't blame you, John! After seeing how good he's doing lately, I don't think you would want to run the risk of getting on his bad side."

John shook his head soberly, though the smile on his lips bore evidence that he was teasing.

"Absolutely *not*. Even after all these years, he still scares the life out of me!"

After agreeing to give him some time alone with her father, she walked toward the outside steps that led to her mother's art studio on the second floor of the marina. She hadn't been inside for several years, and when she entered it was immediately obvious that no one else had, either. The room remained much as it had been for the past decade, and two unfinished paintings covered in a light coating of dust still sat abandoned on their easels.

For Molly, it was a sad reminder that tomorrow is never a guarantee—that sometimes we have no choice but to leave things undone.

...

John found Bill Edwards sitting in one of the old wooden rockers on the back porch of the marina store. He chose one for himself and sat down next to the older man, who was busy tying and untying sailors' knots with a short length of cotton rope, his movements so ingrained and second nature that he could have easily done them with his eyes closed.

John spoke, wondering if the sound of his voice would bring the tying to an end—or at least pause it.

"It sure is a nice afternoon, isn't it? Nice day to be out on the water."

"Yes, it is. And yes, it would be," Mr. Edwards grunted, his hands never stilling.

John spoke again, taking his time not to smother his father-in-law with too many questions. He had made that mistake more than once in the past, and when it had happened, Mr. Edwards had simply gotten up to walk away without saying a word. Theirs was a tenuous relationship, never very familial feeling—hence the fact that John still used such a formal title for the man, even after all these years. "Mr. Edwards, when was the last time that you sailed?"

Mr. Edwards made more grunting sounds and scratched his head a couple of times before coming up with an answer. "Twelve or thirteen years, I suppose." He continued tying his perfect knots as he mumbled and grumbled, appearing to be somewhat irritated or, at the very least, frustrated.

"Well, the reason I'm asking is that I'm curious about your plans for your old schooner."

The aging sailor stopped his task and dropped the rope on the ground beside his chair. John was expecting him to get up and walk away—or worse. Bill Edwards didn't seem at all pleased that the old sailboat had been brought up in conversation.

"Why are you bothering me with questions about my father's boat?"

"Well, Sir—" John felt his footing slipping out from under him.

Maybe this wasn't a good idea, after all. Still, unless he asked, he would never know.

"I was hoping that I might be able to get her restored for you." He paused, wondering what his father-in-law would say. "With your permission, of course."

"And tell me, John—just what do *you* know about restoring a vessel like the *Afton*? Or *any* vessel, for that matter?"

"Sir, to be perfectly honest, I myself know very little about it," John admitted. "But there are people that specialize in that kind of thing, and I was thinking that I could hire someone for the work. I found a company in Charleston dedicated to wooden boat construction and restoration, and I know that they would do her justice."

Bill Edwards didn't speak, just stared out over the black water as memories of the boat and of his father flooded his mind. At last, he broke his silence and gave John a piercing stare, a hard set to his jaw as he spoke. "I don't want a bunch of out-of-town know-it-alls banging around in my shop *or* on *my* boat."

"No, sir—they wouldn't be doing the work *here*. She would have to be transported up to their yard in Charleston," John explained, hoping that he might have *some* shot at winning Molly's father over. "I would be covering all expenses, of course."

The old man reached down with his large hand and lifted the length of rope from the dock boards, rising up from the chair more quickly than John would have imagined possible. He turned sharply on his heel and walked back into the store.

As the creaky screen door slammed back against its frame under the force of his pull, he spat words over his shoulder, his loud, harsh voice ringing out behind him. "That boat is not leaving this property. Not while I'm still above ground, anyway! And, *so help me,* she'll not be taken anywhere even after *that*. The answer is *no*!"

John really didn't know what to say next, but he knew better than to push any further. "Okay, Mr. Edwards. I respect your decision, and I understand your feelings about it," he said with a nod of surrender. "But if you ever change your mind—"

"I *won't*. You can be sure of that. Now be on your way!"

Molly's father had ended the conversation abruptly, on his own terms and with the last word, an art that he had mastered long ago. John left it alone, knowing that to try and continue convincing Mr. Edwards would only make things worse. He said goodbye, promising that he and Molly would stay in touch. He was turning to leave when Mr. Edwards spoke again, this time through the worn, tattered screen on the rusting door. A single yellow light bulb burned above him, casting an odd shadow that made him look even larger than he already was.

"Let me tell you something, John. Before you run off from here and never come back, okay?" "Yes, sir," John managed, feeling certain that he should be steeling himself for a verbal beat-down.

"Don't you *ever* let Molly come down here by herself again. It's not safe for a woman to travel the highway alone these days. You should know better than that, boy!"

John looked down at the ground, avoiding eye contact as Mr. Edwards gave him exactly what he deserved to hear.

"Yes, sir. It won't happen again, and I'm very sorry that things worked out like they did."

"*I'm* not the one you need to be saying you're sorry to, John."

"Yes, sir. I know," John admitted, wondering how much his father-in-law might have guessed. His mother had certainly known enough without his having to tell her anything, and Mr. Edwards was a sharp man—no denying that fact. "And I'll tell her as many times as it takes."

"I didn't want my Molly to marry some big city hot shot, but she did it anyway when she married you. Because it seemed to make her happy, I had to learn to be okay with it," he said, his stare unbending and the set of his jaw determined. "Lately, though, she hasn't seemed all that happy. And it's *your* job—above everything else—to make sure that she is."

John nodded, feeling shame wash over him. "Yes, sir. I understand—and, believe me, I'm working on that."

"You'd better be doing more than *working* on it, son. Don't let her down again. I *mean* it—do you understand me?" Pausing for effect, Mr. Edwards continued, "One last thing, and then you be on your way."

"Yes, sir?"

"Y'all be careful driving back today. And the next time you come down, you make sure my granddaughter is with you. You do that, and then maybe, just maybe, we can talk about that boat."

"Yes, sir. You can count on it. We'll see you soon!" John knew that now was the time to make his exit and not overstay even by as much as a moment, so he went straight to the car.

Seeing that Molly was still in her mother's studio, he tapped on the horn and waited for her to come out. They agreed that she would follow him to the airport so he could return the rented Cadillac, and they'd drive back to Atlanta in her car—*together.*

She went back to the studio and locked the door, then dashed into the store to give her father a long hug, repeating her instructions to him not to overdo it and gently reminding him of his promise to her. Merely nodding and dismissing his daughter with a wave of his hand, Bill Edwards's face was impassive—and less than reassuring—as Molly left her father to follow John.

Molly was traveling close behind the rented Cadillac, trying not to lose him as they drove to the airport about ten miles north of town. She knew the road well, but she was focusing on John. She half-smiled at the realization that, while nothing was quite settled with her father *or* her husband, it felt like her heartbeat was finally catching the right rhythm.

Suddenly, it was clear to her how out of sync her heart had been. No wonder she had been unhappy and at odds with everyone, including herself. Maybe this was the beginning of something new, something right. As much as she loved Savannah and hated leaving her dad alone, she was looking forward to the ride home with John, knowing they would have each other's undivided attention.

Thirty minutes later, John was driving Molly's car north on I-16 when she spoke.

"John, I really want to thank you again for coming down here to help me with Dad. Truthfully, I've missed you, and I'm *so* glad you're here."

He smiled at her and reached for her hand. "Thank *you* for wanting me here. And thank you for giving me the chance to make things right between us."

They drove along in silence for the next forty miles, both just happy they were there together.

"I've been thinking that I should take some time off—away from the firm. Time to be with *you*. Alone."

Molly was thrilled at the idea of a vacation! It had been *years* since they'd been anywhere together, just the two of them. She was happy, and he could hear it in her voice.

"Oh, John! Are you serious?" She looked like a schoolgirl who had just been asked to the dance. "I think that's a *wonderful* idea! What did you have in mind?"

"I want to go sailing—like we used to," John replied, taking his eyes off the road to watch the reaction on her face. "I found a boat for hire in Key West and made arrangements for us to keep her as long as two weeks if we want."

Much to his delight, Molly's eyes danced with joy. "Really, John? You're serious about this?"

He laughed, sharing in her excitement. "*Of course* I'm serious. If you're onboard, that is—no pun intended. We can leave from Atlanta next Saturday and be out to sea by Sunday. What do you think?"

She was overjoyed at the idea of being alone with her husband for two whole weeks, doing something both had always loved so much. It was a chance they hadn't had in so long and something they both needed. But . . .

"What about Afton, John? We can't just leave her."

John smiled his most winning smile and said smoothly, "No worries, my love. I've already worked all of that out with Katie."

"Wow, John! I'm impressed. You really *are* serious about this!"

"Absolutely—it's something that we should've done a long time ago, and I know it'll be good for us. Michael and Joan are handling things at work right now, so it's a good time for us to go—while we have the opportunity."

Molly smiled, then leaned across the seat and kissed him on the cheek. "Then I would *love* to!" She stayed close, resting her head on his shoulder as hope swirled in circles around them both.

The remainder of the drive was spent deep in conversation, making plans for their upcoming trip. They were both looking forward to visiting Key West again, having only been there once before, so long ago on their honeymoon. They had talked many times in the past about going back, but it had never worked out. Now, it seemed, their thoughts were synchronized as they dreamed together of sand, of water, and of sailing.

...

When they arrived back in Atlanta, late on Sunday afternoon, they went straight to Brad and Katie's house, both anxious to see Afton. She was just as excited to see them, running straight into John's waiting arms.

"Daddy, I missed you!"

He stood up, holding her tightly. "I missed you, too, baby girl! So very, *very* much!"

"Daddy," she said, holding his face between her petite hands, her expression suddenly serious. "Can we go get some ice cream?"

John laughed, happy to be holding his daughter again. "We sure can, sweetheart. I think ice cream sounds like the best idea *ever*."

After stopping off for ice cream on the way home, they all unpacked their bags, relieved to finally be together again, all in their rightful place. John went into Afton's room to say goodnight, and she surprised him by calling him over to the bed.

"Daddy, tell me that story again . . . the one about the thing I used to do and say every night when I was little."

"Well, if I remember correctly, you'd want to get into your pajamas *all by yourself*. I think you were about three . . . and, depending on the pajamas, you could do it alone, just like a *big* girl. Then you'd run and hide your little bunny." He smiled at the memory. "And I'd say, 'Aaaaaftonnn—are you ready?'"

The little girl giggled. "I remember, Daddy. I remember! And then I'd say, 'Ready, Freddie!' And you'd always say, 'Hey! *I'm* not *Freddie!*' And we'd laugh, and you'd go look for my bunny." She smiled, then furrowed her brow seriously. "I don't know why I didn't give him a name—poor little bunny. I still have him somewhere in my closet."

"And then, when I found your little bunny, I'd tuck the two of you in and turn off the light. And you'd say, 'See you when the sun wakes up!'"

"I remember, Daddy." And with childhood innocence she asked, "We have fun together, don't we?"

"We do, baby girl. We do." John got up from the side of the bed and went to the closet, looking in the topmost forgotten spots. Sure enough, there was the little bunny, just waiting to be found again. "*Look* what *I* found!" He brought the little bunny over to her.

They both smiled, and he tucked her in, just like she was three again. As he turned out the light, he heard her little voice pipe up. "See you when the sun wakes up, Daddy!"

"See you when the sun wakes up, sweet girl." *See you when the sun wakes up.*

John walked out of her room and into the bedroom he shared with Molly. For the first time in a very long while, John knew he was *exactly* where he was supposed to be—with his girls, at home. He sighed deeply and let the moment seep into his soul like a good rain on parched earth.

He walked around to his side of the bed and laid his keys and phone on his nightstand, listening to the sound of water running in the bathroom and knowing he had a few minutes before Molly would be ready for bed.

After scrambling around in drawers as he tried to find a match or lighter, he finally found one and lit each of the many candles in their bedroom. He dimmed the lights and looked around in amazement, realizing how long it had been since he'd last made the effort toward a special evening for Molly. He stifled a surge of guilt and focused on the task at hand.

When Molly at last walked out of the bathroom, John was waiting for her in bed. Rambling on about something barely discernable, she broke off midsentence when she saw him, her jaw dropping in surprise. Her eyes locked with his, and she touched her hand to her heart, her shaky smile telling him more than words could express at that moment. She crawled onto the bed next to her husband, and John pulled the covers over them both as they lay facing each other.

"I found this letter on the bed," he whispered, holding up the worn pages for her to see. "Do you remember when I sent it?"

Her eyes pooled with tears. "Of course I do, John. I could never forget that. I missed you so much when you went back to college, and the letters from you were like my air."

"Close your eyes," John murmured. "I want to read it to you again tonight, and I want you to feel it again, feel how much I missed you. Feel how much *I have missed you* in these past days we've spent apart."

She smiled at him and closed her eyes as he began to read. "My dearest Molly, the days feel like years since I've seen you. I want to hold you so badly, and I keep thinking about our last summer night on the beach in Savannah."

John continued to read on as the candles burned low. Neither of them noticed.

Late into the night, John finally fell silent and watched his beautiful wife sleep. He got up and blew out the few candles that were still burning.

He crawled back into bed and wrapped his sleeping Molly within his arms—finally at peace.

Finally at home.

CHAPTER FIFTEEN

JOAN WAS STUNNED TO SEE JOHN WALK INTO THE OFFICE EARLY ON MONDAY MORNING. Dismay edged her voice when she spoke.

"What on earth are you doing here, John?"

"I work here—*remember?*"

She noticed a slight change in his demeanor, and she realized he could probably detect how caught off guard and nervous she was. She tried to compose herself before she spoke again, hoping she might convince him to dismiss her surprise.

"*Of course* you do—don't be absurd! It's just that I thought you were taking some time off," she insisted. "Getting *away* from the office."

"I am, John—trust me. But there are a few things I need to clear up before I leave town, and I wanted to go over the reports from this past month, particularly the financials from the Bahamas deal. Are there any issues that need to be addressed?"

Joan responded quickly, hoping to expedite his departure and give him no reason to suspect even the slightest complication—or anything *else* that might potentially delay him. "Nothing comes to mind. I'll see to it that you have a copy of the report by the end of the day."

He thanked her and went into his office to log onto his computer.

John used most of the morning to weed through an enormous backlog of email correspondence, pleasantly surprised to find an email from his old college friend Ben, the subject line simply reading, "G'day, mate."

The message explained that Ben was in Atlanta for about two weeks on an assignment at the Georgia Aquarium, heading-up a team installing an exhibit of marine life that existed in and around Australia's Great Barrier Reef.

Ben expressed his eagerness to see him if he had some free time over the next couple of weeks. The two had not seen one another since John's visit to Sydney the summer after graduation from UGA, and he was excited to read that his old friend was in town. He responded, telling Ben that he would very much enjoy seeing him while he was here, included his mobile number, and asked his old friend to call him so they could make arrangements.

A few minutes after ten o'clock that morning, Michael walked into John's office and took a seat, his mood noticeably unsettled.

"How are you doing, John—*really*?"

John responded to the question in an upbeat manner and with a smile he could hear in his own voice. "Honestly, Mike? I feel like I'm better than I've been in a *really long* time. Thanks for asking."

Michael stared at him, searching his face for signs to the contrary. "I'm glad to hear that. I've been a little concerned—and so has Joan. I thought you were going to take some time off."

John laughingly answered, "What's the deal? If I didn't know any better, I might think that everyone around here is trying to get rid of me or something!"

"There's no *deal*, John." Michael raised his hands as though he was trying to calm his partner. "We just know that you've been under *a lot* of stress lately, and we want you to take a break. You deserve it. Don't worry about this place, buddy—it'll still be here when you get back."

John shuffled through some papers on his desk, already shifting his focus and ready to move on. "I'm going away with Molly for a week, maybe even two if things are going well. I've rented a boat in the Keys so that we can go sailing. To be perfectly honest, Mike, I wish we could leave today."

"Then what's keeping you here?" Michael asked, his voice eager. "There's certainly nothing pressing going on right now that *I* can think of."

John paused his paper shuffle to reply, studying Michael for a moment. "I need to tie up a few loose ends before I go, and we have this 'awards gala' thing on Friday. I feel like I should be there. As of now, our plans are to leave town Saturday morning."

"Okay, then," Michael said with a shrug. "Suit yourself—God knows *I* wouldn't let some silly plaque keep me away from the Keys for a whole week!" He looked at John and waited for a response, but when none was forthcoming Michael rose from his seat and began to leave. "Well, then, if you'll excuse me, I have to go to my office and start interviewing for a new assistant."

John looked up sharply. "What happened to Erica?"

"I wish I knew," Michael said, shaking his head with mild annoyance. "She left the office last Wednesday, and I haven't heard from her since. I've tried calling her several times but get only voicemail." He smirked. "Too bad, too. I'm going to miss that one." He left John's office and made his way down the hall to his own.

John imagined the lobby's seating area attendees would likely resemble that of a modeling agency's casting call more so than qualified candidates awaiting an interview as the administrative assistant to a CFO. Slightly amused, he continued poring over the sheets of paper laid out before him.

. . .

That same morning Erica Payne checked her luggage at Hartsfield-Jackson International Airport in Atlanta, gathered her boarding pass, and took the underground train to concourse D as she made her way toward gate 17. An hour later she was seated aboard Delta flight 743 bound for Paradise Island, Bahamas.

John buzzed Joan and asked her to come into his office. Without responding, she got up from her desk and moments later took a seat across from John. He was *all* business, leveling his gaze at her over the storied surface of his desk.

"I need for you to catch me up, Joan. How do we look on the Bahamas deal?"

She responded without hesitation, her answer clearly well in hand. "Twenty percent of the full loan amount has been transferred and dispersed into the four working accounts, as agreed. After the initial stages of the project are complete and inspected, the client will then be able to request subsequent draws against the remaining amount to continue the project."

John stared at her quizzically. "I understand how the process *works,* Joan. What I'm asking you is if everything *looks* okay with it."

She blinked, looking slightly insulted, as though he had questioned her intelligence or maligned her character in some way. Or was he just imagining that?

"Everything looks *fine,* John. Stop worrying. The loan origination fees *alone* were a tidy sum and have already been deposited into the firm's account." She waved her hand dismissively, and Joan noticed that he seemed relieved that the transaction had gone so smoothly. Had this been two weeks earlier, she knew him well enough to know that he would have already been scouring the roster for the next potential client. But for today he seemed content just to let things *be,* for a while.

"Will there be anything else?" Joan asked. "If not, I *do* have other business to attend to." She got up from her chair to leave the office.

"Wait, Joan," he said, surprising her. "I was under the impression there were to be only *three* working accounts for this client, yet you said there were four."

A look of annoyance flashed across her face. "*Yes,* John. A *fourth* account was added at the client's request. It happened while you were off 'finding yourself,'" Joan almost sneered as she said the words. "If you'll recall, you said only to contact you in the case of an emergency, and this was hardly that."

"Fine, then," he allowed. "Can you send me an updated report that will reflect the change, please?"

Once again, Joan appeared to have her feathers ruffled. "I suppose I can do that, but are you really going to keep worrying yourself with the minute details around here, John? You're supposed to be on vacation, for goodness sake!"

He shrugged off her words with a dismissive smile. "I suppose you're right. Just do me a favor and keep a close watch on this thing for me while I'm away."

"Of course. You know I will—I am your eyes and your ears. That's my job, after all, isn't it?"

As she neared the doorway, John called one last thing to her. "Oh, and by the way—what happened to Michael's new assistant, Erica?"

Joan paused for a brief moment, her previous look of annoyance replaced by a cool smile as she spoke. "I haven't the slightest idea. Your guess is as good as mine." And with that, she disappeared.

John finished a rough draft of his acceptance speech and decided to print it so Molly could give it the once-over and let him know if it needed any polishing. When he had finished, he logged out of the system and left the office. He had promised Molly that he would come home early to get ready for their dinner plans at Atlanta Fish Market with Brad and Katie, and he noticed, with pleasure, that he was beginning to feel like his old self again.

On the drive home, his cell phone rang.

Unknown Caller.

John typically ignored these calls yet this time felt compelled to answer.

"John Callaway," he said.

The voice on the other end was unmistakable, and his smile broadened when he heard it.

"What's goin' on, mate?" Ben said, and John was glad he had played against character and actually answered the phone. He would have hated to miss *this* call.

"Ben! I was hoping to hear from you! All is well—how are you?"

"Can't complain, mate. Gonna be in town for a few more days, and I was hoping we could get together and catch up, maybe have a bite?"

"Of course! Hey, listen—Molly and I are meeting some friends out for dinner at six, but we would love it if you could join us. I know that Molly would love to see you again."

Ben agreed, and John gave him his home address so they could all drive to the restaurant together. Both men signed off, and John thought how nice it was going to be getting together again with old friends.

As he pulled up in front of the house, John was greeted by the happy sight of his wife and daughter. Molly sat on the steps and was watching Afton as she rode her bicycle in the driveway, happily pedaling in slow, meticulous circles as the training wheels kept her steady. It was a gorgeous early summer day in the Southland, and his girls were taking full advantage of it.

John parked his car and joined his wife on the step beside her. After giving her a kiss, he began to tell her about Ben's visit. "I've asked him to join us for dinner tonight if you don't mind."

She smiled brightly, her blue eyes sparkling in the sunlight. "No, I don't mind, silly! I would *love* to see him again—his stories always made me laugh!"

"Me, too," John agreed. "Good." He put his arm around Molly and gently kissed her forehead.

How could he have been so careless to put this woman—and this life with her—second to *anything*?

Ben arrived shortly after five o'clock, seeming as happy and care-free as ever, looking much the same as he had in their youth, with the exception of having grown a full beard.

Maybe it really is the tea, John thought with a smile.

"It's so great to see you, Ben! You have no idea how surprised I was to get your email!"

"Likewise, John. It does me good to see you both—still together and happy, from what I can see—and have a look at this house would you!" Ben held is arms wide and with mock concern said, "Are you laundering money for the bloody cartel?"

"If it were only so easy!" John responded jokingly.

They spent most of the next hour catching up and reminiscing about the summer they had spent in Savannah so many years ago. Molly began laughing as the story was retold about the day they had all gone sailing together and Ben had fallen overboard *before* they had even pulled away from the dock. As he listened, John was struck by the sudden realization of just how much he had missed the sound of Molly's laugh. It was contagious, and by the end of the story Ben and John were laughing hysterically right along with her.

Their evening with Ben and the Sutherlands was extremely enjoy-able, and everyone was in full agreement that they should get together more often. Of course, Ben pointed out the fact that he would need a little advanced notice on the next one if he were to attend. He also invited everyone to come visit him in Australia.

Naturally enough, his invitation spun the conversation in a new direction, and the Sutherlands seemed excited about the possibility of taking a vacation to the Outback. John himself had always wanted to return with Molly and experience it together. Bearing that in mind, he told Ben he would be in touch and he could expect some company in the near future. Ben was glad they would be coming and told them how much he looked forward to it.

At the end of the evening, John and Molly waved Ben off as he drove away from their home, telling him that, if he had any more free time during the week, they would enjoy seeing him again. He told them that he was behind schedule on the exhibit and would likely be too tied up to have a break but invited them both to drop by the aquarium if they got the chance.

"Thanks for dinner. I'll return the favor when you make it over my way. Have we got a deal?" he asked with a wide grin.

"You're on, Ben. We'll be looking forward to it," Molly replied, taking John's hand in her own.

Ben looked at them both, shaking his head in undisguised pleasure. "You two . . . Good luck on that trip of yours. Be safe—no falling overboard!"

· · ·

Once they were alone in their room that night, John's mind was flooded with old memories. He continued telling Molly more about the trip he had taken to Australia after college, reiterating that he was looking forward to seeing it again but with her this time. Molly was thrilled about the idea, as well, peppering him with questions that seemed to feed both of their excitement.

· · ·

On Friday evening, John dressed in his custom-tailored tuxedo and waited at the bottom of the stairs for Molly to come down. She looked radiant in a dark-blue evening gown that was embellished with shining sparkles in just the right places, and a nervous excitement washed over him as she descended the staircase to join him.

"Belle of the ball," he breathed.

"Well, thank you, sir," she replied, with a shy smile that only made her more beautiful. "And might I add that *you* are the most handsome man I ever did see!"

He laughed. "*You* might add that, but I'm not sure anyone else would agree."

"They don't have to," Molly said with a coy shrug, "but they'd be quite mistaken."

The gala was being held at the Fernbank Museum in Atlanta, which had been lavishly decorated for the occasion. There was a buzz in the air, and the list of corporate elites in attendance was extensive, not to mention impressive. John was honored that he had been singled out in this influential group, and he was sure that his father would have been, too. Molly was standing near him at the back of the room as they waited to be seated when Joan and Michael approached.

Much to Joan's obvious pleasure, the dress she'd purchased specially for this auspicious occasion was the first thing everyone noticed, and Molly complimented her on her choice.

Joan waved off the compliment and turned to John. "Congratulations, John. I'm very happy for you tonight. You're well deserving of this honor, and I'm glad you're finally getting recognized for all we've accomplished."

Her meaning was thinly veiled at best, and Molly wondered if her husband had caught the implication.

"Thank you, Joan. It's a nice feeling, and I'm glad to be here tonight to celebrate this with all of you."

Michael stepped forward, accompanied by a leggy blonde whose flash and lack of modesty was extremely out of place, especially in *this* conservative a crowd. "Congratulations, buddy. Good job."

He put out his hand to shake John's, and John leaned in to speak so no one else would overhear. "Please tell me that she at least knows how to *turn on* a computer."

Michael laughed at the remark. "She knows how to turn on much more than a *computer*, John. But, *relax*. She's not who I hired—she's my date."

John felt somewhat relieved by what Michael had just told him. Unfortunately, his relief was short-lived.

"Just wait until you see who I *did* hire, though. She's stunning!" Michael gave a thumbs-up and a big smile as he spoke.

...

The five of them were shown to a reserved table near the front of the banquet room, and they each took their appointed seats. After the evening's director of ceremonies made brief introductions from the podium on stage, dinner was served. Their table etiquette dissolved into light conversation throughout the meal, thankfully requiring little concentration, a fact for which John was grateful since his mind was already adrift at sea.

After the dinner plates were cleared and replaced with coffee and cocktails, the guest speaker took the podium. John watched in admiration and awe as baseball legend Hank Aaron began to speak. John had grown up watching the man play for the Atlanta Braves and had always respected his accomplishments, along with his ability to overcome adversity, and John was thrilled at the chance of getting to meet a living legend. A well-produced highlight reel of "Hammerin' Hank's" celebrated baseball career was shown on two large screens at the front of the room, ending with loud applause and a standing ovation. Once again, Mr. Aaron spoke, going on in detail about how challenging it had been for a black man to play professional sports in the 1950s, especially in the South. He talked about the importance of having a positive attitude and earning the respect of his teammates and peers, and it stood out to John that there was no evidence of animosity or resentment anywhere in his speech. When Mr. Aaron concluded, he was once again honored with a resounding ovation.

At the end of the formal part of the ceremony, the achievement awards and recognitions were handed out. A short introduction that included John's accomplishments at Callaway was read before John took the stage to accept the award for CEO of the year. When he stepped up to the podium, he paused for a beat before beginning to speak, taking time to look over the sea of faces staring back at him.

"I'm greatly honored to be here tonight as the recipient of this prestigious award. I have spent the better part of a week preparing a speech that would best describe to you my gratitude for having been chosen from among you. But—now that I stand here, holding this in my hand—it is clear to me that there is really only one person who is responsible for making this possible."

Joan stole a quick look in her compact mirror, making sure her lipstick was perfect and not a hair was out of place, preparing to stand at any moment. Her chest puffed up with pride as she awaited the next words that would surely come, and Michael reached over to pat her hand lightly while John continued.

"For more than twenty years, she has stood beside me without complaint, through the ups and downs, the mergers and takeovers, and the countless late nights. She has sacrificed herself and her time just as much as I have—if not more." He paused, swallowing the lump of emotion in his throat. "Tonight, I owe everything that I have accomplished in my business *and* in my life to my beautiful wife, Molly. I could not have done this without you, and for that, I thank you. I love you."

His last words were punctuated by yet another standing ovation, and John began to make his way back to the table, where Molly sat, overcome with emotion as tears filled her eyes. Next to her, Joan sat in stunned silence for some time before rising and walking away from the table without a word to anyone. She strode out of the banquet hall and to the front door of the museum, gave her valet ticket to the attendant, and waited for her car to be retrieved.

Joan's hasty and insulted departure went unnoticed by John, who could see only Molly.

"Are you okay?" he asked, his voice hardly audible over the sound of the applause that still rang out.

"Are you kidding? Mr. Callaway, I'm honored and moved, and these tears are only the best kind," she whispered back, as he hugged her tightly and kissed her.

More applause broke out, finally bleeding into the music of a brass band, and people began to make their way toward the large dance floor in the center of the room. John smiled and looked at Molly.

"What do you say we skip this part and go on home to celebrate and start packing?" he asked, giving her a conspiratorial look.

"Why, my dear man, I do think that's the second-best thing I've heard all night."

CHAPTER SIXTEEN

THE CESSNA CITATION TOUCHED DOWN AT KEY WEST INTERNATIONAL AIRPORT JUST AFTER ELEVEN O'CLOCK ON SATURDAY MORNING. The flight down from Atlanta had been a quick and pleasant one, and John had once again been Charlie's co-pilot, a role he both highly enjoyed and took great pride in. His father had never learned to fly, and it was one skill that he felt a sense of ownership in, something that he could truly claim, apart from his father.

For the last thirty minutes of the flight, Molly had busied herself taking digital photographs from the window of the jet, the crystal-clear water and coral reefs below almost surreal in the morning light. Their approaching view was both beautiful and awe inspiring—almost too much to bear—and John had a difficult time remaining focused as Charlie landed the plane.

After taking a taxi to the Casa Marina Hotel to check into their suite, John and Molly were happily surprised to find that it was the very same room where they had spent their honeymoon so many years before. The suite had been newly renovated, but the perfect ocean view remained just the same, and they were both ecstatic to be back.

Originally built in the 1920s, the hotel was a beautiful classic. Its design had been the vision of the late Henry Flagler, the railroad magnate and entrepreneur who had been so influential in Florida's renaissance during the early part of the twentieth century. The grand

old hotel had recently undergone a complete multi-million-dollar restoration, and not a single detail had been overlooked.

They decided to have a seaside lunch at the resort's open-air café,
then give the owner of the boat a call to get the final details about its
location and make arrangements for its inspection.

"John, I really want to thank you for making this happen for us,"
Molly said, smiling across the table at him. "I mean—*look* at this.
We're *really here* doing this!" She spoke excitedly. "I know it wasn't
easy for you to leave the office like you did, but the past week and a
half with you have been amazing; and I just want you to know how
much I appreciate it. It means *so* much."

John reached across the small table and took her hand. "You don't
have to thank me, Molly. I'm only doing what I should have been doing all along. I'm sorry that I disappointed you and hurt you the way
I did, and I promise to do my best not to ever let you down again."

Molly looked deep into his eyes, heartened to find the man she
had always loved looking back at her. "I believe you, John. I have no
doubt about that. You're *back*. *This* is the man I fell in love with, and I
have him back. Thank you for coming back to me." She squeezed his
hand, and they both smiled in silence.

When the lobster salads they had both ordered finally arrived,
Molly and John were more than ready to dig in. They ate and talked,
enjoying the view around them and the smell of the sea air as they sat
together at their table, far away from their life at home and finally,
finally able to just *be*.

After they finished lunch, John called Buddy Sullivan, the owner
of the sailboat. He was given directions to a private marina just off
of Roosevelt Boulevard in the New Town section of Key West, and
they took a taxi to meet Buddy and his wife Brenda there, a friendly-
looking couple in their mid-sixties. After all of the introductions were
made, the four of them began walking toward the slip where the thirty-two-foot Morgan was waiting.

Buddy spoke as they strolled along the dock. "How long have you been sailing, John?" he asked.

"Since college. Really, though, my *wife* is the expert—she's the one who taught me," John admitted easily. "Her father owns a marina near Savannah, Georgia, and he's been an avid sailor all of his life. He raised her with sailing in her blood."

Molly flushed under her husband's praise and deflected focus back onto him. "I really didn't have to show him all that much. John was a natural."

They arrived at the slip, and Molly noticed that Buddy seemed almost giddy at the sight of the boat.

"She's a beauty, this one," he said proudly. "Brenda and I have sailed her as far down as St. Thomas, and last summer we took her up to Tampa. The plan was to be at sea at least six months out of the year after I retired, but I've had a few health issues recently. I try to stay as close to shore as I can without having to give up sailing all together."

John looked at the older man, whose bone-deep love of the water was palpable. "I'm sorry to hear that, Buddy," he said sincerely. "She certainly is a beautiful vessel, and I'll care for her as if she were my own."

"I know you will, John. I read people, my boy—and I have a good feeling about you."

John continued his inspection and then he, Buddy, and Molly stepped aboard to have a look below deck. The cabin could easily accommodate up to four passengers, so, with just him and Molly, there would be plenty of room for an extended voyage. Buddy demonstrated the main features of the boat, and then they made their way back up to the dock and began discussing the details.

"How long do you plan on keeping her out, John?" Buddy asked. "Got your destinations all figured out, or are you going where the wind takes you?"

"We plan to be out for at least a week, but a lot depends on the weather, I suppose. I thought we would sail out to the Dry Tortugas first off and then go on to Fort Jefferson. Molly and I went there on a day trip when we were here on our honeymoon, back in '92," John replied, wondering if Buddy would raise objections or if the man was asking merely out of curiosity.

"That's a good place to start, since it's an easy run—only about seventy miles out. The coordinates are already stored on the chart plotter and GPS on board, and I'd imagine you would have no trouble at all making the trip," Buddy said helpfully. "There are a few islands out beyond the fort that you might want to explore, too. Some aren't even on a map. Just be careful. It can get really shallow awfully quick in some places."

John thanked him for the heads-up and told him of their plans to spend the afternoon shopping for supplies and outfitting themselves for the voyage.

"We're planning to set sail first thing in the morning, bright and early," John went on with an excited smile.

"Good plan. Don't let the day get too far ahead of you," Buddy replied with a nod, extending his callused hand toward John.

The two men settled out the last details of the deal and worked out an arrangement for John to borrow one of Buddy's old Jeeps for running errands around the island.

Later in the afternoon, John and Molly returned to the marina and began hauling their supplies down the dock and loading them aboard the boat. They stowed forty gallons of fresh water, enough food to last for up to two weeks, and two sets of snorkeling gear, as well as various other supplies and necessities.

On their last trip to the boat with supplies, Molly started running, a gleeful smile lighting up her face. "First one to the boat chooses dinner!" she screeched, sounding more like their seven-year-old daughter than a grown woman in her forties.

Despite her head start, John passed her in the last seconds, just barely winning. They both doubled over in laughter as they tried to catch their breath. John started strutting like a peacock, savoring his victory, and then suggested that they return to the hotel for a shower before heading down Duval Street in search of a nice place to have dinner. Molly was famished and readily agreed, giving him a well-deserved victory kiss.

An hour later, the two were seated on the Veranda at the A&B Lobster House near the end of Duval, overlooking the harbor and enjoying the perfect spot for winding down their first day of vacation. John ordered a filet and lobster tail, while Molly chose the blackened swordfish. Both devoured their meals, agreeing that this was now their all-time favorite restaurant. The food was outstanding, and the view *alone* was well worth the price of admission.

Molly breathed in deep and looked at John. "Good choice, baby!"

He relished the look on her face, and in that moment he felt like the luckiest man alive.

"Good choice, indeed," he whispered back, his words inspired not by the restaurant but by the woman who now sat with him in the waning hours of daylight. "If we leave now, we can make it over to Mallory Square just in time to watch the sunset."

They had made such great memories there twenty years earlier, amidst that breathtaking scene where thousands gathered each evening to bid farewell to the sinking sun. It had a carnival-like atmosphere, drawing street vendors, musicians, and performers of all types all year long, coming alive every day at sunset—a Key West tradition that was not to be missed.

"I couldn't think of anything I'd like more," Molly said with a smile. "And then maybe afterwards, we can go find the perfect slice of Key lime pie for dessert."

John grabbed her hand and pulled her up from her seat and into his arms, burying his face in her hair and breathing in her scent. "You won't get any argument from me on that one, my love. Let's get out of here!"

Mallory Square was alive and well.

That was the magical thing about Key West—the relaxed attitude that everyone seemed to have and their abandonment of schedules in favor of having a good time. There was no set time to be home, no living by the clock. It was just a place to let go and just *be*.

John had not allowed himself to be so carefree in such a very long time, and it felt great. He was amazed to realize how much of his life he had let pass him by without really *living* it.

"I'm so happy that we're here together and that you've given us a chance to be *us* again," he said, taking Molly's hand and looking deep into her eyes. "I want this to be a new beginning, a turning point in our lives and in our marriage. I promise I'll learn how to be a better husband and father—the kind of man you deserve, and the kind of father that Afton deserves."

As he spoke, Molly could feel herself getting lost in John again. She had missed him, but she promised herself right then and there that she would never let him slip away again.

After the big orange ball slipped from view, the crowd that had gathered to watch began to disperse, making their way back to the many bars, restaurants, and hotels from whence they had come. John and Molly fell in with the crowd working its way back to Duval Street and meandered down to Sloppy Joe's Bar, taking a table near the stage. The place had been one of Hemingway's personal favorites back when he'd lived in Key West in the '30s, and its walls were decorated with pictures and memorabilia from his eccentric and tragic life.

Upon ordering large slices of Key lime pie, John and Molly settled in to listen to a band that had just finished setting up on stage.

"'It is good to have an end to journey toward,'" John read aloud, intrigued by words on a nearby wall. "'But it is the journey that matters, in the end.' Ernest Hemingway had quite the way with words, didn't he?" John mused as he looked over to Molly and took a mental picture of this moment in their journey, knowing there were some moments in life that you wanted to last forever.

When the band took their break just over an hour later, he and Molly settled the check and began wandering slowly back down the street toward their hotel, stopping in several shops and a small museum on their walk back.

The museum held ancient coins and relics that had been found on shipwrecks in and around Key West, ships that had succumbed to the treachery of the reef located less than a mile offshore. The main artifacts in the museum were from the *Atocha*, a Spanish Galleon that had sunk during a storm in 1622, somewhere off the coast of Key West. Loaded to the hilt with a fortune in gold, silver, copper, and other fine jewels, the wreckage had been discovered in the mid-eighties by legendary treasure hunter Mel Fisher. And to date, more than 450 million dollars' worth of Spanish treasure had been found and brought to the surface.

John was intrigued by the history and significance of the story, and while Molly was busy looking at pottery, he purchased two coins from the wreck that had been made into gold necklaces, one for each of them to wear. He also bought a small, pocket-sized book about the various coins and artifacts that had been salvaged from the wreck, and he wrote an inscription on the inside page:

Dear Molly,

> *This is the first day of our time in Key West, a renewal of our life together and our journey to happiness–the day that I bought a treasure for each of us to wear. May this necklace always be a reminder that you are the priceless treasure in my life. I hope you know that I cherish and love you more than anything.*

Love always,
John

After leaving the museum, they flagged down a pedicab and rode the last mile of the way back to the Casa Marina Hotel. They took a short, refreshing dip in the hotel pool and then wrapped themselves in plush robes before going out onto the balcony to sit and let the remains of the day soak in.

While the stars twinkled around them in their seats on the balcony, John reached into his pocket and pulled out the book and necklaces, handing each gift to Molly. She admired them both with fascination, but when she opened the book and saw what John had written inside, she had to bite her lip to hold back tears of happiness.

"I love it, John!" she exclaimed. "I love the book and the coin—but I especially love *you*."

He helped her with the clasp and pulled her into his chair with him, holding her close. They sat together there, holding hands and looking out over the sea as the moonlight danced upon it and the water shimmered like jewels.

"Thank you for everything, babe," Molly said softly. "It's all just *perfect*. So very, very perfect."

CHAPTER SEVENTEEN

THE TWO AWOKE EARLY SUNDAY MORNING TO A BRIGHT AND CLOUDLESS SKY. John stepped out onto the balcony with a cup of coffee as he waited for Molly to shower and gather her things, enjoying the feel of the light offshore breeze ruffling his hair. He couldn't imagine a more perfect day for them to begin their adventure.

Making sure that Molly was still busily getting ready, he quickly used his phone to send a short email before placing it into his bag with the rest of his things.

...

When everything was loaded into the Jeep, they drove to Bahama Village to eat breakfast at Blue Heaven, a rustic building set amidst one of the original sections of Old Town, with an open courtyard and tables set for outdoor dining. It was not at all uncommon for one of the resident roosters to visit the tables in the hope that a stray bread-crumb or two might be found, and the quaint little joint was popular with both locals and tourists alike.

Gamecock fighting had been banned in the town sixty years ear-lier, and a law had been passed against keeping caged chickens. The fact that they now had free run of the restaurant—not to mention most of the town, as well—had only added to the ambiance and the atmosphere that was so undeniably Key West.

John and Molly gorged themselves on omelets and French toast, along with freshly squeezed orange juice and fruit, both in full appreciation of the fact that there would be no meals on ready order while they were out at sea. Once they were full nearly to bursting, they paid their check and left for the marina, anxious to set sail and begin their adventure.

John checked the oil in the small inboard engine that would be used for motoring in and out of port, while Molly began untying the lines that held them fast to the dock. Buddy approached them moments before they were ready to cast off.

"Well, it looks like you two are about ready to get going," he said cheerfully. "I checked the weather report, and there's only a slight chance of an afternoon thunder shower. That's typical down here this time of year, really. Nothing to worry about—these storms tend to disappear just about as quick as they come up."

John reached out and shook Buddy's hand. "Thanks for the heads-up, Buddy. And don't worry about a thing. I'll be taking good care of her."

As Molly walked up to the bow with a ready smile and greeting for Buddy, John added, "*Both* of them." He smiled and nodded in Molly's direction.

Buddy smiled easily in return. "I'm sure you will, son. We'll see you both when you get back. Good sailing!"

As Buddy walked back up the dock toward the old Jeep where Brenda stood waiting, Molly watched him go. "I really like him—and *them.*"

"Me, too," John replied. "That'll be us, one day. Married long—and happily."

The last line was cast off, and they were finally free from shore, with John at the helm and navigating the schooner down the narrow canal that connected the small harbor to the open sea. The cool wind was at his back, and the sun warmed his face. It seemed to John like he was sailing toward paradise, as Molly sat on the bow in front of him and took pictures, wanting to document every possible moment of their trip. She ducked below deck to retrieve her cell phone and made a call to Katie, checking on Afton before they sailed out of range.

She gave Katie the Sullivan's phone number in case of an emergency and told her that they would be able to contact the boat through the use of a marine radio. Katie wished them a safe and memorable journey, then reminded Molly to take plenty of pictures.

"I'm not going to lie to you—I'm *so* jealous!" Katie said with a laugh. "I wish Brad would take me on a romantic adventure sometime, but I'm not sure either of us has the sea legs that you two do!"

"Well, don't worry about the pictures, Katie. I've probably taken more than a hundred already, so I'll have plenty to show you when we get back. It's so beautiful here, and things are really good with John and me. We needed this more than either of us realized, I think," Molly said thoughtfully, before breaking into a grin. "As for a romantic adventure of your own . . . I'll see what I can do about making hints to Brad, okay?"

"Thanks, my friend," Katie laughed. "Oh, and I plan on checking in on your dad later this week."

Molly thanked her again before hanging up from Katie, then making a call of her own to her father, hoping to reach him at home since it was Sunday and the marina would be closed. Much to her surprise, there was no answer. She swallowed a lump of apprehension in her throat and left a message on his answering machine, letting him know that he was to call Katie should he need her for anything and that she would be able to get in touch with them while out to sea.

Probably a big waste of time, she thought, mainly because he rarely, if *ever,* checked his machine.

When she was done making her calls, she stowed the phone away in her purse and reclaimed her position as John's first mate.

A half hour later, they were clear of the harbor and the reef and were heading southwest into open water. John cut power to the engine and Molly released the main sheet, which gave a loud popping sound as a sail cloth emblazoned with a bold red *S* was stretched tight by the wind. The bow began lurching forward, slicing through the small wave troughs in its path. The only sounds being made now were coming from the rigging hardware and the water lapping against the Morgan's sleek hull.

To John, it sounded like the soft, sweet music of a long-forgotten song. He powered up the chart plotter and GPS system, showing that they were approximately sixty-eight nautical miles from the Dry Tortugas and Fort Jefferson, the first stop on their voyage.

...

Erica Payne sat alone at a poolside table at the Atlantis resort on Paradise Island, Bahamas, her bathing suit barely visible under the cover-up she wore, a large white hat shading her face from the harsh rays of the sun. Crossing her legs, she lazily bounced one foot, the patent leather of her high-heeled sandals flashing in the sunlight. She was a vision, picture-perfect for any resort's brochure—and she knew it.

She ordered a light breakfast and pulled her phone from her bag, scrolling through emails and texts, deleting most as she went along. She was pleasantly surprised, however, to see one in particular. After reading it through twice, she saved it into her personal file and began enjoying her breakfast.

...

Early in the afternoon, the first sight of land came into view on the horizon.

"John! I think I see it—is that the fort?" Molly shouted, trying to be heard over the wind.

"I think it must be," John said with an excited smile. "We're still pretty far out, though. And I'm not sure about the depth of the water near the island, so I don't know how close we can get to shore."

He handed Molly a navigational guidebook and asked her to look up the location to see if it gave any information on how to make an approach. She found instructions concerning docking and mooring near the island and relayed them to John, walking him through them to keep things running smoothly. When they were within a half mile, they lowered the sails and reengaged the engine, easing in as closely as they could. About a hundred yards offshore, they dropped anchor in eight or so feet of water before John retrieved their snorkeling gear from a storage locker on deck.

"Ready for a swim, sweetheart?" he asked Molly.

Molly gave him a broad smile. "Absolutely. I can hardly wait!"

The water was crystal clear and pleasantly warm, and on the short swim to the beach they spotted a rainbow of fish and other marine life, including a six-foot nurse shark—even an octopus. Molly was relieved when they finally made it to dry land.

"Seeing that shark was kind of scary," she said with a blush of slight embarrassment. "I do have to admit, though, it was also pretty amazing!"

John laughed. "I'm so glad you liked it."

The rest of the afternoon was spent exploring Fort Jefferson and its surroundings. It was hard to believe that something so grand in scale could have been built so far out to sea, so long ago. Molly continued taking pictures until the battery on her camera began to run low, and after relaxing on the beach for an hour in the late afternoon John suggested that they start making their way back to the boat.

One of the things he remembered well from his marine biology class in Savannah was that sharks came in close to feed at sundown. He didn't bother divulging this bit of knowledge to Molly, however, for fear that she might panic and he would never get her back to the boat. Fortunately for them both, they were safe aboard the Morgan ten minutes later.

After showering off, John began preparing the grill for dinner. He and Molly had made sure there would be no shortage of good food on this trip, and tonight's main course would be grilled Mahi with garlic potatoes. Molly set a small table at the stern, and they dined as the sun sank away into the ocean.

Once they'd cleared away their dishes, the two sat together on boat cushions and watched the stars grow bright against the pitch-black sky.

"You know, I could really get used to this," Molly sighed.

"Me, too. In fact, I think I already am," John said quietly as Molly leaned closer, bracing her back against his chest. "You know, before we left Savannah, I asked your father about possibly restoring *Sweet Afton*."

Molly turned her head to face him, a curious look on her face. "Really, John? What did he say to that?"

"Pretty much what I expected him to say—*No!*"

Molly looked back out at the sea. "Doesn't surprise me, either. Even after all these years, that boat still haunts him. I think maybe now even more than ever. It would probably have been better if he had just gotten rid of it after the accident," she mused. "My mother told me that she tried to get him to agree to it, but he was adamant about keeping it."

"Maybe it's a bit selfish on my part, but I'm so glad he did. It truly is a work of art, and I was hoping that maybe he would allow me to get her restored—so he could see her once again how she was meant to be, not rotting away in some old shed," John said, the disappointment plain in his voice. "Who knows, maybe we could even have gotten the chance to sail her again."

Molly was quiet, and John knew she was probably thinking about her father and the fact that he was now in the twilight of his life.

"Surprisingly, he actually *did* say before we left that maybe we could talk about it next time we go down for a visit. He made me promise to bring Afton, as well, so I think it would be a good idea to take her there as soon as school is out for the summer."

"I think that would be wonderful, John," Molly said, hope creeping back into her heart. "Let's do that. I really want Afton to have the chance to see him again, and I think I'd like to have another look in my mother's old studio, too—maybe try to organize some of her things."

"We will. I promise." John kissed the top of her head and tightened his arms around her shoulders. She kissed his hand.

"I love you, John."

"I love you, too. So very much."

CHAPTER EIGHTEEN

IN THE EARLY, DARK HOURS OF MONDAY MORNING, A LIGHT RAIN BEGAN
TO FALL. John awoke and thought for a moment that it might help
wash away some of the dried sea spray that had already accumulated
on the surface of the boat. Whether it did or not, it didn't matter.
What *did* matter was that it was cool and calm on the water, and he
pulled himself closer to Molly and was soon asleep again.

Nearly three hours later, John and Molly were awakened by what
sounded like a low-flying plane overhead, and they quickly scrambled
to the deck to investigate. They made it out just in time to see a small
seaplane land and taxi up to a long dock adjacent to Fort Jefferson.
After the plane was secured, four passengers and the pilot unloaded
and began to walk toward the old fort.

Molly, of course, documented the entire scene in pictures, intrigued at the sight of these unexpected newcomers to their secluded
little enclave. John's own curiosity was piqued, as well, but for reasons
far different than his wife's. He had always had a fascination with all
types of aircraft and had been particularly interested in seaplanes for
quite some time. Seeing this one—here, now—made the wheels in his
head begin to turn, but he decided he would keep these thoughts to
himself.

For now, at least.

The rain was gone now, but it had done little in the way of washing the boat as John had hoped it might. The heat was beginning to

rise, so he began the process of readying the boat to get underway. He lifted anchor, loosened and raised the sails, and within minutes the Morgan was once again gliding west across the clear turquoise water.

John wanted to see some of the other smaller islands out beyond the fort that Buddy had suggested they explore. There was a steady breeze from the southeast filling the sails, and the traveling was good. A pod of four or five bottlenose dolphins surfed along just in front of the Morgan, taking full advantage of the steady push from the bow. John pointed them out to Molly so that she could see them and capture the scene with her camera. He loved seeing her enjoy the experience—it was like watching a little girl at Christmas.

When she put the camera away, Molly looked up at him and blew a kiss. He played along, caught it, and patted his heart with his hand. Flashing before him in his mind's eye were those effortless days of joy with her in years gone by.

Synchronized hearts.

That's where they were today.

Back to the beginning.

John looked at his phone out of habit—and curiosity. As he had expected, there was no service. At first, the thought of being disconnected from the firm—and from the rest of the world, for that matter—had made him feel uneasy. But as time passed, he had actually begun to feel more liberated.

For the first time in a very long time, it was beginning to feel okay to be out of touch. He began to truly relax, feeling confident in Michael's and Joan's abilities to handle most any situation that might arise at the firm. And—worst-case scenario—if they *couldn't*, he would take care of it when he returned. For now, he knew beyond a shadow of a doubt that there was nowhere else on earth he would rather be than on *this* boat, with Molly.

Miles away at the Callaway headquarters in Atlanta, two men in dark suits stepped from the elevator and approached Joan's desk.

"How may I help you gentlemen this morning?" she asked.

The man who appeared to be in charge spoke up. "We've come to speak to Mr. John Callaway Jr."

Keeping her face impassive as she gave both men the once over, Joan answered, "Mr. Callaway is away from the office at present, and I'm afraid he can't be reached. I am the chief operating officer. May I ask what business this is regarding?"

Neither man's expression seemed to change.

"When do you expect him to return?"

"I can't really say. He's out of the country on vacation." Joan narrowed her eyes. "Who did you say you were again?"

The man doing all the speaking produced a card and handed it to her.

"Donald Copeland, FBI," Joan read aloud. The other gentleman produced a card of his own and passed it over to Joan. "Jeffrey Smith, Internal Revenue Service, Special Branch," she read, alarm rising up within her.

Copeland spoke again. "Who is in charge of the firm during Mr. Callaway's absence?"

Joan could hear the unease in her voice as she spoke, and she knew that the men standing in front of her could hear it, as well. "That would be Michael Bloom, Chief Financial Officer. He is also Mr. Callaway's business partner."

"Is Mr. Bloom currently available?" Copeland asked. "We would like to speak with him."

Joan could feel her alarm give way to irritation as she replied to his tedious method of inquiry—and his dismissal of *her*. "Mr. Bloom has not yet made it into the office this morning. If you wouldn't mind telling me what this is about, perhaps I can help you?"

Smith finally broke his silence. "When you speak to Mr. Callaway or Mr. Bloom, will you please ask them to contact us? The matter is one of extreme urgency."

"Of course," Joan replied.

The two men returned to the elevator and disappeared.

After watching them leave, Joan immediately picked up the office phone and dialed Michael's cell, relieved when he answered on the first ring.

"This is Mike."

"Where are you right now?"

"I'm about to pull into the garage at the office—why? What's up?"

Joan's voice was low but direct. "Meet me at the coffee shop on University in ten minutes. We need to talk." She didn't wait for Michael to respond. She put the phone back on the receiver, picked up her purse, and left the building, telling no one where she was going or when she might return.

...

After about thirty minutes under sail, John and Molly approached another small island that appeared to be deserted and was mostly covered in mangrove trees. There was a small beach area on its northern side, but the water seemed too shallow to get very close. They decided to continue westward for another hour, and if they found nothing more of interest, they would return and attempt to maneuver the boat closer into shore. Just as they'd hoped, they headed southwest for another forty minutes, and two small landmasses came into view.

John checked the chart plotter to see if he could identify the islands and get a quick fix on their position, but neither of the tiny land masses appeared on the plotter or on the GPS map. His curiosity got the better of him, and he decided to sail in closer for a better look. Molly was napping on the foredeck when John rang an old-fashioned brass bell that was mounted next to the helm.

"Land-ho!" he shouted, making Molly jerk awake in mystified panic. "All hands on deck!"

She looked back at John, trying to reorient herself, and he pointed in the direction of the two small islands. The larger of the two islands was roughly three acres in size, and John figured the smaller one was only about half that size, positioned about five to six hundred yards to the southwest. Both islands were mostly protected by a thick stand of mangroves, and several dozen medium-sized palm trees shaded the larger of the two.

John and Molly both worked quickly to lower the sails and start the inboard engine. John wanted to maneuver the boat around the area under power, not knowing how shallow the water was or if maybe there was a reef lurking near the surface. There was a fairly deep channel that ran between the two islands, and John was able to ease the boat to within fifty feet of the shore, much closer than they'd been able to approach the last island. The current running through the channel where they'd be mooring the boat was swift, so John set two anchors, one fore and one aft; and, while the anchor ropes stretched tight, the boat still held steady in her place.

They gathered some supplies, food, and their snorkeling gear and made the short swim up to the sandy white beach. Molly was still a little shaken at the idea of having to swim among sharks, but the picturesque island scenery had been incentive enough for her to gather her courage.

"This is beautiful, John! Can we live here forever?" she asked, only half-joking.

They both laughed as they put all their things down on the blanket they'd carried along in a waterproof bag. After eating a quick lunch of sandwiches that Molly had prepared before they'd left the boat, they set out to explore the tiny oasis. About a mile offshore, they saw a large fishing boat cruising along, and John noted that, other than the boat and the plane from earlier this morning, they had seen no other people all day.

"I guess this really is what one might call a getaway!" he commented to Molly with a smile.

"I know," she replied, basking in the warmth of the sun on her skin and relishing their solitude. "Isn't it great? It's just you and me on our very own private little island." She jumped into his arms and kissed him playfully.

Paradise was certainly getting more interesting—and paradise-like—by the minute. If memories were like anchors for the soul, then anchors were being cast in deep waters this afternoon, firmly mooring John's and Molly's souls together.

They made love there on the shore, their bodies entwined as they lounged and talked. Eventually, they decided to walk the shoreline, following its edge as it snaked its way through the stand of mangrove trees. They waded through shallow, crystal-clear pools full of fish and crabs and other creatures. John thought that, if he had a net, he could probably scoop up something delicious for dinner.

"Wow, look at all these fish! I bet Ben would love it here!" he exclaimed.

Molly laughed. "No doubt he would. But, I have to say, I'm definitely glad that he didn't come along on this trip!"

"Me, too, but it might be fun to come back again someday and bring him along," John replied with a laugh of his own.

"John, if you bring me back here again, I don't care *who* comes along!"

Just in front of them, a large stingray shot out toward the open water and startled them both. Molly screamed and ran up onto the beach, the water splashing madly up around her as she moved.

"It was just a *stingray*, Molly! Come back!" John called after her, shaking his head and smiling.

"*Just* a stingray? There's no *just* about it! That thing was monstrously huge! Didn't you *see* that?" she called back.

John laughed as he waded back to shore to his spooked wife, scooping her up into his arms and carrying her around the last of the mangrove trees to the safety of the powder-white sand. Theirs were the only footprints they'd seen since arriving an hour earlier—just one more reminder that, as far as accessibility was concerned, they'd arrived somewhere far out of reach from the world at large. Here, they were at the proverbial "end of the line."

"You know, I'm not sure that many people even know about this place or ever come this far out," John remarked. "I'm glad that *we* found it, though. I feel like an explorer—or maybe like Robinson Crusoe! Except for the fact that I'm on this salty piece of land with a beautiful woman, I have a boat, and I can leave whenever I want. Okay, so maybe *not* so much like Crusoe."

Molly laughed. "Maybe more like Gilligan!"

"Hey, now! I'm gonna get you for *that* one—*MaryAnn*!" John ran in her direction, and she sprinted off down the beach as their laughter was swept up in the wind.

"You're gonna have to be faster than *that* to catch *me*—John *Gilligan* Callaway!" she shrieked gleefully.

...

Michael Bloom sat stunned by what Joan had just told him. "None of this makes any sense, Joan. I don't understand why John would even *consider* doing anything like this," he said, shaking his head in disbelief. "He has no reason to."

Joan's voice was calm as she spoke. "I don't either, Mike. Could be the stress at home with him and Molly—or maybe he just got bored," she ventured. "Who knows? At first, I thought it was just a simple mistake, and I fixed it. But then it somehow got changed again. I didn't want to confront him about it, though. I just suggested that he take some time off so that you and I could figure things out. I *certainly* wasn't expecting a visit like I had this morning."

"This is just all too much, Joan," he insisted. "It just doesn't seem like John, at all. What are we supposed to do now?"

"Well, the one thing that you *are* going to need to do *for sure* is separate yourself from all of this. You'll need to cooperate with these people and make sure they know that you're not involved in *any way* and that you had absolutely no knowledge that anything at all was amiss."

Michael stared blankly at her as the words hit his ears, still making no sense to his confused brain. "I just can't believe this is happening. I think we need to call John. I mean, surely there's a reasonable explanation for all of this—there *must* be."

Joan's voice turned up a notch. "I've already *tried* to call him, but his phone goes straight to voicemail. *Wherever* he is, there's either no service or he's turned his phone off altogether. I have no way of reaching him." She slid Agent Copeland's card across the table in front of Michael. "I'd suggest that you take some time to gather yourself and then call this man to set up a meeting. Meet me back here tonight at six, and we'll talk about what we should do next."

Michael stared at the card lying on the table before him and shook his head, the words on the card blurring under his unblinking gaze.

...

John and Molly reached the northern side of the island, finding its exposed edges to be mostly coral that was razor sharp and dangerous. As he warned Molly to be careful, she took photos of the natural beauty that seemed almost beyond imagination, seemingly undiscovered and somehow untouched by progress and civilization.

"Hey, Molly!" John called out to her, watching as she lined up her next shot. "How do you feel about staying out here for a couple of days?"

"Are you kidding me? I would love that—I already told you I want to move here!"

CHAPTER NINETEEN

MICHAEL BLOOM SAT ALONE IN THE CONFERENCE ROOM AT CALLAWAY, WAITING FOR COPELAND AND SMITH TO ARRIVE FOR A NINE O'CLOCK MEETING, LEAVING HIM UTTERLY CONFUSED AND INTENSELY NERVOUS. The wait gave him just enough time to feel exasperated with the facts—and suppositions—running rampant through his mind.

Joan, meanwhile, sat calmly at her desk, intently eyeing the elevator area, and when the two men stepped from the elevator, she joined them and led the way to the conference room. The predictably suited men introduced themselves to Michael and informed him that, although this was an informal interview, it was being recorded. They encouraged him to be truthful and to answer their questions both fully and directly. Michael agreed, and the small red light blinked to life on a digital recorder they'd brought in with them, adding to Michael's uneasiness. The men spread several official-looking documents out onto the table in front of Michael, and Mr. Smith, from the IRS, spoke first.

"Do you recognize what these documents are?"

Michael looked them over. "Well," he said, clearing his throat, "they appear to be authorizations for money transfers. And judging by the amounts listed, I assume they're from the deal we most recently closed on a development project in the Bahamas."

"Do you recognize the signature on these documents?" Smith prompted.

Michael looked at the name neatly written at the bottom of the page. "Yes."

Smith produced a second set of documents that appeared to be identical, then continued speaking. "Do you recognize the signature on the *second* set of papers, Mr. Bloom?"

This time gulping slightly before he spoke, Michael once again answered in the affirmative.

"Yes."

...

Erica Payne entered the First Caribbean International Bank and approached a teller at the front counter, producing identification and a withdrawal slip with an account number written into the blocks provided.

"I would like to make a withdrawal, please," she said without hesitation.

The teller looked closely at the photo on the ID and then back again at Erica. "Of course, ma'am. I see that there is not an amount listed on the slip. How much would you like to withdraw?"

Erica flashed him a perfect smile. "*All* of it."

The teller gave her a tentative look before he replied. "I see, Miss Payne. However, you *must* understand that, due to the *substantial* amount of your request, I will need to get the manager's approval and certain arrangements will need to be made to accommodate your wishes."

Erica continued to smile as she tried to mask her annoyance. "Certainly. I will be waiting."

"I appreciate your patience. Please give me a few moments." The teller excused himself and entered a small, glass-walled office in the center of the lobby. He presented the withdrawal slip to the branch manager, and Erica watched the senior man's eyes go from reading the slip of paper upward for a quick scan of the lobby. When he saw her, she winked. He practically jumped up, nearly tripping over the teller in his haste to leave the tiny cube and approach her.

"I am Patrick Bryan, the bank manager," he said when he reached her, extending his hand. "Miss Payne, I presume?"

It was a rhetorical question, of course, but she responded with a glorious smile. "Please, Mr. Bryan, call me Erica."

"Yes, of course, Miss . . . uh . . . *Erica.*" He laughed and blushed like an addle-brained schoolboy with a crush. "Harold has informed me that you wish to make a rather large withdrawal from your account. Is that correct?"

She moved in a step closer to him and gently straightened his necktie, then patted his chest lightly as she broadened her smile and lowered her eyelids suggestively. "*Harold* has informed you correctly. I wish to withdraw *all* of the funds from my account."

Much to her satisfaction, the man was entranced by her stunning beauty and the attention she was showing him. For a moment, he seemed lost in her gaze, forgetting his place and abandoning his professionalism as hormones overtook him. He blinked and returned to his senses, clearing his throat gruffly.

Erica smiled, pleased at the effect she was having on him.

"And how do you wish to receive the funds?" he asked.

She gave a throaty laugh. "Why, *in cash*, of course—*Patrick.*"

"Very well. I will need a little time to process the transaction and gather the funds. Can you come back at noon?"

Erica was not happy to leave the bank empty-handed, but she knew better than to let her displeasure show. "Anything for *you*, Pat." She turned and walked through the large revolving door, triumphantly assuming success and knowing, without a doubt, that all eyes were still fixed firmly on her.

John and Molly awoke to another perfect day in paradise.

"Molly, let's try to catch a fish for lunch today," John suggested as he held up a crude net he'd made from one of the bags that had held their swim fins. "Sound like a plan?"

"Okay," she said, looking somewhat doubtful. "I have to say, though—the chances of you *really* catching an actual fish with that thing are pretty slim. But it'll be fun to watch you try."

"Wanna bet?" John said with a wink.

"*Maybe*," Molly replied playfully. "Depends on what we're betting."

After finishing breakfast, the two jumped into the water and swam back to the shore of their tiny island oasis. John beat Molly to the beach and turned around just in time to see a sleek black fin slicing through the water directly behind Molly.

"Molly, watch out!" he yelled, but just as he did the fin disappeared under the surface as the shark darted away. Molly came up onto the sand, shaking water out of her ears.

"What, John?" she asked, looking puzzled. "Did you say something?"

He felt a tinge of panic but tried not to show it. "Oh, nothing—I was just messing around."

"Well, don't do that again! You almost scared me to death!" She teasingly punched him in the arm, and he bent down to pick up a handful of seaweed, dropping it on top of her head before he gleefully ran off toward the mangrove shallows, with Molly hot on his heels.

When Molly finally caught up to him, John was already knee deep in the water, standing motionless as he stalked a fish. She started to approach him, but he held up his hand to hold her off.

He really is on a mission to catch a fish, she thought in surprise as she watched him focus intently on the water in front of him.

John quickly scooped his makeshift net down into the water, bringing it back up only to see that it remained empty. He repeated the process several more times before finally admitting to Molly that it was harder than he had expected—not that he was throwing in the towel, by any means. She found a shady spot underneath one of the palms and settled in to watch the show.

After another hour, John was still without success, and Molly offered to swim back to the boat to make sandwiches.

"*No!*" John yelled out, somewhat forcefully.

"*Wow*—okay," Molly said, feeling the need to back off. "I didn't mean to hurt your feelings. I was just trying to help."

John apologized for his harshness and asked her to give him just a few more minutes to try. The last thing he wanted was for Molly to get back into the water where he had seen the shark earlier. He wasn't quite sure how to handle the whole situation yet, but he needed the chance to work out a plan.

As he watched and worked things over in his mind, a large fish swam up to within a foot of where he stood. He took a swift stroke at it and—to his own surprise, and certainly to Molly's—came up with a flopping redfish securely caught within his net. He ran toward the beach as Molly stood, jumping up and down and clapping in excitement. He stopped and took a bow, grinning from ear to ear with pride at his accomplishment.

Once he'd reached the shore with his catch in hand, John took a length of nylon cord from the waterproof bag they'd brought ashore and made a small loop in one end, running the other end into the fish's mouth and out through its gill. He fed it back through the loop that he'd tied and pulled the slack through until it was tight before he secured the loose end to one of the mangrove branches and then eased the big fish back into the water. It would be a little while before they were ready for lunch, and John wanted to keep him alive and fresh.

"Wow, John. I honestly didn't know you had it in you!" Molly exclaimed in undisguised amazement.

"You didn't think I had *what* in me?" John poked, feigning insult.

"The whole survivalist thing—all this being out on the water, out in the elements and so far away from civilization. Finding and catching our food . . . All of it," Molly replied. "I must say, I'm very impressed. And *quite* turned on," she continued with a smile.

John had begun to gather some driftwood for a cooking fire later, and he flashed a knowing grin over his shoulder at Molly. "You'd be surprised at what people are capable of doing when they really put their mind to it." He paused. "Both good *and* bad." With those words, he walked farther down the beach and away from her.

As she watched him go, she sat back down under the palm, that very same feeling of uneasiness she had experienced on the pier in Savannah less than two weeks before beginning to spread over her again. She couldn't quite explain it, but something just didn't feel right. She wished that she had a working phone, so she could call home to check in on her dad and Afton.

She sat staring out at the water, lost in thought, until she had almost thoroughly reassured herself, having shaken the feeling of dread for long enough to continue on and attempt enjoying the rest of the day with John. She walked in the direction he had gone, hoping to find him easily and help him gather more wood. She spotted him on the northern side of the island, sitting on the edge of the coral rocks, as he stared off into the distance.

She approached him and spoke. "Hey, you! What are you doing over here all alone? I was getting worried about you."

He turned and looked at her, his expression sad and distraught. "I was just thinking, Molly. Thinking about everything that's happened lately and wondering what to do next."

She was perplexed, and she knew it was plain on her face. "What do you mean, 'What to do next'?"

"I don't know . . . I just wish we didn't have to ever leave here. Everything is just so perfect, and I'm afraid for it to end."

"It doesn't have to *end*, John," Molly said quietly, still wondering where he was going with all of this. "But we certainly can't stay here *forever*. We have a daughter at home—remember?"

"*Of course* I remember—don't be silly!" he said. "I just . . . I wish things weren't so complicated." He rose from his perch, losing his footing on the slippery surface as he stepped across the algae-covered rock to reach where Molly stood, his right leg grazing the razor-like coral that had been exposed during low tide. He regained his balance and stood still for a moment as he tried to figure a way out of his predicament.

"Are you okay? Did you get hurt?" Molly asked, worry furrowing her brow.

John looked up at Molly. He had only slid down a few feet or so, but the coral was dangerously sharp. "I think I'm alright—I just scraped my leg a little," he said, trying to ignore the searing pain in his leg.

From what he could tell, his best route of escape would be to go into the water and walk around the edge of the outcropping, back to the sand. It was only a short distance, and he was soon back on dry land, but by then his leg felt like it was on fire from the stinging salt water.

"John, you *are* hurt!" Molly exclaimed.

He looked down at his battered limb. While it was only a surface scrape on the side of his right calf, it was a long one, about ten inches, and bleeding profusely. John spoke in a calm voice, trying to reassure his wife.

"It's really not that bad, Molly. I'll take care of it when we get back to our supplies—no worries," he said, giving her a smile that he hoped would calm her down.

He put his arm on Molly's shoulder, and they began walking back to where they'd set up camp earlier.

"John, is there something that you need to tell me?" Molly asked, looking at him with concern. "Because if there is, now is the time."

He was looking away from her as he replied. "No, love. There's nothing that I need to tell you. Just forget I said anything, okay? Really."

The wary feeling had returned to the pit of Molly's stomach once again, and this time she feared it would not be so easy to let it go.

...

When they returned to the area where the driftwood had been stacked, Molly found the small first-aid kit in their waterproof bag.

"Let me put some of this antibacterial cream on your leg. It's the best we can do until we can get back to the boat and tend to it properly, John."

Giving her no argument, he sat on the blanket as she applied the medicine to the wound.

"John," Molly said hesitantly, "I—I have a bad feeling."

He looked up at her. "What do you mean—*bad*?"

There was an audible nervousness in her voice as Molly answered. "I don't really know how to explain it to you. It's just this strange feeling that something is wrong or that something bad is going to happen—like something is chasing me and is right on my heels. And, even though I'm running, I just can't get away from it."

John listened silently as she confided her fears.

"I had the same feeling last week when I was at the pier on Tybee, and now, with *this* happening—well . . . it makes the feeling even stronger."

He tried to reassure her. "Baby, I'm sure that everything is just fine. And don't worry about my leg—it's really just a scratch," he said with a shrug. "Hardly even hurts anymore."

She was still kneeling beside him, looking at him without speaking, as if she would start to cry at any moment.

"Look, Molly, please don't worry so much," John murmured, as he placed his hand gently on the middle of her back. "Besides, if anything were wrong, Buddy would have called us on the radio."

She didn't seem convinced, and John's words did little to ease her anxiety. "I don't know, John . . . Are you sure that the radio even *works* this far out? I mean, nobody even really knows exactly where we are. *We* don't even know!"

"*Of course* the radio works. I heard the weather report on it this morning before we swam ashore. And, believe it or not, I do have a pretty good idea of where we are." He could tell she was genuinely worried and would probably not be able to relax again until she confirmed that all was well at home and with her father. "I tell you what, babe—after we eat, I'll go back to the boat and make a call to Buddy and Brenda to check in and make sure that everything is fine, okay?"

"Okay," Molly said with a deep sigh. "Thank you."

John began to build a fire with the driftwood they'd gathered and continued placing larger pieces on the flame until it was fully ablaze, wanting a hot bed of coals for roasting the fish. A half hour later, the fire was getting close to ready. He pulled his dive knife from its sheath and walked down to the water's edge to retrieve his prize, leaving Molly behind to prepare the rest of their dinner on a blanket they'd spread out over the sand. When he reached for the rope to haul in his catch, it was quickly pulled taught, then came a sharp tug before the nylon cord was yanked from his hand.

He still has plenty of fight left in him . . .

John reached back down just under the water's surface to put his hand on the line again. It was noticeably slack and felt distressingly light. Fearing that the fish had somehow escaped, John gave the line one last tug. What he saw on the end of the frayed cord shocked him at first, taking him a moment to register what he was looking at. All that remained was part of the large fish's head connected to a short piece of spinal bone that was noticeably cleaned of flesh and meat. One large, black, bulging eye stared at him, seemingly in terror.

"*What* the . . . ?" he gasped.

Molly saw what dangled at the end of the rope and hurried down to where he stood.

"What happened to that fish?" she asked, panic heightening the pitch of her voice.

Thoughts of the fin he'd seen slicing through the water earlier that morning raced through John's mind. "I'm not sure," he said, hoping his words were convincing enough. "I guess it could have been a sea turtle or another fish or something."

"Or a *shark!*" Molly exclaimed.

"Or a shark," John admitted reluctantly, though he kept an edge of doubt in his tone in an effort to discourage her suspicion. "But I think it's *really* unlikely that it was a shark, Molly. They usually don't come in this close to feed this early in the day—unless, I suppose, there's a free meal just there for the taking. My guess is that the fish was in distress, and whatever had him for lunch could tell."

Molly's agitation was clearly at the surface. "That *scares* me, John. I don't like this—not one bit. I'm ready to leave. *Now,*" she said, turning to go back to their blanket and pack up.

He put his arm around her and could feel her trembling. "Molly," he said as he looked into her eyes. "It's *okay.* I'm not going to let anything happen to you—you can trust me on that. *Don't worry.* Besides, nothing can get to us on dry land, now *can* it?"

Her words were shaky. "I suppose you're right—but we *are* eventually going to have to get back to that boat."

John had been thinking about the fifty feet of open water and the swift current where the boat was moored, the same place where a large shark had come within just feet of Molly earlier that morning without her even being aware. More importantly now, he was thinking about the wound on his leg that would add to their challenge of escaping.

"Don't worry, baby," he said, even as troubling thoughts flooded his mind. "You're going to be just fine—don't I *always* take good care of you?"

In retrospect, he wondered how his words actually *sounded.*

They gathered their things and slowly began walking back toward the boat, neither of them eager to get back into the water just yet, least of all Molly.

As they neared the water's edge, each stopped dead in their tracks, dumbfounded at what they saw—or *didn't* see. Where the boat had stood fast just hours before, they saw only an empty channel of swiftly moving blue-green water.

Molly screamed in panic. "Oh, *my God*, John! What *happened*? Where's our boat?"

He was just as puzzled as he scanned the horizon for some sign of the Morgan, finally catching sight of a flash of the red hull in the distant waves.

"*There!* Look over there!" He was pointing toward the smaller island on the other side of the channel. "I see it!"

The beautiful sailboat was loose, keeled over on its side at about a forty-five-degree angle up against the beach, and she appeared to be taking on water.

Instead of being reassured that they'd spotted the boat, Molly was even more upset. "What are we going to do, John? How are we going to get home? We're stranded here!" Her panic level seemed to rise with each word she spoke. "*No!* This *can't* be happening!"

John used all of his resolve to remain calm, knowing that his alarm would only serve to make Molly even more hysterical than she already was. He stood at the edge of the surf with his hands on top of his head, feeling helpless, as he stared across the water at the flailing sailboat.

"It's going to be okay, babe. Just give me a minute to think."

CHAPTER TWENTY

JOHN SAT ON THE SAND AT THE WATER'S EDGE. IT WAS GETTING LATE IN THE DAY, AND THE WINDOW OF TIME TO REACH THE BOAT BEFORE DUSK WAS QUICKLY SLIPPING AWAY. He thought again about the shark—or perhaps *sharks* would be more accurate, since they were not usually solitary creatures. Sharks were known for hunting in packs, like wolves, with one making the initial bite to test the prey. Then, once blood was in the water, a frenzy would ensue.

This could go from bad to worse very quickly.

Understandably, Molly was still shaken and had sunk down into the sand next to him, her face buried in her hands as though she could not bear the sight of the scene in front of them. John could see her occasionally look up and search his face for some sign of comfort. He knew she was scared—and, truthfully, so was he. Concentrating and desperately trying to come up with a plan, John knew he had to make this situation turn around quickly.

"What are we going to *do*, John?" she asked again. "Are we *really* stuck here? We haven't seen another person or even another *boat* for almost two days now. *What are we going to do?*" Her frantic voice slowed ominously. "This is *bad*, John. This is *very* bad!"

John's tone was quick and sharp as he answered. "I'm *thinking*, Molly—just *let* me *think*!"

She put her head back down on her knees and began to sob quietly.

Erica smiled as the handsome gentleman at the jewelry store placed two Rolex watches on the glass counter in front of her. He was well dressed, wearing an expensive cream-colored linen suit with a crisp light-blue shirt, and he spoke with a slight accent.

English, she thought, *or maybe even Australian.*

He presented himself as quite sophisticated and very well polished. Indeed, he was the perfect face for such a refined establishment as this.

"You really can't go amiss with either choice. The platinum with diamond bezel certainly makes an elegant statement, while the 18-karat gold is a timeless classic," he said with a smile that could have easily been used in a toothpaste ad.

"I couldn't agree with you more," she replied, her own smile stunning enough to match his. "*Sold.*"

He was obviously surprised that she had made her decision so quickly—and easily.

"Very good. Which one would you like?"

She was quite enjoying this. "Why, *both*, of course," she said, with her trademark wink and flashing a luminous smile.

His smile broadened. "Excellent. I'll get this taken care of for you right away. And how will you be paying today?"

Erica never broke eye contact with the man. "Cash."

"Of course. Is there anything else that I can help you with?"

"Maybe—perhaps we could discuss it over drinks later," she replied flirtatiously.

"I am quite sorry, miss, but I'm afraid that won't be possible this evening. I am already spoken for, but I *am* flattered that you asked," he said, bringing her little game to an early—and certainly unexpected—end.

"Hmm, what a shame," she said, with a pretty pout. "In that case, could you please tell me where I might find *Louis Vuitton?*"

Later that afternoon while Erica was returning to her suite at the Atlantis, one of the lobby desk attendants called out to her, catching her just as she was about to walk by.

"Ms. Payne, may I speak with you for a moment?" he said with hushed urgency.

She turned sharply and walked over to the counter, looking at the man's nametag. "Yes, Thomas?"

The man spoke discretely. "Ms. Payne, I wanted to inform you that a gentleman came to the desk earlier this afternoon and was inquiring after you."

"Who was this mystery man, and what did he want to know?" she asked curiously, beginning to grin as he replied. Perhaps she had an unexpected suitor . . .

"He wanted to know if you were a guest at the resort and, if you were, how he might contact you," Thomas said.

"And what did you tell him?"

Thomas appeared to be somewhat offended by her question. "Of course, Ms. Payne, I told him that I was not permitted to divulge any information regarding our guests. Protecting their privacy and acting with discretion is our policy, and we *strictly* adhere to it."

"I see," she said, her expression giving away nothing further. "Did this gentleman leave his name?"

"No, Ms. Payne, he did not."

"Thomas, if he should return, will you please call my suite and let me know?"

"As you wish, Ms. Payne," he replied with a respectful nod.

She began to walk away but then turned back as another thought ran through her mind.

"Thomas, what did this man look like?"

"I'd say he was about forty years of age, tall. And he was wearing a handsome suit."

Her shapely eyebrows rose in curiosity. "Did he happen to speak with an English accent?"

"Not that I recall, ma'am."

Her lively smile faded. "Thank you, Thomas."

"Of course, Ms. Payne."

Moments later, Erica entered her suite and went directly to the small safe located in the bottom of a cabinet that also contained a television and a minibar. She punched in the combination and quickly emptied its contents into one of the new Louis Vuitton bags she had purchased earlier in the day, before hastily gathering her clothes and some of her other belongings, stuffing only the items that would fit into a separate small suitcase. After departing the room with barely a backward glance, she took the elevator directly down to the pool level to avoid having to exit through the lobby.

She left through a side exit, making her way back to the front of the building, relieved to notice an idling cab awaiting its next fare. She hastily opened the door, slinging her bags into the backseat ahead of her.

"Drive," she ordered the man behind the wheel.

The driver sneered at her, using his rearview mirror, before offering a curt reply. "Where to, ma'am?"

"Anywhere away from here," she said simply.

...

Heavy, dark clouds had moved in from the west and hung low over the small piece of paradise that now firmly held the Callaways captive. John heard thunder rolling in the distance as he examined the wound on his leg. It was painful, but the bleeding had stopped—for the most part, at least. He took off his shirt and began tearing it into narrow strips, planning to make a temporary bandage in an effort to help control the last of the bleeding, which might allow him a better shot of getting through the water undetected by any hungry sharks in the area.

Ironically—or maybe fortunately, now that he thought about it—when he'd studied marine biology that long-ago summer in Savannah, the week they'd learned about sharks had been the most interesting and fascinating to him. He remembered nearly everything the teacher had discussed on the subject, and he certainly knew that just one drop of blood in the water would be like ringing a dinner bell—especially at *this* time of day, when they started to come in close to feed. He was also not naive to the fact that, although he enjoyed swimming, he was far from possessing any true skill in the sport.

The current was swift and strong, and swimming against it would present its own challenge, even for the most seasoned of swimmers. As he stared out at the water, footage from so many of the week-long shark documentaries he'd watched over the years seemed to play in a constant loop in his mind, particularly the attack scenes.

"What are you planning to do?" Molly asked, coming up behind him.

He went back to wrapping his calf with the cloth strips, hoping his determination would bolster his own confidence, as well as Molly's.

"We have no choice here, really. I'm going to have to swim for the boat," he replied, not looking up at her. "I have to get to the radio so I can call for help, and I need to go *now* before it gets dark and the storm starts."

Molly moved to stand in front of John, placing herself between him and the water that was getting more turbulent by the minute.

"No, John, please!" she pleaded in desperation. "You can't get into the water like this! What about the sharks? What about the storm?" She was shaking her head manically. "*No*, we have to stay here and wait for someone to find us!"

With his leg finally wrapped, John inched closer to his wife, facing her and gently taking both of her shoulders in his hands. "Look, honey," he said grimly—quietly. *Firmly.* "I have to do this. It's our best chance right now. We can't just sit here and wait. You said yourself that we haven't seen another person in days, and we have very

little food and water and *no* shelter from the storm that's coming."
He paused, looking back out at the water. "I'm also afraid that when
the tide comes back in, it could raise the boat off of the sandbar, and
she could drift away and be lost forever. I *have* to go, and I have to
go *now*."

Feeling an odd mix of desperation as well as admiration for his
ability to stay focused, Molly reached out for her husband, wrapping her arms around him and holding on tight. "Please, John—*please*
don't leave me here alone," she begged him, her voice muffled as she
spoke into his chest.

"It'll be okay, Molly. I promise I'll never leave you alone."

John stroked her face, looking down into her eyes before he sealed
his promise with a kiss. Knowing that lingering any longer might lead
to second thoughts and put his chances of beating a storm at greater
risk, he pulled away and quickly waded out into the water.

Molly's breath caught in a half-whimper, half-cry as she watched
him brace against the waves.

For now, at least, John felt that his odds of swimming the channel
and reaching the boat were better than good. But he knew there were
no guarantees, either. When he was about waist-deep, he turned back
to her.

"I love you, Molly. Everything will be okay. I *promise*."

...

Michael Bloom sat in his car in the parking garage at the Callaway
corporate office, staring blankly, without comprehension, at his
phone.

What am I supposed to do now?

The day before, the agents he'd met with had made him sign a
contract forbidding contact with John under any circumstances. He
was also not allowed to discuss any details of the matter at hand with
anyone else, neither *inside* nor *outside* of the firm.

Which would include Joan.

Everything, it seemed, was falling apart around him. Everything was subject to official scrutiny. Unsurprisingly, the hard drives from all the firm's computers had been seized for analysis.

All computers but *one*.

The one that he and *only he* knew about.

It was the laptop on the seat beside him. He stared one more moment at the silent cell phone in his hand and pressed a button on the speed dial.

Knowing there would be no ring, his words were ready when the voicemail recording prompted him

"Hi, Erica. It's me."

...

After spending what felt like twenty minutes in the water, John had covered more than half the distance across the channel. The swimming was difficult, and as he struggled against the incoming tide, he calculated that he still had maybe two hundred yards left before he would be able to stand. He could feel exhaustion setting in, so he floated for a minute, breathing hard and trying desperately to catch his breath. He was basically treading water now, trying to see Molly standing on the opposite beach, but only able to catch small glimpses of her as his body bobbed—at the mercy of the ever-increasing waves.

He looked down into the clear water and could see that the make-shift bandage on his right leg was completely gone. Obviously, the thrashing motion from his hard efforts to swim had torn it loose, making him wonder if he might be bleeding again. It was difficult to tell—he felt numb from the constant exertion, numb all over, almost.

John turned over to float on his back as he paddled with his hands in the direction of the boat, trying hard not to lose any of the distance he had managed to cover so far. For a moment, he closed his eyes, squeezing them shut to shield them from the stinging salt, only to snap them open again as he felt a sudden movement in the water underneath him. It was close, and the force almost rolled him completely over.

At the exact moment he opened his eyes, a bolt of lightning streaked down from the angry sky over the beach where Molly stood. John watched as she turned and ran into the edge of the tree line, a futile attempt to find cover. The thunderclap that followed was instantaneous, almost deafening. John's heart was pounding, his mind racing, battling against panic over the storm closing in all around him, as well as whatever might be in the water below.

That was too close.

He felt the sudden movement pass underneath him once again and ducked his head below the surface of the water, seeing nothing. Still, he could only assume it was a shark coming in for a closer look.

To assume anything *less* threatening might lead to death.

Not waiting for a third pass, John began swimming harder, pushing every stroke as hard and as far as he possibly could. His only hope now was that he might somehow outrun both the lightning and the hungry predator suddenly seeming in relentless pursuit.

As John inched closer to the Morgan, he began to see some of the damage occurring as the beautiful boat floundered in the rough surf. The mainsail was partially submerged on the far side of the vessel, and the force of the water from the constant barrage of waves was stressing the mast and tearing loose some of the rigging that held the lines in place. He knew he must get the sail pulled in close and out of the water completely if there was any hope of saving her from further damage.

A mishmash of items from inside the ship's tiny cabin could be seen tumbling up onto the beach, an obvious indication to him that the interior had been at least partially flooded.

Every stroke now seemed fruitless to John, doing little to benefit his progress or his frame of mind as the strong rip current worked like an anchor, trying to hold him out at sea and far away from safety. As rain began to fall, visibility became almost impossible, diminished to only a few feet in front of him. By now, fatigue had overtaken him to the point that the shark's presence only moments before seemed more like a distant memory, an odd observation of some strange being that had no true bearing or consequence on his survival. He felt disoriented, his body weighted and dull from the physical exertion. Yet at the same time his mind was pushing him to fight on and keep moving.

The war between body and spirit raged.

John knew that if his feet weren't able to touch bottom soon, it was likely he would never again feel solid earth beneath him. His movements became mechanical, his only thoughts focused on Molly and Afton and the rising ache that he may never see them again. With his eyes closed tightly against the stinging salt water, he continued swimming.

Right arm, left arm, kick.

Right arm, left arm, kick.

He mindlessly repeated the pattern until he was jolted by the realization that his hand had brushed against something solid. He instinctively pushed away, and his foot touched the sandy bottom.

John opened his eyes and could see that he was only about twenty feet from dry land.

And he was *alive*, more alive than he had ever felt before.

He stood and began to wade through the waist-deep surf, scrambling and stumbling as he tried to run toward the safety that the shore would at least temporarily afford him.

John stood on the beach, shielding his eyes from the rain that was now sheeting down onto him—the island where his precious Molly was stranded no longer visible in the torrential downpour. He was powerless now, left only to hope and pray that she was safe and sheltered somehow from this storm.

Molly was huddled down underneath the brown palm fronds of a tree that must have been blown down in a prior storm, a make-shift haven that was aided, albeit poorly, by the beach blanket she'd pulled over her head. While it did little to keep her dry, it did at least provide somewhat of a buffer between her eyes and ears and the torrent that seemed to engulf the small, salty piece of land she now inhabited alone.

She prayed that John was safe, that he had somehow managed to get across the channel before the storm came down on them.

That his leg was not bleeding or hurting too badly.

She refused to give in to the reality of what was actually happening, refusing to allow her mind to focus on the very real danger they were both in—refusing to believe that there could truly be a shark out there capable of taking away the most important part of her life.

She struggled not to think of all of these terrible things, instead replacing the thought of a doomed future with the beauty of dreams—dreams of John and of Afton and of home.

Oddly, her mind wandered back to a stormy night when Afton was just four years old. Her little girl had been terrified of strange noises and the darkness of the hallway, so Molly had made a game of encouraging Afton to overcome her fears. Molly had called it their "One Brave Thing a Day" game, which often meant doing things like walking down the hallway in the dark or going into a bedroom before the lights were on. Whenever Afton did the "brave thing," she got a prize, like a piece of candy or an extra book read to her at bedtime. Afton had caught on quickly and enjoyed the game, where doing brave things in her little world equated to receiving rewards. They had been playing the game one stormy night when John came home from work. Afton heard the garage door, alerting them to his arrival, so Molly had encouraged her daughter to go downstairs all by herself. Afton had been tentative at first, but when she had heard her daddy's voice, she had run all the way, flying into his arms.

Now, alone on the island, Molly repeated the words she would have used to help her little girl face her fears. "You can do this one brave thing, just like Afton," she said aloud to herself. "John will be back soon."

She was huddled in solitude, willing courage to seep into her bones, as she brushed the moisture from her face one more time, a mingling of rainwater and salty tears.

...

John scrambled to climb aboard the wounded Morgan. He had little strength left, and it took all of it to heave himself up and over the side rail suspended about six feet above his head. The boat was being rocked violently back and forth on its side from the churning surf that had been kicked up by the sudden storm. Once he made it onboard, John lay there for a moment, gasping for breath before he gathered himself and mustered enough strength to make an attempt at entering the flooded cabin.

He could see most of their personal belongings floating in three feet of water, and hope surged through him like a strong wind as he thought about the radio.

Could it still be intact? His mind raced. Although the radio itself was primarily waterproof, it still needed the boat's battery to power it, and the antenna would need to be in place to transmit signals over any significant distance. From what he could see, the antenna was secured to the top of the mast, and the mast was in immediate danger of being torn loose from the deck by the heavy sail that was now completely submerged.

Suddenly overcome with the need to hear a voice—*any* voice—he yelled out loud, "Help me!"

It was hopeless, really, if he stopped to think about it. But he still couldn't just give up. Knowing there was no one around to hear him, much less *help* him, he yelled out again.

"Get up, John! Help *yourself*!"

He hurried into the cabin and searched the galley drawers for a knife he could use to cut the sail away from the mast. He quickly found one and made his way toward the rigging ropes and cables that were all tangled about the deck. He tightly grasped the mast pole itself, locking one foot underneath a section of rail, then hung himself over the side of the small ship and began cutting loose everything that he could reach.

After nearly ten minutes of desperate attempts at making some sort of progress, he could finally see part of the sail coming loose and beginning to float out and away from him. It didn't seem to be pulling down on the side of the boat as hard now, but he knew he couldn't stop. He continued to cut as he inched his way along the hull until, at last, the sailcloth was completely free. With the immediate threat finally at an end, he collapsed from exhaustion.

Twenty minutes passed in a blur, and John was suddenly startled awake by another loud clap of thunder. The storm was directly over him now. He was glad that it seemed to be moving quickly, and he hoped it had moved completely away from Molly by now. As he strained and squinted in an effort to see across the channel, he could only make out a few of the taller palms near the center of the island.

It would be dark soon.

He needed to move.

...

Molly felt the rain ease up, relieved to find that it was now nothing more than a steady drizzle. She crawled out from underneath her makeshift shelter and began looking toward the area where she had last seen John in the water. Her visibility was limited to a couple hundred yards; and, as she scanned the distance in hopes of seeing *something*, she was disheartened to see absolutely nothing. The other island, the sailboat, and her husband had *all* vanished behind a dark wall of wind and water. The storm that had just passed directly over her was enormous, and the thunderhead seemed to stretch out for miles in every direction.

Suddenly desperate, she broke out into a run, running flat out until she was knee-deep in the water.

"John!" the sound of her voice was a fever-pitched scream that seemed to go nowhere, swallowed up by the wind and the rain. She was knocked from her feet by a crashing wave that reached up as though it were alive, grabbing her and pulling her down. She panicked as thoughts of what else might be in the water with her rushed into her mind, and she clawed her way quickly from underneath the foamy surf, falling onto the wet sand in a sobbing heap. She lay there crying out for help in a voice that could barely be heard by her own ears, shock overtaking her as sheer panic and fear robbed her of the ability to think clearly.

But she couldn't give in. She couldn't.

She *had* to pull herself together, *had* to survive this ordeal.

She and John both still had a life to live—*together*.

...

John found his way back into the boat's flooded cabin, noticing, with no small amount of relief, that she sat up a little straighter in the water now, mainly due to losing the sail but also in part to the rising tide helping to lift the hull off of the sandbar. He stood in thigh-deep water surveying the damage, utilizing what little remaining daylight was left before heading straight for the radio—only to find that it had no power.

Rather than giving it up as a lost cause, he decided he would work on it before writing it off completely. But first, he needed to search for items that might aid in their rescue—or, more immediately, their survival. He located a small LED flashlight and the safety bag that included a solar blanket, a small first-aid kit, and a flare gun, along with three medium-range flares. Moving quickly, he also gathered all the fresh water that was available and the food items that had been stored in waterproof containers.

The rain outside was still heavy, and although the cabin was anything but dry, it did offer at least some protection from the worst of the storm. He placed everything he had hopes of salvaging onto the galley table and then hoisted himself into the highest bunk.

John needed rest, even if it was only for a little while until the storm passed. For the first time since he'd left Molly standing alone on the island, he felt the searing pain in his leg again. It wasn't good, but he knew that, as long as he could still feel it, that pain meant he was alive.

For now, at least, that was enough for John.

Within seconds, he was out cold.

CHAPTER TWENTY-ONE

Buddy and Brenda Sullivan were finishing an early dinner out on the afterdeck at Louie's Backyard in Key West, enjoying the pleasantly cool evening as they dined. The breeze had picked up a bit over the past hour or so since their arrival, and some lightning could be seen far off to the southwest. To most everyone else, it was a relief from the humid nights they'd been having.

But to a seasoned sailor like Buddy, it meant something else.

It meant that, somewhere between Key West and Cuba, there was a very large storm, and he knew that John and Molly were most likely in the midst of it. Feeling a sense of dread closing in, he asked for the check.

"I want to get back to the house and make a call to the Callaways on the radio," he said, his eyes serious as he looked across the table at his wife.

Brenda gave him a surprised look. "Do you think there's something to worry about?"

Buddy patted her hand reassuringly, despite knowing that she could read him well enough to see through his words. "I'm sure it's nothing, but it wouldn't hurt to check on them. With any luck, they chose to sail north, which means they may have missed the storm altogether."

"I hope you're right, Buddy," she said, glancing out at the sky and the water. "I would sure hate for them to be caught out there in *that*."

As the final words left her lips, a bright flash of lightning cut through the sky and a large gust blew in, tugging the umbrella on their table. Buddy was able to grab it just before it became completely airborne.

"Me, too," he replied, speaking up to be heard over the wind. "Let's go."

Over the next hour, Buddy made a dozen failed attempts to raise the boat using the ship-to-shore radio, leaving him more and more convinced that something was wrong. While he knew there could be many explanations for why John was not answering his calls, the worst-case scenarios seemed to crowd out any of the more non-threatening possibilities.

Stop it, Buddy. They've probably just left the boat to explore the beaches, simple as that. You're overreacting, he chastised himself. *Or maybe they've docked at one of the dozens of marinas to the north and are out enjoying a nice dinner together. Maybe they sailed farther west, out past Fort Jefferson, and are out of the range of the repeating tower.*

Although his gut was telling him something entirely different, he'd failed too many times to justify continuing to try and decided to let it go for the night. He would try to reach them again in the morning.

...

Molly continued to peer out into the darkness across the channel, hoping for *some* sign that John had made it to the boat and that he was all right. Although the rain had stopped completely by now—at least, where she was, it had—she was still unable to make out anything on the distant shore.

"Please, God. Please let him be okay," she prayed out loud. "I *need* this man—I really need him. And he needs me, too." She gathered all her strength to scream out again. "*John!*"

John awoke. He wasn't sure just how long he had been out, but it had to have been several hours. His shorts had partially dried, and the pain in his leg had grown much more severe in that time. He must have been more spent than he'd realized.

As he tried to move his leg, pain sliced through him and stopped him from getting up. He gritted his teeth to steel himself against the agony he was in—he didn't have a choice here. He needed to try to clean the wound as best as he could, which meant moving. He certainly could not afford an infection—not out here, definitely not now.

His leg had grown stiff from lack of movement, and his muscles were fatigued beyond anything he'd ever experienced. John forced himself out of the bunk and onto the floor, holding his right calf up out of the dirty water that remained in the flooded cabin. Fortunately, much of the rocking movement had stopped now, and the Morgan was only slightly listing to one side. He searched in the first-aid kit for some alcohol and antiseptic, but he was going to have to make do with only a small tube of medicated ointment and some sterile wipes. As he continued rummaging through the drawers and cabinets, he found half a bottle of 100-proof Puerto Rican rum.

"Thanks, Buddy—I think," he muttered under his breath. He hadn't taken Brenda for a hard-liquor woman, though one never knew. More than likely, however, Buddy was the one who chased a day at sea with the amber liquid.

John braced his leg on top of the table and pressed his back against the galley counter as he began pouring nearly half of what was left in the bottle directly onto the slice in his leg. As the alcohol seeped into his wound, the pain was so intense he thought he might pass out, screaming with an intensity he didn't know he was capable of. For a moment, he considered downing the last of the rum to numb himself, but he realized it would be self-defeating. He didn't need his senses to be dulled in any way right now; he needed to stay as sharp as he could, and he might need the rest of that rum later. Using his teeth to tear the packages, he opened several of the medicated wipes and placed them directly over the affected area. He found an ace bandage in the kit and wrapped it firmly around his calf muscle to completely cover the surface of the wipes.

He needed to get out of here—*soon*.

Molly stirred under the damp blanket. Her eyes opened as her ears registered the sound of what seemed to be the screech or the growl of some kind of wild animal. Erring on the side of caution, she lay motionless under the old broken palm, listening intently for another sound, but she heard nothing except waves sliding back and forth upon the shore.

Deciding she must have dreamed it, Molly sat up and peered out into the blackness, trying to adjust her eyes to the dark. She had never known a night so long and so dark—it seemed almost surreal.

There was not a star in the sky nor a light on the water. There was *nothing* out here, nothing but darkness and endless night.

And her. She was alone and helpless, so she started to pray.

...

John looked at his watch—5:55 a.m. Dawn would be breaking soon, and then he would better be able to assess his situation and see that Molly was okay. He *prayed* that she was.

John made his way up the five steps that led to the deck and was speechless at what he saw. The boat was no longer caught between the sandbar and the beach. Luckily for him, the incoming tide had lifted the boat enough that the outgoing tide was able to pull it away from shore, which explained why the boat was sitting up straighter in the water. The seven-foot keel had cleared the bottom, and the boat was now floating freely and being dragged out into the open sea.

All around him, the sky was turning a hopeful shade of pink with the first of the day's light coming over the horizon. John was beginning to see the shapes and outlines of the shoreline, guessing he was maybe a thousand yards out, moving quickly with the tide and the current.

Hopefully, his luck would hold.

He went for the ignition button to try to start the tiny engine, and, while it turned over, it refused to fire. John continued spinning the starter until he heard the battery begin to weaken. Not good. He would need battery power if he had any hope of using the radio.

Think, John. Think.

He needed a solution. As he went back down the companionway leading into the interior, he saw air bubbles coming up through the water.

And it was getting deeper.

The boat was still sinking, and the only explanation that came to mind was that the hull might have been compromised when she was being battered against the sharp coral near the shore. The bilge pumps were not working, either. Obviously, a circuit board had been fried, which would also account for the dead radio.

Think, John. Think, he mumbled to himself again, scrubbing the back of his balled-up fist against his damp forehead in frustration.

He went back upstairs and took another look around. He could see well enough by now to know that the boat had traveled at least another couple hundred yards in the last five minutes or so, and the Morgan was currently positioned so that only a portion of the other island was visible, the island where he had left Molly.

...

Fully awake now and standing at the water's edge, Molly watched intently as the far island began to take shape in the morning light. She still couldn't see John or the boat and was growing more impatient as she waited. She had a sense of what her grandmother must have felt so many years before as she had so anxiously awaited news about her grandfather. The apprehension she was feeling about the unknown was almost more than she could bear.

The poetic words of "Afton Water" echoed in her mind, and Molly could almost hear her grandmother's voice, as if she were right there with her, reading them aloud.

In times of stress, Molly had always found a calming peace in those words.

"Please, Lord," she whispered now, "let my John be okay."

When the sun cleared the horizon, the other island was in full view. The morning was crystal clear, without even the slightest sign of a cloud in the sky, much less the torturous storm from last night.

Molly stood in disbelief as she looked across the channel, and then confusion gave way to panic.

Could this really be happening?

The sailboat—and John—were nowhere in sight.

She fell to her knees as sobs and screams escaped her lips, ripping through the empty world around her.

"Help me, John! Help me! *Please!*"

...

John grabbed the flare gun, quickly loading a flare before firing a shot and hoping there would be a boat near enough to see the bright red flame as it fell through the morning sky. He wished then that he had thought about doing it before the sun had had a chance to get up as far as it already had.

Too late now—but, at the very least, he hoped Molly would be looking in his direction and see that he was still there.

She must be going crazy, wondering what's happened to me and if I've made it to the boat. Or if there even is a boat to make it to . . .

John knew he had a decision to make, and it was one he needed to make sooner rather than later. With every passing minute, he was being carried farther out to sea by the pull of the outgoing tide.

He had two choices.

He could stay aboard and try to salvage the boat—and, if that proved to be impossible, hold onto the slim hope that he would be rescued before she completely sank. Or he could abandon ship now and try to make it back to land.

From what he could tell, neither option seemed to be much in his favor.

He thought of the promise he'd made to Molly that he would not leave her alone. He couldn't break his word.

With that in his heart and forefront in his mind, John's decision seemed clear—he would have to leave the temporary safety of the flailing vessel.

He found a small, self-inflatable life raft under one of the seat cushions on the deck and quickly pulled the yellow cord attached to the side and let it go, hearing a loud bang and then a whooshing sound as the tubes inflated almost instantly. He smiled in spite of himself—the raft had performed just as advertised. He tied a length of rope to a grommet on the top tube and threw the orange rubber ring over the side, dropping supplies into the raft, tossing in everything he thought he could fit, along with himself, without sinking.

When he'd loaded up, he grabbed his journal and the logbook. He ripped out a page and quickly jotted down his and Molly's names and a rough idea of their location, then sealed the message in a Ziploc baggie and pinned it to a small bulletin board above the galley table. With any luck, the boat would be found while it was still afloat and help would come soon after.

Task completed, he lowered himself into the tiny raft, cut the rope loose, and began paddling with the dinghy's sad little three-foot plastic paddle.

After twenty minutes of hard effort, John had not put more than fifty feet of distance between himself and the Morgan. It was quickly becoming obvious that, by merely keeping pace with the larger boat, he was still being dragged away from shore. He couldn't possibly paddle the bulky, overloaded raft hard enough to fight against the current. Every muscle he had felt like it was on fire, and his body was screaming for relief.

How was he going to manage this?

He was not in the office boardroom, a place that he knew well how to control. This wasn't his element out here. He wasn't in control of this wild, wide-open ocean where he was just a small man in a life raft, getting farther away from the refuge of land by the second.

Farther away from Molly.

Farther away from hope.

John looked back and forth from the Morgan to the shore, trying to gauge the distance.

Fifty feet back to the boat and maybe three thousand back to dry land. That boat is going to sink, eventually, he thought. *On the other hand, it's morning—prime breakfast time for sharks.*

"Do it, John!" he said aloud, wasting not even another second before he dove over the top tube of the inflatable boat and began to swim.

...

Buddy Sullivan sat in his small home office, with the radio mic in his hand. He'd been calling the Callaways every fifteen minutes for the past hour, still with no luck. Becoming more worried than frustrated, he took off in the old Jeep, firmly set in his decision to head down to the docks to see if anyone who had been out on the water in the past couple of days might have seen them.

Chances were slim, but he had to at least try.

Miles away, Molly lifted her head to look at the sky.

John's searing flare had long since settled into the water on the far side of the opposite island, and she had not seen it. Still trying to get her mind to understand what could possibly have happened, she knew for certain that John wouldn't have purposefully left her out there all alone.

She shook her head, trying to clear it. At this point, there was no way of knowing if he had even made it across the channel. The thought left her nauseated, and a sense of panic and dread washed over her. Without any hope coming to the surface, Molly was left fearing the worst.

...

Buddy walked along the harbor's docks, casually speaking to each of the local fishermen and shrimpers he knew. Most of them never ventured more than fifty miles from Key West, but he wanted to find out if anyone might have spotted the Morgan heading out of port so he would at least have a general idea of what direction they'd sailed.

Unsurprisingly, no one had anything to report.

Deciding he might have better luck on dry land, he wandered into the Green Parrot on Whitehead Street, a favorite local hangout that was always packed with colorful characters ready for conversation. It was still early in the day, even by Key West standards, but a couple of the diehards were already leaning across the scarred old wooden bar top as they nursed their beers.

Buddy couldn't quite figure out if they were here early or *still* here this late.

After a few minutes of conversation, he concluded that neither of the bleary-eyed patrons had any clue about the possible whereabouts of the Callaways and turned to leave in frustration. He'd almost made it to the door when he heard a groggy voice speak out, and it stopped him in his tracks.

"I might have seen a boat like the one you're talking about."

Buddy turned to see a man stretched out on a bench in a dark corner of the saloon, his forearm over his face to shield his eyes from the rays of morning light coming through the open windows—obviously an offense to his hung-over state. By the looks of him, Buddy could only assume that the man had resorted to the hard, wooden bench rather than stumbling home to bed for the night.

As Buddy approached, the man sat up slowly, his effort visibly focused on not throwing up. He rubbed his face and forehead, no doubt feeling the full impact of the previous night's revelry. The man had only one eye fully open when he spoke again in a low, gravelly voice.

"I flew some Yankee tourists out to Ft. Jefferson a couple days ago and dropped them off for the day. I saw a boat moored about a hundred yards out. Had a man and woman onboard." He paused and swallowed a belch. "Could've been your boat. Don't know for sure, but be glad to take you out for a look after breakfast, since I don't have another charter booked until this afternoon."

Buddy's first reaction was surprise—not that the Callaways might have actually been spotted, but that this man was functionally capable of landing a floatplane in the open ocean. Too late, he realized that his thoughts were plainly displayed on his face.

"I'm not always like this, you know," the other man said wryly. "Last night was kind of a . . . celebration of sorts, I guess you might say."

Buddy raised his eyebrows. "I see, Mister . . . ?"

The man held out his hand. "Dennis."

"Nice to meet you, Dennis," Buddy replied as he shook the man's clammy hand. "Buddy Sullivan."

Breaking grasp, he wrote his number on a napkin and told Dennis that if he saw the same boat again, a phone call would me much appreciated.

"Sure, sure," Dennis said with a slow nod. "But are you sure you don't just want to go have a look?"

Buddy began to walk away. No way was he getting in a plane with this disastrous character of a man.

"Maybe some other time, Dennis."

"Sure thing." Dennis began to lie back down on the bench, easing himself into position.

Buddy paused again at the doorway, giving the drunken pilot one last look. "By the way—what were you celebrating last night?"

A dry chuckle came from the dark corner.

"I finally got my pilot's license!"

CHAPTER TWENTY-TWO

JOAN TAYLOR DINED ALONE AT A SMALL UPSCALE BISTRO IN DOWNTOWN ATLANTA.

Four full days had passed since she'd last spoken with John, and it had been two days since the government's goons had visited her at the firm.

Out of character for her, Joan found herself at a loss for what to do next. She couldn't contact John, and the office was off limits—for now, at least.

She finished her meal without tasting it, paid the check, and left.

Her mood was almost melancholy as she wandered along Peachtree Street, gazing into the picture windows of the local boutiques, restaurants, and jewelry stores. She thought of the diamond bracelet she'd bought herself on John's account the week before; and, while it was not her style to wear something so extravagant, she had done it to make a point.

And it had certainly accomplished that.

She'd wanted to remind her boss that he, alone, did not control everything—that she, too, had power. And she wanted to be sure he didn't forget that she was quite capable of asserting that power, should she feel the need.

On the surface, at least, John had seemed unfazed when she had shown it to him. But she knew that, deep down inside, his stomach had tightened into a strained knot, but not at the extravagance of the gift.

Of course not—he had that amount of money and more to toss around without much consideration. The diamond bracelet had been a mere drop in the bucket.

No. Joan knew that the knots in his stomach were caused by something far more disturbing to the mind of John Callaway Jr. than mere diamonds could ever be.

And that was that, although he was CEO of Callaway, the control was not solely in John's hands.

An hour later, Joan found her way back to her car. As she drove, she placed a call on a prepaid cell that she had purchased at a convenience store a few days earlier.

Her very own "burner phone."

The call was picked up immediately, without greeting.

Wasting no words of her own, Joan spoke in very short, precise sentences. "Did you do as you were instructed?"

"Yes."

"Were there any—complications?" she asked, darting a glance in her rearview mirror.

"No."

"Did anyone question you?"

"No."

"Are you safe?"

A pause on the other end made her jaw tighten.

"I'm not sure," the voice said at last, sending a jolt of adrenaline pulsing through Joan's body.

Knowing better than to show her hand, Joan kept her voice calm and steady, wanting to convey nothing but confidence and total control.

"Explain," she said coolly.

"I'm not sure, but I might have been followed."

Joan found herself looking again in the rearview mirror, an almost visceral response to the words infiltrating her ears. She managed to keep her tone from altering as she spoke again. "Go to the place I told you about," she instructed the person on the other end of the line as she pulled up to a red light and braked to a stop. "Do *not* speak to anyone you don't have to. Do not draw any attention to yourself. Remain there until you hear from me again—understood?"

"Understood."

Joan ended the call, pounded the steering wheel hard with her fist, and yelled out in frustration.

"*Idiots!* I am surrounded by utterly incompetent *idiots!*"

A man crossing the street in front of her stared as she continued with her rant. The light switched to green, and she floored the accelerator, almost hitting him, gritting her teeth, as she snarled through the windshield at him.

"*Another* imbecile! *Get outta my way!*"

She'd let herself lose her composure, and Joan was far from pleased that a stranger had seen her acting out. She looked at herself in the mirror, disgusted at what she saw looking back at her.

"You'd *better* take care of this, Joan," she reprimanded herself. "Are you hearing me?"

She drove on, feeling herself regain control.

A moment later, her personal phone alerted her to an incoming call.

Michael.

She paused for a moment, wondering if she should let the call go through to her voicemail. In light of recent developments, she decided to answer.

"I hope this is important, Michael. I'm hardly in the mood for idle chitchat."

"And good afternoon to you, too, Joan!" Michael quipped, her cold mood chilling his patience further, considering the circumstances.

She rolled her eyes, wishing he were astute enough to read her tone. Knowing Michael, however, she had little faith in his abilities.

"Get to the point, Mike," she snapped. "I don't have time for games. And neither do you, I would imagine."

A pause hung heavy over the line before he spoke.

"Okay, Joan. You're right. No games. I'm concerned about the extent of the allegations against John and the firm. None of this makes any sense at all. There's no motive for him to have even *thought* about doing what they're accusing him of doing." Another pause. "Unless . . ."

Joan was unimpressed by his sudden rally of support for John. "Unless *what*, Michael?"

"*Unless* he did it *for* someone else. Or maybe even . . . *because* of someone else."

Joan turned onto the street that ran along the front of John and Molly's home, her eyes fixed on a plain gray panel van with blacked-out windows that was parked in the driveway. She held her stare and spoke in a sarcastic monotone. "Michael, you'd be surprised at what some people are truly capable of."

"What exactly is *that* supposed to mean?" Michael huffed.

"It simply means what it means, Mike. Don't worry yourself unnecessarily. Just stay focused."

With that, Joan ended the call.

She continued driving past the house, her speed neither slowing nor accelerating, as she tried to avoid drawing any attention to her presence. Still, she wasn't overly concerned that she might have been seen. She could easily think of a dozen or more plausible explanations for her whereabouts when it concerned John.

Her phone rang again, and it momentarily startled her. Michael again.

No doubt he was angry that she had ended their conversation so abruptly moments before.

This time, she chose not to answer and pressed the red button, instantly routing the call to her voicemail. About a minute later, a chime sounded to indicate there was a new message awaiting her retrieval. But she was in no rush.

It could wait.

Michael could wait.

She had bigger things on her mind at the moment. Besides, she hadn't fully decided just how she was going to handle Michael Bloom at this point. For now, he would keep. Joan rolled her eyes and exhaled in a huff.

...

Erica Payne stepped off a luxury sport boat that was now docked at a private slip in South Miami, handed a thick bundle of crisp hundred-dollar bills to the captain, and gave him a wink as she collected her bags. She offered a waiting cabbie an address, tossing another hundred into the front seat beside him when he paused and looked at her to make sure that she was serious about her destination. He shook his head and grinned.

"Wha-tever ju say, pretty lady!" he laughed, his Cubano accent thickly coating every word.

A half hour later, the driver pulled to a stop in front of a small second-rate motel in an older part of the city.

"Welcome to Miami!" her driver exclaimed with a sarcastic chuckle.

She gathered herself and her luggage, standing frozen in disbelief as she faced the front of the old building.

Hardly the tourist destination, she mused as she walked into a cramped lobby area that had certainly seen better days.

She paid in cash and penned a fictitious name onto the register. The desk clerk handed her an old-school key attached to a faded orange plastic circle, a poor attempt at mimicking some type of tropical fruit. She stared at it for a minute, not exactly sure what to do next. She was completely out of her element in such a seedy joint.

No one was there to carry her luggage to her suite.

There wasn't a concierge.

Certainly not a spa or even a restaurant.

She was unaccustomed to such a low standard of living, and she cringed at the thought of having to spend even a single night in this wretched place.

Her feeling of being out of place was hardly one-sided.

Erica was a striking woman who commanded attention, even amidst her own kind, so her presence here was certainly noticed when she exited the dirty little office and stepped out onto the street. Just across the way, several old men sat in worn wooden chairs, taking shelter from the scorching sun under a scant awning as they played dominoes and checkers. As she stood in the relentless heat and glaring sunlight, one of the men looked up, the broad smile he flashed her revealing only a partial set of teeth, two or three of them ironically glinting gold.

How odd!

The flash of gold reminded her of the gleaming Rolex clasped temptingly to her wrist. She was suddenly aware that all eyes were on the watch and not *just* her—another feeling that she was unaccustomed to.

She walked quickly to the corner of the street where she found a cab idling, literally throwing her bags into the backseat before she climbed in and tossed a fifty at the driver as he sped her away.

...

Michael walked into his condo in midtown and wandered aimlessly from room to room for a few minutes before finally plopping down in the center of his sofa. He sat in silence, staring up at the ceiling, his mind reeling, feeling a sense of panic, dread, and confusion—all at the same time.

He needed to do something—but *what?*

After ten minutes, he rose to his feet, walked to his desk, and began rummaging through the drawers, frantically searching for a small scrap of paper with a phone number scrawled on it. He dialed the number but received no answer, cursing under his breath at his lack of success.

He stalked into his bedroom and hurriedly packed a light bag, retrieving his passport and a small stack of cash from a bedside safe and tucking them safely away into the inside pocket of his jacket. He had been told—or rather, *warned*—by Agent Copeland that leaving town was unadvisable and they would most likely want to speak with him again in the very near future.

Logically, such a "suggestion" left him no time to spare, and ten minutes later he was speeding south on I-75.

...

After a brief meeting, Joan walked back to her car and once again used the burner phone to place another call to the number she'd dialed before.

"Hello?" a reluctant voice answered.

"Did you do as you were instructed?" she questioned, again wasting no time—or breath—on a greeting.

"I tried to, but the local riffraff hanging around that dump didn't exactly make me feel safe."

Joan's pulse quickened as her blood pressure rose.

"You listen to me, *Erica*. Everything that we're trying to accomplish here hinges on you doing *exactly* as you've been instructed. We've been over this dozens of times!" she fumed. "He's already en route and is planning to meet you there sometime later tonight, so pull yourself together. Be a big girl for once and do as you are told! *Are we clear?*"

There was a moment of silence before a submissive reply came over the line. "Yes."

Joan clenched her eyes shut as she tried to mask the rising impatience in her voice. "We are very close to having what we both want—and what *one* of us, at least, *deserves*. I need you to hold it together.

He'll tell you what to do next once you've given him what belongs to him. *Please*, do me the favor of telling me that you *are*, in fact, competent enough to understand such a *simple* instruction!"

"Yes, Joan."

"Good. And, Erica, just one more thing—this is to be our last conversation. I *do not* expect to ever see you or hear from you again!"

She allowed no time to reply, simply turning the phone off before tossing it into a large Dumpster behind a closed-down strip mall on I-75.

...

Michael's first inclination was to fly, but even if he didn't fly commercial but instead used Charlie, a flight plan would still have to be filed. The FAA had become a stickler on such things, post 9-11, and he needed no one to know of his destination, least of all the FBI or the IRS. Stopping just south of the city, he filled his tank and hurried back onto the interstate, carefully keeping his speed just under 80 mph, in hopes of avoiding being stopped. He estimated that he would arrive in South Florida sometime after midnight.

He would just have to figure the rest out once he got there.

CHAPTER TWENTY-THREE

MOLLY CONTINUED TO SEARCH THE SHORELINE OF THE SMALL ISLAND JUST ACROSS THE CHANNEL FROM WHERE SHE STOOD, WISHING WITH ALL HER MIGHT FOR EVEN A GLIMPSE OF HER HUSBAND OR OF SOMETHING— ANYTHING—THAT WOULD MEAN JOHN HAD BEEN ABLE TO MAKE IT TO SAFETY.

She saw nothing.

No boat, no debris, and—most importantly—still no John.

She tried to control her breathing as panic once again began to engulf her.

How can this be happening?

She was becoming disoriented in her surroundings, and what had seemed like a perfect paradise, only the day before, was now beginning to feel like an inescapable prison. Feeling left with no other choice, Molly went in desperate search of some sign of life besides her own. She ventured along the shoreline over to the opposite end of the tiny sliver of land, which now felt smaller and much more confining than it had felt when they'd first arrived.

She shaded her eyes, looking far to the north and then to the east, studying the horizon and searching for any shape at all that could possibly be a boat or a plane—*any* sign of civilized life. Water was the only thing visible to her—empty water, wherever she looked. It literally felt as though she were the last remaining person on Earth, isolated from everything she had ever known.

It was a helpless and hopeless feeling.

After all she and John had been through together, Molly could not bear facing the possibility of life without him—or, God forbid, Afton's life without *either* of them.

She made her way back to the spot where they'd planned to have lunch the day before. She rummaged through the sparse provisions they'd laid out on the checkered tablecloth, once again spreading it out on the sugar-white sand. Under other circumstances, it might have been a scene from a travel brochure, enticing visitors to some faraway tropical paradise.

Ironically, this place was indeed far away.

And it was definitely tropical.

But it was no longer *paradise*, by any stretch of the imagination.

Molly took stock of the items laid out before her: the fillet knife that John had used on the fish he'd caught the day before, two bottles of spring water, and four slices of bread. Although the bread was sealed in a bag, condensation was forming from the heat of the day, and the moisture was making the bread soggy. Mold would soon follow, so she quickly rationalized eating three of the slices before they became of no use to her.

How long would she have to wait for someone to find her?

She chewed the bread, the damp gumminess of it seeming tasteless and solid as she swallowed.

Did John make it to the boat and call for help?

Anxiety did nothing to make the bread go down any easier, but she knew that she needed to eat *something*.

She kept her eyes trained on the horizon and the endlessness of the water. The empty, cruel expanse of blue gave her no answers and no hope. She drank only a few sips from one of the bottles of water, just enough to swallow the bread and stay coherent. Her mounting thirst made her want to finish the bottle, but she still had enough lucidity to realize it might be some length of time before she was found.

She needed a plan.

It was now up to her, alone, to save herself.

John was fatigued far beyond what he would have once defined as complete exhaustion, in a normal world, even under the most stressful conditions. But for the extremes he was now being forced to endure, how could he have even begun to prepare himself?

He reached out, grabbing hold of a frayed piece of cable that was still attached to the shattered mast, the mast that was being dragged along behind the tiny, wounded ship. Sharp pieces of wire repeatedly punctured his skin as he slowly pulled himself toward the flailing Morgan, the very same vessel that had stood so proud and steady beneath his feet less than two days before. The boat was still partially afloat, with enough of her above water to offer temporary refuge and reprieve from the mayhem that surrounded him.

His hands seemed permanently cramped, and the dozens of tiny cuts felt like shards of glass embedded into his skin. Yet he continued pulling himself along, hand over hand, until he reached a bent and broken piece of railing that hung low against the battered hull. He managed to loop his arm through the railing and drooped against it like a rag doll for several minutes, trying to catch his breath and regain some measure of strength.

Somehow, John needed to get his leg onto the rail and propel his body up and over the side. While he dangled there, contemplating his next move, he felt something brush against him below the murky surface. It startled him into motionlessness, every single part of his spent body frozen in fear.

Could it be part of the tangled mess of lines and sailcloth that had been above the waterline?

Or could it be . . . ?

There—he felt it again!

It was quicker and more deliberate this time, nudging him not so gently and forcing him up against the hull.

John's fight-or-flight instinct finally engaged, and he felt no pain, no fatigue—only pure, primal energy. It gave him just enough to lift his body clear of the water and onto the lower deck of the small sailing yacht.

He lay there on his back, immersed in about two inches of water and staring up at the sky, thanking God in a whisper and hoping it could be heard in heaven above the deafening pounding of his heart. He closed his eyes to avoid the stinging saltwater just moments before utter exhaustion knocked him unconscious.

As John floated into oblivion, the Morgan was pulled farther out to sea by the swift current of the outgoing tide, now locked firmly in the grasp of the Gulf Stream.

Each passing moment took him farther out—and farther away from Molly.

. . .

Molly walked back to the dead old palm and pulled away the wet blanket she'd used as shelter from the storm, hoping it might be able to dry out in the morning sun.

Looking up at the sky, she realized she had no idea what time it was—nor would she unless she somehow miraculously learned how to read the position of the sun. Or unless someone rescued her.

Until then, she supposed that time was irrelevant, in the grand scheme of things. What would it matter if it were ten in the morning or ten o'clock at night? Seconds, minutes, hours—they all seemed the same out here, all alone.

Still, she *was* curious. The sun was almost directly over her head now, and she tried to guess . . . *Did that mean it was noon?*

She wished, now, that she were wiser about such things.

She wished she were wiser about *so very many* things.

Like venturing off on the open unfamiliar water on their own.

Molly shook her head in silent self-reprimand. There had been no way of knowing.

Trying to shift her focus to more useful thoughts, she rifled through the small first-aid kit that she'd used to treat John's leg wound and inventoried its contents.

Five medium-sized Band-Aids, one large piece of gauze, a small pair of dull scissors, four aspirin, and the remnants of a tube of medicated ointment.

She placed all the items along with the remaining water bottles and her last slice of bread into the waterproof bag they'd used to bring their things ashore.

How long can I survive here with so little? Two or three days?

Her thoughts wandered back to John. Was he even still alive?

She wondered what Afton might be doing at that very moment, her sweet little girl certainly oblivious that anything might be amiss.

What about her father? If she were gone, who would look after him?

Molly sank to her knees in the sand and wept.

...

Michael Bloom pulled into a service station on the south side of Ocala, his mind completely preoccupied as he swiped his credit card on the gas pump, just as he had done so many times before.

Reaching for the pump handle, a sickened feeling washed over him, and he snatched his hand back as though he'd been burned.

How could he have been so careless and stupid?

He frantically began punching the cancel button on the small keypad. After several attempts, the command went through, but he had no idea how such things worked. Would a canceled transaction still register on his account if he was being tracked? He reached in through the car's passenger-side window and retrieved a vintage Atlanta Braves baseball cap, pulling the bill down low and leaving his sunglasses on as he entered the convenience store to pay the attendant in cash.

Walking through the door, he stopped as his eyes adjusted, his mind registering that he recognized the person standing in line at the front counter, someone he never would have expected to see at such an out-of-the-way place. His flight instinct propelled him back out the door, as quietly as had come in, making his way to the car, hoping he had remained unnoticed. Within seconds, he was back behind the wheel, with the engine running. As he pulled away from the pump, he heard a loud pop and then a banging sound near the rear of the car.

What the–?

He looked in the right sideview mirror to see the gas nozzle still firmly in place where he'd left it and a now-detached length of black hose dragging uselessly on the ground alongside his car. Michael cursed under his breath for making such a stupid mistake, now racking his brain for a call to action.

His prevailing thought being the possibility of a camera recording his visit—not to mention the idea of his credit card being processed and leaving a paper trail. There was *no* way, at this point, he could risk returning to the store and being seen. He pulled over a few blocks down the street and disengaged the nozzle, tossing it into an alleyway before he ducked back into the car and floored the accelerator, his pulse racing as he merged onto the Florida Turnpike.

Traveling south, Michael's mind was reeling.

Should he continue as planned?

Should he turn the car around and hurry back to Atlanta before anyone even realized he'd left?

Should he try to contact Joan?

No, he had already made too many mistakes for one day.

You're smarter than this, Mike! he thought, disgusted at himself. *No more slip-ups–use your head!*

He reached over to the passenger seat for his phone and scrolled through his recent call log, selecting a number and putting his call through.

Erica wandered through the boutiques and shops along Ocean Drive, feeling at home in this ultra-chic section of Miami known simply as South Beach. A block down the sidewalk, she entered the lobby of the Clevelander Hotel, where she'd booked a room a few hours earlier, approaching the elevator just as her phone rang.

The number displayed on the screen was one she didn't recognize, yet she had no choice but to answer.

"Hello?" she said quietly, relief flooding over her as she recognized the voice of the man who answered.

"Well, hello, beautiful. I hope all is well in sunny Miami. I should be arriving in town sometime around midnight and will meet you at your motel."

She gave a throaty, sarcastic laugh in reply. "Yeah—about that filthy little fleabag motel that you chose for me . . . you won't find me there. Not in *this* lifetime, anyway. I now have lovely accommodations at the Clevelander in South Beach. You can meet me here, instead."

She heard the sound of his frustration in the form of his fist pounding the steering wheel.

"Erica, that is *not* what we discussed! These things were all planned out for a *reason!*"

Erica narrowed her eyes in annoyance and huffed. "Don't take an attitude with me! I don't know what the big deal is, anyway! It's *just* a hotel! Really, you'd be wise to rethink your tone if you want to get your hands on what's tucked away in my room!"

There was a pause on the other end.

"Erica," the voice said, now sounding more patient, even if only slightly. "I need for you to listen to me very carefully. Go to your hotel right now and gather your things—*especially* what's mine. Leave as quietly as you can without checking out or being noticed. *If* that's even possible for you! Get into the next taxi you see and tell the driver to head south toward Homestead, and then call me back at this number. Once you're en route, I will give you an address where we can meet. *Do not* deviate from what I have just told you—are we perfectly clear on that?"

She clenched her jaw and gritted her teeth. "Crystal!" she hissed. She broke the connection before he could respond.

. . .

John awoke with a gasp and spat out a mouthful of saltwater onto the deck. By now, the level of water inside the boat had risen at least another six inches, creeping into John's airway and then into his lungs. He rolled over and rose onto his knees, heaving as he desperately struggled to take in air at the same time as he tried to expel the water. He finally caught his breath and leaned back against the helm in disbelief at how close he had just come to drowning—and in only a few inches of water, at that. John stared blankly at the horizon stretching out before him with no land in view, the hopelessness draining the remainder of strength from his waterlogged body. All the while, his mind drifted in and out of subconscious thought.

The sea cannot be tamed nor contained. At best, it can only be reckoned with . . . it owes no explanation for what it gives or for what it takes. It just is.

CHAPTER TWENTY-FOUR

MOLLY SAT ALONE AT THE EDGE OF THE SURF, HER EYES FIXED ON THE
TINY ISLAND ACROSS THE CHANNEL TO THE SOUTH. It was the last place
she had seen her husband, as he swam out of sight toward the flailing
sailboat. She wished there were some way she could make the swim
herself. Instead, she was left to wonder if John might be in danger and
unable to signal for help.

She still had no way of knowing if he had made it safely across.
Those waves had been so rough during the storm and the current so
swift . . .

*Even an accomplished swimmer would have stood little chance of making
it to the opposite shore.*

She shook her head in frantic defiance of her own thoughts.

"No!" she yelled out into the emptiness.

She knew her husband, and she knew what he was capable of
when he set his mind to something.

"He *absolutely* made it! He promised me that he would and that
everything was going to be okay. He said he would never leave me,
and I'm holding him to it!" she said in determination. "John Callaway
does not give up."

Her words were swept away with the breeze, out onto the water
that pushed and pulled at the sand underneath her.

He'll be back soon. Any time now, he'll pick me up and take us home.

Molly forced a small smile and held her stare as the sun slowly
began to sink back down into the distant waves. The gentle warmth

of an incoming tide washed over her legs, and she remained still and quiet in her chosen spot. A single tear made its way down her cheek and onto her chin before falling off into the water. The sea slipped beneath her, sweeping pieces of her away with it as it went back out, pieces of her energy, pieces of her faith.

Pieces of her hope that John would come back to her.

Then, as if on some sort of cosmic timer, the last light of day faded to black, and Molly was once again wrapped in darkness.

Another day had gone.

...

John now sat upright with his back braced against the Morgan's portside gunwale. The boat was beginning to list onto her left side, and he could tell from her position that seawater had most likely filled the cabin—if not yet completely, he knew it soon would. With night closing in, he realized his chances of being visible to rescuers would be next to nothing.

Keeping her afloat until morning became his most immediate concern as he searched for a way to purge water from the doomed vessel. He filled his lungs with air and held his breath as he slid down into the darkness of the flooded cabin, hoping the venture would help him assess the extent of the damage *and* to retrieve a five-gallon bucket filled with rice. The bucket's weight had initially been his reason for leaving it behind when he had first made his choice to abandon ship the day before, but now he was grateful for its presence.

Once he'd made it back to the deck, John removed the lid, his aching fingers struggling to complete his task. When he'd opened the bucket, he emptied out the rice and used the container to bail water from inside the cabin. It was a slow and laborious process, but certainly a necessary one. After about twenty minutes, John was relieved to see he'd cleared out at least three inches' worth of water, and he felt a sudden surge of energy to keep bailing.

Bucket after bucket of water, he poured over the Morgan's side, repeating the grueling process time and again, all the while ignoring the spasms in his tortured muscles.

If I can somehow find the leak, maybe I can also figure out a way to stop it. The thought gave him a moment's pause before he shook it away to refocus. *First things first, John. Stop figuring and just keep moving!*

John's body was fully engaged in his work, but his mind was singularly focused on Molly and what she must be going through, stuck back on the island all alone. He was sure she was hungry and afraid. Even worse for her, he knew, would be the worry she was feeling over what might have happened to him. He wanted so much to believe that maybe, somehow, she had been rescued and taken somewhere safe and dry—*and* that a search party was already hard at work looking to rescue him, as well.

He had to believe it would only be a matter of time before he would be reunited with the only woman he'd ever loved, the only woman he would love forever.

More than anything, he wanted to hold Molly close and never let her go.

Please, God, let me have that chance.

He tried to imagine what his sweet little Afton would be doing at that very moment—probably getting ready to be tucked into bed and hoping for good dreams. She would, of course, be oblivious to the danger that her parents were in, so very many miles away from her.

Images of his wife and little girl played like a slideshow in his mind, comforting and distracting him at the same time, as he continually repeated the never-ending cycle of refilling and emptying the bucket that had now become a permanent fixture in his hands.

After two more hours, John could feel the Morgan now resting vertically—just as she should. He had managed to lower the water level in the cabin to just above his ankles, which righted the ship—finally. Miraculously.

A great accomplishment for anyone, he thought, *no matter what their condition or level of physical prowess!*

Still, he could see air bubbles rising to the surface in more than one area of the cabin floor, a subtle but cruel reminder that his work was far from done. A gallon jug of fresh water sloshed about under the galley table near his feet, and he reached down to pick it up, opening it carefully and lifting it to his lips for several large gulps before tightly replacing the cap. Fortunately, he'd overlooked it when he'd hurriedly loaded the life raft with supplies two days ago. And now, that single plastic jug represented life to him in that moment, and so it had become his most precious possession.

John rummaged through the dark cabin, hoping to salvage anything that could possibly help him find his way out of this mess, his eyes lighting on a small, waterproof LED flashlight tucked away in the back of a galley drawer. He flicked it on, finally able to see the debris that now littered the entire interior of the once beautiful Morgan. He bounced the beam around, shining the sliver of light in every open space he could find, in hopes of discovering the hull breach.

From the profusion of air bubbles, John could only assume the leak was coming from *underneath* and not from the sides. His best guess was that the rupture had probably occurred where the boat's keel was attached to the bottom center of the hull. If that turned out to be true, there would be no way to repair the damage while the boat remained in the water.

John's only choice, as this point, was to continue bailing water so he could buy as much time as he could and hope for rescue before the boat was claimed by the sea—for good.

Guilt weighted his arms as he worked, and self-blame settled heavily upon his heart.

If only I'd thought to secure her better in the channel or had sailed somewhere else, instead.

If only . . .

Molly crawled her way back underneath her faithful palm, re-claiming it as her place of refuge. A light rain began to fall, and once again she used the blanket as a makeshift covering from the elements, though it seemed to do little in the way of actually keeping her dry. After having spent two full days with only sparse shade, her skin was so badly burned from the sun that it had taken on a purple hue, and heat radiated from her body like an oven.

Although she felt chilled, the cool rain eased some of her pain and made it slightly more tolerable. Small comfort though it was, it was at least something to hold on to.

...

Weak and hungry, John worked on through the night, a night that was beginning to feel like it would have no end.

In an effort to assess how quickly—or how *slowly*—the boat was actually sinking, he used his dive knife to make several hash marks on the table leg at roughly one-inch increments. He timed the rising water with his watch, measuring how long it took the water to rise to meet each tick mark.

His crude form of measurement was far from exact, due to the rocking motion of the vessel, but he guessed the boat was going down at a rate of about four inches per hour—and that was in *calm* seas. His body desperately needed a reprieve, and he tried to use the numbers he had estimated to gauge just how long he could break for rest with-out completely losing her to the deep.

It was too risky.

He was too tired, he knew, and stopping might put him in danger of falling asleep without waking up in time to save her. Instead, he continued on, occasionally slapping himself in the face to stay alert. And though he was rapidly dehydrating from constant exertion, losing fluids through his sweat, John tried to conserve the only drinking water left to him in his one remaining jug.

His muscles were tight and cramped, and he began to wonder which would be worse—dying from pure exhaustion or drowning.

He shuddered at the thought of both.

"*No!*" he grunted.

If he was going down, he was going down *fighting*.

He kept his pace steady, knowing that eventually morning *would* come, and he had to believe that help would soon follow.

CHAPTER TWENTY-FIVE

ERICA EXITED THE CLEVELANDER HOTEL IN SOUTH BEACH AT ELEVEN
THAT NIGHT. She found a waiting taxi and told the driver to head
south toward Homestead.

As she watched the lights speed past the windows of the moving
cab, her lips were drawn into a thin line of grim dissatisfaction. She
was far from pleased with the new arrangements that had been forced
upon her, but this was only a temporary setback. Soon enough, she
would be making her own decisions about when and where she came
and went.

She had waited too long, worked too hard, and given up far too
much to be without her personal freedom, as well.

With any luck, that last phone call would, indeed, be the end of
her entanglements with Joan Taylor. She was more than ready for
two things: to be rid of Joan and to live the life she had been dreaming
about for as long as she could remember.

Once she was safely out of Miami Beach, Erica called the number
back, just as she had been instructed.

There was no answer.

While she considered her next move, a text came through with an
address just outside the city of Homestead, along with an appointed
arrival time. She gave the information to the driver, and he entered
the address into a dash-mounted GPS. Their estimated time was forty-five minutes, depending on traffic.

She looked at the clock on the dash.

Forty-five minutes meant a premature arrival, and she was tired of being scolded for not following instructions to the letter. Although it was dark, she asked the driver if there was a more scenic route he could take, hoping to kill some time. He obliged by exiting the bypass and working his way through the crowded streets of Little Havana, then heading on down through the towns of Coral Gables and Leisure City. There were certainly parts of the area that were beautiful; and, while Erica might enjoy coming back one day under *different* circumstances, she was hardly being robbed of much if she never returned.

Soon enough, she would be able to travel and live almost anywhere in the world.

It was a thought that made her smile in the darkness of the cab, and she closed her eyes and tilted her head back as thoughts of the drastic changes that her life had taken lately—and the even more drastic ones that lay ahead—flooded her mind.

Sure, she might miss a few friends and acquaintances from her old life in Atlanta. But, with no real family left to speak of, she felt like she wasn't having to sacrifice all that much. In a way, they were simply casualties of war. She had searched desperately for a way to escape the abusive relationship that still haunted her, and she'd needed a new start.

If that meant she had to reinvent herself to find it, then so be it.

A nervous excitement had begun to creep through her when the driver told her that they were getting close to their destination.

...

Just north of Miami in Boca Raton, Michael Bloom once again stopped to fill his car with gas, picking up a roadmap of South Florida and the Florida Keys, while he paid—*in cash*—for his fuel. He wasn't familiar with the area he was driving through, and the idea of using the car's navigation system left him feeling paranoid about the possibility of being tracked.

Now, more than ever, he wished he knew if anyone was even aware that he had left Atlanta. He figured someone was bound to realize it soon enough—but, by then, it would be too late for him to even think of going back. He saw road signs ahead for Miami Beach and Homestead and knew he was getting close.

He merged onto Highway 1, continuing southward with renewed focus and determination.

Soon.

...

Back in Atlanta, Joan used the janitor's code to enter the offices of Callaway Development. It was after hours, and the firm was still officially off limits—for now. She certainly didn't want to have to answer questions about her visit from her favorite agents—or from anyone *else*, for that matter. She had mistakenly underestimated the sense of urgency and quick response from the federal agencies involved in the investigation and hadn't been fully prepared the day they'd arrived.

Joan didn't like admitting to *anyone* that she had been caught off guard, even for a moment.

Not even to herself.

There were still a couple of things left undone, some "loose ends" that demanded her immediate attention, and she needed access to the offices in order to tie them up, effectively tidying things away.

First things first.

She went to her desk, immediately noticing the missing computer and empty filing cabinets. No matter—that was not her purpose in being there. She opened her desk's top drawer and took out a small screwdriver, then slid a chair up against the opposite wall and stood on it to reach an air vent cover. After carefully removing the four screws that held the cover in place, she set it aside and reached up into the ductwork. She felt around the dark space until her hand touched a leather pouch.

She'd hit pay dirt.

She withdrew the pouch, re-secured the vent cover, and moved the chair back to its original position, taking great pains to leave no trace of a disturbance. She couldn't risk even the slightest detection by anyone curious enough to look.

Sitting at her desk, Joan opened the pouch and removed several color-coded USB thumb drives.

Green means "Go!"

Closing her fingers tightly around the green drive, she smiled and dropped it into her purse.

Joan then entered John's office and walked around his desk, running her hands over its rich, smooth surface and feeling the elegance of the wood. She had stood in this very same spot and done this very same thing countless times in the past, even when it had belonged to John Sr., many years before. She took a moment to sit in John's chair and reflect on the fact that—in her mind, at least—inheriting it would have been her due, after all she had done here.

So many times she had imagined what it would feel like to finally own it.

"*Someday,*" she whispered as she rose from the chair.

Joan had intimate knowledge of that desk and its history, and she considered it an old, dear friend.

And, like an old friend, she knew its secrets.

All its secrets.

Placing her hand against a decorative raised panel on its right side, she simultaneously pressed the panel and ever so slightly slid her hand. The panel sprung open, revealing a small hidden compartment. Removing the contents, Joan inspected them and then replaced them, along with the leather pouch she had just retrieved from the air duct. Over the years, she'd learned that a similar "hidden compartment" feature was built into many presidential desks, guessing that such compartments were more of a novelty or a curiosity than an actual security measure.

It had been accidental, really, her discovery of this little hideaway.

Joan had found it one day while she'd been polishing the desk, not long after she'd first come to work for the firm. But she'd kept its secret to herself for all these years, never revealing what she had found to *anyone*.

So far as she knew, she was the only person still alive who even knew of its existence.

...

Erica's taxi pulled up exactly at the appointed time.

She took a look around and then questioned the driver. "Are you *sure* this is the correct address?"

"It's the address that you gave me, ma'am."

She reopened the text message and verified it again.

"There *must* be some mistake," she said, shaking her head in frustration. That could be the only explanation, surely.

They were parked in front of an old, abandoned shopping mall that was partially destroyed. The driver explained that the sad-looking structure had been severely damaged during Hurricane Andrew in '92, and the owners had been in litigation with the insurance companies for years. All the while, it had been left largely untouched, though it had become a favorite hangout for misguided youth as well as the perfect hideout for homeless Cuban refugees.

Erica studied the crumbled walls and exposed wiring. *No way* was she going to allow herself to be dropped off and left alone in a place like this!

She told the driver to take her back to Miami immediately, handing him a hundred-dollar bill as he began to drive away.

Her phone chimed, alerting her to another text message.

"Tell the driver to let you out at the end of the last building. Once he has left the parking lot, I will pick you up."

Her fingers rapidly tapped out a response. "Are you here? Are you watching me now?"

Another chime.

"Do as you're told."

The words made her blood run cold.

Clutching the now-silent phone in her hand, she gave the driver a new set of instructions.

He turned to look at her uncertainly. "Are you sure?"

"Yes," she said with more determination than she felt.

When the taxi pulled to a stop, Erica looked nervously around as she opened the door and placed her foot carefully on the ground. She took a deep breath and stepped completely out of the car, bags tightly in hand as she stood there alone in the shadow of the building, waiting to be picked up.

She hoped that she wouldn't have to wait long.

She had a bad feeling about this.

...

Joan left the building through a side door that opened onto the street. It had been intentional—she knew that by not parking her car in the building's garage she would avoid using her key card, ensuring there was not a record of her whereabouts. It was better this way, leaving no evidence of her comings and goings. She refused to be taken by surprise or caught off guard by anyone, ever again.

Joan Taylor was too wise for such displays of incompetency.

Back at her BMW, she opened the trunk and lifted the cargo mat to reveal a laptop she'd hidden away in the spare tire well, along with two more prepaid cell phones and a small metal lockbox. After unlocking the box, she reached into her purse to remove the thumb drive she'd retrieved from the office and stowed it safely inside—secured now, in its place, with her passport and ten thousand dollars in cash. After giving the items a long look, she closed the lid and relocked it, patting the hard, cold metal surface of the box as she slid it back into the wheel well.

Once she'd pulled away and was on the road again, Joan dialed a number into the prepaid phone she'd taken from the trunk.

It rang only once.

"Yes?" a male voice on the other end said.

"Is it done?" she asked.

There was a hesitation. "I'm pulling up now. Are you sure there's no other way?"

"Are you *kidding* me?" she fumed in reply. "Of course there's *no* other way! Now, do what you've been *paid* to do and don't make me regret coming to you for this."

There was another pause before an answer came. "Yes, Joan."

"You *idiot!*" she shrieked. "Never, *ever* use my name again! Call me back as soon as you're finished." She gave him the number of the last spare prepaid phone resting in the trunk. Furious at the level of stupidity she was having to deal with, she pulled to a stop behind the first fast-food restaurant she saw. She quickly wiped the phone clean of her fingerprints and threw it into a nearly empty Dumpster, watching in satisfaction as it smashed into pieces against the side.

"I knew you were a weak and stupid man the first time I met you!" she hissed under her breath. "And you certainly haven't done anything to prove otherwise!"

CHAPTER TWENTY-SIX

A DULL SILVER SUV WITH BALDING TIRES AND DARKLY TINTED WINDOWS
PULLED UP TO THE CURB, JUST IN FRONT OF WHERE ERICA STOOD WAIT-
ING. She watched cautiously, remaining motionless in the shadows
until the window was lowered halfway down.

"Well, come on," a familiar voice said at last, flooding her with a
sense of relief. "Get in—what are you waiting for?"

Erica forced a smile as she stepped forward and out of the shadows. "I wasn't sure it was you. Can't blame a lady for being careful."

He laughed and pretended to look around with exaggerated suspicion. "Of course it's *me*. Who else would it be?"

Erica opened the rear passenger door and began to put her luggage on the seat.

"Which one of those is mine?" he asked, halting her movements.
"I want it up front with me."

"*Fine*," she huffed. "Whatever."

As Erica reached out for the handle on the Louis Vuitton case, he
quickly spun in his seat and grabbed her by the wrist, squeezing hard
for effect. "Listen carefully because I'm only gonna tell you this *once*.
Don't ever even *think* about doing me wrong, do you understand?"

Erica struggled to loosen his grip. "Stop it, you jerk! You're hurting me!"

She had a slight advantage over her aggressor because of his awkward position, pinned behind the steering wheel and strapped into

the driver's seat, so she was able to wrench herself free from his grasp. Glaring at him more out of anger than fear, she hissed again.

"Don't *ever* touch me again! Do *you* understand?"

He grinned, a very obvious and very poor attempt at covering clearly intended malice with playfulness.

Erica was not amused.

She masked her annoyance—and her slight fear—by taking stock of her new surroundings. The worn-out vehicle reeked of sweat and stale cigarettes, and she could also detect the faint smell of alcohol. It was painfully apparent that this was his only means of transportation. Why else would he have driven it all the way down here from Atlanta?

She hadn't liked Greg Kline from the moment Joan had introduced the two of them. She'd known too many men like him before and always made it a point to steer clear. Now, her dislike was turning to contempt at the way he was treating her, like she was somehow inconsequential in of all this.

Greg Kline was hardly one to be trusted, and she watched his every movement closely as he rolled away from the decrepit mall and back onto the main highway.

"Why are we going this way?" Erica demanded as he headed south toward the Keys. "Where are you taking me? I want to go back to Miami right now!"

He put his hand on the headrest, next to her face, so close that she could smell him. Not liking any part of him being anywhere near her, she leaned away. He grinned at her reaction.

"*Relax*, gorgeous. I'll take you where you need to go. I just thought we could head down toward Key Largo, maybe catch a glimpse of the ocean and then sort this whole thing out. Who knows, you might even end up liking it. And we can watch the sunrise together." His dry laughter was sickeningly fake.

Erica slowly turned her head to look over at him. He puckered his lips into a kissing face, which only sickened her further.

"What is there to sort out, Greg? You take me back to Miami. You take your money. We never see each other again. End of story."

"Oh, it's the end of *your* story, all right," he muttered.

"Better yet, Greg—why don't you just drop me at the next town we come to, and I'll find my *own* way back."

He stared at her but remained silent, his eyes never returning to the road as he floored the accelerator, gaining speed.

"You *are* an idiot!" she spat, her eyes growing wide. "Do you *really* want to get pulled over for speeding? You've obviously been drinking—and tell me, just how *do* you plan on explaining the fact that you have $2 million *in cash*?"

...

Michael Bloom pulled into the drive-thru lane of a popular chain restaurant on the south side of Miami, the fact that he hadn't eaten since sometime around noon now too much to ignore. Once he'd been handed the grease-stained paper bag filled with his order, he parked in a dark space near the corner of the parking lot and practically inhaled his burger and fries. He studied the map he'd bought earlier in the day, his fingers leaving small spots of oil from his dinner. From what he could tell, he was approximately 150 miles away from Key West.

At this time of night, traffic was on his side, and his guess was that he could make it there in three or four hours. He'd been running flat out on heightened nerves and excitement up to now, and until this very moment, he really hadn't realized how tired he actually was. He closed his eyes to ease the sting of fatigue and fell almost instantly asleep.

Greg Kline continued driving recklessly and at high speed, despite multiple warning signs that screamed "Work Zone" and "Danger," posted all along the route. The road narrowed to only two lanes, flanked on both sides by bright orange cones. Heavy construction equipment sat idly hulking all along the shoulder, and large piles of gravel had been dumped at regular intervals. But nothing seemed to faze the crazed man whose foot controlled the fate of the car. He was a maniac with no regard for anything or anyone—including himself.

"I take it back, Greg," Erica shouted at him, "you're not an idiot— you're just *crazy*! Stop and let me out right now!"

His foot pumped the accelerator again and then immediately slammed on the brakes, lunging them both forward and up against the dash. Erica looked over at him, simultaneously stunned and sickened at the over-exaggerated grin that seemed permanently affixed to his face.

"See what happens when you don't shut up, doll? Now—*ssshhh!*" He slowly put his index finger to his lips.

Erica watched his reckless, radical behavior in horrified shock. A glint of something caught her eye on the driver's side floorboard, and she focused on what appeared to be the nose of a revolver resting beneath the brake pedal. The gun had most likely been dislodged from underneath the driver's seat during the sudden jolt. Greg's eyes followed her gaze, and he quickly reached down with his left hand to pick it up. With his attention momentarily distracted, Erica took her chance and grabbed the steering wheel with both hands, giving it a hard jerk.

The top-heavy SUV made a sharp turn to the right and began skidding sideways. Greg gave up fumbling for the gun, in an attempt to regain control of the vehicle, but Erica held tightly to the wheel as they continued to slide, narrowly missing one of the large tractors parked alongside the road. Greg swung wildly with his right fist and connected squarely with Erica's cheekbone and left temple.

The flash of bright white that suddenly clouded her vision blocked out everything.

And then the world went dark.

. . .

A tapping sound on the window woke Michael with a start. He looked up groggily into a harsh beam of light shining into his face and lifted his hand to shield his eyes, trying to see.

"You can't sleep here," a commanding male voice said.

"What?"

The voice spoke again. "I *said* you can't sleep here. If you don't move along, I'll have to call the police."

The police?

Michael looked again and could now see that it was the fast-food restaurant's manager standing next to his car.

"No problem," he said, feeling nearly sick with relief. "I think I must have dozed off after I ate."

"Well, sir, you've been out here for a couple of hours now, and it looks like you're a long way from home," the man said, his voice gentler now, but still firm. "I hope you get wherever you're headed soon, but you need to get going, okay?"

"No problem. Thanks for the wake-up call, so to speak," Michael said with an embarrassed smile. Now fully awake, he waved the man off and left the parking lot to continue his journey toward Key West.

Falling asleep like that had been a *huge* mistake.

Michael banged the steering wheel with the palm of his hand in frustration as a multitude of thoughts screamed through his mind.

Now that was beyond stupid, Mike! Really dumb! What if that guy had called the police? How would that look to the FBI when they came asking questions, which they would. You know very well they would. And if you'd gotten caught, what would that mean for ever having a shot at finding John and getting the truth about what's really going on at the firm?

"Not smart. Not smart at all," he said aloud as his palm pounded the steering wheel again.

. . .

Erica's eyes fluttered open. She had been momentarily knocked unconscious by the blow from Greg's fist. Still feeling hazy, she looked around and tried to reorient herself. The driver's seat was empty, but the engine was idling, and the door stood open. Her ears picked up the sound of movement at the rear of the vehicle.

Moving carefully to avoid being noticed, she tilted the rearview mirror slightly so that she could see what was going on at the back. She watched breathlessly as Greg rummaged through an assortment of tools and what looked to be building supplies, and she could see that he was holding a length of rope in his mouth and a roll of duct tape in one hand, while the other hand roamed in search of God only knew what else. Not waiting to find out his intentions, Erica eased her left leg over to the driver's side, reached over with her hand to maneuver the gearshift into reverse, and floored the accelerator with her left foot.

As the motor revved, Greg Kline looked up in shock at the rear of the SUV that was now headed straight for him.

It was the last thing he would ever see.

. . .

Erica heard a sickening thud when the rear of the SUV impacted Greg's body, and she felt a hard bounce as the spinning rear tires climbed up and over the obstacle that now seemed almost negligible. Increasing her speed, she continued racing backward across the gravel construction site. Because of her position in the passenger's seat, she was unable to reach the brake pedal in time to stop the large vehicle's momentum, finally coming to a sudden halt when the rear end smashed directly into a bright yellow piece of heavy equipment. Both front airbags deployed, and the engine sputtered before it finally gave out.

Erica sat dazed in utter disbelief. It was almost too much to process. And really, she didn't have time for it.

She had to get out of there—*now*.

After a moment, she composed herself and stumbled out of the car, grabbing hold of the only bag she could reach, the Louis Vuitton. A cloud of dust settled over the gritty makeshift parking lot and onto Greg's mangled body, which now lay motionless in the gravel. Erica was grateful that traffic was minimal at this hour; and, as far as she knew, no one had witnessed what had just happened.

She made her way to the edge of the highway and began walking north.

She'd only gone about a hundred yards along the roadway before a large delivery truck slowed to a stop just ahead of her. She was leery of accepting a ride from a stranger, and she certainly couldn't say a word about the body she'd left lying in the gravel behind her; but, more than anything else, she knew she needed to put distance between herself and what was now, undeniably, a crime scene.

When Erica reached the truck, a gentle voice with a soft country accent spoke up.

"Ma'am, are you okay? Can I take you somewhere or call somebody for you? You really shouldn't be out here walking alone, not at this hour, anyway."

He seems nice enough, she thought, assessing the man sitting in the driver's seat of the truck. Who knew how far she would have to walk to find a bus station or even a taxi at this hour? Deciding to take him up on his offer, she gave him a slight nod and reached up to open the massive door on the side of the truck. The man grabbed her hand to help her climb up and into the cab next to him.

"Where are you headed, ma'am?" he asked kindly.

Though she was still a bit frazzled, Erica's instinctive charm kicked in, and she gave him her winking smile. "Wherever you're going is just fine with me."

The driver smiled back, and she could see him blush.

. . .

They both remained silent for the next half hour as they continued traveling north on Highway 1. The left side of Erica's face had swollen up nicely, thanks to the force of Greg Kline's fist, and she wondered what her knight in shining armor might be thinking about her appearance.

He finally spoke, dispelling some of the awkwardness. "My name is Tully, ma'am."

"It's lovely to meet you, Tully. I'm Erica."

He nodded and just smiled for a moment. As he looked more closely at her, his smile was replaced by a small frown of concern.

"None of my business, ma'am, but would you like me to take you to a doctor or something?"

"No!" she snapped.

"I'm sorry, ma'am. I just thought . . ." he stammered.

Erica softened. "No, Tully—*I'm* sorry. I'm not angry with you for asking. It's just that, well . . . I guess I've gotten used to this. You'd think I'd have learned by now."

"I'm *real* sorry to hear that, ma'am," Tully said, his face serious. "You deserve better. You're a real good person. I can just tell."

She smiled. "Thank you, Tully. That's really nice to hear," Erica said quietly. "I'm glad to know there's at least *one* good guy left in the world." Watching the grin return to his face, she continued to lay it on. "And to *think* he convinced me to come down here as sort of a second honeymoon!" She shook her head. "He promised me things were going to be *different* this time . . ." She let the words trail off and turned to look out the window, satisfaction setting in, as the scenery sped by.

Things had turned out differently, indeed!

. . .

Tully drove into downtown Miami and let Erica out at an all-night diner, refusing to take the $200 she offered him for his kindness. Still insisting, she laid the bills on the seat and slammed the door shut before he could protest any further, and walked toward the restaurant. As soon as Tully's truck had turned the corner onto the next block, she went in search of a cab, flagging down one that she saw idling in front of another restaurant nearby.

She opened the door and slid into the backseat, barely glancing at the driver as she gave him her destination.

"Clevelander Hotel, South Beach."

CHAPTER TWENTY-SEVEN

As Buddy and Brenda Sullivan sat in their kitchen having their morning coffee, Buddy's mind churned heavily with thoughts about his failed attempts over the past two days to reach the Callaways by radio.

He couldn't shake the feeling that something wasn't quite right. He highly doubted the possibility that the Morgan might have malfunctioned, considering its newly installed electronics. But anything was possible, he supposed, especially when two amateur sailors were at the helm.

Even if that were the case, though, surely John would have had the sense to return to port once he realized there was an issue. At the very least, he would have tried to contact Buddy by phone.

No, Buddy knew in his gut that something was wrong—terribly, terribly wrong.

He was also not naive to the fact that, in most cases, the open sea was rarely forgiving.

As Buddy sipped the last dregs of his coffee, he heard the thud of the newspaper as it landed firmly on the wooden floorboards of the front porch. The rusty hinges on the old screen door made a familiar squeak when he walked out to retrieve the paper—a sound that, while Brenda constantly asked that he oil it, was the sound of home for him, a sound that he loved hearing.

The morning light was beginning to bathe the town in soft pink, and, as so often was his habit, Buddy sat down in one of the porch's large rockers to watch as night gave way to day. With the sky's colors growing more intense, he was reminded of an old sailors' rhyme he'd learned not long after moving to the Keys, nearly a decade earlier.

"Red sky at night, sailors' delight. Red sky in morning, sailors' warning," he whispered into the still air.

Buddy opened the paper and quickly scanned its small print for anything that might ease his mind about the missing couple and his sailboat, but he saw nothing. He thumbed to the pages containing details about the weather forecast and read through its predictions— mostly sunny for much of the day, giving way to clouds and heavy rain late in the evening and throughout the night.

Not at all what he wanted to hear.

Buddy could no longer just sit and speculate about the Callaways' whereabouts—he needed to make an all-out effort to locate them. He walked back inside, tossed the paper on the kitchen table for his wife to read later, showered quickly, and then set out toward town in search of anyone who might know anything at all about the missing couple—or his Morgan.

...

Michael sat idle in traffic for the better part of an hour, just north of Key Largo. He'd hoped to be in Key West by daybreak; but, with the way traffic was going, he'd really be lucky to make it there by noon. At this point, he couldn't tell what the holdup was—probably an accident or road construction. Whatever it was, the result was the same, and everything was pretty much at a standstill.

After a few minutes of crawling forward by mere inches, he spotted flashing lights ahead that seemed to be heading in his direction. He squinted his eyes as they came closer.

Ambulance—lights flashing, no siren.

That can't be good, he thought.

Once it had passed by, traffic began creeping its way south again. After about a half mile at what felt like a snail's pace, a flatbed wrecker escorted by a sheriff's cruiser passed him in the oncoming lane. Chained down on the flatbed was a mangled old Chevy SUV.

Michael could only imagine what the other car must look like.

Up ahead, a little further off to the left, were a half-dozen police and sheriff's vehicles parked in a crude semicircle near some heavy equipment that sat silent and still in a graveled clearing alongside the highway. Yellow crime-scene tape sectioned off an area just behind the cars, a fair sign that something very bad, and probably fatal, had just happened.

The sight of it sent a sudden chill up Michael's spine.

Fortunately, the officers seemed to be focused fully on the immediate area and paid little attention as traffic crept along, and he was flooded with relief that cars were not being stopped, for whatever reason.

Once he'd passed the scene, the flow of traffic increased to normal speed, and he was back on his way.

And not a moment too soon, in his estimation.

...

Molly emerged from under the old blanket and dried palm fronds, hoping that the prayers she'd whispered the night before would have been answered and that this hellish nightmare would be over when she awoke.

But the light of morning revealed no change.

Her situation had not improved; it might have even become worse, judging by the negligible amount of clean drinking water left in her bottle. Knowing she desperately needed help, she walked along the beach looking for signs of life—slim as her chances seemed, at this point.

"Please, John. Please come back for me . . . *please* be okay!"

John opened his eyes to sunlight peeping its way slowly over the horizon. He'd been dreaming of Molly and of Afton and, strangely enough, of his father. The dream had seemed so real that it took a couple of seconds for him to realize it was just that—a dream.

It was almost cruel, the realization that he was still so far away from his family.

He attempted to stand, but the searing pain in his right leg made it nearly impossible. A quick inspection of his wound left him with little doubt that it was infected. Pus was gathering in pockets in and around the cut, and he felt feverish and light-headed. He knew that some of the symptoms he was experiencing were most likely being caused by his lack of proper food and water coupled with his overexposure to the elements, but there was no denying the look and feel of the wound itself.

He reached for the old bottle of rum and gulped down a mouthful before pouring the last of it straight onto his wound. There was a sting, but not like before. And although he was grateful for even the slightest reprieve from pain, he knew it was a bad sign.

The dulled pain meant he'd lost most of the feeling in his leg from the severity of the infection.

He needed a doctor—*soon*.

He rummaged desperately through the boat's cabinets and compartments looking for anything at all that might help him, coming up with nothing more than low-dose aspirin in a box that had been stowed in the head.

At least it was something,

Only five small pills rattled around in the bottom of the bottle. John swallowed three, hoping with everything he had that they would break the fever.

Despite John's best efforts to avoid any further contamination, the water level in the cabin had risen to the bottom of his calf, making it virtually impossible to keep his leg clear of the dirty water. He knew he needed to start bailing again, but there was something driving him to keep searching, to keep plowing through every nook and cranny of the boat looking for—he wasn't even sure what. He just knew he needed to continue looking, and if he passed out from the infection that was setting in, the boat would sink sooner rather than later.

He wanted to check everywhere and everything, and then he would begin to bail again.

John pulled at the seat cushions of the settee adjacent to the galley table and found a set of four additional life jackets stowed in the compartment underneath. A piece of dark blue strap and a shiny gold buckle nestled among the preservers caught his eye, and he reached in and pulled out a lady's purse—*Molly's!*

She'd obviously hidden it in a place that would be inconspicuous to anyone who might decide to poke around the boat while they were onshore. He'd always thought her to be a little paranoid about certain things, but in this moment he was grateful for her cautiousness. He dumped its contents onto the galley table and found two prescription pill bottles, one of which was for Ambien.

Apparently, she'd been having trouble sleeping.

Was that because of me?

John shook the thought aside for the time being and reached for the second bottle.

Amoxicillin.

He remembered Molly taking Afton to the doctor about a month before, when she'd complained of an earache. The doctor had prescribed the antibiotic, not knowing that Afton was allergic, and she'd had a reaction to the medication after the first dose. Molly had gotten a different prescription for Afton the next day, and John found himself thanking God for the fact that Molly hadn't thrown out the old medicine. He opened the bottle, counting out nineteen remaining capsules. He went ahead and took two of the pills, then slid the bottle into his pocket, well aware that the severity of the infection now raging within his body might not even be touched by such a low dosage.

But it was hope.

And—*sometimes*—in even the smallest of hopes lies salvation.

...

Buddy Sullivan walked the docks in Key West harbor until nearly noon. By then, he'd asked everyone he saw if they'd seen or heard anything about the Callaways, but no one had anything to say.

As he approached two men offloading diving gear from a center-console fishing boat onto the dock, Buddy overheard one of the men mention Fort Jefferson. The words stopped him in his tracks.

"Have you fellas been diving out near the fort?" he asked, a note of hope hanging in his voice.

"Yes, sir—we were there until just before the storm hit late yesterday afternoon," one of the two men replied. "Five-foot swells were a little much for this boat, so we came back early. We were supposed to head back out today, but Pop said that there's even worse weather coming in tonight, so I guess we'll be rethinking that one."

"Who's Pop?" Buddy asked.

The man spoke again. "He's the old guy that owns this boat. He seems to know what he's talking about, so I doubt he'll take you out, either—if that's what you're after." He pointed a thumb in the direction of another man up further on the dock, talking to a young couple. "He's the one in the blue shirt and white cap. Good luck."

Buddy nodded his thanks and headed toward the old boat captain.

Turned out that Pop was, in fact, only a year older than Buddy. The man's sun-beaten face had obviously weathered him into old age, long before his time. But if there was anything at all you needed to know *in* or *about* Key West, Pop was definitely your man.

Once the young couple had wandered off, Buddy took the opportunity to introduce himself.

"Pop?" he ventured, holding out his hand to the other man, who grasped his outstretched hand in his own and gave a slight nod of acknowledgement. "I'm Buddy Sullivan. Do you have a minute?"

Again, Buddy was given a nod, though this time, it was accompanied by words.

"Sure. Just cancelled my charter, so I have the whole afternoon!"

Buddy laughed, then got down to the meat of the matter.

"I understand you were out near Fort Jefferson yesterday?"

"Yessir, sure was. What can I help you with?"

"Well, I was wondering if you happened to see a thirty-two-foot Morgan sailboat with a man and woman onboard?"

Pop chuckled. "You're gonna have to be a little more specific than that, my friend. I see a lot of sailboats out at the fort. It's a real popular spot with the sailing crowd."

"The mainsail has a large red *S* on it, so it's pretty hard to miss."

Pop removed his hat and scratched his head as he mulled over an answer.

"No, Buddy, I didn't see anything like that. And I'm sure I would have remembered it if I had." He paused, his bushy eyebrows knitting together. "If they were smart, though, they would have headed back east or north to beat the squall."

"I sure hope you're right," Buddy replied, not feeling much confidence in the idea that the pair had indeed been wise enough to redirect their course in time.

"Most times I am, but sometimes I ain't," Pop said with a dry laugh. He replaced his cap and started to walk away. "I hope, for their sake, they're outta there by now," he said as his steps took him further away. "There's a *real* bad one coming in tonight. Came across the Yucatan a couple days ago."

Buddy looked up at the perpetually blue sky that revealed only the slightest wisp of a cloud, before his eyes wandered back to Pop. He'd almost reached his boat by then but must have sensed Buddy's gaze. Without turning to look over his shoulder, Pop lifted his finger and pointed to the sky.

The man spoke truth, and he was sure of that which he spoke.

CHAPTER TWENTY-EIGHT

AFTER MORE THAN TWO DAYS OF ISOLATION, MOLLY'S PANIC BEGAN TO GIVE WAY TO QUIET DESPERATION. She hadn't eaten a thing since those three slices of soggy bread, and she had drunk very little. Her mind was starting to feel numb to her circumstances, and she wondered if she might be experiencing some type of traumatic shock. She had been wandering for hours on end, back and forth along the shoreline, in constant search of any sign of life other than her own.

Without much cloud cover, her skin was at the mercy of the sun, and her feet were becoming tender from the constant abrasion of sand and shells. Earlier that morning, she'd thought that she might have seen a large boat or a ship in the far distance. But it was getting harder to tell, especially with her vision growing fuzzy from the constant glare of the sun reflecting off the water.

As it neared noon, Molly retreated into the cooler, shaded area of the tree line and stretched out atop the picnic blanket to lie on her back, closing her eyes to rest.

Surely someone will find me today, she thought, as sleep shrouded her.

It was the first time she'd allowed herself to admit that maybe her worst fear was being realized and that John might not be coming back for her, that someone else would have to rescue her.

A few minutes passed, and she was awakened by a sudden sound. It was one she didn't recognize, but it seemed to stand out in stark contrast to nature—the only sounds she had heard in days.

Molly sat up and looked out but saw nothing on the water in front of her. She looked up through the sparse canopy of trees above her and spotted a white contrail as it painted the clear blue sky. A commercial jet was passing directly overhead but still miles above her and so very far out of reach. She knew it was useless to think she might possibly be seen from that distance, but it gave her an idea.

What if another aircraft flew over–at a lower altitude?

She moved from her resting place and began to work.

...

Michael crossed over several bridges and was now driving south along Roosevelt Boulevard in Key West. As he drove, he dialed the number on the piece of paper in his pocket, frustrated to receive no answer—*again*.

He pounded the steering wheel.

He pulled in at the first marina he saw and asked the attendant if he knew someone by the name of Buddy Sullivan, a name whose corresponding phone number John had given him to use in case of emergency.

At the time he'd scribbled them down, he'd had no reason to believe he would ever need to use the information, but he was glad now that he'd listened to John.

It wasn't much to go on, but at least it was a start.

The young attendant said the name was familiar, but he wasn't sure where Sullivan kept his boat and had no idea how to reach him. Michael thanked the boy and handed him a twenty-dollar bill with his number written on it, just in case he thought of anything later that might help Michael in his search. The boy thanked him and suggested a few more places for him to look where he knew a lot of sailboats usually docked.

Armed with a few ideas, Michael continued driving down Roosevelt toward Old Town, stopping to check out any promising-looking spots along the way.

...

Buddy Sullivan walked into the Green Parrot Bar on Whitehead, hoping to spot his new "friend" Dennis, the alcoholic seaplane pilot. While he might have appeared to be an incompetent fool, Buddy had still liked him and how eager he had seemed to help. Buddy wanted to check in with Dennis again, to see if he'd possibly seen or heard anything useful since they'd spoken last.

Seeing no sign of him, Buddy asked one of the bartenders where he might be found.

"You might try Captain Tony's down on Greene Street," the muscled barman said, nodding a square jaw in the direction of the door. "If he's not flying, Dennis is usually either here or there."

Buddy thanked the man for the information and set out toward the other bar, near the end of town. When he arrived at Captain Tony's, it was in full swing.

It was, after all, Wednesday afternoon in Key West.

This was one of the very things Buddy had loved about the Keys from his first visit. It was a given that everyone was there to have a good time, and rarely was anyone in a foul mood.

It seemed today was no exception.

Buddy worked his way through the crowd, searching the patrons' faces, but Dennis was not among them. He edged up to the bar and asked if anyone there had seen him. A woman sitting near the end directly across from him spoke up in a deep, seductive Southern drawl.

"You just missed him, darlin'."

Buddy was having a hard time hearing her over the crowd, so he snaked his way around to the opposite side, to get closer. Up close, she was much older than she'd appeared from a distance, and he guessed her to be in her early seventies, at best. The woman's makeup was heavily caked on, exaggerating her features and expressions, accentuating, rather than masking, her age. She wore an excess of costume jewelry and a blonde wig that was at least two decades out of style. Her wide smile revealed bright red lipstick smearing the surface of her stark white dentures.

A second before he'd approached, she'd inhaled a full drag from her long, thin cigarette, and as she spoke, a stream of smoke escaped from her painted lips.

"Ah said you just missed him, baby," her gravelly voice rattled. "He had to go to work. He flies people around the Keys in that air-o-plane of his." She waved her cigarette back and forth above her head, giving a visual to match her words. She took another long drag and clamped a veiny hand around Buddy's forearm. "I'm Sandy Gale, darlin'. What's *your* name?"

Buddy answered, and she smiled again.

"Ah *like* that name . . . *Buddy*. Makes it sound like we're already good friends."

"Well, thank you for that, Sandy," Buddy replied, feeling uncomfortable but hesitant to leave before he got the answers he needed. "Any idea where Dennis keeps his plane?"

Sandy tightened her grip on his arm. "It's Sandy *Gale*, baby. You can't use one without the other!" She let go of Buddy's arm and picked up her drink. "If somebody calls for Sandy, Ah don't even hear it."

He apologized for the unintentional blunder.

"It's okay, shugah—you didn't know." She patted his shoulder and went on speaking. "He parks that plane of his out on the north end of the island, somewhere off Roosevelt. I don't know the exact place, but as far as I know it's the only one out there. Why don't you just take a seat and have a drink with me 'til he gets back?" She patted the empty stool beside her.

No longer uncomfortable, Buddy found himself amused by her outspoken, flirtatious personality, so he was gracious when he spoke.

"Thank you, Sandy *Gale*. Maybe some other time. Right now, I really need to try and catch Dennis before he leaves."

She took the last drag on her cigarette and crushed it out into the ashtray, the ashes still smoking, as the other hand removed a fresh one from the pack in front of her on the bar. "Okay, baby—better hurry along, then." She lifted her glass and toasted the air. "And don't you worry none, dahlin'—he never has more than a beer or two before he goes to work."

. . .

Buddy drove north on Roosevelt Boulevard, looking left at every possible boat dock and marina for any sign of Dennis or his float-plane. He glanced up at the sky around him occasionally, just in case the sloshed pilot had already made it airborne.

He highly doubted that Dennis had had time to take off in the short time that had passed since he'd left the bar . . .

But then again, it *was* Dennis—*hardly* a pilot who seemed to do things by the book!

. . .

Michael continued working his way south along Roosevelt, looking at every sailboat he saw docked there. He saw a long dock with several boats and what appeared to be an airplane parked out at the very end, so he pulled into the graveled parking lot, just as a man was securing a motor scooter to a steel pole with a chain and padlock. Michael walked toward the man and noticed that he seemed to be in a hurry, as though he was trying to make it onto the dock without being seen. Michael quietly approached and spoke up from behind him, obviously catching the other man off guard.

"Excuse me, but can I ask you a question?"

Dennis stopped suddenly and slowly turned around, his voice uneasy as he replied. "Sure, I suppose."

Michael detected a faint smell of alcohol on the man's breath. "Do you know a man who keeps a sailboat around here somewhere—named Buddy Sullivan?"

Dennis's posture relaxed, and his clouded expression cleared in relief.

"You're not from the FAA?"

Michael's confused expression was enough to answer Dennis's question, and he smiled.

"Yeah, the name sounds familiar." Dennis scratched at a scruffy jawline as he waded through his foggy memory. "Yeah, yeah," he nodded. "I *do* know him. Met him yesterday at the Green Parrot. He was asking if I'd seen his sailboat, all worried about the people who took it out. Nice enough fella, though. He a friend of yours?"

Michael felt his pulse quicken. "How do you mean—*worried?*"

"I don't know," Dennis said, shaking his head and shrugging. "Like, he hadn't heard from them in a few days, and he seemed concerned. You know, we've had a couple real bad squalls roll through the past week or so."

Michael's anxiety rose with every word that left the man's lips. "Do you know how I can find him? I have his number, but he's not answering."

Dennis shook his head. "Not real sure. You might try some of the marinas closer to downtown. But then again, some people moor their sailboats just offshore because of the shallow water inland, so he might not be at a docking marina at all." He paused thoughtfully and scratched his jaw. "I guess you could check with the harbormaster in town. He might know where to find Buddy."

Michael shook Dennis's hand gratefully, finally feeling a glimmer of hope that he might be getting somewhere.

"Thank you for your help. I really appreciate it. If you happen to see him, would you please ask him to give me a call?" he handed

Dennis a twenty with his number written on it. "Next round is on me, okay? Thanks again."

Michael walked back down the dock and toward his car, more concerned and more confused than ever.

. . .

Buddy spotted the floatplane and saw Dennis nearing the end of the dock. Making a sharp turn onto the gravel, he nearly sideswiped a Lexus with his Jeep and quickly jumped out of his vehicle as it jerked to a stop, hurrying down the pier toward where Dennis now stood performing his preflight inspection.

Dennis looked surprised to see him, and before he could speak, Buddy launched into his questions. "Hey, Dennis—you haven't seen or heard anything yet, have you?"

Dennis shook his head. "No, sir, I haven't, but I'll be on the lookout. What do you think is going on?"

Buddy took a deep breath, suddenly realizing he was a bit winded from the dash down the dock. All this stress wasn't doing his blood pressure any favors, either.

"I wish I knew, Dennis. They left here on Sunday morning, and I haven't been able to reach them since."

Dennis went back to his inspection, working his way to the tail of the plane. "*Sunday*? Man, they could be halfway to Mexico by now!"

Buddy stood in silence, a multitude of scenarios playing out in his head.

"It's funny you stopped by asking like you did, though," Dennis said, breaking into his thoughts. "Another guy just came by here and was looking for you—said he's friends with those people who took your boat out."

Dennis had Buddy's full attention now. "What do you mean? *What guy?*"

Again, the head shake. "Don't know his name. He left just before you walked up. You *literally* just missed him. Said he's been trying to get in touch with you." Dennis pulled the twenty from his pocket. "He said if I saw you, for you to give him a call at that number." He handed it over to Buddy, his fingers barely leaving the bill as he added, "Uh, I'm gonna need that back when you're done."

Buddy nodded as he dialed the number scrawled on the twenty, then crushed the bill back into Dennis's hand as the phone rang.

...

Twenty minutes later, the three men stood on the pier in front of Dennis's plane. His charter to Little Palm Island was running late, but he'd decided he would give them ten more minutes. Michael had introduced himself and told Buddy that he, too, had been unsuccessful in his attempts to reach John about an urgent business matter. Dennis agreed that after he'd dropped his passengers at Little Palm, he would help search the area for as long as the fuel—and the weather—held out.

Buddy sat up front at the controls alongside Dennis, while Michael balanced on a small jump seat at the rear. The two middle seats were occupied by a young honeymooning couple en route to Little Palm Island.

Thankfully, it was only a short flight from Key West, and the search for John and Molly could begin soon.

CHAPTER TWENTY-NINE

ERICA WAS ENJOYING A LATE LUNCH POOLSIDE AT THE CLEVELANDER HOTEL IN SOUTH BEACH. She was casually eavesdropping on the conversations going on around her, taking particular interest in the table directly behind her. A good-looking middle-aged couple and their oddly average-looking son sat savoring afternoon cocktails and each other's company, laughing easily while discussing an upcoming trip on their private yacht to the British Virgin Islands.

Erica used the direct sunlight as an excuse to reposition her chair, a fortuitous move that granted her a full view of the group in question. It only took a moment for them to notice her, and—judging by the flushed cheeks on the couple's fair-skinned son, coupled with the unabashed once-over from his father—*noticed*, she was!

Having spent her honeymoon on St. Maarten a little less than three years ago, Erica remembered a favorite dining spot with an incredible Caribbean view. She used this tidbit of local knowledge to ease her way into the trio's conversation and spoke with her eyes sparkling brightly.

"I hope you don't think me rude, but I couldn't help but overhear that you're planning a trip to the Islands."

The son was the first to offer a reply, the friendliness of his voice eagerly welcoming her into the conversation. "We sure are. We leave tomorrow for a three-week trip."

Erica's voice was thick with envy. "Oh, *my*—that sounds like an absolutely *marvelous* vacation!" she exclaimed, her hand fluttering to her chest daintily. "Should you find yourself in St. Maarten, you *must* go to Oceans 82. The food there is *divine*, second only to their sunset views."

By then, the younger man was clearly losing his composure, so his father took the lead.

"We're certainly expecting it to be unforgettable, and thank you for the recommendation. It will actually be the maiden voyage for our new boat, *Law Man.*"

Erica tried her best to conceal the shocking jolt of negative energy immediately coursing through her body, and she managed to hold her smile. "What a *clever* name. I'm assuming, then, that you're in law enforcement of some kind?"

The couple laughed, and the man's wife finally spoke.

"*Heavens* no, dear. Charles is an attorney just up the way in Palm Beach."

Erica's tension eased, and she feigned laughter. "How wonderful for you all!"

The wife spoke again, smiling brightly. "Would you care to join us, dear?"

Erica was taken aback for a moment.

Can it really be this easy?

Her reply was almost too hasty. "Yes!" she exclaimed.

Flashing her a grin, the young man stood and slid back the chair next to his. "Please, do join us."

Erica politely accepted the invitation and took her place at their table, realizing now that more effort would be required if she was to secure passage aboard their yacht, ultimately slipping quietly out of the country.

Introductions were made all around, and another order of drinks was requested. The alcohol having helped put her at ease, Erica had inadvertently offered up her real name, Lyla Cain. Immediately realizing her misstep, she hesitated to course correct, now believing her initial oversight could work in her favor—an abused woman in search of anonymity, somewhere far away. She soon learned that Charles Hamilton and his wife, Celia, were celebrating their fortieth wedding anniversary on the upcoming voyage and that they—along with their son, Miles—would be shopping for a vacation home in the Caribbean. Fate seemed to be on her side and she had to suppress a child-like desire to giggle with excitement over her good fortune.

"How about you, dear—what brings *you* to Miami?" Celia asked.

Erica's lack of hesitation and ready reply rose from her expertise as a professional liar. "Well, to be completely honest, I've recently gone through a rather lengthy and *nasty* divorce. So, I decided to take an extended leave of absence from my interior design business to re-center myself and to recharge."

Miles and Charles seemed to hang onto Erica's every word.

Celia, on the other hand, clucked her tongue in womanly concern and laid a gentle hand on Erica's arm. "I'm *so* sorry to hear that, dear. I'm sure that better days are in your future, just around the corner. You'll see," she said, lifting her glass in a toast to Erica.

"Thank you, Celia. And please don't be sorry. I'm *already* having a better day, having met you all!"

"The pleasure is ours to have met *you,* sweetheart," Charles replied, his son's agreement echoing seconds behind.

"Thank you all so very much," Erica said, again, as they all clinked glasses.

Here's to you, Lyla. Here's to you . . . she smiled to herself.

. . .

An hour passed, and the conversation flowed as easily as if they were all old friends. Erica took special care to give as little detail as possible about her real life, in the hopes of avoiding an unexplainable blunder.

"I would love to hear more about your design business, my dear," Celia said, looking at Erica in interest. "I might need to call on your expertise if we buy that vacation home we're looking for. *If* you're feeling up to it, that is."

Erica was barely able to conceal her excitement. "I would be more than happy to help you with that, Celia. In fact, I'm planning to spend at least a month in the area; so, should you find the perfect getaway, I would be glad to come have a look and discuss ideas," she enthused.

Celia clapped her hands in delight. "Aren't you just a *doll!*"

Erica sparkled under the older woman's praise. "Thank you. And so are *you* all," she replied, winking at Miles.

The younger man nearly choked on his drink.

Conversation wound down as Charles called for the bill and reminded his family of an upcoming meeting with their new yacht captain to discuss the details of their itinerary. Much to Erica's pleasure, Celia seemed reluctant to break away.

"If we must, Charles," she said glumly, standing to give Erica a hug. "Forgive my husband for cutting our time short, dear. You'll find he's *quite* the stickler for details."

"No need to apologize for that—I am, too!" Erica said lightly, waving off the older woman's apology.

Celia's face brightened as a thought occurred to her. "If you don't already have plans, would you care to join us back here for brunch tomorrow, before we leave—say, around eleven-thirty or so?"

"No plans," Erica said, shaking her head. "And that sounds absolutely lovely, Celia. I'll be looking forward to it."

"Us too," said Miles.

The group parted, and Erica left the Clevelander, deciding that a shopping trip was in order. Since she'd left her suitcase in Greg Kline's filthy SUV the night before, the only clothes she had were the ones she was currently wearing.

And *that* would certainly not do.

After Charles and Celia Hamilton concluded their afternoon meeting with the captain and crew of *Law Man,* they decided on a casual stroll along the private dock—if for no other reason than to satisfy their own curiosity about the other yachts being kept there. Charles's observations about the other boats and chatter about their upcoming trip seemed to fall on deaf ears, and, while Celia might have been present beside him, her mind seemed anywhere else. Now that he thought about it, she'd been particularly—uncharacteristically—quiet since they'd left the hotel earlier that day.

Charles looked at his wife with concern in his eyes. "Is everything alright, dear? Your mind seems to be miles away."

"I'm okay," she murmured unconvincingly. "I just can't get that poor girl Lyla off my mind, that's all."

"Why? She seemed fine to me."

"Yes, she did *seem* fine," Celia allowed. "On the surface, at least. But didn't you notice the swelling on her cheek? Or the bruise?"

Charles shook his head. "Bruise? I didn't notice any bruise. Are you sure it wasn't just a shadow?"

"Yes, I'm *sure,* Charles! She'd tried to cover it with makeup, but it was most definitely there." She paused thoughtfully. "It's probably why she never took her sunglasses off."

"This *is* Miami, dear—everybody wears sunglasses!" he laughed, still unconcerned.

"It's not funny, Charles!" Celia snapped, her frustration rising to the surface. "I'm afraid that she may be in real trouble—maybe even in danger! I've known women like her before, women who are used to hiding abuse. The bruise and that swelling were very recent," she went on. "She might not be as completely rid of her ex as she wanted us to believe!"

Charles put one hand gently on his wife's shoulder and used his other hand to hook his index finger under her chin, tipping her face up so he could look straight down into her eyes. "I'm sorry I laughed, dear. I can see how upset you are by all of this."

"I *am* upset. I just feel like we need to help her somehow."

Charles pulled her closer and hugged her. "You're a good woman, Celia Hamilton!"

...

Having gotten her shopping done by early evening, Erica happily returned to her suite at the Clevelander and went about removing price tags from her recent wardrobe additions, then began organizing cosmetics and essentials into a new set of luggage. The television was on in her suite, its ambient noise providing a nice distraction from the quiet.

Too much silence allowed her mind the freedom of wandering back to Joan and to Greg and to the speculation about which of them had betrayed her, maliciously planning her demise. For all she knew, it wasn't just *one* of them—it was *both* of them, acting in collusion.

She had her suspicions. But in this case, she hoped she was wrong.

Working her way through the stack of clothes, she thought about tomorrow's brunch with the Hamiltons. Best-case scenario, she could avoid resorting to plan B, which would include having to put Miles to use. He *seemed* smitten enough, and he was nice. But he was *far* from her type. She shuddered at the thought but didn't feel ready to dismiss the idea entirely, just in case everything else failed.

When she'd finished packing her things, she unzipped the Louis Vuitton bag and removed three one-hundred-dollar bills from one of the stacks, placing them into her wallet. She paused to look at the driver's license tucked in front, still in disbelief of all that had happened since she had been *that* person.

After choosing one of her new dresses for dinner, she used the bathroom mirror to touch up her makeup. Her cheek was still sore to the touch, but at least most of the swelling had gone down. And after a few masterful strokes with a blending brush, her black eye was hardly visible.

The local news theme played on the television in the adjoining room, leading straight into an intro by a well-coiffed anchorman whose stilted voice made her blood run cold.

"Good evening. And now, tonight's top story: The Monroe County Sheriff's Department and the Miami police are searching for a person of interest in connection with an apparent hit-and-run fatality on US Highway 1, just north of Key Largo. Wanted for questioning is Dr. Lyla Cain, an Atlanta psychiatrist who was reported missing from her home and practice late last month by her husband. As of this broadcast, Mr. Cain was unavailable for comment."

Erica stood frozen in front of the mirror, watching the reflection of the TV directly behind her, as the story continued and a picture showing Dr. Cain filled the screen, taken from a two-year-old *Atlanta Medical Journal* and featuring a very blonde Erica Payne, formerly known to the world as Dr. Lyla Cain.

"If you have any information leading to the whereabouts of Dr. Cain, you are urged to contact your local law enforcement *immediately*. We will bring you updates about this ongoing story, as they emerge."

Erica sat on the edge of the bed in stunned silence. Obviously, the authorities had thoroughly searched Greg Kline's vehicle and inspected every inch for fingerprints. Given the circumstances surrounding the scene, they'd been quick to process any possible evidence found—certainly *not* to her advantage. She'd known, of course, that it would've happened eventually, but she wasn't prepared for this type of news so quickly. Her only hope now was that the Hamiltons had somehow missed the news and would be oblivious to the situation.

If not, she would have to think of another way out of this tangled mess.

At this point, she knew, it didn't matter that Greg Kline's death had been in self-defense. It was far too late for her to try to explain to the police everything that had happened thus far. Besides, now that the public had been informed about her true identity and her general whereabouts, the police were no longer her biggest fear.

It would only be a matter of time before *he* found her.

CHAPTER THIRTY

JOHN STRAINED TO LIFT HIMSELF UP AND OFF THE WATER-SOAKED BUNK, THEN ONTO THE COMPANIONWAY FLOOR. He had been resting for forty minutes, every two hours, using a wind-up alarm clock to wake himself at the appropriate intervals.

The breaks between the grueling labor of bailing water from the cabin, however, seemed to do very little in the way of easing his fatigue, mentally *or* physically.

After each rest period, he climbed the short three steps to the deck and scanned every inch of the sky in hopes of seeing even the slightest sign of possible rescue. All day long, the results had remained exactly the same—*fruitless*.

During the mind-numbing repetition, John tried his best to use each second to its full advantage, keeping a close watch on any changes in the Morgan's condition, as well as on her position in relation to a sea chart plastered across the cabin wall.

Without any visible landmarks, however, he had no way of knowing how far he had actually drifted away from Molly.

As far as the boat's condition, the best news was that—according to his crude calculations, at least—the leaks hadn't gotten any worse. If there *was* a bright side to things for the day, so far *this* was *it*.

That, and his discovery of an unopened, smashed granola bar among the many otherwise useless other items stashed inside Molly's purse. Taking his time to chew and savoring every bite, he couldn't remember a time when anything else in his life had tasted so good.

The wind continued to pick up as the day went on. Every once in a while, a heavy gust would cause the boat to list severely to one side and then violently rock and shake as it righted itself again. Up until now, John had been somewhat able to remain in denial of the Morgan's danger, but with the large storm approaching, he was facing facts and realizing his rescue was far from guaranteed.

Can I really last another night, alone at sea, in a sinking ship? he wondered.

If he was being realistic, John had to admit that even one large wave could flood the vessel beyond his ability to recover it.

And if that happened, it would *all* be over.

...

Molly kept a vigilant watch on the sky and on the water surrounding her, remaining in a constant state of silent prayer, no longer allowing her thoughts to turn to hopelessness and fear.

"You can do this, Molly—this *one* brave thing!" She kept repeating this simple phrase, over and over, to assure herself that she did, indeed, have the courage she needed to survive.

As she studied the sky to the west, rows of dark clouds were stacking one on top of the other, building into a thick black wall that seemed to reach the stratosphere. The wind was coming in stronger now, too, and an occasional arc of electricity sliced through the entire mass of clouds and down into the sea. The scene looked surreal in comparison to the cloudless blue sky to the east, back in the direction of Key West.

...

Twenty miles east of Fort Jefferson on a southwest heading, Dennis, Buddy, and Michael searched the ocean below for the lost Morgan.

"I met your friend Sandy Gale at Captain Tony's today," Buddy said to Dennis. "She's who told me where to find you."

A huge smile spread over Dennis's face. "Miss Sandy Gale Bourgeois!" He pronounced the last name *boo-ZWAH*. "That woman is a handful, but as sweet as the day is long!"

Buddy laughed, "*Handful* is an understatement—maybe more like *two* handfuls!"

"You know, she was somewhat of a celebrity back in her day," Dennis said, catching Buddy's interest. "Yessir, she was a semi-famous lounge singer back in New Orleans. Sang at all the great clubs from Miami to Los Angeles, and she was married for a while to a famous actor, back in the 1960s. Don't remember which one, though. Man, she was even engaged to some oil sheikh from over there in the Middle East, but she broke it off when he wouldn't agree to live with her in New Orleans!" Dennis chuckled. "Can you imagine?"

Buddy shook his head in disbelief. "Nope. Really can't," he murmured, thinking back to the woman he'd met earlier in the day, a woman who was most likely *still* perched boozily right where he'd found her on that very same barstool.

"She's been after me for years to name this plane *Sandy Gale*, as sort of a tribute to her," Dennis drawled. "She claims I even agreed to it one night, but I can't say as I recall promising anything like that. Been drinking, though—so, you never know." He gave a quick glance to Buddy and winked.

Dennis lowered the plane's altitude as he approached the fort, preparing to circle it. Fortunately, many vessels had cleared the area ahead of the impending storm, so it made the search for the missing craft somewhat easier.

"Boys, I'm going to make a low pass near the fort," Dennis piped up, raising his volume to be heard over the noise of the engine. "If you see anything that resembles what we're looking for, just give a holler."

Michael and Buddy nodded, their eyes scanning the water below.

"That stormfront to the west looks to be about sixty or seventy miles out, so we'll have about an hour, at best, before we'll need to head back."

After several low passes, Buddy felt confident that his boat was not among the few that remained in the area.

"What do you want to do, my friend?" Dennis asked, glancing at Buddy.

"I'd like to head a little further west if we can. I told the Callaways they might want to explore some of the untouched areas at the outer reaches of the Tortugas," Buddy replied, not yet ready to give up.

Dennis nodded hesitantly. "We can look a little further out, but that's going to put us right up against *that* before long!" Dennis nodded in the direction of the ominous black wall of clouds looming on the horizon.

"That looks pretty bad," Michael said anxiously. "Are you sure it's okay to be out here?"

"I don't have radar, but as long as we stay out in front of it, we should be fine," Dennis replied, his words still not doing much to calm Michael's concerns.

Michael slid forward to the edge of his seat, his eyes narrowed and his brow furrowed in worry. "*Should* be?"

Dennis chuckled at the sick look on Michael's face. "We'll be fine."

After a thorough search around several of the outlying islands, the small plane was now less than thirty miles out ahead of the storm. Dennis suggested that they start thinking about heading back but agreed to swing a little farther to the south and take a different line on the return leg, knowing there were still a few remote outcroppings they could safely check.

...

Molly felt a chill as the temperature suddenly dropped several degrees ahead of the storm front and large drops of rain began to fall.

She wished she had some type of container to capture it, knowing she now had only a few sips of drinking water left in her bottle. With marble-sized hail mixed in with the rain now pelting her, she ran toward her makeshift shelter under the old palm, covering as much of her body as she could with the rain-soaked picnic blanket. The downpour soon entirely gave way to the hailstorm, and the sound was nearly deafening, like radio static being broadcast at full volume. With her hands over her ears, Molly curled into a ball, doing her best to make herself as small as possible as she tried to drown out the storm with her fervent prayers.

...

With the storm now nearly on top of Dennis's plane, he was finally able to convince Buddy and Michael that they'd exhausted the area and they would need to head inland before visibility went down to zero. He banked the plane left thirty degrees and began making his turn. Michael was sitting on the low side of the aircraft and looked out the window, just in time to catch a glimpse of something. With the rain pouring in sheets, he wasn't exactly sure what he saw, but it looked unnatural and out of place in its surroundings. He reached up and squeezed Dennis's shoulder to get his attention and pointed.

"Down there!" he exclaimed. "I think I saw something!"

Dennis gave a look in the direction of Michael's finger but didn't spot a boat. He didn't really see anything if he was to be perfectly honest.

Michael shouted out again. "Down *there*—on that small island! I saw something! We have to turn around and take another look!"

Buddy agreed, and, against his better judgment, Dennis banked the plane in the opposite direction to head back for a second pass.

Flying lower this time, they approached the larger of two small islands positioned close together.

Buddy pointed it out first. "There it is! I see it!"

Dennis's eyes picked out something, right where Buddy was pointing. "Yes, I see it, too!"

And there it was.

On the bleached white sand of a small beach below them, the word HELP was spelled out in large letters, with what looked to be dead palm fronds and seaweed. Dennis turned the plane one more time and prepared for landing. The waves were beginning to white-cap, and the surf was pretty high, closer in. As adrenaline made him feel more sober than he'd ever been in his life, he looked for a place to set the plane down in calmer water, between the two islands.

The hailstorm had been violent but brief, and now only a steady rain fell, an occasional clap of thunder encouraging Molly to remain in her hiding spot. Dennis's plane made a rough water landing, hopping and skipping several times before stopping as he taxied as close to shore as he thought was safe, trying to get a closer look at the island through the heavy downpour.

...

When Molly first heard the sound of the engine, she assumed it might be another bout of hail moving in closer. When the noise continued, without an accompaniment of pelting ice, she lifted the blanket and was amazed at what she saw less than a hundred yards in front of her. She jumped to her feet and ran toward the plane, screaming wildly and waving her arms.

Michael saw her first. "My *God!* That's Molly! Stop the plane!"

Molly never slowed as she ran straight into the water, falling face first into the oncoming waves but quickly regaining her footing. She was now waist deep in the water, wading out to the plane as Michael opened the door to help her, grabbing her hand and pulling her onto the pontoon, then into the cabin.

Molly was shaking uncontrollably and talking so fast that she was incoherent, all the while trying to figure out why John wasn't there with them. Michael tried to calm her, knowing that she was experiencing some type of shock.

"Molly, slow down, sweetheart," he soothed. "You're okay. I just need you to take some deep breaths and talk a little slower for me, okay?" He pulled a blanket from behind the seat and wrapped it around her before going on. "Molly, sweetheart—where's John?"

Shivers wracked her body as she spoke. "He's gone. He left me here. *He left me*. He's gone on the boat."

Michael, Dennis, and Buddy stared at her with incomprehension.

Finally, Michael spoke again. "Molly. Honey—what do you mean *he left you*? John wouldn't just leave you here like this!"

She shook her head, trying to make it all make sense in her own mind, as well. "The boat—the boat got loose. John swam out to catch it, and he disappeared. He's *gone*! He's *lost*! We *have* to find him—*now*!"

"When did the boat get loose, Molly?" Buddy broke in. "In the storm? Did the boat get loose in the storm?"

She shouted urgently, wishing they would stop questioning her and start looking. "*No*! Two or three days ago." More shivers rippled through her. "I don't know where he is!" she sobbed. "*Please*, Michael! Please help him. We *have* to find him!"

Buddy stared silently at Michael and gave him a knowing look, both men hoping to avoid upsetting Molly further.

"I hate to say this, but we need to leave right now," Dennis said grimly, looking out as the force of the wind whipped the sea into a frenzy. "Once we're in the air, I'll make a radio call to the Coast Guard and report John and the boat missing, and they'll begin a search."

The men agreed, taking their seats and buckling Molly in, her shivering frame now frozen in silence as the plane began to move.

CHAPTER THIRTY-ONE

JOHN WAS COMPLETELY EXHAUSTED AND BECOMING DELIRIOUS. The Morgan was now within the full grip of the raging torrent, and he was having a more difficult time standing as he worked to bail water out of the cabin and onto the deck. As the water level continued to rise around him, John again felt the searing burn from the re-introduction of salt to his infected wound. He reached into his pocket and removed the pill bottle, rushing to swallow two capsules washed down by several large gulps of water. The Morgan shifted violently onto its side, causing him to lose his grip on the jug, and it fell into the water at his feet. He grabbed it up as quickly as he could, but it was too late, and his once-clear, pure spring water became contaminated with sea and filth.

In that moment, it felt to him like a death sentence.

Testing the dirty water from the jug with his lips, John instantly spit a rancid mouthful out and hurled the ruined remains as hard as he could against the cabin wall. He screamed out a list of indecipherable words and began tearing into the cabin in a violent rage, pulling apart anything and everything he could and blindly throwing items out of the cabin onto the deck.

Among them was the bucket he'd been using to bail water, and the moment the bucket left his hands, John realized his mistake and scrambled up the steps, desperately trying to retrieve it. It was futile, and he watched in horror as the bucket tumbled over the Morgan's side and out of reach. From his kneeled position at the top of the steps, John allowed sheets of rain to wash over him as he looked to the stormy sky, already dark as night, and pleaded with the heavens to deliver him from this torment. He closed his eyes and lowered his head, overcome with defeat. There was a loud crack, and he was suddenly thrust backward, tumbling down the steps and onto the floor. Dazed and disoriented, he gathered himself and attempted to stand. Water was now coming into the cabin from the bow at an alarming rate.

His mind raced. There had obviously been a collision, but with what?

He could feel the Morgan making a counterclockwise turn as the bow began dipping into the sea from the inundation of floodwater.

John once again pulled his weight up the steps, climbing until his head was above the hatch so he could see out. Visibility was less than fifty feet through the thick veil of raindrops, but it was there, right in front of him—*land*.

Or at least the resemblance of it, from what he could make out.

He reentered the cabin and began rifling through the cabinets and drawers, filling Molly's purse with anything he could get his hands on. He fastened a life vest around himself and grabbed a second, holding it under one arm and wrapping the purse straps tightly around his other arm as he prepared to abandon ship.

Back out on deck, John estimated that in the short time it had taken him to prepare the boat had drifted another fifty yards from where the impact had occurred. From his vantage point, he could see the shoreline being overrun by crashing waves that looked to be several feet above his head. The sight hastened him, leaving him with no alternative but to abandon the sinking boat one final time. With no further time for thought, he lept over the side railing and into the water, kicking and paddling his way toward *terra firma* in an ultimate struggle against a strong current fighting to hold him at sea.

As John neared the irregular shoreline of the small outcropping, he began to decipher shapes and could see that his beacon of hope was little more than a sparse patch of vegetation growing over an exposed coral head. A lone palm stood near the center, its meager frame barely supporting the few tattered fronds that clung to it, while a sparse collection of plants, bushes, and thorny vines littered the remainder of the tiny island like abandoned trash. Jagged rocks and sharp coral elevated the half-acre plot of land only a few feet above the surface of the water.

Managing to work his way to the downwind side of the outcropping, John labored toward a small spot between the rocks that seemed somewhat protected from the direct assault of the crashing waves. Grabbing hold of the pointed end of a jutting rock, he was able to get one knee onto the coral, feeling its sharp edges tearing into his flesh as he climbed his way out of the water and onto the base of the island. Once he'd reached a safe place to hold up, he positioned the extra life vest beneath his legs, in an effort to shield himself from further abrasions, his exhaustion finally overtaking him and dragging him into an unconscious state.

...

Dennis landed the plane in relatively calm seas, just before the storm made landfall in Key West. On the return flight, he had radioed the Coast Guard to report John and the boat lost at sea, only to be told that a proper search could not be launched until the weather had cleared the area, which would most likely be first light the following morning.

Going against Molly's wishes, Michael, Buddy, and Brenda took her to Lower Keys Medical Center in Key West, where she was treated for severe dehydration and exposure. The attending physician advised that Molly be admitted for observation overnight, just as a precaution, so she could be monitored and quickly rehydrated. Her burned skin was treated, and she was given a sedative that pulled her into the oblivion of sleep, far out of reach of her panic and shock.

Michael agreed to stay by her side until further arrangements could be made, sending Buddy and Brenda off with inexpressible gratitude and his promise to call them first thing in the morning with an update. In return, he asked that they contact him immediately with news—*any* news—they might hear of John.

...

Dennis caught up with the Sullivans in the lobby area as they prepared to leave the hospital.

"Hey, Buddy! I'm glad I found you. How's she doing?"

Buddy's response was precluded by Brenda. "She's definitely been through a lot, but the doctor said she should be just fine in a day or two. Physically, at least. Right now, what that poor girl needs is rest, and plenty of it."

"That's really good to hear," Dennis sighed, the concern clouding his face clearing just a bit. "I can only imagine how she must be feeling, though."

Buddy nodded his head in agreement.

Dennis paused a moment before speaking further. "Hey, listen. I was thinking . . . I don't have anything scheduled for tomorrow because of this crazy weather, so if you would be willing to help chip in for gas, I'd be more than happy to keep looking. It sure couldn't hurt to have as many eyes as possible out there."

"That's mighty good of you, Dennis," Buddy said, extending his hand to the younger man. "Tell you what—I'll cover all the costs if you take care of the flying."

With a plan in place, the two shook hands and parted company, agreeing to meet at the fuel dock at first light.

Buddy and Brenda made the drive home in silence, Buddy's mind berating him for ever having decided to lease out the Morgan. He wished now that he'd at least held the Callaways off for a few days to

wait out the unstable weather, but that was the nature of the Keys—
beautifully unpredictable.

...

As the night wore on, Michael struggled with the dilemma of calling Joan to give her the news. It seemed wisest, though, to wait until morning, his hopes grasping at the slim chance that by then he
might have more information—and better news—about John and his
whereabouts.

Nor did it seem prudent to alert Agent Copeland to the fact that
he'd left Atlanta.

He paced the hallway, periodically checking in on Molly while she
slept.

Around seven the next morning, a nurse found Michael in the visitors' lounge and told him that Molly was awake and asking for him.
He thanked her and headed to Molly's room, relieved to see her sitting propped up in bed, sipping orange juice through her cracked lips
with a straw. She reached out for his hand and held it tightly.

"Thank you so much for saving me, Michael. I really don't know
what I would have done if y'all hadn't come along," she murmured,
her eyes serious as she held him in her gaze. "Michael, it was horrible
out there all alone! Please, *please* tell me that John is safe!"

"You don't have to thank me, Molly," Michael said, squeezing
her hand. "I'm just glad you're alright. And I promise that everybody
is doing *everything* they can to find John."

Molly's eyes began to water as she spoke. "He *has* to be okay,
Michael. He just *has* to be! We have to look for him—he can't be out
there like this. Please tell me that we can find him and that he's going
to be okay!"

Michael let go of her hand and walked to the window, staring out
into the damp darkness rather than having to face the desperation in
her eyes.

"Molly, I really need to talk to you about something, but I'm not sure if I know how. I definitely don't want to stress you any more than you already are—that's the last thing you need right now."

"What are you talking about, Michael?" Molly demanded, the volume of her voice testament to her rising level of anxiety. "Is it about John? Did they find him? *Tell me*!"

CHAPTER THIRTY-TWO

JOAN OPENED THE TRUNK OF HER CAR AND TOOK OUT THE LAST REMAIN-
ING PREPAID CELL PHONE, HER FACE SET IN GRIM CONCERN AS SHE DI-
ALED THE NUMBER FOR THE PHONE SHE'D GIVEN TO GREG KLINE.

He was supposed to have used it to contact her after he finished
dealing with Erica, and she had expected a call from him two nights
prior or at the *latest* by early yesterday morning. It was now nearing
daylight, and there had been nothing but radio silence. While the
phone continued to ring unanswered, concern amplified into anxiety.

Ten minutes later as she watched the rising level of hot water filling the bathtub in her modest one-bedroom condominium in Lenox
Hills, she hoped her mind would be eased after a long soak. While the
tub filled, she retrieved the purloined green thumb drive and inserted
it into a USB slot on her laptop, then signed into an online bank account at First Caribbean International Bank. She selected a sub-list of
account numbers and reviewed the balances. A withdrawal transaction for $2 million had been processed on one of the accounts, show-
ing the current balance as zero. She moved on to the next accounts,
initiating a wire transfer for the remaining funds in each to be moved
to a second bank in Grand Cayman. Just as she clicked the button to
complete the transfers, the prepaid cell phone beside her buzzed, the
unexpected sound startling her. She grabbed the phone and answered
it immediately without bothering to glance at the caller ID.

"*Where are you?*" she demanded, her voice booming over the line.

The male voice that replied was one she did not recognize. Definitely *not* Greg Kline.

"Ma'am, may I ask who I'm speaking with?"

Joan felt her blood run cold, and she was stunned into silence.

"Ma'am—are you there?" the voice asked.

Joan barely managed to calm herself before answering. "Yes. Yes, I'm here. Who is this?"

"Ma'am, this is Lieutenant Baldwin with the Monroe County Sheriff's Department. Do you mind telling me with whom I am speaking?"

A surge of adrenaline shot through Joan's body like a speeding bullet. She could feel her pulse race, and her head suddenly felt light, sending the room spinning. Panicked, she disconnected the call and threw the phone into the half-filled tub of water before collapsing into a heap on the tiled bathroom floor.

...

Molly's pleading continued for Michael to tell her what was going on, but he remained pensive, staring out the window as he spoke. "Molly, I really don't know where to begin. There's just *so much* that doesn't make *any* sense."

"What are you *talking* about, Mike? *Where is my husband?*" Molly's voice was practically a shout by now as hysteria threatened to overtake her. She threw her empty orange juice container in his direction. "You have to tell me!"

Bewildered by her sudden outburst, Michael turned to look at her. "I honestly don't know, Molly," he said quietly, shaking his head. "I *swear* I would tell you if I knew anything at all."

Molly's eyes narrowed at him. "What are you talking about, then? What's this *big thing* that you're afraid to tell me? What could possibly be worse than the fact that John's still out there somewhere?"

Michael moved away from the window and sat down in a chair in the corner of the room, facing her full on before he began.

"Molly, I didn't come down here with any knowledge that you and John were in any sort of physical danger. The timing of my arrival here was pure coincidence."

Molly's eyebrows knit in confusion. "I don't understand at all, Mike. If you didn't know we were missing, then why *did* you come here?"

Michael slapped his palms down hard on the arms of the chair, gripping them tightly in his hands before he released them again and launched himself to his feet. "Because I needed to talk to John about some things that have been going on with the company, and I couldn't reach him on his phone!" His shoulders slumped in defeat and frustration. Michael walked back toward the window, as though there might be some solution waiting for him on the other side of the glass panes.

Molly watched him, taking a moment to lower her voice and regain some semblance of composure. "What kind of *things* could be so urgent that they warranted you driving *a thousand* miles to talk to my husband while he's on vacation? What was *so* important it couldn't wait?"

Tired of shouldering the burden of hiding information, Michael blurted out, "John is in trouble, Molly! I think he's done something really stupid, and *none* of it makes a bit of sense!"

Molly swallowed hard and leveled her gaze at this very distraught, very unfamiliar version of Michael Bloom. "Tell me what you're talking about *right now*, Michael. I want to know *everything* you know—*everything*. No exceptions."

Michael exhaled loudly, turning to face her again. "Okay. It all seemed to start a few weeks ago when our Bahamas deal was being finalized. John seemed a little different—around the office, at least."

Molly listened intently, as the past few weeks replayed in her mind.

"What do you mean by *different*, Michael?" she asked.

"I really can't put my finger on it, Molly—believe me," Michael replied, shaking his head slowly. "I've been wracking my brain, trying to sort all of this out and piece it back together. He just seemed distracted—*totally* out of character for him when it comes to business, as you well know!"

Molly didn't blink as her mind tried to process where he might be leading.

Michael went on. "Joan noticed it first and brought it to my attention. She told me that he'd made several careless mistakes she'd had to fix. It wasn't a huge deal, but, God knows, nothing is *ever* lost on her!"

"What kind of mistakes?" Molly asked.

"Like, accounting mistakes. I reviewed and signed off on every part of this deal, and nothing was at all amiss when it left my desk, but . . ." His words trailed off.

"But *what?*" Molly prompted.

Michael's face was a somber mask. "But a couple of days ago, the FBI and the IRS showed up at the office, wanting to speak to John."

Molly was unable to hold back a gasp of alarm. "What on earth for? Why would the *FBI* need to see John? *Or* the IRS?"

"I wondered the very same thing when Joan told me about it, and then I had to meet with them myself."

Molly pushed on. "Well, what did they want?"

"This is where things *really* start to not make any sort of sense," Michael said slowly, choosing his words more carefully with the hope of not upsetting Molly any further. "The agents showed me multiple wire transfers that John signed off on, showing large deposits into an account I was totally unaware of. The money in question, $5 million, was illegally diverted from a portion of the construction funds on the Bahamas development and deposited into accounts at a separate bank."

Admittedly, Molly had no idea how such things worked, but none of it made any sense to her, not when it came to John.

"Michael, it must have been an honest mistake. You know John better than *that*. There's got to be a perfectly logical explanation for all of it, and once John's back, he'll be able to clear it all up. You'll see." There was a surety to her voice that belied the lack of confidence she was actually feeling.

"Here's the thing Molly," Michael replied, his gaze dropping to the floor. "One of the accounts totaling $2 million lists the owner as my former assistant Erica Payne."

Hearing the woman's name hit Molly's heart like an arrow, and she felt a knot of dread forming in the pit of her stomach. "What are you saying, Mike? What does that mean?"

"I honestly don't know what it means, Molly," Michael admitted. "But in all likelihood, it means that someone who was a total stranger to the firm—and to me—just a few weeks ago has somehow disappeared without a trace, along with *at least* $2 million of the company's money. And by the looks of it, John has something to do with it."

Molly's voice rose in the white heat of anger. "You *know* good and well that John had *nothing* to do with this, Michael!"

"What else am I supposed to think, Molly?" Michael snapped. "I *told* you none of this makes any sense!"

"Give me your phone!" Molly demanded, thrusting her hand out at him. "I'm calling Joan, and I'm going to get to the bottom of this nonsense for myself!"

Michael shook his head, making no move to do as she was demanding. "Calm down, Molly, please."

"*Calm down*? How can I calm down, Michael? I don't even know if my husband is *alive*—and now *this*? I need my clothes! I need to get out of here right now. I have to find John!" Molly's shoulders began to shake as uncontrollable sobs overtook her.

As he watched his friend's wife in quiet desperation, Michael realized he was completely at a loss as to what to do next. Now that Molly knew everything, he was sure she would contact Joan—and the FBI—at her first opportunity. He had no doubt he would be in serious legal trouble for leaving Georgia *and* for disobeying the gag order from the FBI, but he resigned himself to deal with that when the time came.

For now, though, his main concern was to find John.

After all, even more than being his business partner, John was his friend.

CHAPTER THIRTY-THREE

"SEE YOU WHEN THE SUN WAKES UP, DADDY!" AFTON'S VOICE RANG CLEARLY IN JOHN'S EARS, AND HIS EYES SPRANG WIDE OPEN.

As his eyes adjusted and reality clicked back into place, he realized it had only been the cruel tricks of his mind playing jokes on him, teasing him with images of his daughter and their little game. In all actuality, his situation was dire, growing more hopeless with every passing second. He was still stranded alone on the edge of the earth, left to his own devices on the crude crags of rock and dirt where he'd passed out sometime during the night. The only thing between him and the sharp, wet rocks were the two life vests he'd managed to salvage from the Morgan. He felt the strap of Molly's purse still bound to his wrist, thankful he had somehow managed to hold onto it.

Flooding rain had given way to a light drizzle and now that, too, was beginning to ease up. The sun was making its climb up and over the horizon, and for now he allowed himself a moment to lay sprawled beneath the cool, narrow shadow of the lone palm. He knew full well that this reprieve would be short-lived; and as the sun traced the sky throughout the day, he, too, would have to move and follow the only shade that the tiny speck of ground afforded him.

As he lay still, John tried to focus his mind enough to assess the entire situation before him. He swallowed thickly, his throat parched and his gritty tongue reminding him that he'd lost the only fresh water available to him, and he had no way of knowing when—or *if*—another drop would ever come. Second-guessing himself, he wondered if he'd made the right decision in leaving the boat when he had.

What if the Morgan is still afloat somehow, and the Coast Guard would have been able to locate it?

John had all but forgotten about the injury to his leg, until he tried to sit up to take a look around. The pain was so severe he thought he might vomit or pass out. He dug deep down into his right pocket to find the pill bottle and took two more antibiotics, finding the tiny capsules almost impossible to swallow without water to ease their passage down his dry throat. Against his better judgment, he dipped his left hand into the ocean and allowed a few drops of the salty water to wet his tongue and throat, just enough to swallow the medicine. He'd heard stories and had also seen a movie once about men going mad and eventually *dying* from drinking salt water while they were lost at sea.

He hoped he wouldn't share their fate.

He closed his eyes and prayed with all his might that Molly was okay, forcing himself *not* to imagine her any other way but safe and dry. He knew he needed to hold on to his hope of seeing her again if he was to survive this hellish nightmare. His stomach gnawed at him, reminding him of hunger and the fact that he had eaten virtually nothing in days.

How much longer can I last like this? Without food, without water, without proper medicine? And without Molly?

John wanted to cry, but the tears wouldn't come. It angered him that he had put himself and Molly in this predicament. Such a foolish attempt to repair a marriage that should have never been broken to begin with had possibly cost them their lives.

"Please, God, help me get through this! Help Molly!" he shouted aloud toward the sky above, then rolled onto his knees and pulled himself up by grabbing onto the low mangrove branches above him.

Now standing, he removed the life jacket that was buckled around his body and tossed it, along with the other life jacket and Molly's

purse, onto the next ledge up. For him, at least, this was the proverbial "higher ground," even though it was less than five feet above
the sea at its tallest point. He pulled himself slowly up on top to get
a better look at what was to be his temporary home. It was much as
he had expected—rough and raw. There was little there to sustain
him or even protect him from the elements. He did, however, find
two small plastic bottles caught in the twisting limbs of a mangrove
tree, along with a six-foot length of braided nylon rope—*similar to ski
rope*—tangled within the foliage of a tropical bush.

He placed his scavenged items at the base of the lone palm, alongside the life vests and Molly's purse.

Walking along, John also gathered what little driftwood was available into a small pile for a future signal fire, wondering if he might
find a way to light it if the need arose. He found a longer piece of
wood still floating but near enough to the water's edge that he could
grab hold of it. He laid it out in the sun to dry, hoping to fashion it
into a crude crutch to help take some pressure off of his tortured leg.
He was again growing tired and weak but continued scavenging the
areas he could get to for anything at all he thought might be of use.
Best-case scenario, he would soon be found, and this task would have
only had to serve as a distraction while he waited. Worst-case scenario—he would have to use what he already had and what he could
find to survive for an undetermined length of time.

...

Erica Payne meticulously applied the final touches to her near-
flawless makeup before making her way downstairs to the hotel's
poolside restaurant. She was anxious to see the Hamiltons again but
was equally apprehensive, not yet knowing if her secret had been
found out.

She cautiously surveyed each of the tables, hoping to see the couple and their son before she, herself, was noticed. If they were already

there in anticipation of her arrival, it was a fair assumption that all would be well. Still, the fact that she was a few minutes early might well explain their absence. She eased herself into the shadow of a vacant pergola nearby, trying to blend into the scenery until she was sure it was safe to be seen.

Much to her relief, she saw the Hamiltons a moment later as they were being seated by a hostess in the far corner of the open-air restaurant. She gave them a few minutes to situate themselves and observed a waiter placing a menu in front of each of the four chairs, allowing herself the trace of a smile as a sudden sense of relief flooded her. Exiting through the rear of the pergola, she quietly made her way toward the Hamiltons' table.

Miles was the first to notice her approach, and he quickly moved to stand, reaching for her hand at the same time as he slid her chair back from the table. His handshake felt a bit clammy, most likely from nervousness, but Erica ignored it and presented a perfect smile.

"I am *so* glad you were able to join us, dear!" Celia exclaimed, breaking the momentary silence of the table. "And, oh my! Don't you just look *lovely*!"

"She sure does! Uh, I mean—yes, you do!" Miles exclaimed, making no attempt to disguise his enthusiasm.

Erica responded cheerfully, her smile radiant. "Well, thank you *both* so very much. You're *too* kind, really."

Charles Hamilton partially stood to his feet from the far side of the table, greeted her with a smile of his own, and invited her to sit. Never one to argue with a man with money, she was quick to obey.

After pleasantries were exchanged all around, the waiter appeared at the table to take their orders. When it was Erica's turn, the waiter cocked his head a bit as the two made eye contact, and she felt the stare of recognition in his eyes. The cold sweat of panic came over her, and her hands began to shake. Worse still, her voice quivered when she spoke, and she stumbled over her words as she tried to recall her order.

Celia could sense her uneasiness and saved her the effort. "I believe she would enjoy the same as I ordered," the older woman said, her words sure and strong to Erica's ears.

The waiter commended her choice, thanked them, and retreated in the direction of the kitchen.

Celia spoke again, her face the picture of concern. "Are you alright dear? You seem as though you've just seen a ghost."

Erica's mind was reeling, but Celia's words brought her back to attention.

"Yes, yes. I'm fine. I'm sorry—it's just that our waiter reminded me of someone I used to know. And not under very pleasant circumstances," Erica replied, offering no further explanation.

Celia assumed she was probably referring to her ex-husband but did not press her to reveal anything more.

Erica rose from her chair, murmuring an apology as she stood. "Will you all please excuse me? I'm sorry, but I'm not feeling very well."

"By all means, of course we will, love," Celia replied.

Miles and Charles both stood as Erica made her way from the table toward the exit.

"That poor girl," Celia said as she also excused herself from the table to follow Erica.

"What's going on, Dad?" Miles asked his father.

"I'm not really sure, son, but I'm going to let your mother handle it as she sees fit. One day you'll understand there are some things only a woman knows how to deal with—and for that, I'm grateful!"

...

Erica was in her hotel room, hurriedly packing her cache of new clothes into a bag. In her haste, she hadn't fully closed the exterior door, and she heard a light knock as it was gently pushed open.

Seeing movement out of the corner of her eye, she whirled her entire body around.

"Lyla, dear, it's Celia. May I come in?"

Erica hadn't even had time to answer before Celia Hamilton's face peered past the door into a room that was now in complete disarray. The Louis Vuitton bag was sitting on the end of the bed directly between where the two women stood facing each other. The bag was unzipped, and it would have been easy for someone to notice its contents should they have chosen to look. Erica practically leapt forward, quickly placing a garment on top of the neat stacks of hundred-dollar bills before zipping it closed. In the rushed process, she inadvertently caught part of the fabric in the shiny zipper, struggling desperately with it for a moment before Celia gently placed her hand on top of Erica's.

"Let me help you with this, dear," she offered kindly. "You seem very upset, and I'm afraid you're only going to make matters worse by forcing it."

Erica had no time to react before Celia slid the zipper back open, but, fortunately for her, Celia simply tucked the fabric back inside the duffle without looking and reclosed it. On the edge of tears and knowing she was most likely on the verge of being caught, Erica stammered, "I'm sorry, Celia. It's just that—"

Celia stopped her with a hushing sound and gave her a motherly hug. "It's okay, dear—you have nothing to explain. I have a good idea of what you're going through, and it's understandable to be upset."

Erica was somewhat puzzled by Celia's assumption, but she seized the opportunity to play into it without hesitation.

"I just need to get away from this place, Celia. This was a bad idea from the start."

Celia nodded. "I completely understand, and that's why I wanted to come speak with you."

Erica, still intrigued, continued to listen, wondering if there might be some useable information to be gained. Or, perhaps, an ideal solution about to emerge.

"You said yesterday that you needed some time away and that you had no real agenda, am I correct?" Celia asked.

"Yes ma'am," Erica agreed with a nod.

Celia gave her a warm smile. "Well, Charles and I have discussed it, and we want to offer you an invitation to travel with us, at least to our first port of call in St. John. You can decide what you would like to do from there."

Erica felt her heart flutter but did her best to suppress her excitement. "That sounds absolutely wonderful, but are you sure it's really okay?"

Celia hugged her again. "Certainly, my dear! In fact, I *insist* that you join us!"

...

An hour later, the captain gave the crew of *Law Man* some last-minute instructions and ordered that the docking lines be let go. As they prepared to get underway beneath a near-perfect sky, Erica sipped a cocktail on the yacht's foredeck alongside the Hamiltons, inwardly toasting her successful escape.

CHAPTER THIRTY-FOUR

BUDDY SULLIVAN OCCUPIED THE CO-PILOT'S CHAIR IN DENNIS'S SEAPLANE. FOR THE PAST THREE HOURS, THE TWO HAD BEEN FEVERISHLY SEARCHING THE WATER BELOW, MAKING LARGER AND LARGER SWEEPS AWAY FROM THE AREA WHERE THEY HAD FOUND MOLLY THE EVENING BEFORE. The Coast Guard search had initially been delayed due to bureaucratic red tape, so it had only recently gotten underway.

Dennis spoke to Buddy through his headset. "We have less than an hour's worth of fuel left. I'll need to head back to Key West soon."

Though disappointed, Buddy understood that there was little margin for error when it came to fuel, and he simply acknowledged Dennis with a thumbs-up.

By then, they were in the heat of the day, and moisture-laden clouds were beginning to build and turn a dismal gray. More bad weather was in the forecast, adding to the pressure to locate John *sooner*, rather than later.

"Do you think we'll be able to come back out after we refuel?" Buddy asked Dennis.

"I'm not sure yet. It'll mostly depend on this front closing in. Right now, it doesn't look too bad, but you know as well as I do how quickly that can change out here," Dennis replied. "We can look at the radar when we get back and make a determination from there."

Buddy didn't acknowledge Dennis with a response this time. Instead, he kept his concentration trained on the endless ocean below.

Molly was awakened by the doctor's voice beside her hospital bed.

"How are you feeling today, Mrs. Callaway?" His demeanor was genuine and kind.

Molly yawned as she spoke. "Please, call me Molly. I feel all right, I suppose. Physically, I think I'm fine. But my nerves are a little on edge, due to the circumstances."

The doctor placed a stethoscope on her chest. "That's completely normal," the doctor assured her. "It's my understanding that you've been through quite an ordeal."

"I guess I have, but I won't consider it really over until I've found my husband and I know that he's okay!" Molly replied.

"Molly, I can't see any reason to keep you here any longer," the doctor said as he continued his examination. "So, if it's alright with you, I'm going to prescribe something to help you relax and let you go home."

Molly was relieved to hear that she would soon be free from the confines of the hospital, and she had no doubt it was audible in her voice.

"Thank you, doctor! That sounds perfectly fine to me. My husband's business partner is here, and he can take me wherever I need to go."

"Very good, Molly. Just give us a bit to get your release processed, and we'll have you on your way."

...

Mere minutes later, Michael walked into Molly's room, with Brenda Sullivan following close on his heels. Brenda leaned down and hugged her neck tightly.

"We just spoke to the doctor, dear, and he said you're free to go. That's such wonderful news!"

Molly forced a small smile. "Yes, and not a moment too soon. Please tell me you've found John?"

Brenda patted Molly's hand. "Everyone is doing everything they can to bring him home, sweetheart."

Next to her, Michael nodded. "The Coast Guard is out there looking right now, Molly, and so is Buddy, along with his pilot friend."

Brenda handed Molly a bag. "Here are some clothes for you, dear. I picked up a few things this morning that I thought you might be able to wear. And when you're ready, you're certainly welcome to come to my house and wait for your husband there."

"Thank you so much, Brenda—for everything," Molly said quietly, unable to fully express the depth of her gratitude for the other woman's thoughtfulness and encouraging words.

Brenda smiled. "You are *so* welcome, Molly. Now go on and get dressed so that we're all ready when they release you. I've already given Michael my address."

...

After the tedious process of her release was complete, Molly was relieved to sink into the vastness of one of the reclining chairs in the Sullivans' living room, her skin still radiating waves of heat that left her chilled and shivering. She asked to use the phone, as there were several calls she was desperate to make.

The first, of course, being to Katie Sutherland. She desperately needed to hear Afton's voice and let her friend know what was going on. Katie was devastated when she heard the news but promised Molly that she would make sure Afton remained unaware of the situation for the time being. Molly thanked her for that and did her best to hold back a flood of emotions when she was finally able to speak to her daughter. It wasn't an easy thing to do, but she remained cheerful during their brief conversation and reminded her little girl that she would see her very soon.

The second and third calls were to her father and to John's mother. They each insisted on coming to Key West immediately, but Molly held them off, letting them know that nothing more could be done, at the moment. After she promised them both that she would call often to keep them updated, they reluctantly agreed to stay put until further notice.

Molly was especially relieved that her father seemed understanding. Bill Edwards had never *once* flown in a plane and she knew full well that, should he get the notion in his stubborn mind, he would try to drive himself from Savannah to Key West—*alone*—in his old truck.

Her final call was to Joan Taylor.
No answer.

...

Sitting behind the wheel of her idling car in Atlanta, Joan literally did not know which way to turn.

This was new territory for her, and she wasn't at all comfortable with the fact that she was losing control of the situation. Being one who never left *anything* to chance, she reprimanded herself for choosing Greg Kline to play such an important role in her tangled web of deceit. It was painfully obvious by now that he'd somehow been unsuccessful in his task to deal with Erica, and she was left to assume he was now most likely in police custody somewhere in South Florida. She certainly had not planned for *this* scenario, and she was left scrambling for a way to deal with the fact that when pressed he would most likely talk. The coward would cave the minute he was put in the position to save himself.

...

Joan had met Greg a little over a year before after finding his handyman flyer attached to a crowded bulletin board in her favorite coffee shop. Needing some minor renovation work done in her condo, she'd chosen him over the others because of a picture attached.

He had a look she found oddly attractive. Admittedly, her personal life had always been kept very private, and meeting a man this way somehow seemed like a good idea to her. He'd spent several weeks on and off completing his work, and she'd kept adding more tasks to keep him around after that, especially after learning details about his unsavory past. He'd spent a year in prison for insurance fraud some five years prior, his flimsy justification being his need to cover the cost of two ex-wives who demanded exorbitant child support and alimony payments. Fortunately for him, one of the women had mysteriously disappeared shortly before he'd been incarcerated—albeit under questionable circumstances.

The promise of a million dollars and the chance to escape the daily rigors of construction work were all it had taken for the ex-felon to agree to take part in Joan's plan. She'd kept him in the dark for the most part, disguising the plot as nothing more than simple greed.

Dr. Lyla Cain, on the other hand, had known of Joan's motive from the beginning, and the thought of doing away with her altogether had come to Joan later, after she'd begun to consider her more of a liability rather than an asset. It had taken little time for Greg Kline to consider and accept Joan's additional offer to double his payday, providing further confirmation of Joan's suspicion over the strange circumstances surrounding the disappearance of the former Mrs. Kline.

...

It had taken Joan months to fabricate Greg's construction and development background so that it would pass scrutiny with both John and Michael. Though she had never truly liked Michael Bloom as a person, nor as John's business partner, she couldn't deny his abilities and his keen eye for detail. He would make no mistakes when he was tasked with adding all of the numbers involved, carefully reviewing every digit to ensure that it made sense for the firm to pursue such a large deal and that their risks were minimal. Much to Joan's credit, she had been able to present the counterfeit development deal to Michael in such a way that he fully believed it to be his own idea. Having already falsely vetted many of the particulars herself, Michael's trust in her blinded him to the possibility of her deceit, and he had been excited and anxious to pitch the plan to John.

Which he did—with *great* enthusiasm.

...

Joan entered a part of the city she'd visited only once before, a place she'd hoped to avoid in the future at all costs. Her shiny new BMW 7-series looked extremely out of place on these dodgy streets and was noticed by everyone as she passed by. When she'd been here the first time, it had been with Greg. Somehow, the area seemed even seedier than it had before, now that she was all alone. Navigating her car down a dirty alleyway behind a dilapidated strip mall, she pulled up alongside a large steel door that guarded the rear entrance of one of the few remaining businesses. She checked her surroundings as carefully as she could before getting out of the car, then walked to the door and pressed the button twice on a buzzer off to the side of the doorframe. While she waited, she caught sight of a surveillance camera mounted just below the roofline above her and was staring up at it when the door was suddenly swung open, revealing a very large man.

"Whaddaya want?" he demanded.

Joan squared her shoulders and leveled her gaze before she replied. "I need to speak to Mr. Oz. We have some paperwork to discuss."

The hulking man nodded and stepped to the side to let her through, closing the door heavily behind her. He turned without further words and led her down a hallway, leaving her to wait in a small, dingy room that was empty, aside from a small collection of filthy chairs. She remained standing until a second buzzer sounded and the man returned to usher her into a large, elaborately decorated room that bore an odd resemblance to a themed luxury suite at a Las Vegas hotel.

The irony was almost amusing—almost.

A man's voiced echoed strangely from somewhere inside the dimly lit room. "So, you're *back*. Was there a . . . *problem* . . . with your package?"

Joan answered as she tried to discern the man's whereabouts. "No, not at all. But I need another—just like before."

A pause hung in the air before a reply came. "For the same person—a Dr. Cain, as I recall?"

Joan's eyes could finally make out the figure of a man sitting on the end of a long sofa, tucked deep into the shadows of the room. Feeling the need to assert herself, she took several steps in his direction.

"That's far enough!" the man said abruptly, stopping her short.

He had been just as elusive on her first visit, never allowing himself to be fully seen.

"No, this time it's for me," Joan said, hoping to keep the discomfiture from seeping into her voice. "I've recently discovered that I may have the need to disappear—permanently."

"I see," the man said simply. "So . . . you'll no doubt be needing a passport and an out-of-state driver's license, as well as a new social security number and credit cards."

"Yes, I need *everything*. And I need it right away."

The man gave a dry chuckle. "Slow down, slow down . . . For *quality* things such as these, one must be *patient*. And naturally, very well funded."

"When, then? And how much?" By this point, Joan was almost pouting.

"Three days. Fifty thousand," the man said coolly.

The amount, both of time and of money, was one Joan would not bend to. She shook her head. "A hundred thousand . . . in *one* day!"

The man chuckled again, his languid manner almost agonizing. "My, my—aren't we in a *hurry*? Very well, then. *Done.* Let's say, to-morrow afternoon at five." There was a short pause, and then he added, "All cash, used bills. Now, *go*."

Joan rolled her eyes as she turned to leave. "Whatever . . . weirdo," she muttered under her breath.

CHAPTER THIRTY-FIVE

JOHN CALLAWAY LAY ON HIS STOMACH ATOP THE TWO LIFE PRESERVERS, HIS SHOULDERS AND ARMS STRETCHED FAR OUT OVER THE ROCKY EDGE OF THE SMALL ISLAND. His hands held still, just above the water's surface, as hundreds of small silver fish crowded together just beneath him in the sparse pockets of shade the jagged ledge afforded them. Once again, he plunged his hand down into the school, hoping to grab hold of at least one of the elusive creatures. But just like it had in the dozens of attempts before this one, his hand came up empty as the fish all darted away together in a perfectly synchronized instant.

Thunder could be heard rolling in the far distance, and John looked long out into the horizon. Soft gray clouds were beginning to billow to the west, and the wind was occasionally kicked up by a gust. He turned his focus back to the schooling fish that were merely inches away from his grasp. Despite fighting to keep his thoughts on the task at hand, John's mind kept straying to a heaping plate of Miss Martha's soulful Southern cooking and a very large glass of her perfect sweet tea.

If only I had my old cast net from Savannah, he mused.

Looking further down underneath the ledge, John could see something waving back and forth in the current, partially buried beneath the white sand. It was a faded blue, with something metallic along the exposed edge. He reached for the long piece of driftwood still drying in the sun and used it to retrieve the curious object from the ocean floor. Once he'd dragged it to the surface, he was able to determine that it was a tattered section of plastic tarpaulin, measuring about three feet by four feet, with one lonely metal grommet remaining fastened to the corner. He spread the piece of tarp out on the ground underneath the solitary palm and used it as a place to lay out and inventory his possessions. Foremost placing his dive knife in the center of the tarp before he began removing the items from Molly's purse, he took time to appraise each object for its usefulness. He searched her wallet first, finding a receipt from their last shopping trip to the supermarket, along with her driver's license, credit cards, and $600 in cash. A shopping trip that had taken place just before they'd loaded the boat in Key West.

If only, he thought.

Next, he found a small case containing nail clippers, tweezers, a small pair of scissors, and a lightweight metal nail file. Appreciating the potential value of these items, he immediately placed them near the center of the tarp, alongside his knife. He then found a small container of dental floss. He pulled its length from the spool and visually measured it to be less than three feet. He would have liked to have had more, but this was reality, so he wound it around a small stick and added his find to the growing pile. Several papers and Molly's passport were near the bottom of the small bag. John opened the soggy passport and was instantly mesmerized by his wife's picture, her blue eyes staring out at him from there on the page, causing his emotions to build, and his dry throat tightened even more.

The splat of a heavy raindrop hitting the tarp pulled his attention away from the photograph and dragged him back to the present. He felt another drop hit his arm, followed by another onto the tarp and then another. Quickly grabbing one of the plastic bottles, he used his knife to slice the top third of it off, allowing a larger opening in which the raindrops could be collected. He placed his newly modified receptacle on the ground, away from the tree, and raked sand around its base to keep it from tipping. He bent his head backward, looking up to the sky and opening his mouth, expecting a temporary reprieve from his torment. A single drop found its way to his now thick tongue, and then, just as quickly as it had begun, the rain ended.

John desperately reached for the plastic bottle, only to find it, too, completely dry. Anger overtook him, and he hurled the bottle into the bushes below. He took the pill bottle from his pocket, counted what remained, and stowed it back inside Molly's otherwise empty purse before zipping it closed. He leaned the purse against the base of the palm in the narrow alley of shade and used it for a pillow, keeping his head tilted upward so he could still view the water, keeping a lookout for a passing boat, ship, or plane.

He lay without movement for the better part of an hour, noticing white contrails from commercial aircraft lingering in the sky above him and tracing them with his mind's eye, all the while trying to imagine where those white streaks might be leading to—or away from. At one point, he even saw a ship, but it was so far out that he was unable to determine if it was Coast Guard or not. Knowing he was most likely closer to Cuba than North America, he entertained—even welcomed—the thought of being picked up by the Cuban authorities. Those circumstances could be dealt with, but the ones he was facing now—he was not so sure. He dozed.

. . .

A deafening crack of thunder startled him awake. The soft gray clouds he'd fallen asleep to sometime before now loomed almost overhead and had turned to a dark purple, so dark that they were almost black. A flash . . . and then another loud *Bang*! He scrambled for the remaining plastic bottle and sliced it the same as he had the first, once again placing it in the open where it could receive the most exposure to this saving rain—or so he hoped.

Looking at the tarp and everything that lay upon it, John's slightly delirious mind was reeling. He quickly snatched up the items, stuffing them back inside Molly's purse, then took four slender sticks from the driftwood pile and pounded them a few inches into the hard ground as best as he could to form a square shape slightly smaller than that of the plastic sheeting. With this done, he cut a small slit into each corner of the tarp, carefully placing the four slits onto and over the tops of the four stakes so each corner was supported. The tarp now hung mostly flat, just a couple of feet above the ground, and John placed a palm-sized rock in the center of the tarp, its weight pulling the sheet down to form, in essence, a large funnel. On the underside of the tarp beneath the rock, he made a small hole using the tip of his knife and placed the plastic bottle directly beneath the hole.

And then he waited.

...

Buddy Sullivan walked through the front door of his Key West home utterly exhausted, and he knew that exhaustion was probably as plain on his face as his own nose. Brenda would be worried about how it was all wearing on him, he knew, but there was nothing to be done for that, not until they knew more about John. As Buddy passed through the front room, he saw Molly stirring slightly in the recliner. She looked restless but seemed to be dozing. He was taking careful steps so as not to disturb her, hoping she wouldn't awaken to ask questions about her husband—mainly because he didn't have any answers for her. Certainly not any she would want to hear, at least.

As Buddy entered the kitchen, Michael rose quickly from the place he'd claimed at the table next to Brenda, and his wife paused mid-sentence, no doubt in anticipation of what Buddy would have to say. He looked at them both with a defeated posture and, without speaking, shook his head.

Michael spoke up with genuine concern, "What do you mean? He couldn't have just vanished!"

Buddy knew in his heart of hearts that not only was that entirely possible, it was beginning to look probable. Trying to remain positive, Buddy finally spoke. "I can assure you that I won't stop looking until he's found—or that I'm satisfied that there really is no hope. The Coast Guard is continuing their search through the night from a cutter, but the air search is temporarily suspended due to the weather. It's certainly too unstable for Dennis's plane, but as soon as it's safe and if there is any daylight, we're heading back out."

"I'm going with you!" Michael insisted.

"That's a good idea, Michael," Buddy agreed. "An extra set of eyes can make a huge difference, especially in these conditions."

A few minutes later, Buddy was seated at the table showing Michael a navigational map, outlining the areas that had been covered so far and making note of more places to check once they could resume their search.

Brenda, meanwhile, had busied herself making lunch for the four of them. She was a bundle of nervous energy, and having somewhere to focus her mind had been imperative.

The landline phone mounted on the kitchen wall rang loudly, startling them all.

"Buddy Sullivan," Buddy spoke into the receiver after he'd hastily snatched it up.

A pregnant pause hung heavily in the air of the kitchen as Buddy listened to whomever was on the other end.

"Well, what could that mean?" he demanded, his face becoming solemn. "I see. Well, then—what will you plan to do next?"

Michael and Brenda both stood motionless, hanging on Buddy's words, as he continued to ask questions and nod his head.

Unable to bear it any longer, Michael interrupted. "What's going on, Buddy?" he asked as his pulse began to quicken.

Buddy held up a finger to Michael so he could continue the conversation. "I see. Well, please call me as soon as you have confirmation. Thank you." Buddy ended the call, hanging the receiver back on the cradle.

Buddy turned around to face his wife and Michael, trying to keep his voice down as he began telling them what the call was about. "The Coast Guard has located a life raft drifting about 120 miles southwest of Key West, roughly thirty-five miles west of Cuba."

"Is John okay?" Michael exclaimed.

"I'm not sure. The raft was fully loaded with supplies, but there was no one onboard."

"That poor boy . . . and girl," Brenda sighed as she motioned toward the front room where Molly was resting in the recliner, her heart breaking for the couple.

"What's going on? Where's John?" a frantic voice suddenly called out.

The three looked to the kitchen doorway, where Molly now stood, holding onto the doorframe for support. Michael reached for her, but she pushed him away.

"Tell me what's going on right *now!*" Molly demanded.

As Buddy relayed what they had just learned from the phone call, Molly shook her head in confusion.

"What does that mean? Please, tell me what that means!" she cried, desperation clear in her voice.

"The Coast Guard seems to think there's a chance John may have drifted into Cuban waters and was perhaps picked up by a patrol," Buddy said, hoping, even as they spoke them, that his words might keep her from breaking down. And that they might actually turn out to be true. "They're trying to get information from them now, but you know how difficult that can be."

Molly's face looked almost hopeful for a moment, but that look was short-lived. "Of course, it could also mean . . ."

Buddy hesitated and kept his words slow and his tone even. "It could also mean that John never made it onto the raft, at all."

A tear formed and ran down the length of Molly's face, clinging to her chin in defiance of gravity, refusing to let go.

"But Molly, sweetheart, that could be a good thing!" Buddy rushed on. "It could mean that he's still on the Morgan and the raft just got away from him somehow in the storm." He'd added the last part on his own, in an effort to calm Molly. The Coast Guard had not mentioned that, at all. He knew, at best, that scenario was unlikely.

...

John kneeled in front of his makeshift cistern. Of the few raindrops that had found their way onto the tarp so far, none had collected in his bottle. He thought of the first bottle he had so hastily thrown away, wishing it were close by now, in case he might possibly capture more than he was anticipating. Thunder and lightning were closer together now, letting him know that the worst of the storm would soon be upon him. The steadiness of the drops being caught within his crude water trap was increasing, and he clasped his hands around the bottle to keep it upright as it slowly began to fill. No longer able to resist the temptation, he removed the less-than-half-full bottle from beneath the tarp in hopes of gorging himself on it. One large mouthful in, he spat the water from his lips as salt assaulted his tongue. He realized too late that the initial collection had been laden with dried salt from the surface of the plastic.

Silently cursing his own stupidity, John carefully emptied what remained in the bottom of the tarp and started the process all over again, as the cool rain continued to wash everything clean.

After only a few minutes, he'd collected another half bottle, which he cautiously tested with the tip of his tongue. Though not quite pure, it was far better than the first batch, and he allowed a swallow to ease down his constricted throat. Discarding the remainder, he once again placed the bottle under the tarp to begin refilling. Halfway through the process, the rain started to lighten before ending altogether, and John held the bottle steady beneath the slow drip until it was filled to the brim. With shaking hands, he put the bottle to his lips and drank.

He stopped only long enough to shake two more antibiotics into the palm of his hand, chasing them down with more of the water that seemed to hardly touch the level of thirst he had reached.

As the last drops were consumed, he began to weep with the sudden realization at just how *little* it could take for a man to be truly happy.

CHAPTER THIRTY-SIX

THE HAMILTONS—CHARLES, CELIA, AND MILES—ALONG WITH THEIR GUEST, KNOWN TO THEM AS LYLA CAIN, ENJOYED AN EARLY DINNER ON THE AFT DECK OF LAW MAN. The ninety-foot motor yacht was cruising comfortably through the dark blue water at a steady twenty-three knots, roughly 120 miles southeast of Miami. The conversation was kept light and fun, with Celia making every effort to accommodate their guest and newfound friend.

"If the weather is good, the captain says we should reach St. John in about three days," Charles told the group as the dinner plates were replaced with four large slices of Key lime pie. No one wasted any time in devouring their dessert as the stories and laughs continued. On more than one occasion during dinner, Miles Hamilton's hand had managed to graze over Erica's bare leg—not likely an accident. She'd been successful in maneuvering herself away from his advances thus far, but he was growing bolder, and she was hoping to avoid a scene. He was in the process of subtly inching his chair closer to hers when the ship's first mate interrupted their gathering.

"Mr. Hamilton, sir, the captain has asked that you please join him on the bridge."

Charles responded without hesitation and excused himself from the table.

"Hurry back, dear. You don't want to miss our first sunset at sea," Celia implored.

What on earth could that be about? Erica wondered anxiously.

Miles could not have been less interested in the matter and continued bantering with his new crush. Fifteen minutes later, Charles Hamilton returned, a look of concern etched on his face as he stood beside the table without moving to reclaim his seat.

"What's the matter, dear? Is everything okay?" Celia questioned.

Charles was obviously distracted, delaying his response. "Oh yes, dear. I'm sure everything is fine. We just need to make a quick stop in the Bahamas, and then we'll be on our way."

Celia seemed puzzled. "The Bahamas? Is there a problem with the boat?"

Charles reassured her as best as he could without going into detail. "Oh, I'm sure everything will be fine . . . just a technical difficulty. It will be sorted out quickly enough," he said, his eyes cutting to Erica.

She suddenly felt nauseous. Until that moment, she'd had no concern at all that this unplanned detour had anything to do with her. Now, she was absolutely sure it did.

...

Joan used her personal cell phone to call Michael. It had been two days since she'd hung up on him, and she was beginning to wonder why she'd not heard back from him. It was unlike Michael *not* to pester her, and, considering the circumstances, she would have expected more from him at this point. She listened as the call went directly to his voicemail without ringing—not even once.

Frustrated, she ended the call without leaving a message, her mind whirling as she wondered what to do next. Even as she glanced back down at the phone in her hand, thinking she might try again to reach Michael, it rang and vibrated, the suddenness of it startling her. She didn't recognize the number on the caller ID, so she let the call continue unanswered. A minute after the ringing stopped, a familiar chime indicated a voice message.

Giving in to curiosity, she retrieved it.

"Miss Taylor, this is Agent Copeland. I need to speak with you as soon as possible. The matter is urgent. Please return my call." His voice was dry and monotone, much like his personality.

She was in no hurry to speak with him and, in fact, would try her best to avoid him altogether.

If that was possible.

. . .

Wanting to make sure no loose ends were left to dangle, Joan drove to the Callaway office building. She felt a sense of urgency to clear the secret drawer in John's desk of its remaining contents, in the event that she may not have the chance to return. She circled the building once and avoided the parking garage, instead choosing a space at a nearby pay lot. Walking down the opposite side of the street from the office building, she tried to go unnoticed by anyone who might recognize her. Just before stepping off the curb to cross the street, a dark SUV with tinted windows—followed by the same gray van she'd seen in John's driveway—pulled to a stop in front of the main entrance. She pivoted, quickly entering a small cafe, and seated herself at a table by the window with a clear view of the office door. A waiter immediately appeared at her table, but she quickly dismissed him, saying she needed a moment to decide.

. . .

After a few minutes, she watched as Agent Copeland and an un-identified man in a similarly generic suit exited the SUV and walked through the large revolving door into the lobby of the building. She only had a partial view through the window, due to the obstruction of the van, but she could see the two men speaking to the security guard at the front desk. She watched the guard pick up the phone and nod his head several times before hanging up. After that, he led the two men over to the elevator and accompanied them onboard. Once the doors had closed, she wasted no time leaving the cafe and getting back to her car. Her heart raced as she tightly gripped the steering wheel, her fingers wrapped around it as though she were strangling it. Blindly shifting the car into drive, she sped away from the lot, with no real destination in mind.

...

Erica sat on the end of the queen-sized bed in her beautiful state-room, staring at the Louis Vuitton bag on the dresser in front of her. She replayed the past two days in her mind, wondering how she'd allowed herself to be trapped on this boat with literally nowhere to run.

Everything to this point had all seemed to work out perfectly for her.

Perhaps *too* perfectly.

Had one of the crew recognized her?

Or perhaps it was the captain himself.

Then again, maybe she was just overreacting, her guilty conscience rearing its ugly head.

Either way, she needed a plan—and a quick one, at that.

She scanned the room, not knowing exactly what she was looking for, but she knew she would know it when she found it. Making her way around the entire cabin, Erica pressed on the walls, then looked inside the cabinets and closets. Because of limited space, even on a vessel this large, engineers were very creative in designing storage compartments. There were large drawers beneath the bed, two on each side, just a few inches above floor level. The drawers were about three-feet wide by two-feet deep. With this noted, she removed blankets from one of the drawers and wiggled it free from its track. Once the drawer had been removed, she was happy to see a four-inch gap of empty space between the floor and where the bottom of the drawer would rest, once it was replaced.

Erica worked quickly, placing the stacks of bills beneath the bed, her mind rolling over the fact that if she were caught with the money, a self-defense plea would hold little weight.

Right now, this hiding spot might very well be her only option. Besides, the person being sought for questioning was Dr. Lyla Cain. The few who knew her as Erica Payne, an employee of Callaway Development, were accounted for—as far as she knew. After she finished placing the stacks, she added her passport, credit cards, and everything else that identified her as Erica Payne.

There was a light knock on the door.

"Lyla, dear . . . are you okay?"

She frantically worked the drawer back onto the track as she answered, trying to keep her tone as even as possible. "Yes, Celia. Thank you. I just think I may have gotten a little seasick."

She heard the knob rattle on the locked door, so she hurried to put some of her clothes into the bag, then sat it back on the dresser. Rushing into the head, she splashed water onto her face and then flushed the toilet.

"Well, dear, you know the best thing for seasickness—short of being back on land, that is—is fresh air," Celia's disembodied voice said through the door. The knob rattled again.

Erica exhaled as she crossed the floor of the room and opened the door to let Celia in. The older woman reached for her arm, her face clouded with concern. "You poor girl! Let's get you up on deck and feeling better. We'll be in port soon."

Erica forced a wan smile. "Thanks."

. . .

Michael paced back and forth on the front porch of the Sullivans' home. It had been several hours since they'd heard from the Coast

Guard; and, having never faced a dilemma even remotely close to this, he was having a hard time even conceiving what to do next. He weighed the pros and cons in every possible scenario, but the odds were never once stacked in his favor, no matter what the outcome. After much self-debate, he gave in and went to his car, cranked the engine, and powered on his phone.

Joan answered on the first ring, "Where are you, Michael?" she demanded without greeting.

"I'm in Key West, Joan," Michael responded coolly.

"Key West? What are you *thinking*? The FBI is looking for you, you know!"

"I had hoped they wouldn't be—but it may not even matter, after all."

"*Of course* it matters, Michael! Don't be foolish!" she snapped.

"There's been an accident, Joan. It involves John and Molly." His tone had taken a more solemn note.

"What do you mean? What kind of accident?"

"A boating accident," Michael replied. "Molly is okay for the most part, but . . ."

"But, *what*?" Joan was almost yelling.

"But John is still missing. The Coast Guard is searching, but things don't look too good right now."

There was a pause before Joan spoke again. "What exactly do you mean by *missing*?"

"There was a storm about a hundred miles off the coast a few days ago. John and Molly were separated, and Molly was found—alone—on an island, suffering from exposure. She told us that John was injured and had swum off by himself to try and save the boat, but she never saw him again." Michael's voice began to get shaky. "This afternoon, the Coast Guard called with news that they'd found a life raft loaded with supplies, but John was not in it. That's all we know for now."

The severity of Joan's initial shock was settling down a bit as she listened to Michael recount the story of how John Callaway had come to be lost at sea. Her thoughts swirled around the idea that maybe, somehow, this tragedy could work to her advantage.

What better scapegoat could there be?

CHAPTER THIRTY-SEVEN

A LIGHT DRIZZLE WAS ALL THAT REMAINED ON JOHN'S SIDE OF THE STORM. HE WAS DISAPPOINTED BY THE FACT THAT THE RAIN HAD BEEN SO BRIEF, AS HE DESPERATELY NEEDED MORE WATER. On the other hand, he was grateful for what he did have and tried to remain positive as slow drips continued filling the bottle beneath the tarp.

He took some time to examine his leg. Although it was not healing, it didn't appear to be any worse. Fortunately, the doses of amoxicillin seemed to be staving off further infection. He didn't feel as though he had a fever, but it was hard to tell with the level of sunburn he was experiencing. As the mist gathered on his skin, his body jerked with a chill.

He needed food.

The hunger that gnawed at his empty stomach seemed to grow as if awakened by the realization that he couldn't even recall the last bite of food that had crossed his lips. Once again, he went off to search the jagged edges of his desolate temporary home for anything he could scavenge. The storm had pushed more debris toward the tiny island, but so far none of it appeared to be of any use. While surveying the shallows, he observed the small silver fish still amassed there by the thousands, studying their movements as he tried to figure a way to get his hands on them. The water churned suddenly, followed by a violent splash as a tail slapped the surface of the water. A few seconds later, two more surprise attacks were sprung on the unsuspecting fish, which had swiftly become a meal to a much larger fish. Seeing this invigorated his spirit, empowering him to take action.

John searched the further recesses of the small island, a difficult task that meant traversing through the thorny brush and tangled mangrove limbs, for anything that might help him create a makeshift spear. The driftwood pieces were not feasible, nor were the gnarled, crooked branches of the mangrove trees; and so, he continued hacking his way through to the other side of the tiny island. It was slow going, given the size of his dive knife. He would have given anything for a machete.

The opposite shore was sandy, a stark contrast to the hard, sharp edges of the coral he'd been dealing with thus far. The soft slope permitted easy access into the water, and he waded along the rim into the knee-deep surf, allowing the saltwater to clean his wound. Feeling something unnatural beneath his foot, John reached into the sand and found a short length of coax cable. He pulled it free, surprised to find that a section of fiberglass radio antenna was attached at one end, broken off to a length of about four feet. The slender rod was splintered where the break had occurred. With the antenna in hand, he made his way through the dense brush and back to the lone palm.

He could see the large fish, most likely a dorado, still feeding near the rocky ledge.

Time to make good use of his fortunate find.

John removed the nail file, which was about five inches in length, from the small case in Molly's purse. He pressed the flat base of it down into the shattered end of the mast, allowing roughly half of the pointed end to protrude, then gathered the splinters around the file with his hand. He used his free hand to wrap the full length of the dental floss around the splinters to hold the file tightly in place. Though his hands stung from the fiberglass shards, he took solace in the fact that his task was now complete.

Holding his breath in anticipation, he measured the spear's sturdiness by pressing the tip against the palm tree. It gave only slightly when moderate pressure was applied.

The beginnings of a smile tugged at the edges of his parched lips.

This would do quite nicely.

Once again, John lay on his stomach atop the life jackets, his arms outstretched over the water. This time, however, his hands held a weapon, a means to hunt. And so, it began.

The beautiful, large fish were wary of his looming presence and shied away from the edge at first. But he continued to hold his position, not flexing a muscle or blinking an eye, as he allowed the creatures to slowly feel more at ease. After a while, they began to swim in closer. One even bumped the side of his spear with its tail, but John was not in a good position in which to strike. Suddenly, a school of the tiny fish came rushing toward him, closely pursued by a large dorado. John slowly eased the spear back a few inches, and then, at the last moment, he quickly thrust it forward, impaling his prey clean through, near the base of the dorsal fin. The strong fish froze stiff, showing obvious signs of a fatal strike to the spine. This was a fortunate mishit for John, since the fish was much larger than he could have handled had a fight ensued. John quickly grabbed hold of the tail and, using his last reserves of strength, hoisted his catch from the sea. Dragging the fish over the rocks, he estimated its weight to be at least thirty pounds.

Though the sun now hung low near the horizon, his day had just gotten brighter.

Tonight he would sleep with a full stomach.

Not wanting to soil the tarp, he found a flat spot in the rocks on which to clean his catch. Taking knife in hand, he made an incision behind the gill until his blade found bone, then turned the blade on its side to work his way along the ridge of the backbone all the way to the tail, removing the entire side of the fish in one complete piece. He laid the fillet, skin side down, on the flat rock and worked his knife between the skin and the flesh of the fish, sliding his knife forward from the tail until the skin had been completely cut free. Once done, he held up his prize and admired the beauty and purity of this pristine white fillet.

He divided the entire slab into eight equally sized pieces, barely able to slow his movements as he surveyed his bounty. He chose one and bit into it, the texture noticeably chewy but the flavor good. He took another bite before his ravenous hunger seemed almost to consume him, driving him to devour half of the eight large slices in mere minutes.

Temporarily sated, he continued working on the remainder of the fish until he had twelve pieces of what could be considered "prime sushi" laid out before him. He wished he had a fire on which to grill or smoke some of the meat, but that would have to wait. He'd not yet figured out a way to create a flame.

Using the six feet of nylon rope he'd found earlier in the day, he threaded the fillets onto it so that they hung down evenly in a neat row. He dipped the meat into the ocean, allowing it to be drenched in salt water, before tying the rope between two limbs of a nearby mangrove tree to be dried out—and hopefully preserved.

His stomach quieted, John rested.

...

Miles away in Key West, Molly was growing restless. The light of day was beginning to fade, and nothing more had been reported about her husband. She felt totally helpless as she sat in quiet solitude, waiting for word.

Not unlike the cliché, she was hoping for the best yet fearing the worst.

The front door opened and Michael stepped inside, taking a seat on the sofa opposite from her in the Sullivans' front room.

Not wanting to be overheard, he spoke quietly. "I just got off the phone with Joan, and I told her everything that was going on."

"What did she say?" Molly asked.

Michael cleared his throat and lowered his voice to just above a whisper. "She said that the FBI is looking for John . . . and me. They were at the office today."

Molly's volume elevated as she replied to the words that seemed unbelievable to her. "This is ridiculous! I'm calling them right now to find out what's really going on!"

Michael nodded his head in defeat. "I understand how you feel, Molly. I would like to know that, myself. Can you do me one favor, though?"

"What?" Molly asked.

"Can you *not* tell them that you've seen me—for now, at least? I think that, under the circumstances, it's best for me to get back to Atlanta. Hopefully, before they realize I'm gone."

Molly nodded without hesitation. "Sure, Michael. I can do that. But remember—at the end of the day, it's my husband I'm most worried about right now."

Michael stood to leave. "Understood."

Through the front window, Molly could see Michael speaking to Buddy Sullivan on the porch. She couldn't hear what they were saying, but she watched the two shake hands before parting.

Picking up the handset of the Sullivans' phone, Molly placed a call to Joan.

. . .

Seeing a Key West phone number on her caller ID, Joan assumed it to be Michael again and answered on the first ring. "What *now*, Michael?"

There was a brief pause.

"Joan, it's Molly." Molly's voice wavered as she began to cry.

Joan softened her tone to reply. "Oh, my dear girl. I'm so sorry. I just spoke to Michael, and he told me what's happened. It's horrible, Molly. Just horrible."

"What am I going to do, Joan?" Molly implored, her voice labored. "I can't lose him. I just can't!"

Joan chose her words carefully as she tried, in her own way, to comfort Molly. "Calm down, dear. We're not sure of anything yet. For all we know, John could be on his way back to you as we speak."

There was another pause from Molly's end of the line. "I'm just not so sure, now. They found—" a sob broke Molly's words. "They found a life raft, and he was hurt and . . ."

"Molly, I need for you to calm down and listen to me, okay?"

Molly didn't respond.

"I need you to call me the *very minute* you hear anything at all about John. I'm handling things here in Atlanta, so I need for you to handle things down there, okay?" Joan said, her voice even and her words succinct. Now was the time to stay levelheaded.

She could hear Molly blowing her nose.

"Joan, what's going on with the company?" she sniffled. "Michael told me that the FBI—"

Joan cut her off, her voice sharper this time. "Molly, like I said, I'm handling things here. There's nothing for you to worry yourself with right now. So do what I ask, and we'll talk again soon."

"But Joan!"

The line fell silent.

Molly dropped the phone into her lap, put her face in her hands, and wept.

CHAPTER THIRTY-EIGHT

IT WAS NEARING 7:00 P.M. WHEN LAW MAN ENTERED PORT AND PRE-
PARED TO DOCK IN NASSAU, NEW PROVIDENCE ISLAND, IN THE BAHAMAS.

Erica stood alone at the stern, gripping the railing so tightly her
knuckles were beginning to turn white. Celia approached her from
behind, gently placing a hand on Erica's shoulder.

"Dear," she murmured, "Charles has asked me to let you know
that there are some people here who need to speak with you."

Erica remained silent, biting her lower lip in an attempt not to
show emotion, as Celia continued. "I can't imagine what this is all
about, and I'm sure that it's all a misunderstanding. You just be yourself and be truthful, and you'll be fine—you'll see."

Erica wanted to laugh out loud at the sheer absurdity of what
Celia had said.

Instead, she remained stoic and simply nodded in agreement,
wondering if Celia could see the tears that pooled in her eyes.

A man in a suit, accompanied by a constable, met Erica at the top
of the gangplank. With a hand on each of her arms, the two men escorted her down the ramp and toward a waiting car. *Law Man's* first
mate followed closely behind with her luggage and her purse. Before
entering the vehicle, Erica managed to glance back over her shoulder
to see the Hamilton family standing there together, watching everything unfold.

Miles gave her a small wave, trying to go unnoticed by his parents,
and she returned his gesture with her signature winking smile.

He blushed.

The car ride was silent, and the plain sedan found its way to the center of the city, pulling to a stop in front of an official-looking building. Erica was let out and once again escorted by the two men, in the same fashion as before. This time, however, she was led into a small, plain room containing only a steel table that was flanked on either side by a bench bolted to the floor.

Erica asked the men several times what this was all about and if she was under arrest, but she was met only with silence.

The door slammed shut behind them, leaving her there to wait and wonder.

...

Fifteen minutes passed, and the door swung open to allow a dark-skinned man wearing a badge and a friendly expression to enter the room. Staying silent, he sat down across from Erica and placed a manila file on the table between them.

He smiled.

Erica's first observation of the man was of his physical presence— namely, the perfect teeth that somehow managed to outshine her own.

She complimented him. "What a lovely smile, Mister . . . ?"

The man's expression became serious as he finally broke his own silence. "I am Captain Pinder of the Royal Bahamas Police Force. I want to ask you some questions—with your permission, of course?"

Erica tried her best not to appear nervous, but it was a struggle, given her anxiousness to find out the extent of what he knew.

"Well, Mr. Pinder," she said, pausing for effect as she corrected herself. "I'm sorry, *Captain* Pinder—what is it that you would like to know?"

Resting his forearms on the table, he leaned forward.

"I would like to know what your involvement is with one Gregory Kline, of Atlanta."

Erica mimicked the captain's movements by leaning forward onto the table, smiling as her next words left her lips. "I want an attorney."

The man's eyebrows lifted slightly. "If you are referring to Mr. Charles Hamilton, I'm afraid he is already back at sea and can be of no help to you." Captain Pinder's broad smile returned, while Erica's expression remained unchanged, save for the clenching of her jaw muscle, which, in turn, caused her cheek to twitch slightly. "However, if you are speaking of someone else, I'm certain that can be arranged." He patted his hand twice on the steel table, stood, and left the room, failing to take the manila file folder with him.

Fairly sure that she was being observed but unable to contain her curiosity, Erica used a fingernail to lift the cover of the file. Inside were graphic photos of the alleged crime scene in Key Largo, including several pictures of Greg Kline's mangled body. Feeling nauseous again, she withdrew her finger and let the file close, then pushed it away from her side of the table.

Once more, she waited.

. . .

John sat with his back against the lone palm. Now that he'd eaten, his only thoughts were of Molly.

Surely she's been found and is safe by now—but why haven't I been saved? Why has there not been a boat, a plane, or another human within miles for days now?

He couldn't help but wonder if, perhaps, the weather was playing a large part in hampering his rescue. But there wasn't a hurricane to contend with—just typical tropical weather. As far as he could tell, anyway.

He needed to know that Molly was okay. She didn't deserve this— any of it. Guilt's weight rested heavily upon him as he resigned himself to spending another night alone and unaware of anything else going on in the world outside of the miniscule space he'd confined himself to. Before allowing himself to rest, John removed the plastic bottle from beneath the tarp and studied it. It was less than half full. Feeling confident about being rescued soon, he drained it, using the last swallow to take two additional antibiotic pills. The water now only carried with it a hint of salt. With each fill, it was becoming fresher. He reached over to feel the consistency of his hanging fish. It was still somewhat spongy, but he knew that by tomorrow the sun would do its work and he would be able to enjoy his fill of dried fish sticks.

...

Over an hour had passed since Captain Pinder had left Erica alone in the room to wait. She was growing restless, and she needed to use the bathroom. Rising from the bench, she moved to the door and tried the knob out of sheer curiosity.

She was hardly surprised to find it locked. Left with no alternative, she knocked on the cold surface of the door several times without getting a response.

She began banging harder, sharper, in a demand to see someone so that she could be let out.

After a moment, she heard the jingle of keys and watched as the doorknob was turned from the outside. She took a step back to allow the door to swing open.

A man in a dark suit entered and asked her to have a seat. She didn't recognize him as being one of the men she'd seen when she was being led through the building earlier.

"Are you my attorney?" she ventured.

The man merely smirked, again instructing her to take her seat on the bench, this time more insistently.

Erica refused to comply, her feet rooted to the floor where she stood. "I demand to use the restroom!" she fumed. "I have not been placed under arrest! If you're my lawyer, then get me out of here—*now*!"

The man's voice remained infuriatingly calm and unwavering as he replied. "We will get to all of that in a moment. Right now, I need for you to take your seat, Dr. Cain."

Erica reluctantly did as she was told, anxious to find out the depth of her troubles.

The man sat down on the bench opposite her, neatly folding his hands together on the table in front of him. It was then that he finally introduced himself.

"My name is Donald Copeland, and I am a lead agent with the FBI. Would you like to tell me why you think it is you've come to be here today?"

Erica's mouth suddenly went dry. "Am I under arrest?" she stammered.

Agent Copeland's response was quick and matter of fact. "Not at the moment. But let's give it some time, and we'll see."

Being a trained psychologist, Erica knew exactly what he was trying to do. He wanted to come across as non-threatening, almost nonchalant, in his attempt to garner information from her—classic reverse psychology tactics, something she was well versed in.

Realizing her responses would need to be indirect without seeming too vague, she began.

"I assume this is about that man who was killed on the highway in the Florida Keys—am I correct?"

Agent Copeland nodded. "Tell me the nature of your relationship with the man."

She arranged her expression into one of confusion. "*Relationship?* I don't understand what you mean. There is no relationship!"

Copeland smirked. "Then tell me, Dr. Cain, exactly how did you come to be a passenger in his vehicle?"

Now reeling, she barely managed to maintain her composure as she replied. "I met him a few days ago in Miami, at a restaurant near my hotel. We talked for a bit and then took a drive to watch the sunset at some place he knew. He asked me to go to the Keys with him later that night, but I turned him down." She shrugged. "I suppose he went anyway."

The agent watched her carefully. "Did you see him with anyone else at any time after you refused his offer?"

Feigning innocent frustration, she chose her next words with caution. "Look, I told you—he asked me to go with him, but I refused. He took me back to my hotel, and I never saw him again—end of story!"

Copeland shrugged his shoulders. "Simple as that, huh?"

She leaned forward to speak, slowing her speech and deliberately emphasizing each of her words. "Simple. As. That."

The agent calmly reached into the inside pocket of his suit jacket and produced a small digital recorder, placing it upright on the table between them. He pressed a button near the top of the device, and a small red light began to flash.

"Where's the money?" he asked suddenly.

Erica feigned ignorance and annoyance, narrowing her eyes at him. "Money? What are you *talking* about? What money? He didn't have *any* money, as far as I knew!"

The agent nodded, his clear skepticism a direct contradiction of the movement, before he spoke again. "What do you say we start this again? This time, from the beginning—*Erica*."

At the sound of the name being declared, Erica felt her jaw clench and her face twitch. A direct punch to her stomach could not have felt worse than the blow she'd just been dealt.

"I want an attorney—*now!*"

...

It was nearing midnight as Lyla Cain sat anxiously at the interrogation table, now alongside the only lawyer she'd been able to procure at a moment's notice. He was less than ideal; but, under the current circumstances, he would have to suffice. Working on an ancient laptop, the barrister typed out the last paragraph of an agreement that, if accepted, would allow his client to escape prosecution—in exchange for full disclosure.

The document was handed over to Agent Copeland for review. The tentative agreement was conditionally accepted, based on the testimony to be given and the level of her involvement in the death of Greg Kline.

This time in the presence of her attorney, Agent Copeland again engaged the recorder.

He spoke a few words, and then she began.

"I first met Joan Taylor a little over three years ago. She had been referred to me by a colleague who no longer felt able to treat her. Joan wasn't crazy. Well, at least on paper, she wasn't. In fact, she was extremely intelligent. Her mental anguish stemmed more from resentment."

Agent Copeland interrupted. "Resentment? How so?"

"She felt that she had been somehow wronged—first, by her father. Then once again, later in her career."

"I see. Please continue," he said.

"Shortly before I began treating Joan, I had gotten married. The relationship was violent and abusive, almost from the start. Though I kept my personal life very private, Joan was quite intuitive and quickly picked up on it. Soon, I found myself confiding in her, just as she was confiding in me."

"How often did you counsel Joan Taylor?" Copeland asked.

"In the beginning, it was once a week. But later it became twice per week. I had stopped charging her for the extra sessions over the past year, feeling somewhat guilty for using much of that time to discuss my own issues and abuse. Eventually, she approached me with an idea, a so-called 'way out' of my predicament. It was a chance to start over—a new name, a new life, a new me."

"Why did you feel the need to go to such extremes?" the agent asked.

Her expression changed, as though a light had gone out inside of her. "Because my husband told me that if I ever left him, he would kill me—and I had no reason to doubt him."

She continued speaking for the better part of an hour.

By the time she spoke her last words, the last remaining measure of her resolve was spent.

CHAPTER THIRTY-NINE

THE MORNING WAS OVERCAST AS DENNIS AND BUDDY STOOD IN CON-
VERSATION NEAR THE FLOATPLANE AT THE FUEL DOCK.

"What are you thinking, Buddy?" Dennis asked, his voice somewhat hoarse and a bit shaky—no doubt after another night of revelry
at the Green Parrot or Captain Tony's.

"I really don't know what to think, Dennis. The authorities seem
a little less hopeful after finding the empty raft, but since there's been
no sign at all of my boat, I'm not sure that all hope is lost."

Dennis nodded. "Well, I'm willing to have another look as soon as
these clouds lift if you're up for it."

Buddy was grateful for Dennis's ready offer of help and agreed
to go with him at the first opportunity. Finalizing their plan, Dennis
said, "I'm flying a couple of guys up to Marathon to meet a fishing
party, but I should be back by noon. Maybe by then the weather will
have improved."

The two men shook hands and parted.

...

A violent commotion jerked John awake, and he was momentarily
disoriented.

He'd slept much harder than he'd expected.

In front of him, more than a dozen squawking seabirds were engaged in a frenzied fight over John's hanging fish fillets. He attempted to scare them off by yelling, but little more than a slight squeal escaped from his constricted vocal chords. He reached over to the pile of driftwood and slung several pieces into the flock, yet this did nothing to stop the vile creatures from ravaging his food supply. Steadying himself, he stood and hurried toward them, wildly swinging his makeshift crutch and finally driving them away. With the flock now cleared, he angrily surveyed the damage.

On his scale, it measured catastrophic.

Only a few small pieces of the drying flesh remained threaded on the nylon rope. Hastily plucking the remainder, he decided to eat them now rather than later, accepting the reality that he would have to land a second fish if he wanted to eat again on this day.

Checking the bottle still positioned beneath the tarp, he was dismayed to see that it held less than one inch of water. There had been little dew during the night and zero rain showers. Observing the gray sky above him, however, he felt that it all but guaranteed another downpour. And, based on this rationalization, he swallowed the liquid along with two more of the remaining six antibiotic capsules.

Now with spear in hand, John began making his way along the edges of the coral and scouted for dorado. Only a few of the small baitfish were gathered in schools at this early hour. He hoped the heat of the day would bring more of the tiny fish to the sanctuary of the shadows and crevices of the jagged rock, which would certainly encourage the dorado to feed once again. Using one of the life vests as a seat cushion, he positioned himself in such a way that he could thrust the spear in multiple directions when the time came and then settled in to wait.

Buddy and Brenda were sitting on their front porch, doing their best to engage Molly in light conversation and distract her from the harsh reality she'd been thrust into. Despite Brenda's insistence that she remain behind and continue to recover, Molly was dead set on going along with Buddy and Dennis when they resumed their search for John. Buddy agreed with his wife, however, knowing that any flight out with Dennis did not automatically guarantee a round trip. Finally giving in to their wisdom, Molly reluctantly agreed to stay behind with Brenda in Key West.

"I don't understand why we haven't heard anything from the Coast Guard today," Molly murmured.

"I'm sure they're doing what they can to find John, but there's a lot more ocean out there than I think you realize, Molly. The Gulf Stream itself is a tricky thing. It can carry a boat or a person many miles in a short period of time," Buddy explained. "That, along with the weather that we've had the past few days, has complicated things even further."

Molly's expression appeared shut down. Brenda lightly laid a hand on Buddy's arm in a way that let him know he'd probably said enough. Sensing he'd upset the situation further, Buddy excused himself from their company, saying he was going to meet Dennis and would be back as soon as he could.

Brenda offered to make lunch, but Molly remained silent, showing no interest in food.

...

Despite a light drizzle, Dennis was airborne an hour later and on a southwest heading with Buddy in the seat beside him. "Any word at all on the Coast Guard search, Buddy?" he asked.

"Not a word," Buddy replied.

Dennis shook his head. "It's odd to me that no debris has been spotted. That leads me to think that your boat is most likely still afloat, but if that's the case, the Guard should have found it by now. Unless, of course, the Cubans got to it first!"

Buddy winced. "The Coast Guard said the same thing. Makes me wonder if they might be more certain of that possibility than they're letting on, which would definitely make them less eager in their search."

"Well, I hope that's not the case. But you know as well as I do that if it turns out to be true, then it's a whole different ballgame," Dennis observed.

Buddy nodded his head in silent agreement, his eyes trained on the water below.

They continued their course at an altitude of a thousand feet and flew beneath the clouds.

...

It was just after noon and although it was still overcast, John could begin to see more small fish gathering close to the rocks beneath him. He hoped that larger fish would soon follow, as fatigue and thirst were wearing on him. It seemed that the more he tried to focus on the task at hand, the more his mind wandered aimlessly through a melancholy cloud of random thoughts. His mood perked up a bit, however, when the water less than ten feet in front of him began to swirl. He adjusted his stance closer to the edge so that he would be able to make a solid strike as soon as the opportunity presented itself. Another swirl, and then a flash of green and silver sped past—just out of reach of the tip of his waiting spear.

John could feel the last reserves of adrenaline coursing through his veins, feeding his muscles and sharpening his hunting instinct. He tried to control his breathing so that he would be able to remain steady and sure on the slippery rocks on which he stood. For a moment, he thought he heard a faint buzz, similar to an engine sound, far to the east. But it quickly disappeared, swallowed up in the thick clouds.

The water calmed, but John's focus remained constant, as he knew full well that his next chance at a target might be his last. The buzzing returned and, for an instant, he swung his head in the direction of the sound. Almost at the same time, a large dorado made its presence known just to the left of where John was standing. A quick twist of his body caused John to lose his footing, which sent him headfirst into rocks and coral on the ledge beneath him. An instant flash of white light blinded him just before he lost consciousness.

· · ·

Dennis attempted to make radio contact with the Coast Guard on several occasions, but to no avail, given the fact that his radio range was greatly diminished by the poor conditions. He and Buddy were hoping for an update or—even better—news that John had been found. Rain began pelting the windshield of the aircraft, and visibility became limited to just a few hundred feet. Left with little choice, they made the decision to return to Key West until conditions improved.

· · ·

Molly was sitting on the front porch swing at the Sullivans' when Brenda brought a cordless phone out to her. "Molly, dear, your friend Katie is on the line for you. She says it's urgent."

Molly quickly grabbed the phone from Brenda, fearing the call had something to do with Afton or her father. "Katie, what's wrong?" Molly's voice rose with dread.

"I'm not exactly sure, but something weird just happened," Katie replied, sounding miles and miles away to Molly's panicked ears.

"What are you talking about?"

"Well, I was just watching the news, and there was a story about a missing lady, a doctor of some kind from Atlanta. She's been taken into questioning somewhere down in the Bahamas, and—get this— her real name is Lyla Cain, but she's been operating in Atlanta over a number of weeks under the assumed name of Erica Payne!"

Hearing the name made Molly nearly drop the phone. "*What*? But Erica worked for Michael—she's not a doctor!"

Katie went on to relay more of the little information she knew. "It doesn't make sense to me, either. But, apparently, this woman's husband reported her missing more than a month ago."

"This is crazy, Katie!" Molly exclaimed, rushing on to tell her friend about what was going on at the firm. She asked about Afton and then told Katie she needed to make some calls and would be back in touch.

Disconnecting from the call with Katie, Molly dialed Michael's cell.

He answered almost immediately. "Please tell me you have good news?"

"Well, I have news," she replied, "but I'm not quite sure what to make of it."

As Molly repeated what Katie had just told her, Michael listened silently, replaying the past month's events over in his mind while he tried his best to make sense of it all.

His attempt was unsuccessful.

"Molly, as soon as I'm back in Atlanta, I'm going to contact the agent who questioned me. I'll try to find out more of what's going on, so please sit tight until I call you back—unless, of course, you have news of John. In that case, call me immediately!"

Molly agreed to wait, albeit reluctantly.

The wind speed was increasing, driving taller waves and smashing them into the tiny island where John now lay drifting in and out of consciousness. The continuous thrashing caused his limp body to be pushed around on the sharp pieces of exposed coral, further aggravating an already dire situation. There were moments when his eyes would open and he would attempt to move, but the pain in his body and the severe concussion prevented any advance toward safety. Tightly wedged into a crevice only a few inches above the water, he was once again at the mercy of an angry sea.

CHAPTER FORTY

MOLLY PACED THE KITCHEN FLOOR WHILE BRENDA BEGAN MAKING PREPARATIONS FOR AN EARLY DINNER. She was trying her best to explain to Brenda the series of events that had unfolded over the past weeks, but it was difficult, especially in light of the fact that she was so unclear about everything herself.

"Molly, honey, it sounds to me like you should call the authorities yourself and get to the bottom of all this. If nothing else, it might be a good idea to let them know what's going on right now with your husband," Brenda suggested.

She knew Brenda was right, and it was taking all of her resolve not to do that very thing. Even so, she was torn, having made a promise to Michael to wait. She didn't necessarily want to get him into serious trouble if it could at all be avoided.

Still weighing her options, she asked Brenda if she could use a computer she'd seen on a desk in another room, wanting to search for any information available on Erica Payne's capture. Brenda obliged and a few moments later Molly was reading through several news articles she'd found on Google. The first showed a picture of Dr. Lyla Cain and gave a brief overview concerning her disappearance from Atlanta nearly five weeks earlier. Although both the picture and the article seemed surreal, it was most definitely the woman she'd seen John leaving the restaurant with that awful day. The article went on to explain that she was a well-respected psychiatrist who'd practiced in Atlanta for almost four years. There were some quotes in the article from a few of her colleagues and even one from her husband, all pleading for her return.

The second article had been posted only a day before, and it gave more information about the doctor and her recent apprehension in the Bahamas—detailing the events of the hit-and-run near Miami and naming the victim as one Greg Kline, a native of Atlanta who was known to work frequently in construction. Lyla had been sought in connection with the incident that was now being labeled a homicide. It took only a split second for the name Greg Kline to register with Molly. She'd heard it mentioned several times in the past few months when John had spoken about the large development deal for the resort in the Bahamas. Subsequent articles were more of the same, just a redistribution of the facts by different news outlets. One article, however, did mention the fact that Dr. Cain had been frequently using an alias and had been apprehended aboard a private yacht bound for the British Virgin Islands.

A bewildered Molly continued scanning articles for the better part of an hour, unable to find a story or any information linking Erica— *Lyla*—to Callaway Development. And there was no mention at all of the $2 million Michael had told her about. One article *did* state that she was in the custody of the FBI and had been transported back to Atlanta for further questioning.

Molly wanted answers. She needed to know how the authorities might be trying to tie her husband to this tangled mess of deceit— and now possibly even murder. It made no sense whatsoever, and she needed her husband now more than ever. Certainly, he would be able to fix things, just as he always had. She reached for the phone and quickly dialed a number.

Fifteen minutes later when Buddy Sullivan walked through the front door of his home, Molly practically leapt from the chair she'd been sitting in and rushed toward him. "Buddy, please tell me that you have John!" Her plea was soaked in desperation.

Buddy looked sullen, and Molly's eyes began to well with tears.

"I wish I could tell you that I did, Molly, but I can't. I'm at a loss, to be honest. Between my searches with Dennis and the Coast Guard's, we've covered several thousand square miles. He's just not anywhere to be found."

Molly stood shaking in silence, using all of her might to hold back the flood of emotion that she felt she was drowning in.

Watching her carefully, Buddy went on. "There's still a very good chance that he was picked up by the Cubans, so it might be a good idea to try to contact the State Department. Maybe it's time to get them involved. Surely they would have a better chance than us at finding out if that's the case."

Molly nodded. "I'll contact the authorities, then, if you really think that will help."

Breaking into their conversation, Brenda walked into the front room to announce that dinner was ready, and Buddy brought her up to speed on the situation.

"I've already made a call to our pilot, Charlie, who's on his way now to Key West," Molly said after Buddy finished speaking. "He should be here in about an hour and a half. I think it's best that I go back to Atlanta to check on my daughter. I may even bring her back with me when I return first thing in the morning."

Although he was somewhat surprised that she would leave under the current circumstances, Buddy agreed to drive her to the airport and pick her back up when she returned. She made him promise to call her should there be any news of John—good *or* bad. After a quick meal with the Sullivans, Molly was taken to Key West International, where she only had to wait a short time for Charlie's arrival.

...

On the return flight back to Atlanta, Molly did her best to update Charlie on the accident, leaving out the details and developments that were transpiring at the firm. She wanted to be careful about divulging any information she, herself, wasn't exactly sure of. Sensing her uneasiness, Charlie asked her no further questions but still offered any assistance he could provide, and she graciously thanked him for his concern.

Once they arrived back at Brown Field, Molly asked to use Charlie's phone, wanting to call the Sullivans for an update. With anxious hope, she waited for good news, but there was none to be reported. The weather had deteriorated even further in the search area, and the Coast Guard's effort had been suspended. Still, Buddy reassured her that he would continue to search on his own for as long as it took and that he would pursue the Guard in urging them not to give up. Molly thanked him again and said she would most likely see them the following day.

After thanking Charlie and reminding him of her tentative plan to return to Key West, she retrieved her vehicle from its parking spot inside the Callaway hangar. Now behind the wheel without access to a phone, she made her way toward Katie's house, feeling blind and disconnected, oblivious to the fact that she was driving without a license or identification.

Before anything else, she needed desperately to see Afton. Once she'd had a few moments with her daughter, she would call Michael to let him know she was back in town, with plans to speak with the FBI.

She pulled into Katie's driveway just as the kids were getting home from school. The second she saw her mother, Afton ran and practically dove into Molly's waiting arms. Molly barely noticed her own fatigue or the pain she'd been suffering from the sun exposure that had burned and blistered her skin, as she squeezed her little girl tight.

Katie hurried to greet Molly and help her into the house, and once the kids were settled the two women found a quiet place to talk.

"Katie, what am I supposed to do?" Molly asked her friend, desperate for some guidance. "I can't make any sense at all out of what's going on!"

Katie held tight to Molly's hand, searching her heart for the right words, but none would come.

Molly's voice was shaky as she went on. "I can't even bear to think of what might have happened to John or what he might be going through right now. I can't, Katie—I just can't!"

Katie did her best to keep Molly calm by reminding her that as long as she had hope she still had John.

...

After contacting Michael and getting Agent Copeland's information, Molly steadied herself and made the call.

Copeland answered on the first ring.

"Agent Copeland, my name is Molly Callaway. My husband is John Callaway."

He seemed professional and interested without sounding overly eager when he replied. "Yes. Mrs. Callaway. I've been trying to reach your husband. Have you spoken with him?"

Molly replied hesitantly, wondering if he might really be as uninformed about everything going on as he seemed. "No, sir. I haven't. Actually, there's been a terrible accident." She recounted the events of the past week to Copeland, noticing that his voice seemed to have taken on an anxiousness that hadn't been present before.

"Tell me where you are, Mrs. Callaway. I would very much like to speak with you in person."

She thought for a moment and decided it best to move the situation away from Afton for the time being, agreeing to meet at the Callaway offices in an hour.

Borrowing Katie's cell phone, she used it to call her father while she drove to the meeting. She was disappointed, but not surprised, that the call went unanswered.

Probably just as well, since she had nothing new to report, anyway, and it would have only worried him further.

She decided next to call Joan, thinking it might be a good idea for her to meet at the office, as well. It couldn't hurt to have Joan's input and for her to help fill in any of the missing details Molly might not have the answers to.

Besides, next to John, no one knew the inner workings of the firm better than Joan.

"Joan Taylor," the voice on the line said coolly.

"Hello, Joan, it's Molly."

There was a pause. "Hello, Molly—I'm sorry, I didn't recognize this as your number."

"It's not," Molly replied. "I had to borrow my friend Katie's phone. I'm back in Atlanta."

Joan's voice rose an octave. "Atlanta? Can I assume, then, that John is with you and all is well?"

Tears constricted Molly's throat for a moment, keeping her silent as she tried to regain her composure. "I wish that were true, Joan. But no, he's not. And I'm only going to be here for a few hours. I came to get Afton, and then we'll be heading back to Key West first thing in the morning. Right now, I'm on my way to John's office to speak with the FBI."

Molly could sense agitation in Joan's voice when she replied. "The FBI! Why would they want to speak with *you*? Are they aware of what has happened to John?"

"Yes, Joan," Molly sighed wearily. "I've already spoken to Agent Copeland on the phone, and he requested this meeting. I felt like you should be there, too, if you can."

Feeling a sense of urgency to stay in control of the situation as much as possible, Joan agreed to the meeting and began to hang up.

"Wait, Joan," Molly said. "There's something else."

"What is it, Molly?" Joan asked, no longer masking her aggravation.

"They found Erica—or Lyla—or *whatever* her name is!" Molly replied.

There was no denying the fact that Joan was obviously unsettled, as she began stumbling over her words. "Wait—what do you mean, 'they *found* her'? *Who* found her?"

"The FBI, Joan! They found her somewhere in the Caribbean. She was on a boat or something, and now they have her! It's all over the news!"

There was no response from Joan—only silence.

Curious, Molly glanced at the display screen and saw the words, "Call ended."

CHAPTER FORTY-ONE

DUSK BEGAN TO SETTLE OVER THE DAY AS JOHN FOUGHT THE URGE TO GIVE IN TO SLEEP. The occasional wave drenching his body served as a sobering reminder that his next breath may very well be his last. His mind was drifting back and forth from conscious to subconscious thought, and the images that flooded his mind were as real to him as anything he'd ever seen.

Molly, in a yellow sundress, stood at the edge of the sea peering out, her arms folded tight against her body, her face racked with anguish and despair. His outstretched arm strained to touch her, but the distance was too great. She fell out of focus—then out of sight.

He was looking down from a high bridge, his attention drawn to an old man who was casting a net from the bank of a river. As the net was released, the man looked up at him, and those piercing, dark eyes locked with John's as he felt his entire body being entangled in the net. He struggled to free himself but only worsened his predicament. He fought the tug on the retrieving line, as its pull tried to force him over the railing and into the depths below.

A salty wave slammed fully into John's face, granting him a momentary reprieve from delirium. The water that remained in the shallows around him was now stained pink as the wounds from his flesh drained freely. He reached above his head and tried to find a handhold, a way to pull his body back to the relative safety of higher ground. The rocks around the lowest edges had been worn smooth by the constant wash of the tide, and he was unable to secure his grip. He let go, and once again his body settled into the crevice.

His eyes closed tightly against the sting of salt as his shrill screams for help were swallowed up by the emptiness around him.

See you when the sun wakes up, Daddy!

Afton's words seemed so real to him that his mind wrestled with the logic that they were only imagined. His eyes fluttered open, and he fully expected to see his daughter there with him. His only greeting was from yet another wave. And, this swell being larger than the ones before, it managed to lift his entire body from the rocks and set him adrift. He gulped air into his lungs in an attempt to stay afloat, as his limbs were so battered and weak they were useless in any attempt to tread water. While the current pulled him away from the tiny island, his singular focus was trained on the lone palm. It was more than a reference point to him; it was a beacon of light in his otherwise dark and murky world.

With his last measure of hope and resolve now drained from his mind and body, John gave into the reality that now lay upon him like a heavy, inescapable weight. His last murmured words were to Molly and Afton as he allowed himself to be wholly swallowed up by the unforgiving sea.

Beneath the waves, there was no salty sting, no pain, no struggle.

Only quiet emptiness.

As the light in John's mind grew dim, he imagined what felt like a pair of strong hands guiding him to some other place, a place of safety.

A voice reached his ears and, though he couldn't make sense of the words, they somehow brought him comfort.

And then, at last, all was dark.

...

In Atlanta, Molly was escorted into the conference room at the Callaway offices. She was introduced to Agent Copeland first, followed by several of his colleagues. Joan had not yet arrived, but Copeland was clearly anxious to begin.

"Mrs. Callaway, thank you for meeting with us today. I'm sorry it is under such grim circumstances. Has there been any news of your husband?"

Molly cleared her throat before speaking, hearing the somber tone of her own voice. "Unfortunately, no, there hasn't been." She paused. "Can you please tell me what's going on?"

Agent Copeland nodded, his face softening a bit with understanding. "I'm sure you have a lot of questions. I'll certainly do my best to tell you what I can, based on what we know so far."

Molly listened intently as the man laid out the details based on the information that had been collected from Erica Payne, the woman formerly known to the world as Dr. Lyla Cain.

"First and foremost, Mrs. Callaway—"

Molly interrupted him. "Please, Agent Copeland. Call me Molly."

He nodded and continued. "*Molly*, there are details I am not at liberty to disclose to you at this time. But, I *can* tell you that we recently apprehended a female who was first sought for information on the role she was alleged to play in an extortion scam involving your husband's company. We later found out that this same individual was connected to a hit-and-run homicide in South Florida—albeit it under a different name. After intense interrogation and further verification, we have learned that she was, in fact, a psychiatrist who had been treating Joan Taylor for the past three years. We have also learned that she was making an attempt to flee from a violently abusive husband."

Molly listened anxiously as he went on, her spinning mind silencing any questions that might have risen to her lips.

"It was our first thought that your husband was somehow involved in the illegal transfer of funds under the guise of a large development deal in the Bahamas I'm sure you're familiar with."

Molly nodded, finally finding words. "Yes. John has been working on this deal for months, but he would *never* do anything criminal."

Copeland gave a curt nod before going on. "That being said, in light of recent testimony by the woman in custody, we have reason to believe that the documents bearing your husband's signature were forged by his COO, Joan Taylor."

At his words, the color drained from Molly's face. "*Joan?* That's *crazy*! They've worked together for too many years to count. What reason could she possibly have to do something like that?" Molly's head was spinning, and her hands began to shake. "That doesn't make any sense! You must be mistaken—I've just spoken with her, and she's on her way here now! She'll be able to explain everything, I'm sure!"

Agent Copeland glanced silently at one of the other gentlemen in the room, sending him to the lobby to await Joan's arrival.

"Molly, I appreciate that this is a lot to take in, but hear me out. Maybe then, you'll understand things more clearly."

She took a sip of water from a glass in front of her as she tried to sort through her thoughts.

"According to the sworn testimony of Lyla Cain—known to you as Erica Payne—she had agreed to take part in a scheme designed solely by Joan Taylor, which would effectively set things in motion for her to take control of Callaway Development. It was Ms. Taylor's intent to replace your husband as president and CEO, and her original plan engineered Erica's employment at the firm so that she could seduce John. Ms. Taylor believed it would both distract him from his work and destroy your marriage. It was her hope that your husband would lose all credibility when accusations of impropriety were brought forth. According to Dr. Cain, your husband neither initiated nor reciprocated any advances or attempts she made toward him."

Molly could hardly see past the tears that had begun to well in her eyes. "I still don't understand *why*! John has *always* been so good to her, and she even worked for John's father before that!"

Agent Copeland shook his head. "We're not completely certain of Ms. Taylor's motivation at this point, and I'd rather not speculate.

We hope to have those answers after we've had a chance to question her."

Molly stood from the table and began nervously pacing the room, her mind traveling in a thousand directions at once. "There has to be another explanation for all of this—there just has to be!"

"I understand that you're overwhelmed, Molly. Anyone would be," Agent Copeland said quietly.

"What about Greg Kline? What's his involvement in all of this?" Molly asked.

"According to what we know so far, Joan hired Mr. Kline to pose as the head of one of the primary construction companies involved in the resort deal. From what we've been able to discern, both Lyla Cain and Greg Kline were to be paid $1 million each for their parts in the ruse. Dr. Cain has stated that, upon meeting Mr. Kline in South Florida to give him his share of the money, he attempted to kill her and take everything for himself. In the course of defending herself, she unintentionally killed him and then fled the scene. However, the funds were not recovered, and we have yet to determine if this was part of Joan's plan or simply Mr. Kline's own idea of a double cross. Due to Mr. Kline's criminal history, we have reason to believe Dr. Cain's testimony regarding his role in this."

Seeing that she was visibly shaken, Copeland asked Molly if she needed a moment to gather herself. She shook her head and insisted that he continue.

"I must point out that we have only one side of a very elaborate story. And, while we have no reason to doubt its truth at this time, we can't verify that until we have spoken to everyone involved. I truly hope that your husband is found safe."

"Thank you," Molly murmured. "But no one wants him home safe more than me."

One of the other FBI agents knocked on the door and asked to speak to Copeland. He excused himself for a few minutes before returning to thank Molly for her time and understanding. He left her with his card and asked that he be contacted at the first news of John. Drained of energy and emotionally exhausted, she agreed and took her leave.

She walked down the silent halls into John's office, noticing the subtle scent of his cologne hanging lightly in the air around her. Her emotions pinballed from love to anger to hurt and back again. She let her body collapse limply into the soft, worn leather of his desk chair, staring blankly at nothing.

And then she noticed it.

A small sliver of paper jutted out from a decorative piece of side molding on the desk, and she leaned forward to pinch the tiny corner of paper between her fingertips, attempting to pull it free. Unable to loosen it, Molly slid open the adjacent desk drawer to find an oddly large space between the side of the extended drawer and the outer edge of the desk, leaving her puzzled over where the piece of paper might actually be protruding from. She retrieved a sharp letter opener from John's desk to pry the molding free, hoping to loosen the trapped document. By working the opener along the edges of the trim, she was able to remove the entire panel. Her efforts revealed a small, hidden compartment, where she found two paper documents along with a small leather pouch containing several color-coded thumb drives.

Molly frantically scanned a handwritten letter addressed to John's father informing him of the impending birth of a child whom the writer claimed that John Callaway Sr. had fathered. Seeing the letter's date, Molly realized that John Sr. must have been in college, because it was certainly long before he had met and married John's mother, Vivian.

In silent astonishment, she read through the remainder of the letter before moving on to the second document. Reading its official title, Molly's breath caught in her throat, and her mind began to reel.

BIRTH CERTIFICATE

Child's Name: Joan Catherine Taylor

Father's Name: John William Callaway

Molly's vision blurred as shock overtook her.

If she was reading this right, the papers meant that Joan was John's sister. But if that was the case, why had it been kept secret? The only person she felt would have the answer was John's mother—unless she, too, had been kept in the dark.

So many questions in need of an answer, with so few people left to ask. Mystified by her discovery, Molly secured her findings in her purse and left the office to head back to Katie's.

Joan could be left to the FBI to deal with—if she did, indeed, risk showing up.

For now, Molly had other matters to attend to.

CHAPTER FORTY-TWO

IN THE EARLY MORNING HOURS OF THE FOLLOWING DAY, KATIE SUTHER-
LAND RUSHED TO OPEN THE GUEST-BEDROOM DOOR OF HER HOME, WITH
A PHONE IN HER HAND.

"Molly, wake up!" she almost shouted as she forced it into her
friend's hand.

Having slept very little during the night, Molly was in a fog of
confusion as she struggled to wake up. "What is it? What's going on,
Katie?"

"The phone, Molly, the phone—it's for you!"

Molly slowly put the receiver to her ear, still unsure of what to
expect. "This is Molly," she said, her voice thick with dread.

"Molly, dear, it's Brenda Sullivan." Molly sat upright in bed as
words tumbled from her mouth. "Brenda, what's wrong?"

Before Molly could ask anything further, Brenda broke in, "John's
been *found!* He's *alive!*"

Molly felt the room spin around her as both panic and relief flooded her. "Where is he, Brenda? Can I talk to him?"

Molly's rapid-fire questions overwhelmed Brenda's ability to keep
up. "Molly, honey, I need you to slow down and listen to me, okay?"

"Is he alright?" Molly choked out as tears filled her eyes.

Brenda's voice came calm and clear from the other end of the line.
"John's been airlifted to Baptist Hospital in Miami. He has some injuries, and I don't think he was conscious when they found him. Buddy

is on his way back home to get me, and we're driving to the hospital. I think it would be a good idea if you came as soon as you can."

The words had barely settled in the air before Molly thanked Brenda for the update and disconnected the call, tossing the phone aside as she rushed down the hall to wake Afton.

Fifteen minutes later, Molly, Afton, and Katie were en route to Brown Field to meet Charlie, planning to fly to Miami while Katie's husband remained behind with the twins so that Molly could have her friend's support for the trip. Once the preflight checks were completed, Charlie wasted no time getting airborne.

The sun was just beginning to light the low clouds when the plane touched down at Miami International. During the brief flight, Molly had made several attempts to speak with the hospital but was given little information. Wanting to waste no time on the ground, she had also made arrangements for a private car to take them directly to Baptist Hospital.

...

John had been taken from the emergency room to have an MRI and a CAT scan performed. Molly had yet to see him and was growing more worried and anxious by the minute. As her agitation reached its limits, one of the first doctors to treat John finally came out to speak with Molly.

"Mrs. Callaway? I'm Dr. Lindsey. I treated your husband when he arrived here a little over two hours ago."

"Is he okay? Is he going to be alright?" Molly's words were frantic.

The doctor placed a hand on her shoulder to calm her. "Fortunately, most of his injuries are superficial cuts and bruises and should heal fine, but there was some infection in a leg wound." The doctor reached into her outside coat pocket and pulled out a small prescription pill bottle and handed it to Molly. The bottle still contained two capsules. "We found these in his pocket. We aren't sure how many he's taken, but they might well have saved his life."

Tears began to stream down Molly's face as she realized what the pills were, and she silently thanked God that she'd forgotten to dispose of them.

The doctor continued. "What we are most concerned with now is a head injury—he seems to have suffered a severe concussion and was unconscious when he arrived. He's been in and out, but his vital signs are good, all things considered. We'll know more once we've reviewed the scans."

Molly's concern grew deeper with each word the doctor spoke. "Can I see him now, please?"

Dr. Lindsey shook her head. "Not just yet. We will be taking your husband to ICU in the next few minutes, but once he's settled in a room, you'll be able to go in and be with him."

Molly took a minute to calm herself before walking back into the waiting room. She didn't want to upset Afton any further, so she chose her words carefully and said simply that the doctors were fixing Daddy and that they would all be together again very soon.

Molly had only just finished reassuring Afton when the Sullivans approached, and she hugged them both, grateful for their help and care. She apologized over and over for everything that had happened and for the loss of the Morgan.

"Don't apologize, Molly, dear. You've been through so much," Brenda soothed.

"Besides," Buddy teased, adding some levity, "I've been thinking about getting a new boat to replace that old Morgan, anyway."

Molly managed to laugh a little through her tears.

It had not occurred to Molly until that moment to ask where and how John had been rescued.

"I was going to tell you about that, Molly, as soon as we knew John was okay," Buddy said. "It's a bit of a strange thing, actually."

Molly tilted her head in silent confusion.

"Some early-morning fisherman found him unconscious on the end of the pier near Smathers Beach, back in Key West. Not sure how he got there but so far no one has claimed responsibility."

"Is it possible that he swam there?" Molly asked.

Buddy shook his head. "That's not likely, Molly, and I would even go so far as to say it's impossible. The search area was more than a hundred miles from where he was found. The Coast Guard and local authorities are investigating, but the working theory right now is that it may have been someone wanting to remain anonymous. Believe it or not, a lot of clandestine activity still goes on in the straits between Key West and Cuba."

In an effort to distract herself while she waited to see her husband, Molly pondered the possibilities of John's rescue. Coming up with none that were truly plausible, she called her father to give him the news, grateful to find that he actually answered the phone this time. He was happy to have heard from her and told her that he would drive down from Thunderbolt as soon as he finished changing the oil in his old truck.

Insisting that such a far travel on his own would only worry her, Molly's father reluctantly agreed to remain at home until he heard back from her. At eighty-seven years old, the stubborn man and his abilities still never ceased to amaze her.

Moving down her mental list, Molly placed a call to John's mother.

Vivian sounded grateful and relieved when she heard the news that her son was safe but, in light of the fact that the severity of his injuries was still unknown, told Molly that she would be on the next available flight to Miami. Molly apologized for not bringing her along earlier that morning, but her anxiousness to get to John had left her little time to think or prepare. Vivian quickly forgave Molly and reassured her that she'd done the right thing.

As per her promise to let him know if there was any news of John, Molly's final call was to Agent Copeland. The call was routed to his voicemail, so she left a detailed message describing the current situation. With that done, she was left to wait until the doctor allowed her to see her husband.

...

On a private airstrip in Grand Cayman, a chartered plane landed and taxied toward a waiting car, its lone passenger being one Joan Taylor, traveling under her new identity—Laura Hinson. She deplaned with a single piece of luggage and made her way to the car, locating the keys above the visor just as she'd instructed. Once she'd taken her seat behind the wheel, Joan engaged the navigation system and entered the address for Cayman National Bank.

She needed to make a withdrawal—a very large one.

...

Molly walked quickly to her husband's side as he lay motionless and unresponsive in the ICU at Baptist Hospital. She gently lifted his hand and held it, being mindful of the abrasions as she leaned in and softly kissed his bruised cheek.

"John, I'm here," she whispered. Maybe hopefulness was clouding her judgment, but she thought she could feel the pressure of a light squeeze on her palm. Nonetheless, it was a glimmer of hope that spurred her on and she continued speaking to him for the better part of an hour before hearing Dr. Lindsey's light knock on the door to announce his arrival.

He told her, in layman's terms, that, due to the severe concussion John had sustained, some swelling had occurred in John's brain. In addition to causing his lack of consciousness, the swelling was also of great concern, as there could be further complications that might arise. On a positive note, however, there wasn't any noticeable bleeding, so it was more of a waiting game to see if his body would heal itself.

Though Molly was given no guarantees, the doctor felt hopeful that John would soon regain consciousness. Should that be the case, he would most likely not suffer any permanent damage. She thanked Dr. Lindsey repeatedly and rushed out to the waiting room to share the news with everyone.

For the remainder of the day and throughout the night, Molly visited her husband's bedside as often as the doctors would allow. Occasionally, his eyelids fluttered and he made low groaning sounds, proof enough to Molly that he was fighting. His mother came in once during the night and spoke to him, and while he was still unconscious, Molly noticed a distinct change in his facial expression. His heart rate monitor increased, further confirming to Molly that her husband was still with her.

...

The next morning, Molly met Katie down in the hospital cafeteria. She'd not eaten anything in more than a day, and it was beginning to wear on her. The previous night, Vivian had taken Afton to a near-by hotel; and after breakfast, Molly suggested that Katie go there to rest and shower, while Molly promised to do the same once Katie or Vivian had returned later in the day. Molly hugged Katie and headed back to the ICU.

Just as Molly passed the nurses' station, one of the uniformed women looked up and smiled.

"Someone's been asking for you."

As the nurse's words registered in her brain, Molly rushed into John's room to find him being examined by a doctor who was making his early morning rounds. The doctor stepped aside, and John managed a small smile for his wife.

"Hello, beautiful. I've been looking for you." His words were strained and barely audible, but they were there.

Overwrought with emotion, Molly was unable speak. She just held his hand and squeezed tight—she was never going to let go.

...

Much to her relief, John continued to improve over the course of the day. Molly was reluctant to mention any of the things going on with Joan and the company just yet, however, wanting to make sure he was *really* okay and not wanting to overwhelm him with any potentially devastating news. For now, those things would wait.

John's mother visited again, and he asked to see Afton. The doctor told them that, as long as he continued to improve, he could be moved to a private room as early as the following morning and his daughter would be allowed to visit.

From that moment until the next day, Molly never left his side.

CHAPTER FORTY-THREE

THOUGH FAR FROM WELL, ON JOHN'S SECOND DAY OF RECOVERY, HE WAS BEGINNING TO FEEL MORE LIKE HIMSELF. As he began recounting the past week's events to his wife, neither of them were surprised to find out they'd shared many of the same thoughts of each other at the exact same time, despite the fact that they were physically separated and miles apart. These seemed to Molly like the feelings her grandmother used to describe to her when she would talk about kindred spirits.

"Molly, I'm so sorry I left you that day and swam to the boat," John said quietly. "I promise I'll never leave you like that again."

Molly offered a feeble smile. "Fortunately, I don't imagine there will ever be another scenario where you'll have to make a choice like that again." Her lip began to tremble. "I thought I'd lost you for good, John. I've never felt so scared and alone."

John inwardly cursed himself for putting his wife in that position, now realizing all the mistakes he'd made—not just the ones over the past week but also those he'd made over the past few years that had led them to this moment.

Hoping that he might have remembered something, Molly asked again about the details of his rescue.

"Honestly, Molly, it all seems like a dream—a dark dream that I can't fully piece together. I remember standing on the edge of some rocks trying to spear a fish, and the next thing I knew, I was floating in the ocean." John strained to recall what had actually happened, but the images only came to him in split-second flashes. Sometimes there was the image of a man with what he thought to be silvery white hair, but he was mostly out of focus and indiscernible from reality or imagination. "I do remember hearing a man's voice—but that's it. It was unfamiliar, and I can't recall anything beyond that."

. . .

Molly allowed John to rest, taking that time to stop by his mother's hotel room for a shower and give everyone an update. She changed into some clothes she had borrowed from Katie, spent an hour visiting with Afton, and then returned to the hospital.

During the return drive, Agent Copeland called her. He thanked her for letting him know that John had been found alive and informed her that he would wait a few days before questioning him back in Atlanta. He went on to say that an APB had been issued for Joan Taylor, who had apparently been neither heard from nor seen in several days. There was reason to believe she'd possibly fled the country, but that had not yet been confirmed.

. . .

When she arrived back at John's room, Molly was surprised to find Michael there, speaking with John. As she stepped further into the room, it became clear that John had been quite agitated. She turned to Michael for explanation.

"I'm sorry, Molly. I spoke out of turn—I assumed John already knew."

"No Michael, he didn't know!" Molly retorted, not bothering to keep her anger at his thoughtlessness in check. "I was waiting until he felt better. He's been through enough stress already, don't you think?"

Michael looked away from her, his face flushed with shame. "I suppose you're right. Really, I *am* sorry."

As he watched the exchange, John's head ached from the effort of trying to process all that Michael had told him. None of it even sounded plausible, much less factual. Molly asked Michael to excuse them, needing time to speak to her husband alone.

Once they were alone, John spoke. "What's going on, Molly? None of this makes *any* sense to me. It's not possible—not even for Joan. She may be devious, in her way, but she's never been unscrupulous or malicious. I need to speak to her."

"The FBI would like to speak to her, as well," Molly said. "But she's gone."

John snapped back, "What do you mean—*gone*? She can't just be *gone*! Where would she go? And, more importantly, *why*? She has no cause to do anything like this!" His mind swirled with questions that seemed to tangle themselves.

Sensing his increasing stress, Molly decided the time had come to show him what she'd found. "John, take a breath . . . I need for you to see something," she said quietly. "Maybe it will help you make sense of all this."

John's hands shook as he inspected the documents, unable to believe that the words he was reading could be true. But there they were—boldly written in official black ink that was now indelibly printed in his brain.

He had a *sister*—a secret that had been kept from him his entire life.

Knowing his father to be a proud but honest man, John's only explanation was that he had been ashamed of his promiscuity but that, in his own way, he had tried to do the right thing by literally paying for his mistake. Perhaps it had been his father's way of accepting his responsibility to care for his child, while at the same time keeping her hidden.

"I'm sorry you had to find this out this way, but it was something that I felt I could no longer keep from you," Molly murmured. "I found this two days ago, hidden in your office. To be honest, I wasn't sure if you already knew and might be keeping it from me, for some reason." Molly said, feeling the edge of shame creeping in at the suspicion she'd allowed to enter her mind.

John's tone was calm now as he replied. "You did the right thing, Molly. Thank you for showing this to me." He shook his head. "But no, I had no idea at all. This is all just too unbelievable." Once again, John stared at the pages in his hands, still shaking his head in utter confusion.

There was a light knock on the door, and Vivian Callaway peeked in. "How's everyone doing?"

Molly looked at her and offered a small smile before patting John's shoulder and kissing him lightly on the forehead. "I'm going to leave you two alone for a bit," she said, rising from her seat. As she passed by John's mother on the way out, she spoke to her, "I think your son has something he'd like to ask you about."

Vivian had a puzzled look as she approached her son's bedside. John handed the documents to his mother, taking a deep breath before he spoke. "What can you tell me about this?"

Vivian's heart dropped at the sight of the papers she now held, the blood draining from her face.

"Something about your reaction, Mother, tells me that you're not nearly as surprised as I was just a few minutes ago. Have you always known?"

She thought carefully before choosing her words. "No, John," she said, her voice just above a whisper. "I haven't always known. I only found out about a year before your father died—this was a big part of the reason we'd separated shortly before his death. To tell you the truth, I think the stress of all this is what finally killed him."

"Why was this such a big secret, Mother?" John pressed. "What was so bad that it all had to come to *this*? Make me understand, please!"

"John, you have to understand that back in those days having a child out of wedlock wasn't something you even *talked* about. By the time he found out about the pregnancy, your father had already started dating me. And had my parents known about it, they would have put an end to our relationship. So he kept it a secret—from *everyone*," Vivian explained.

"Then how did she end up in his life? In *our* lives?" John demanded.

"According to your father, Joan's mother had given her the details of his identity just before she started college. He strongly believed that her mother's intent was to extort money from him—which, of course, worked." Vivian shook her head in frustration. "Your father let his pride get in the way, and he wanted to keep me from finding out."

"So, how *did* you find out?" John asked, watching his mother's face carefully.

"Evidently, Joan used your father's secret as leverage against him, thus securing her place in the company after college. Purely by coincidence, I'd seen a check amount that had been written to her, and when I saw how much she was making as your father's secretary, I actually accused him of having an affair!" A bitter little laugh escaped her lips before she went on. "It was only after I threatened to leave him over it that he came clean about the whole thing. After that, I couldn't decide if I was angrier about the possibility of him cheating on me or the fact that he'd lied to me for literally our entire life together. That's when I left him."

"But you never divorced him," John said.

"No, it never came to that, John. And to tell you the truth, I had almost forgiven him. He told me he'd figured a way out from under her. I always assumed it was to be some kind of settlement, but he died a week later; and, to my knowledge, the matter was never resolved."

Empathizing with his mother, John expressed his deep regrets for all his father had put her through during their marriage. He also told her of his plans going forward with the company. It was something he'd not yet had a chance to discuss with Molly, so he asked that she keep it between the two of them for the time being. She agreed readily, glad for the glimmer of hope she was seeing in all of this.

"I hope, John, that you'll forgive me for not telling you about all of this myself," Vivian said softly. "I was only trying to spare your father's legacy to you. I'm just so glad that you've finally figured out a way to be happy on your own. I love you, and I'm grateful to have you back where you belong." She learned forward and kissed his cheek.

"I love you, too, Mother." John paused, looking deep into his mother's eyes and smiling. "You've always known what I needed, even when I didn't know myself."

...

Molly was spending time with the Sullivans in the waiting room, excited to be sharing John's progress with them. Once they felt confident that John was no longer in danger, they planned to have a quick lunch and head back to Key West. Tears filled Molly's eyes as she thanked them again for all they had done to help her family find their way back to each other; and, seeing John's mother pass by the window, she excused herself from Buddy and Brenda to make her way back to John's room.

"How did it go, babe?" Molly asked, sitting on the edge of the bed and taking John's hand in hers.

"It actually went better than I could have expected. I feel like a weight was lifted off my mother, and I think I have a better idea of why things happened like they did." He paused thoughtfully. "It also helped me have a little better understanding of my father."

Molly arched a questioning brow at him and waited.

Taking a deep breath, John began to explain all that his mother had told him. Molly had always been amazed at how well John was able to handle adversity. More often than not, he was able to find the good in most situations and in most people. She believed it was one of the major reasons for his success in business.

"How do you do it, John?" she asked, once he'd finished.

"Do what?" he replied, genuinely puzzled.

"Navigate problems so well."

John smiled, and Molly saw a gleam in his eyes. "Calm seas don't make good sailors, Molly."

She smiled back at him. "That just reminded me of something I was told my grandfather used to say. You're quite clever, you know."

John chuckled. "Obviously, so was he." As the words faded so, too, did his smile. In its place was a look of apprehension. "Molly, there's something else I want to talk to you about."

She nodded, feeling a knot grow in her stomach. "Okay—what would you like to talk about?"

He squeezed the hand he was already holding and reached out to grasp the other, his eyes serious.

"You're scaring me, John. What's going on?"

He shook his head and allowed his expression to soften. "Nothing for you to be scared about, babe—quite the opposite."

Molly sat silently, waiting breathlessly for what he might say next.

"There will be some very big changes in our lives, and I'm hoping they're changes you can agree to live with," John said at last.

Molly's heart raced as she hung on his every word.

"I have decided to relinquish control of Callaway Development to Michael—at least, for the time being—until I figure out what I need to do with it."

Molly shook her head. "I don't understand what that means. What are you saying?"

"I'm saying that I don't want it anymore—*any* of it. I've seen what it did to my father and mother. And through all of this, I've seen what it almost did to us. I'm not willing to risk what I now have with you for anything in the world."

Molly's eyes began to fill with tears at his words, tears of the best kind.

Tears of true happiness.

"I'm sorry it took such tragic circumstances for me to finally realize it's not about how much it takes to truly be happy—but just how little."

EPILOGUE

IN THUNDERBOLT, MOLLY CALLAWAY FINISHED PUTTING THE FINAL TOUCHES ON HER CANVAS.

She had fully cleaned out her mother's old studio above the marina store and made it her own. She tried almost every day to spend time there, getting lost in the brush strokes and then finding herself again. Downstairs, John busied himself with the daily details of running the newly renovated marina.

Nearly two years had passed since the couple had chosen to permanently relocate themselves and their now nine-year-old daughter, Afton, to Savannah. The move had been a choice they had never once second-guessed nor regretted, giving them a quiet life of simplicity, and they each cherished every precious moment of it. Molly's father, now almost eighty-nine, had finally given into the idea of an assisted-living community but still spent a lot of his time on the dock, sitting in his favorite old rocker. He still enjoyed telling old stories to anyone who had a notion to listen.

The marina, which included *Sweet Afton* herself, had been gifted to Molly by her father on the day she'd moved back home. The beautiful schooner had only recently been returned to her homeport after undergoing a fully detailed restoration by Charleston Shipworks. The entire project had been documented by *Sail Magazine* and featured on the cover of the previous month's issue. The beautiful sailing ship being hailed as the "Pride of Savannah" now displayed herself proudly at the brand-new docking slip constructed especially for her.

With only two weeks left until summer break, John had made careful plans and preparations for his little family of three to take an extended Caribbean cruise aboard the newly rededicated sailing yacht. He was going through some of the final details when a FedEx envelope was delivered to the door. Noticing the sender as Charleston Shipworks, he quickly opened it. Enclosed along with its contents was a handwritten note.

> *Dear Mr. Callaway,*
>
> *Thank you for allowing Charleston Shipworks the honor of restoring* Sweet Afton. *It was our sincere pleasure to be afforded the opportunity to work on such a masterfully crafted vessel. Enclosed, you will find several documents, including a single photograph that was discovered aboard during the restoration process. It is my pleasure to return these personal effects to you, as I am sure you will find value in them.*
>
> *Sincerely,*
> *T. Hurley*
> *Charleston Shipworks, Inc.*

John sorted through the paperwork that was water-stained and had aged to a dry and brittle brown. Only a few words on the original registration document were still legible. He couldn't make anything out of the other two. Beneath the documents in the stack was a very old black-and-white photograph of an older man with a shock of stark-white hair standing at the helm of the *Sweet Afton*. It had an almost eerie familiarity to it, and though he'd never seen a picture of Molly's grandfather, John thought it must surely be him.

A moment later, Molly came down the outside stairs and into the store, where John stood behind the checkout counter. She held the new canvas in her hands, and she handed it over to him. He looked at it and smiled before hammering a nail into the wall behind him and hanging it. Walking around to the front of the counter to where Molly stood, John slipped his arm low around her waist, and the two stood in silence admiring her latest piece.

It was a simple but beautifully painted sign bearing only two words: *Sailing Lessons.*